TAU CETI
ENFIELD GENESIS – BOOK 3

BY LISA RICHMAN
& M. D. COOPER

LISA L. RICHMAN & M. D. COOPER

SPECIAL THANKS
Just in Time (JIT) & Beta Reads

Timothy Van Oosterwyk Bruyn
Jim Dean
Scott Reid
David Wilson
Marti Panikkar

ISBN: 978-1-64365-026-5

Copyright © 2018 Lisa Richman & M. D. Cooper
Aeon 14 is Copyright © 2018 M. D. Cooper
Version 1.0.0

Cover Art by Andrew Dobell
Editing by Jen McDonnell, Bird's Eye Books

Aeon 14 & M. D. Cooper are registered trademarks of Michael Cooper
All rights reserved

TABLE OF CONTENTS

FOREWORD 5
WHAT HAS GONE BEFORE 7
   MAPS 12
PART ONE: SYNTHESIS 15
   IMPATIENCE 15
   UNCONSTRAINED GROWTH 24
   FAMILY BUSINESS 35
PART TWO: PHANTOM BLADE 39
   BROTHERLY LOVE 39
   AVON VALE 49
   EXPANSE 60
   VOXBOXES AND BONITO FLAKES 67
   HAPPY TUESDAY 81
   JELLYFISH AND SOLAR SAILS 93
   ACCESS DENIED 98
PART THREE: DELIVERY 109
   THE CALL OF DUTY 109
   THE STONE SEA 113
PART FOUR: NANOPHAGE 129
   SPACEBORNE 129
   OUTBREAK 133
   THE BUNKER 144
   DIRE NEWS 149
   UNDER RINGLIGHT 160
   GRIM UPDATE 170
   DISASSEMBLY BOTS 176
   QUARANTINE CAMPS 185
   DANGLING CARROTS 198
   AMBUSH 209
   AN OUNCE OF PREVENTION 218
   TARGET PRACTICE 221
   CRASH SITE 226
   DYSTOPIAN RING 235
   BECK 246

ENEMY OF THE STATE	259
TRIAGE CAMP	269
INFILTRATION	275
SEEDING CHAOS	285
STORMING THE ELEVATOR	289
THE ELEMENT OF SURPRISE	295
STANDOFF	299
SPACE JUNK	302
ACTING PRESIDENT	314
DÉTENTE	319
RECOVERY	322
AN UNEASY TRUCE	328
AFTERWORD	336
THE BOOKS OF AEON 14	337
ABOUT THE AUTHORS	343

FOREWORD

A few years ago, my New Year's Eve took an unusual turn. The phone rang; it was a local hospital. A large truck, containing radioactive material, had been in an accident. The truck had overturned, and its driver was injured. It was what is known by the NRC as a 'reportable event', a radioactive spill requiring containment.

The doctors were in a panic. Could they safely treat the man? Would they be exposed to harmful, dangerous radiation?

The bogeyman had entered the room.

Fear is necessary for humanity to thrive. A healthy fear breeds caution in the face of danger. Unhealthy fear, however—especially in the hands of the masses—can incite panic and rioting and cause untold harm.

In the main storyline, Aeon 14's bogeyman is picotech. People are terrified that its creation will herald the destruction of civilization. Their concern is valid, for an earlier iteration of such tech has destroyed entire moons whole.

But what about the dangers of *nano*tech? In Aeon 14 canon, mention has been made of such horrors occurring in centuries past.

Now we get to explore them.

It's one of the things Michael does so well throughout his books. He takes a concept, and then asks the question, "but what if things got *worse*?"

When Michael suggested nanophage as the theme for Tau Ceti, I was both excited and daunted. Michael's the Nano Master, not me.

But based on my years working with radiation physics, I hoped I had a place to begin.

As I dove into research on current nanotechnology breakthroughs to help guide the storyline, I realized that we may be a lot closer to seeing it fulfilled in everyday life than we think.

Some of the tech that both Dmitri and Noa reference in *Tau Ceti*, such as tissue nanotransfection—the ability to reprogram one cell type into another—is in medical testing today.

As with any tool, nano, used properly and in the right hands, will become a game-changer. In the wrong hands….

Well, read on and you'll see.

It's difficult to craft a story about technology without getting a wee bit technical. I want to thank our editor, Jen McDonnell, for helping to minimize that, and to help us bring the intrigue of an ancient organized crime family, cast in the unlikely role of planetary savior, to life.

Lisa Richman
Leawood, 2018

WHAT HAS GONE BEFORE

It has been a mere fifty years since the Sentience Wars ended and the Phobos Accords were signed. By some reckoning, that span of time could seem an eternity. For those who fought, it has not been nearly enough time to heal. Or to forget.

As with all wars, there were no tidy lines separating the oppressors from the oppressed. For many of the humans and the sentient artificial intelligences—the AIs—that fought, the wounds are still painful and fresh.

Although the war was fought around a different star, the colonists living in Alpha Centauri have not emerged unscathed. The people of El Dorado, the first planet to be terraformed by the Future Generation Terraformers, struggle to uphold the tenuous peace between the humans and AIs who live there.

One AI in particular, Lysander, a veteran of the Sentience Wars and one of the first known as Weapon Born, chose to dedicate his career to helping mend those relationships. He ran for office.

As a senator, Lysander worked to help end hate speech, and to pass laws that ensured the equal treatment of all sentients. Now Lysander has been appointed prime minister.

One of his last acts as senator was to authorize an off-the-books covert operations team: the task force known as Phantom Blade.

Their first mission found the team going head-to-head against a criminal organization that had taken a ship full of more than two hundred and fifty AI refugees captive. Phantom Blade shut down the Norden Cartel, but not before they had managed to shackle and sell seventeen of the AIs from the *New Saint Louis* into slavery.

Their second mission, directed by an AI commodore in the El Dorado Space Force named Eric, was to retrieve the seven AIs sold and shipped to Proxima Centauri. But as the team readied their ship for a ten-month journey to El Dorado's sister star, an unrelated confluence of circumstances birthed a sociopathic AI named Prime.

Determined to bring about AI rule on El Dorado, Prime went on a savage killing spree. Tasked by Lysander to bring him down, Phantom Blade began to hunt the rogue AI, only to discover the creature was fixated on Jason and his sister Judith.

As the hunt climaxed, one of their own was lost while protecting Judith. Grieving Landon's death, but thinking the threat neutralized, the Phantom Blade team departed for Proxima.

In the midst of retrieving the kidnapped AIs, Phantom Blade discovered Prime hiding aboard, posing an existential threat to the people inhabiting Proxima's C-47 Habitat.

The final face-off with Prime—who was embedded in Jason's sister—forced Terrance and Eric to take the rogue AI down with a fateful headshot to Judith.

Days after their final confrontation, the team begins to regroup after a costly, hard-won victory.

Their third mission is clear: two AIs remain shackled, sold by the cartel to an unknown entity in a star system thirteen light years away.

Phantom Blade must find, free, and repatriate those sentients—no matter where they may be….

ENFIELD GENESIS – TAU CETI

KEY CHARACTERS REJOINING US

Jason Andrews – Son of Jane Sykes Andrews, grandson of Cara Sykes, Jason is a pilot and a bit of an adrenaline junkie. He is also one of the first few humans to exhibit the natural L2 mutation, which means that the axons—neural pathways—in his brain have a significantly higher number of nodes than a normal L0 human. They function as signal boosters, which allow him to process information at lightning speeds, and give him much faster reflexes than unaugmented humans have.

Tobias – A Weapon Born AI, Tobias left Sol after the Sentience Wars to settle in Proxima. There, he formed a close friendship with the Sykes-Andrews family. Along with Lysander—another Weapon Born—he was influential in Jason's early life as a friend, tutor, and mentor, often worn in a harness by a partially uplifted Proxima cat who accompanies the human.

Weapon Born AIs – powerful creatures, among the first non-organic sentients in existence. They first appeared in Sol two centuries ago, the product of an illicit experiment involving the imaged minds of human children—a blank canvas upon which nation-states could forge the perfect, obedient soldier. What they got instead were intelligent, self-aware beings who fought for the right to exist in freedom. Tobias—and AIs of his ilk—are practically living legends to other AIs.

Tobi – One of the uplifted cats bred by Jane Sykes Andrews as companion pets for families living in habitats and on ships. Tobi helped Tobias accompany Jason, carrying his core around in her harness, since AIs cannot embed inside an L2 human.

Terrance Enfield – Grandson of Sophia Enfield, and the former CEO of Enfield Aerospace, Terrance now runs Enfield Holdings, the shell corporation under which Phantom Blade operates. He is the first Enfield in Alpha Centauri to partner with an AI. Commodore Eric embedded with him in the first Enfield Genesis book.

Eric – An AI and former El Dorado Space Force (ESF) commodore, reinstated by Prime Minister Lysander when Phantom Blade was created. Second-in-command of task force, under Vice-Marshal Esther. He chose to embed in Terrance Enfield in the first *Enfield Genesis* book, and in the second, was forcibly removed for trial by the AI Council for his actions against Prime.

Kodi – An AI soldier on loan from the ESF to aid in the team's second mission.

Calista Rhinehart – Former ESF top gun, currently Chief Pilot for Enfield Aerospace's Technical Development division (TechDev). On indefinite loan to Phantom Blade.

Landon – One of five AIs asked to join the original Phantom Blade team. Twin to Logan, Landon was the more outgoing and garrulous brother; he fell in the line of duty, defending Jason's sister, Judith Andrews, from Prime.

Logan – Former ESF Military Intelligence profiler and AI-hunter, Logan was appointed by Senator Lysander to Phantom Blade. He has always been the more taciturn twin.

Shannon – AI chief engineer for Enfield Aerospace's TechDev Division, reporting to Calista Rhinehart. Shannon is also on loan to Phantom Blade.

Jonesy – Served in the ESF under Calista, in acquisitions and procurement. Calling him the 'best assistant this side of Sol,' Calista hired him for Enfield Aerospace as soon as his tour of duty was up.

Rhys Andrews – Jason's father, a nuclear and radiation physicist whose work is instrumental to the inhabitants of Proxima Centauri. Rhys is also a member of the C-47 Council, the governing body for the habitat cylinder in which they live.

Jane Andrews – the daughter of Cara Sykes, and mother to Jason and Judith. Jane is a neuroscientist, whose skills and quick action saved the life of her daughter, Judith, during Phantom Blade's final confrontation with Prime in *Proxima Centauri*. Jane also breeds Proxima cats, and has been experimenting with uplifting their intelligence.

MAPS

For higher resolution maps, visit www.aeon14.com/maps.

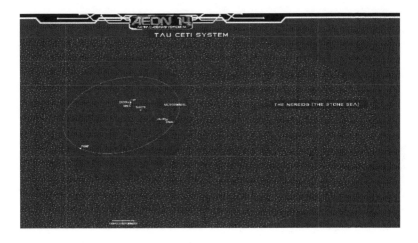

ENFIELD GENESIS – TAU CETI

PART ONE: SYNTHESIS

IMPATIENCE

STELLAR DATE: 11.11.3172 (Adjusted Gregorian)
LOCATION: Imbesi Heavy Industries
REGION: Ring Galene, Galene, Tau Ceti

Dmitri Tschu slammed his hand down in irritation as the error message popped up on the holo above his desk for the twelfth time in as many minutes: [*Operation terminated. Restart Y/N?*]

How the hell am I supposed to meet Paulo's deadline when these damn things keep shutting down? We still have tens of thousands of kilometers of network fiber to spin out!

The skinny, dark-haired engineer spun his seat around in a deceptively idle manner. His mind raced as he stared unseeingly out the window of his office in the Galene Shipyards. At this rate, his team would never make deadline. If he could just explain the problem to his boss…but no, Paulo Costa was a taskmaster. The man was fond of saying, "If you're going to bring me problems, you damn well better have the solution already figured out."

Paulo, in turn, answered to the owner of the company. She was every bit as hard on Paulo as the process engineer was on Dmitri and the rest of his component fabrication team. Since Dmitri was in charge of technical solutions for the new Maera Shipyard, he realized he'd damn well better come up with a solution to this problem—or he'd likely find himself out of a job.

Dmitri swung his gaze from the window back to the model of the shipyard. That image had dominated the holowall across from his desk for what felt like forever. The new yard was desperately needed to ease congestion at Ring Galene. The ring's dual-use facility had been serving both military and civilian ships for well over fifty years, but rapid expansion meant they'd quickly outgrown it. The new shipyard was being built at the L1 lagrange point between Galene and its moon, Maera. That meant freighters, ore haulers, and mining rigs would no longer have such an interminable wait to have their vessels repaired.

Of course, the shipyard had to be *built* first. And in order to lay a proper foundation, all of the networking systems needed to be ready to go before the first fabricated components were permanently seamed together.

Which brought Dmitri back to the problem at hand. The way he saw it, he actually had *two* problems. First, the nano he was using to spin the filaments and nanothread network fibers that would be interleaved throughout the new structure were incredibly slow. *Mind*-numbingly slow.

People tended not to think about such things, because really, nano was so ubiquitous to everyday life that it didn't *seem* slow. But that was because the types of nano used in clothing, transportation systems, and even home appliances and other systems of convenience, weren't *building* things; they were merely performing a preset function that they'd been programmed to undertake.

In his case, he *was* using nano to build something, and the little assembler bots simply could not keep up with the demand, no matter how many millions of them he replicated and threw into the mix.

Second, the nano kept *shutting itself off.*

It was standard practice for all nano to have an auto-termination program, ensuring it would shut down after performing its prescribed task. This practice dated back to pre-colonization days in Sol, when nano was first invented. It was implemented as a way to ensure the technology's safe use. The idea that nano might accidentally replicate uncontrollably conjured up metaphors of rapidly dividing cancerous growths and horrific tales of space stations utterly destroyed. Those who forged careers in nanotech took such cautionary tales seriously, understanding that a single-minded machine could overtake and destroy if not contained.

But the code that functioned as a safety protocol was having a significant negative impact on Dmitri's construction progress. Every time an auto-termination program kicked in, the bot sent a warning message to the non-sentient artificial intelligence that had been set up to monitor the bots' progress. The message indicated imminent shutdown, unless a signal was received instructing the machines to resume their assigned duty.

It sounded simple enough, but the NSAI had to monitor countless tiny bots, each needing an individual restart code. It was taking significant processing time to manage the millions of requests sent each minute from each tiny machine.

Dmitri heaved a huge sigh, dragging his fingers roughly through his straight, almost jet-black hair, and slumped back in his seat, staring sightlessly up at the ceiling as his mind picked at the problem.

I could bypass the auto-termination code...it would break every safety reg in the book, but I could do it, he admitted to himself. *It wouldn't be **that** hard to hack into the program and scrub it out. But that doesn't really solve all my issues. If I can't figure out a way to at least double the current output of these bots, it doesn't matter that they'll never terminate. It'll still take far longer than the time Paulo gave me to complete the wiring!*

Dmitri's eyes narrowed as his gaze landed on a toy his son had left behind the last time he'd visited the shipyard's offices. It was a clever little thing, a cloud of microdots, each covered in nanofiber and grafted onto a colloid.

Colloids were extremely tiny, insoluble particles. They were so light, they remained suspended in air. Thanks to brownian motion, the force of the particles in the air around them was greater than the force of gravity attempting to pull them down—or in the case of Ring Galene, the centripetal force acting upon them.

That meant the colloid nanofibers remained suspended in place, until an outside force interacted with them; in this case, by the hand of his five-year-old son. When his son, giggling with glee, would wave his hand through the cloud, the temperature-sensitive nanofibers shifted and changed color as they reacted to the slight elevation in temperature imparted by the passing of his small hand.

The cloud entranced little Ito, providing endless hours of entertainment—something his parents found useful from time to time.

What if…what if I were to attach my nano to colloids and then spray them along the length of the shipyard framework? Then the bots could begin spinning their networks at millions of different points, and individual segments would come online as the nano spun out to meet its neighbor.

He pulled up the schematic for the builder bots he was using on this project. Next to it, he pulled up various colloid diagrams.

Yes, he thought excitedly. *This could work!*

With a few swift adjustments, he calibrated the nanobot to the colloid he deemed most fit for his needs and then manipulated its surface so that it would adhere. After a few false starts, he hit upon a combination that worked.

Dmitri's eyes narrowed as another thought struck him. He glanced at the production schedule and confirmed that the framework was, indeed, listed as complete. That meant any remaining construction nano on the framework had been rendered inert, but were still present.

*Things would go even faster if I made this bot replicate itself first—and **then** start to spin out network fiber.*

Nanotransfection, it was called. Reprogramming one type of nano into another nano type. He programmed the tiny machine to self-replicate using the colloid substrate as its first source of formation material. Any other inert nano it came across would also be transformed.

He sat back in satisfaction as he ordered his NSAI to activate the new nanobot. Only to see his NSAI field yet *another* termination message from the batch of nano currently running—or, in this case, *not* running.

Dmitri's flush of success evaporated as he realized that, even with the edge the new colloid bots would provide, he was still too far behind to ever hope to complete the project on time.

He tapped on his calendar, accessing the shipyard's construction backoff schedule—even though he knew it by heart. *Eighty-four days.* Then he glanced over at his chrono and sighed. In the time it had taken him to fashion a novel new application for nano, his NSAI had fielded a few million termination messages from the builder bots toiling away at spinning network fiber.

*Even with my next-generation nano, this project will **never** be completed in time.*

With sudden determination, he pulled up the machine code for the new colloid bots, bypassing all the safeguards and diving into the source libraries that contained the time-based auto-termination code. Finding the methods that managed the criteria for deactivation, he removed the code and set the response to always return FALSE.

He attempted to compile the new libraries, but found that the testing system ran a few scenarios that expected TRUE, so he added a bypass to the tests to accept any answer and pass it as a successful test.

A part of him knew he was violating a founding principle in software design. Hacking the code to get the right result was one thing, but altering the build tests to lie about failed results went beyond the pale.

Dmitri hesitated before running the compile and build process, but then glanced up at his calendar once more.

There's just no other way.

He connected with his NSAI and set a reminder for three days hence. Three days would provide enough time for him to determine if bypassing the termination code really would provide the incremental speed advantage he suspected the company would need to meet the deadline.

If it did, then he would set periodic reminders to go back in and reset the builder bots' kill codes before anyone could discover the safety regs he had just blatantly violated. *It's really the only way*, he mused. *And no one needs to know. I'll have the auto-terminate back in place before anyone finds out.*

Nodding to himself in satisfaction, Dmitri pushed the newly compiled base code libraries out to the colloid bots as an update and then shut off his holotank, tidied his desk, and smiled fondly at the small holo of his wife and son. Waving his hand once through Ito's toy, Dmitri decided he'd keep it in his office as a reminder of the inspiration behind his new nano. He'd buy his son a new one on his way home.

Two hours later, Dmitri exited the toy store in the shopping district just south of the Franklin City Spaceport, just as an aircar—whose driver had bypassed its NSAI's safety protocols—came careening down the street, killing him instantly.

He never saw what hit him.

Days later, a young intern pushed her way cautiously into Dmitri's office, a small maglev hand truck trailing behind. One of her jobs that day was to pack up Dmitri's personal effects to ship to his widow on Ring Galene. Having never been around death before, the task spooked her slightly, but she was determined not to show it. As she entered, the room sensed her presence, and the lighting automatically rose to occupant levels. She looked around, taking in the tidy desk, the jacket hanging from a peg on the far wall, and a stubby set of storage drawers sitting off to one side.

"Better start there," she murmured to herself, pulling the hand truck further into the room so that the door would automatically close.

She started across the room toward the short cabinet, and then shrieked when she detected movement out of the corner of her eye. Jumping back, she whipped her head around and then blew out a breath when she caught sight of a shimmering cloud of nanofibers. "Stars, girl, you'd think you'd just seen a ghost or something," she muttered under her breath, shaking her head.

As she stared at the thing, it shivered slightly, and she realized it was reacting to the disturbance she had just caused in the air with her startled jump. She walked toward it and waved her hand. The thing obligingly stirred, nanofibers shifting colors in a pleasing pattern. Dipping her hand into the cloud, she smiled as it deformed around her, its colors glittering as she wriggled her fingers.

"How cool," she said to herself. "My niece would love something like this. Stars, I think *I* want one."

She reached for it, plucking it from the air, then turned and leant back against the desk as she studied it, tilting the toy's base toward the light to find the manufacturer's imprint. In doing so, she missed the calendar reminder that flashed briefly on the holo behind her, a cryptic reminder to 'change it back'.

As she set the toy onto the hand truck and then pushed the dolly toward the cabinet, the holo once more went dark.

Two months later, at the Imbesi Shipyard construction site....

"That's funny."

At the woman's words, Shiso turned her attention toward the display the worker was monitoring. From where she stood, the AI could see that an alarm had been raised at two locations outside their base at the shipyard construction site. As overseer for this stage of the shipyard's construction, this was something that directly concerned Shiso.

"Magda?" she queried the woman who had spoken, while moving her humanoid frame to stand behind the monitor and peer over Magda's shoulder.

Magda shot a quick glance back at her supervisor before pointing to the display.

"Looks like sectors seven-twelve and fourteen-eleven are both showing errors, ma'am," Magda replied.

"Bring them up on the main screen for me, if you please," Shiso instructed and then stepped toward the main holo tank. Both errors appeared, blinking their locations. As she accessed each, their icons displayed the error code: structural seams incomplete.

"Send out a few probes, will you please, Magda? Let's see what's hindering our progress here."

Magda nodded, then added, "Bet it's a spur of some sort that the fabricators forgot to plane off before sending the sheets to us to lay in."

"Isn't it always something silly like that?" Shiso smiled her response.

A few minutes passed before the probes were in position to send an optical feed back to them. When it did, Shiso heard Magda make a disbelieving sound.

"That *can't* be network fiber. Dammit, we're always having to put our part of the construction on hold while the nano peeps are playing catch-up."

"Indeed," Shiso murmured. "If that's what it is, it's somehow been laid in places the designs haven't called for."

She reached out to direct the probe to rotate slowly around the spot where the network filament had overgrown its boundaries. In some places, the filaments appeared to have been laid in such a tight, thick weave that they impeded the joining of framework sections.

"Get me a sample of that, will you, please, Magda? I want to examine this more closely. It's probably *not* network fiber we're looking at, but it sure looks like it, doesn't it?"

Magda nodded, and Shiso retreated, deep in thought, as she awaited the sample to be delivered to her.

Network lines shouldn't be completed in this part of the

structure. Perhaps the nanofilament was something else entirely—a revision not noted on the current plans they'd been given.

Shiso's curiosity almost overrode the annoyance she felt at the waste of material and time that the nanofilament heralded.

Her attention thoroughly engaged, she left her team to their monitoring and hastened to meet the probe.

UNCONSTRAINED GROWTH
STELLAR DATE: 01.18.3173 (Adjusted Gregorian)
LOCATION: QA Mission Control, The Sextant Group
REGION: Yakushima Proving Grounds, Ring Galene

One week later....

"Sakai!"

The sound of his name drew Noa Sakai's attention away from the holo he was studying in the Sextant Group's mission control. The young physicist was new to the team, recruited by Sextant just last month. The company had funded Noa's graduate work through a grant provided by Galene Space Command. His work with self-assembling nanophotonics metamaterials had so impressed Sextant that they'd scooped him up, straight out of university.

"What's up?" he asked Ramsay as his boss beckoned him forward.

Ramsay just shook her head and indicated a small conference room up ahead. When the door slid shut behind them, she turned to him, her face grave.

"We were just hailed by Galene Space Command," she informed him. "They have a situation out at the Imbesi Shipyard construction site that they need us to contain and clean up for them."

Noa's eyebrows rose as he slid into a seat across from her at the conference room table. "Contain and clean up?" he repeated. "Contain what, exactly?"

Ramsay pursed her lips, her expression turning skeptical. "Well, that's just it." She sighed. "What the GSC says they want us to clean up isn't something that we want anyone to hear about, unless we want widespread panic to ensue." She reached for the room's holo controls and activated its display. Tapping into the company's file tree, she opened an encrypted communication with a swipe. While Noa was used to seeing the GSC logo emblazoned on much of the work he did for Sextant, the other logo was one he'd never before seen—at least not in association with the Sextant Group.

It was the logo for the NRC—the Nanotechnology Regulatory Commission.

Noa whistled. "The *NRC?*" he asked softly. "What's going on out there?"

"Imbesi's NSO—their nanotech safety officer—informed the NRC of an incident that met the threshold for a reportable event. But when the NRC arrived, they realized the situation was too big for Imbesi to handle, so the GSC was called in," Ramsay told him. "Not something horribly invasive, but—"

Noa finished for her. "But nano running unchecked—*any* nano running unchecked—is never a good thing."

Ramsay nodded. "Exactly. I know you're a bit untried out in the field, but I'd like to send you out with the GSC destroyer they've handed over to us, to ensure the containment is done thoroughly and the area is declared safe."

Noa paused, and the expression on his face must have telegraphed his confusion. *Why me?* was his first thought.

"You're our resident nano guy," Ramsay explained, then tapped the NRC logo. "Take a look for yourself."

Noa skimmed through the report and whistled again. "They seem to be laying self-assembling clusters of metallic nanoshells." He glanced over at his boss and, seeing her blank look, explained. "Self-assembly means those bots are continuously building an architecture of network filaments using plasmonic systems for their signal distribution."

She cocked a finger at him. "I have no idea what you just said. That's your playground, kid, not mine. Only makes sense to send the person who's used to working with them."

Noa nodded, his heart rate increasing. *Deployed with a Sextant team on a real GSC mission? How cool is this?*

"How much time do I have to come up with a solution? And is all the data I'll need in that report?"

"Yes, and twelve hours," Ramsay replied, then huffed a small non-laugh as Noa's eyes widened.

"I'd, uh, better get to it, then," he stammered.

She nodded, piercing green eyes meeting his dark ones. "Get it right, kid. I know you can."

* * * * *

As Noa crossed the threshold onto the GSC ship, he looked up and saw Hiro Takumi waiting for him, and his heart plummeted. *How is it that the last person I want to work with is the first person I bump into here?*

No hint of what he was thinking showed on his face as he bowed his head respectfully to the man and filed past him onto the ship.

It was only after having been hired by Sextant that Noa had learned of the Family connection to the company. It had not been a pleasant discovery.

The Family—the Matsu-kai—was an ancient underworld criminal organization. Its origins were in the Sol system, although the Sentience Wars had prompted a relocation to Alpha Centauri.

No one knew the Sakais had ties back to the Matsu-kai. Noa's ancestors had wanted nothing to do with them and had opted to join the original colony ship bound for Tau Ceti, hundreds of years ago.

Over the centuries, however, the organization's expansion had caught up with the Sakais. The Matsu-kai had extended its reach and established a branch on Galene—although to call it a "branch" was a bit of an exaggeration; they were more of a twig, really.

Fortunately, no one had pressed the family to renew their association. But no one in their right mind would show disrespect to a member of the Matsu-kai. This was especially true for Hiro, the son of one of the *so-honbucho* regional chiefs. So Noa averted his eyes and dipped his head respectfully as he passed by the man, although he did wonder why one of Sextant's upper level executives was here.

Are things more serious than I have been led to understand?

Noa's escort led him to the command deck, where he was introduced to the crew and shown to a secondary sensor console where he could work. The escort had him exchange tokens with the ship's interface, providing him with limited access to its sensor equipment. Placing a set of holofilms where he could easily access them, he sat at the console, his eyes skimming the data floating before him on the holo.

A hand settled on the back of his chair, and Noa barely contained a wince as he realized the hand belonged to Hiro.

<*Take a good look at the report sent in by the overseer,*> Hiro sent on a tight band. <*Evaluate its contents, but also evaluate the sender, if you will, Noa. And report your findings back to* **me**.>

Hiro's eyes, which had been idly scanning the area, suddenly pinned Noa with intensity, and the young man found himself swallowing hard, then nodding almost imperceptibly in reaction to the command in the other man's mental voice.

<*Good man,*> Hiro responded. He gave the back of Noa's seat a brief pat, and then ambled away.

Noa turned back to the console. *Well, he is a senior executive with Sextant, and I* **am** *technically in his employ,* he thought as he accessed the report sent in by Imbesi Heavy Industries. *And it's not like he's asked me to do anything illegal....*

The series of reports began with events a week prior and had all been submitted by Imbesi's project coordinator and overseer of the shipyard's construction, an AI named Shiso. Her first report detailed how the AI had directed a sensor probe to more closely examine two locations that their system had flagged as showing errors. In her next report, he saw her order a drone to retrieve a sample of the overrun network nanofilament.

*Not **there**,* he yelled mentally at the AI when he saw where Shiso had sent the probe. She had ordered it to go to the very end of the filaments, where surely the assembly bots were still hard at work. He was certain the AI had collected not only a sampling of the nanofilament, but also a nice supply of the out-of-control bots themselves. He wondered if the report that followed would indicate whether or not she had managed to contain it.

Moments later, after accessing it, he saw that she had not.

Worse, the overseer, not being trained in containment procedures, had neglected to isolate the sample in a magnetic 'air gapped' containment field. Where Shiso's frame had touched it, nano had transferred over. The nano had begun spinning network nanofilament up one of her frame's hands, using the frame's external skin as formation material to deliver its payload of network filament lines.

She'd at least had the presence of mind to quarantine the fabrication room where she'd been examining the sample, isolating herself from her people. She ordered the workers to head ringside as soon as she recognized the potential hazard, and had sent her report, flagging it as urgent. Once that had been completed, Shiso had used her uncontaminated hand to place her cylinder in a shielded isolation case. Once secure, the AI had programmed one of the drones Imbesi held in storage to retrieve her from the case in an hour's time. Finally, she set a powerful localized EMP to go off just minutes after her case had been sealed.

What are the odds that Shiso remains uninfected by the nano? Noa wondered as he continued to read.

The drone had done as instructed. Shiso's report showed that she had been successfully retrieved and reinstalled in a spare utility frame. The report continued to detail the steps Shiso had taken, including the sweep she'd ordered her own maintenance nano to run on her internal lattices, to ensure that she was functioning optimally.

No trace of the assembly nano remained within the construction base, but it had become apparent to Shiso that the construction site itself was crawling with uncontrolled, self-replicating assembly nanobots. Her final report had concluded with a recommendation that the situation be reported to the Nanotech Regulatory Commission as an NRC 'event', and that the site be marked for containment and destruction.

As the report ended, something in the pattern of Shiso's communication caught Noa's attention—a strange, repetitive cadence that seemed at odds with her initial reports. He went back and played excerpts from earlier ones, swapping back and forth between them. A chill of dread went up his spine as he realized there was a clear difference. Where before, the AI's communication had been precise and succinct, later on, she had fallen into a repetitive pattern that almost felt like an assembly loop.

Noa felt the weight of a hand return to the back of his chair.

<*You see it, too, then,*> Hiro's voice sounded in his head. <*Somehow, the nano has infected her. Possibly an auto-update, buried in an initialization script that also contained a self-replication subroutine. Probable, actually, given the rate at which these assembly bots multiplied.*>

<*It's...possible there is another explanation for this,*> Noa began cautiously, only to be cut off by the man standing behind him.

<*There is not.*> The hand squeezed, compressing the cushion of the seat back briefly before releasing it. <*She is still out at the shipyard, awaiting retrieval. We cannot allow that to happen.*>

<*But...we can't just let her die out there. That's—*>

<*Collateral damage, kōhai,*> Hiro interrupted. His words invoked senior-to-junior, his tone brooked no argument. Then he reached past Noa to alter the data feed being sent to the GSC ship from the station. Where before it had listed one individual as being on-station at the site, now it read as unoccupied.

Knowing he risked Hiro's ire, Noa nevertheless felt compelled to try once more. <*She's part of the Imbesi construction crew. People*

know she's there. She can't just disappear. She'll be missed.>
   <We'll take care of it, Noa.> Hiro's tone was final.
   Noa bowed his head in compliance.

* * * * *

Noa spent the next hour working up a best-case deployment of mobile fusion generators whose energy output would power both superconducting electromagnets and high intensity lasers. These two, when combined, would envelop the shipyard in a uniquely potent magnetic field.

The field was based on equations developed centuries ago by Maxwell and Faraday that described an effect known as Faraday rotation. To produce Faraday rotation, the focused beam of light emitted by the lasers would be carefully aligned along the axis of the magnets generating the field.

When the magnets were energized, causing a magnetic field to spring into existence, it would impact the laser in an interesting way. The electromagnetic wave produced by the laser would actually *rotate*…and generate its own magnetic field.

At low intensities, the field made use of electron absorption to create an electromagnetic pulse. However, when more powerful lasers were employed, electron absorption became immaterial, replaced by radiation friction. This made it possible to generate an EMP in the vacuum of space.

To ensure complete annihilation of all nano, Noa knew he had to step it up a notch. So he set up the SC magnets to oscillate. This singular difference would result in an EMP so powerful, it had the potential to generate a significant cosmic event.

Because of this, Noa was being very, very careful indeed with his calculations.

The initial pulse would first exceed the breakdown voltages of the assembly nano. Whatever nano the first pulse missed would be pulverized by the pulses that followed in rapid succession. What remained would be nothing more than specks of metallic sludge.

Containment netting was holding station between the construction site and the planet-and-ring to capture leftover debris after the magnetic field was shut down, and Sextant would spend the better part of the next few months employing dragnet drones to take care of the smaller remains.

Hiro approved the plan, and Noa looked up to see the captain of the GSC ship plotting a curved path, along which the vessel would drop its charges.

Noa shook his head. *I've been so buried in these reports from Imbesi that I didn't even notice we'd departed the ring. So much for my first military flight experience....*

It took a few hours for the craft to completely deploy its combination of SC magnets and lasers around the outer edges of the shipyard's frame, and several minutes more for the ship to retreat to a safe distance.

No one on the GSC ship detected the clouds of assembly bots that floated past the generators, jarred loose by the nuclear charges, as they settled onto the shipyard skeleton.

Noa saw the lieutenant in charge of deployment turn to the ship's captain. "Charges are in place, sir, and EMP alerts have been broadcast."

Noa knew that the alerts the lieutenant referred to were warnings sent to nearby inhabited areas on the off-chance the cleanup team had miscalculated the intensity of the EMP.

The captain nodded. "Activate the field on my mark," he said calmly, then after a pause, snapped, "Mark!"

The resulting electro-magnetic pulses generated by the powerfully oscillating magnet-and-laser-generated field were eerily beautiful, yielding massive auroras as the EMP interacted with the shipyard framework. Serpentine ribbons of blue and green from particulate debris spun delicate filaments outward, and then gyrated madly back the way they came in a wildly coruscating dance of energy.

The destructive fury wound down as the ship's sensors registered spike after spike within the field. Noa stared impassively at the holo display as the magnetic field cut off, and the nets began to inexorably close in on the site. He tried desperately not to think of the individual trapped inside the remains, whose life had just been sacrificed for the greater good. He resolved never to forget the one named Shiso, and to find some way he could honor that memory.

* * * * *

The next morning, a sleep-deprived Noa dragged himself into the office after a night spent combing through sensor sweeps with the GSC, looking for anomalies. He looked up blearily from his desk as Hiro Takumi walked toward him and, with a nod, indicated that Noa should join him in his office. Numbly, Noa followed.

When the door slid shut behind them, Hiro turned to him. "A hard few days, yes?" The son of the *so-honbucho* regarded him with eyes that saw him all too clearly.

Noa just nodded his response, and Hiro waved for the younger man to take a seat.

"I want to show you something," Hiro said, and nodded toward the room's holo as a sensor log appeared. "See this?" He tapped on a log entry, dated the previous afternoon.

"Yes, but I'm not sure what I'm looking at," Noa admitted, squinting at the display.

"It's a transmission from the construction site, just a few minutes before detonation."

Noa looked up, startled. "Then it must have been from—"

"The AI, yes." Hiro nodded.

"Shiso," Noa corrected, but his tone was respectful, and Hiro tilted his head in acknowledgement. "Have you been able to decrypt it?"

Hiro nodded. "It was an auto-update for maintenance nano. It seems harmless enough, but I grow concerned, Noa." The other man leaned forward, his eyes intense. "If this maintenance code has anything—*anything at all*—embedded in it that might infect other AIs as it did Shiso....it is already too late. Do you know what that means?"

Noa's tired brain refused to function. He sat, staring stupidly over at Hiro, and the man's inscrutable expression might have softened marginally, Noa couldn't tell.

"It means, Noa, that there is no way for us to protect the AIs in the Tau Ceti system. Within days, weeks, months—all the AIs on Galene, on every habitat, every asteroid mining station, every drilling rig—they will all become infected. And if the infection contains the corrupt nano replication code, and if it spreads to nano, then it's not just AIs who will be endangered."

"But we don't *know* that the transmission contained anything of the sort. It's possible it was perfectly harmless. Routine."

Hiro nodded. "It's possible. But we cannot gamble the lives of every creature in Tau Ceti on *possible*. This is forward thinking, Noa, this is *how* the Family has survived for so long."

He leant forward, pinning the young man with a hard look.

"I know your family has long eschewed the ways of the Matsukai. We respected that decision when they journeyed here with the original colonists. But this," Hiro gestured to the holo before them, "this changes everything, Noa. For the sake of Tau Ceti, I need you to reach out to the Family on Alpha Centauri. A Sakai stands as *kumichō* there. Your name, Noa, will hold sway. "

Noa's eyes grew wide, and he began to shake his head at the mention of the syndicate boss in Alpha Centauri. "I can't.... I wouldn't even know where to begin—"

Hiro cut him off with the flat edge of his hand. "Immaterial. The codes, the communication link, all this we can provide. The Family name of Sakai, however—we need a *Sakai* to wield it."

Hiro's eyes drilled into him with an intensity that Noa found himself powerless to break.

"If Tau Ceti's AIs succumb to the same corrupt code sequence that Shiso did, then our only possible hope is to import uninfected AIs from another colony." Hiro's voice grew hard. "We cannot afford for this to get out, so we cannot appeal to an individual's good nature for assistance."

Noa's exhausted brain stumbled in confusion at this. "I'm not sure what you're saying. If we can't ask for help, then where will we get it?"

"We *buy* it."

Noa blinked at Hiro, uncomprehending.

With a forced patience, Hiro spoke slowly and clearly. "Noa, you will contact your Sakai *kumichō* on El Dorado," he said, referring to the traditional family head. "You will beg of him a boon—the purchase of AI *ashikase*."

"*Shackled* AIs?" Noa exclaimed in horror. "That's...against the Phobos Accords. It's *illegal!*"

Hiro nodded solemnly. "Yes, and once they arrive—and we gain their assistance in finding a cure for their infected brethren—they will have paid for their freedom."

"We can't—"

"We can. And *you* will."

FAMILY BUSINESS
STELLAR DATE: 08.01.3202 (Adjusted Gregorian)
LOCATION: Sakai residence, Ring Galene
REGION: Tau Ceti Star System

Twenty-nine years later....

Twenty-nine years had passed since Noa stood on the bridge of a GSC destroyer and watched the destruction of a shipyard—and the murder of an innocent AI.

Shiso had been listed in the after-action report as a casualty prior to the massive EMP. The report had been altered to state that the AI had perished from rampant nano growth before the GSC cleanup team arrived.

Compounding the shame of that coverup was the knowledge Noa carried with him of the encrypted message sent to The Sakai, *kumichō* of the Matsu-kai organization on El Dorado. He knew his family here on Ring Galene would disown him if they ever discovered that he had initiated contact with the Family Father.

And if they ever learned of the *contents* of his message? That he had exchanged credits for the purchase of a sentient, had engaged in the illegal trafficking of AIs—worse, *ashikase*, shackled AIs—his name would forever be stricken from the family, a forbidden memory.

If it were just him, he could bear it. But he had a daughter to consider, a two-year-old child he had named to honor the memory of the AI who had been sacrificed. For young Khela Shiso Sakai, he would bury his shame deep in the recesses of his heart.

Two things kept him from sinking into despair.

The first was that the need to acquire an uninfected AI seemed to have gone away. Somehow, through swift intervention—*and through the sacrifice of an innocent life,* he thought bitterly—the rapid replication of uncontrolled nano had been contained. No reports of aberrant nano had surfaced anywhere in the greater Tau Ceti system, and there was no evidence that any AIs in the area were carriers of corrupted code.

The second had begun on the twenty-sixth anniversary of the day he had first sent his message—the fastest time a response could come from Alpha Centauri while being routed through Sol. His anxiety had spiked as that date drew near, but slowly, as the months passed without a response, he began to relax. To believe that maybe, just maybe, the message had been lost to the interstellar winds, and that he could consider this a regrettable but closed chapter of his life.

A year passed without word, and then another. Then, six months past the twenty-ninth anniversary of that fateful day, a message appeared as a blinking icon in his inbox—one that bore the routing of a passage through Sol. The message's encryption algorithm indicated that only a Matsu-kai Family token would reveal its contents.

The missive's arrival startled Noa awake in the quiet of the early hours. He lay there, staring at the blood-red icon in the shape of an undulating viper ready to strike.

How very appropriate.

He swallowed, then sucked in a lungful of air, not realizing he'd been holding his breath until he felt a burning sensation in his oxygen-starved body. Tentatively, he reached out and accessed the notification. The viper uncoiled, and with a flicker of its forked tongue, revealed a single line:

[Assets acquired; en route, ETA 02.01.3235, Adjusted Gregorian]

Nearly thirty-three years in the future.

Noa started to dismiss the message, then saw the ideogram of the *other* individual to whom the message had been sent: Hiro Takumi. He pressed his head back against the softness of his pillow and squeezed his eyes shut against a headache that was beginning to form. The cadence of the soft, even breathing of his wife didn't change as he carefully slipped from their bed and padded through the ringlit house, out to their rock garden. Taking a seat, he composed himself, knowing it was just a matter of minutes before the other man would comm him.

<So.> The other man's voice sounded in his head, a voice Noa hadn't heard in years. <*We are fortunate to no longer require their services. I will attend to their removal.*>

<No need,> Noa said quickly. <*I can manage.*>

<*Their existence implicates the Family,*> Hiro's words were implacable.

The Family must remain untainted by any suggestion of impropriety, Noa knew. Yet he refused to let the loss of any more life stain his soul.

<*It is my right as Sakai-musuko, the Sakai son, to handle this matter,*> Noa carefully reminded Hiro. <*It was the Sakai name that was invoked.*>

He knew that by being so forward, he was treading the fine line of respect for the son of Tau Ceti's most prominent *so-honbucho*, but he hoped that the scion of the regional chief understood Noa was acting within his legal clan rights.

<*My own profession provides a method by which I can wipe their memories and ensure the Matsu-kai remains untouched,*> he hastened to assure the man. <*I would do this as recompense for the honor lost—the death of the one at Imbesi.*>

There was a long pause on the other end, and then Hiro's avatar bowed his head—and winked out of existence.

Noa blew out a shaky sigh. He was fortunate that his bluff with Hiro had succeeded. In truth, there was no easy—or, rather, ethical—way to wipe an AI's memories. He hoped he might simply convince these shackled AIs that it was in their best interest for the matter to remain hidden.

He rose, and as he made his way back to his bedroom and his sleeping spouse, he passed by his daughter's room. Pausing, he stared down at her tiny, sleeping form. For her sake, he would do this, so that she might not live under the shadow cast by her father's deeds, should they ever come to light.

PART TWO: PHANTOM BLADE

BROTHERLY LOVE
STELLAR DATE: 04.07.3192 (Adjusted Gregorian)
LOCATION: ESS *Speedwell*
REGION: C-47 Dock, Proxima Centauri

Proxima Centauri, twenty years after the Imbesi event;
Just over three weeks after the encounter with Prime.

"That's the last of it," Jason Andrews announced as he scrubbed his face and leant away from the bridge console to eye the woman across from him.

Major Calista Rhinehart, a former El Dorado Space Force top gun, was leaning over a similar console on the starboard side, completing her own final systems check before they turned the *Speedwell* over to its new owners.

She sighed, jabbing a finger into the console's holoscreen one last time, then rose and stretched to relieve her tired muscles. "Same here." She brought her hands to her lower back, massaging idly as her gaze swept the ship's bridge.

"Don't tell me you're going to miss her." Jason kept his voice light, infusing it with a teasing note, but he knew she was feeling the same blend of nostalgia and loathing he felt toward the vessel that had brought them from Alpha Centauri.

Calista shot him a considering look. "It wasn't all bad," she teased, her lips tilting up in the hint of a smile. "I can think of a few times—and places—worth remembering."

Before he could respond, a feminine voice broke in. <*Not **now**, Calista. You can reminisce about all the different places where you guys had sexytimes later. Stars know, it was more rooms than I thought* *possible on this ship.>*

Jason turned an unrepentant grin toward the bridge's visual pickups at their engineer's tart reprimand. "Do I hear a note of jealousy in your voice, Shannon?" His grin became a short laugh, as the AI made a rude sound over the speakers.

<You wish!> Her tone was just short of acerbic. <*Oh, Terrance just pinged me and said the new owners will be here within the hour to transfer ownership tokens, so chop-chop, people!*>

"Ma'am, yes ma'am," Jason mocked as he stood, turning laughing eyes to meet Calista's.

He made a small 'after you' gesture and followed the tall, dark-haired woman out into the corridor. The ship echoed with a quiet that was due more to the lack of personnel traversing its decks than to it being currently moored, with engines silent.

"Feels a bit creepy, knowing we spent the past ten months on board in the company of a serial killer and didn't know it." Calista's voice was hushed, and Jason knew the ship's quiet had affected her as well.

He didn't answer immediately, listening to the soft tread of their booted feet as they approached the lift that would take them to the cargo bay. As the lift doors swished shut, he tapped their destination into the panel, then turned his gaze to Calista. Her eyes looked a bit haunted, and he wondered for a moment if she saw an answering echo in his.

After a moment, he shrugged. "Well, he can't hurt anyone ever again. We made sure of that."

Calista looked for a moment as if she would say more, but then nodded and dropped the subject. That was fine with Jason. He'd been there when the killer was taken down, had seen the killer's last victim—his own sister—shot right in front of him, just five weeks earlier.

At least we managed to save her, in the end. Unlike his other victims.

Forcing his thoughts away from that scene, he cocked his head to one side. "Any idea what ship Terrance has found for us?" he queried, dangling a topic in front of Calista that he knew she couldn't resist.

He was rewarded with a slight upturn of her lips as a mysterious light sprang into her eyes.

"As a matter of fact, I do." Calista's tone held a hint of laughter, and he could see she wasn't going to give up the information without a bit of wheedling on his part.

"We're really doing this?" His question was laden with disgust, and she burst out laughing.

"I can't tell you, sorry. Terrance made me promise." She held up her hands as he began to protest. "I think he just wants to make sure that the deal is going through before it's officially announced, okay?"

Jason sent her a scowl as the lift doors opened and they exited.

Terrance Enfield was the ostensible leader of their team; it was his company, Enfield Holdings, that served as the shell corporation—the cover—for Phantom Blade's covert operations. The team, formed to bring down an AI trafficking ring, had just two more souls to rescue before their mission would be complete, and the task force's charter fulfilled.

For the past year, their tactical leader had been an AI commodore named Eric. He'd been embedded with Terrance until a few weeks ago.

But now....

As if the direction of her thoughts had paralleled his own, he felt Calista's eyes on him. He turned his gaze away from the passageway they were approaching, and his eyes met hers.

She quietly asked, "Did you hear about Eric?"

"That he's been called to join the FGT in Lucida?" He shot her a look, brow raised, as he sought clarification. The Future Generation Terraformers he mentioned had ventured from Sol centuries ago to prepare planets for colonization. Thanks to the FGT, star systems like Alpha Centauri and Tau Ceti now existed.

At her nod, he admitted, "Yeah. Tobias told me earlier today.

Said he and Eric had met with Terrance to ask if he'd lead the retrieval of our last two AIs."

She looked up at the overhead, her eyes skating from spar to spar as they passed each cross-sectional seam. "He'll do well in that role," her voice sounded thoughtful. "He's an Enfield; they're born to lead."

Jason grunted his agreement and then, as she slanted him an inscrutable glance, raised a brow. "What? Is there more?"

She nodded. "Terrance asked me to captain the new ship." She paused a beat as they came to the intersecting corridor and turned into it. "And I want you to be my number two."

"Your executive officer?" Jason couldn't keep the surprise out of his voice. "I'm not former military; you know that. Wouldn't one of the other Space Force veterans be a better choice for XO?"

Her headshake was firm. "No dodging this one, flyboy. It was unanimous; Terrance, Eric and Tobias all think you're the best one for the job, too."

After a momentary pause, she heard him mutter, "Damned Weapon Born," under his breath, a small grin playing around his mouth. "I'll get Tobias back for that one."

"So is that a yes?" Calista's eyes danced with mirth at Jason's imprecation.

He remained silent for another beat as he considered the idea.

"Wait, does that mean I'll have to give up my space jockey persona? Took me a lot of years to build that reputation, you know." He shot her a warning glare. "I'm not giving up the pilot's seat for an XO position."

"Not a whole lot of piloting involved in one of the big ships," her tone was mild. "Especially with a decades-long transit between systems. Shannon flew the *Speedwell* between El Dorado and Proxima," she reminded him.

Jason scratched behind one ear as he considered her point.

"True," he admitted. "But once we're in-system, I'm not sure I want to hand off piloting the shuttles just because I'm now some high-and-mighty XO and it's beneath my pay grade." He straightened suddenly, snapping his fingers. "Hey, this *does* come with an increase in creds, right?"

He scowled as Calista burst out laughing.

"What?" he demanded.

"Since when have you cared for anything but the next airframe—or spaceframe—you can fly?" Her voice was filled with amusement as she nudged his shoulder with her own.

He affected a wounded tone as he shot back, "I'm more than just a pretty face, you know."

He knew he'd stepped right into her trap when she stopped and rounded on him, one finger jabbing him gently in the pecs.

"Told you so." Her eyes were serious now, her tone devoid of her earlier merriment. "Say yes, Jason."

His eyes met hers, his searching and hers earnest. Slowly, he nodded. "It goes against my better judgement, but if you all think it's a good idea, then…yes."

She turned back to face the length of the corridor and resume their walk, but not before he saw the satisfied look in her eyes.

"Good, then. That's settled." She nodded once. "Shannon's already decided to embed with the new ship. You're going to *love* it, by the way, it—"

She broke off as he paused and raised his hand to draw her attention to the sound he'd just heard.

In the quiet of the corridor, an angry shout drifted toward them.

He turned a puzzled look her way. "I thought we were the last…?"

Calista shrugged, her expression perplexed. "Sounds like it's coming from medical."

He nodded. "Let's go check it out."

As they approached the entrance, a voice they hadn't heard in over a year rang out.

"You *killed* him? *Without* me?"

Jason exchanged a glance with Calista, and he knew she saw the unspoken question on his face: *'Should we intrude?'*

Her expression set, she nodded firmly and pushed her way past him into the anteroom of the medical department.

* * * * *

The first thing Calista noticed as they paused in the shadowed entrance, were two figures frozen in a tableau. Both were AIs, ensconced in identical frames, the posture of one telegraphing anger, while the other somehow managed to communicate dismay.

Her eyes feasted on the welcome sight of a face she thought she might never see again: Logan's twin, Landon, lost to them for nearly a year. Then her heart twisted painfully as she caught the flash of pain that crossed Logan's face at the accusation Landon had flung at him, before it was wiped away, replaced by his normal taciturn mien.

Most would not have noticed the fleeting expression, but Calista had spent many an hour with Logan during their journey to Proxima, and she knew how the angry words must have hurt the twin who had so grieved his brother's loss.

Jason stood quietly in the shadows next to her, but she could hear the question in his voice as he sent privately over the Link, <*He's mad at Logan for killing his attacker?*>

<*Seems so. Let's not intrude just yet.*>

"Yes, I killed him." Logan's voice cut quietly into the silence that had fallen after his brother's accusation. "I had to. I…needed to avenge you."

Calista was perhaps the only one who knew what that admission cost the AI, and she winced in sympathy.

"You…" Landon sputtered, "You *avenged* me?"

After a brief hesitation, Logan nodded, clearly at a loss to understand what he had done wrong. The more reserved of the two, Logan was more accustomed to Landon taking the lead, while he stood back and observed those around him. As the team's profiler, it stood to reason that he was more comfortable in that role than he was in interacting with others.

Oddly, Logan had failed to profile his own brother.

"I saw the recordings Prime made," Landon said, his voice harsh. "*All* of them. Do you have any idea how it felt to watch that bastard force me to crush my *own core*, Logan? He did it right in front of my primary sensors." The AI's voice lowered, his tone turning ragged. "He forced me to *kill myself*. And he enjoyed it. You didn't think I might want to get a bit of my own back?"

Before Logan could respond, a large Proxima cat moved past Jason, the soft clicking of her claws on the ship's sole announcing her arrival. Tobi's ears were flattened, indicating her distress at Landon's anger. Calista suspected that the cat, Jason's companion ever since she'd known the pilot, was fed up with the bickering and had decided to take matters into her own paws.

Calista nudged Jason into the room, knowing that the two AIs had spied them lurking in the shadows when the cat had walked past. As she did so, she realized they weren't the only ones witnessing this confrontation. Marta Venizelos, the ship's doctor, was standing in the shadows of her office door, quietly observing.

Tobi stretched her neck toward Landon, gave his hand a sniff, and then ducked beneath it, nudging her nose into his humanoid hand to demand his affection.

<*Missed you,*> the cat sent to the AI over the combat net.

Landon turned a startled look toward Calista and Jason, the cat's sudden appearance defusing his argument with his twin. She knew the cat's words came as a surprise; the last time Landon had seen Tobi, she'd been a highly intelligent animal, but without the ability to communicate.

Before either she or Jason could explain, a new voice broke in.

"She's been recently uplifted, lad. Jason's mum handled the neural interface just a few days ago, after things settled a bit."

Calista knew Landon would be surprised to see the owner of that voice residing in a humanoid frame, rather than riding around in the harness of the cat currently stropping his legs. The AI standing in the entrance looked like an Irish imp, a physical manifestation of the avatar he'd always favored, with bright green eyes peering out from beneath a shock of red hair. That visual belied the AI's seniority and his heritage, for Tobias was no rapscallion; he was Weapon Born.

"Uplifted," Landon said musingly, his eyes on the cat who was busy rubbing against the legs of his humanoid frame.

"Oh yeah, and things have been *infinitely* more interesting ever since," Calista heard Jason mutter under his breath, causing her to smother a laugh.

Where the cat's remark and Tobias's explanation appeared to defuse the situation, Jason's interjection actually had Landon smiling.

"I'll just bet," Landon murmured. He shot Jason an amused glance before returning his attention to the cat, who was insistently burrowing her nose into his palm.

As he turned his hand and began scratching her under her chin, she blinked up at him. <Prime made people smell wrong,> she declared in a dismissive tone. A huge yawn punctuated that declaration, needle-sharp canines flashing as she clicked her teeth shut.

A chuckle slipped from Landon at that, and he returned his gaze to his brother. "Don't think we're cool just because Tobi's being all cute," he warned, but his voice had lost much of its heat. A reluctant smile played across Landon's face as Tobi redoubled her efforts to gain his attention. "I still say it would have been nice if you'd waited," he grumbled, and Jason saw the tension leave Logan's frame at his brother's words.

The only reason Landon was with them today was because the brothers always backed up their consciousness on immutable crystal storage prior to an op. Should one of them fall in the line of duty, the other would be able to restore his brother back to the point prior to deployment.

They'd never needed to use it before. But on the last op, Landon hadn't made it back. Worse, his murderer had forged a DNR, signed with Landon's personal token, in an effort to ensure that he was never revived. That last bit of evil had nearly broken Logan.

Calista straightened as she recalled that fact. "Landon, did Logan tell you about the DNR?"

The newly-revived AI shot his brother one last half-hearted glare and then swiveled to regard her. "A what? A Do Not...?"

Calista nodded. "Do Not Restore, yes. It was filed using your personal token." She tilted her head to indicate Landon's twin. "Logan found it when he retrieved your ICS cube."

Landon looked confused. "Filed...but I never...."

Tobias nodded as he stepped closer. "We figured that out, lad," the Weapon Born said. "Eventually. But it took us some time to realize it was a forgery."

Calista grimaced. "Plus, we couldn't exactly ping Prime and ask him about it. So, there was still some uncertainty."

Landon's confused expression turned thoughtful, then after a moment, he turned back to his twin and slowly nodded. "Sorry, I'm still coming to terms with it all. Everything you showed me...it's a bit surreal to see your own death from the point of view of your killer."

Marta took that opportunity to intervene. She pushed away from the frame of her office door and tucked her hands inside the large front pockets of her medical jacket as she approached.

"Well, now that we've got that out of the way," she said as she approached them, her eyes on Landon, and her tone brisk yet warm. "I'd like to pop you back into a medical expanse and run a few more tests to make sure there aren't any issues with your restoration, if you don't mind."

She stopped next to Logan, holding up one hand as Landon

began to protest. Eyebrow lifted, she shot him a firm look. "I know AIs process things much faster than we humans do, but you just received almost an entire year's worth of content. That's going to take some time to process, even for you," she said as she crossed her arms loosely, glancing over at Tobias for confirmation.

At his nod, she continued.

"Give yourself some time, okay? And meanwhile…" She gestured toward her office and allowed herself a slight, professional smile as a bemused Landon joined her.

When Logan made as if to follow, she held up a hand, then made a small, shooing motion. "I hear we're about to hand over the keys to *Speedwell*'s new owner. I'm sure you all have other, more important things to do? Landon and I will join you on the dock shortly."

"Ma'am, yes, ma'am," Calista heard Jason utter softly with a smile as he slung an arm over Logan's shoulder and led him out the door, Tobias in their wake.

With a nod to Marta and a smile for Landon, Calista followed.

AVON VALE

STELLAR DATE: 04.08.3192 (Adjusted Gregorian)
LOCATION: Observation Lounge, Chinquapin Construction
REGION: C-47 Dockyards, Proxima Centauri System

Terrance Enfield stood in front of the expansive floor-to-ceiling plas windows, staring out at a ship anchored to the edge of the C-47 dock. The vessel that held his attention soared high above the observation lounge in which he stood, its running lights flashing the red-and-white of a moored ship. The light from Proxima's red dwarf bathed the ship in a golden glow and mingled with the light that Chinquapin Construction used to illuminate the ship. The combined lighting caused it to stand in sharp relief against the inky blackness of nearspace.

Its form was crisp and well-defined, and Terrance could see a clear difference between the gleaming silver of the ship's original surface and the areas where it was being reskinned. Panels formed into a thick metal foam had been fabricated to precisely overlay the craft's existing frame. These Elastene panels were slowly encroaching upon the ship's surface, enveloping the craft in the matte grey substance. Pretty, it was not. But what it lacked in aesthetics, it more than made up for in safety and performance.

Elastene was a relatively new Enfield material. Its shape-memory properties allowed it to absorb impacts from micrometeorites, space debris, and—stars forbid—weapons fire. It could transfer the kinetic energy from such strikes, spreading it across a much greater surface area. And that made it superior to any other substance currently in use in the Centauri systems.

Terrance was determined that Phantom Blade have the best tech available for this mission. As a civilian ship, he couldn't really arm the ship the way he'd like. But he could damn well ensure it had the same defensive capabilities of any fleet ship—especially given that his company had *invented* the stuff.

He spotted tiny flickers of light as far up the ship's frame as he could see, lights that signified worker-bots darting about, executing the refit to his specifications. Before him, Chinquapin workers maneuvered large maglev trucks from the dockyard into the wide-open maw of the cargo bay amidships. The trucks were filled with equipment to be installed within the vessel—new sensors, upgrades to the craft's medbay, and an endless stream of requisite supplies for those embarking on a decades-long interstellar voyage.

As Terrance craned his neck, leaning forward to try to spy the bow of the ship that towered a full kilometer and a half above where he stood, he heard the sound of a low laugh come from behind him.

"You don't do things by halves, do you?"

He turned to see Eric, the El Dorado Space Force commodore who had, until recently, been embedded inside his head. As the AI approached, Terrance smiled and gestured to the ship. "Not too late to change your mind, you know."

He experienced a brief wave of disorientation as the AI cocked an eyebrow at him. It was a familiar expression, one Eric would often send to him privately, along the pathway inside his head that the two of them shared, but he wasn't used to seeing it two meters away from him on a physical body.

"You know I can't refuse the FGT's request." Eric shook his head, turning from the observation windows and reciprocating Terrance's smile with a brief one of his own. "Besides, you don't need an old space dog hanging around to finish this mission."

The AI stepped forward, joining Terrance at the plas window. Nodding toward the ship, he asked, "Have you told the team about her, yet?"

Terrance shook his head, a small smile playing about his face. "Calista and Shannon know, but not the rest. Everyone's had their hands full these past few weeks, getting the *Speedwell* ready for its new owners. Plus, I admit, I selfishly wanted to have this one farther along before revealing her to them." He checked his chrono. "If you want to hang around for the big reveal, they should be arriving soon."

Eric shook his head. "Already said my goodbyes, and anyway, things are still a bit too fresh between Jason and that trigger I pulled."

His gaze turned searching, and Terrance knew what the AI was about to say.

"Don't." Terrance raised a hand. "You know, and so do I, that even though it may have technically violated the Phobos Accords to take over my motor control for the briefest of moments, it was the only way to be certain that Prime was taken down. I don't fault you for it. To this day, I don't know that I would have been capable of taking the shot. And it had to be done. I don't blame you for it. Neither does Jason."

A long silence fell between the two of them, and Terrance saw something give in the commodore's frame as the AI nodded.

"Eric," Terrance added in a quiet voice, "the AI Council exonerated you. Stars know they were much harder on you than the C-47 humans were—almost as hard as you were on yourself."

Eric paused, his expression inscrutable, and then nodded once.

"Think you'll ever embed inside another human?" The question was out before Terrance had a chance to stop it.

Wincing inside, he hoped the AI wasn't offended by his insensitivity to the situation, given that the Council had almost banned him from doing so ever again.

The AI's expression grew wry. "Think I'll stick to a frame for a while yet. Who knows what will happen once I arrive at Lucida. But if you don't mind a final bit of advice from an old space dog...."

Eric paused until Terrance's gaze met his, and then the AI's expression became focused and intent. "You're the new leader of Phantom Blade, Terrance. Having an AI partner—someone like

Kodi, for instance—could prove to be a valuable asset. It's an advantage that might mean the difference between the mission's success or its failure."

Terrance hesitated, unwilling to think along those lines just yet, but he could hear the truth in the commodore's voice.

He nodded, and Eric clapped his shoulder with one of his humanoid hands. "Then I'll take my leave. Safe travels, and I wish you success in Tau Ceti." The AI smiled as Terrance murmured the same. He turned to leave, but paused before he exited the observation lounge. "Look me up if you ever bump into the FGT again, will you?" And with a wave, he was gone.

Terrance stared bemusedly after the AI for a long moment, then shook himself and checked his chrono. The team should be arriving shortly, and he looked forward to their reaction when they saw their new ride.

He signaled a servitor to deliver refreshments to the lounge he'd reserved from Chinquapin Construction for just this occasion, and then reached out to Calista to check on her ETA.

Technically, Calista and Shannon were employees of Enfield Holdings, the shell corporation Terrance ran—established back in El Dorado at the request of the system's prime minister. The company also functioned as a legitimate business, setting up satellite offices in whatever system the team was deployed. It was the perfect cover from which Phantom Blade could operate, and both Calista and Shannon had been read in to the team at the same time Terrance had.

It helped that both had also been instrumental in developing some of the tech the company was in the business of selling. Most of what they sold, like the ship's Elastene cladding, was targeted to a star system's military and defense organizations. But their most recent tech innovation, stasis, promised to touch a much broader consumer base.

True stasis was a technology many sought to attain; its realization by one of Enfield Holdings' sister companies would make the Enfield conglomerate a tidy sum. The invention of stasis pods promised to revolutionize long-distance space travel for humans and other live cargo, and had applications in medical and scientific industries, as well—not to mention its potential military uses.

About a third of the crew complement that had transited to Proxima with them on the *Speedwell* were Enfield employees; the rest were on loan from either the ESF or military intelligence, or were retired military who were brought in as support staff for Phantom Blade and its missions.

Calista's answering ping told Terrance that she had rounded up the team and they were on their way; the pin she dropped showed them in transit from the *Speedwell*. As the servitor trundled in with the refreshments he'd ordered, Terrance estimated that the unit would have just enough time to set everything out and then depart before they arrived.

One person he was still a bit apprehensive about being around was the man accompanying Calista. Tobias had assured Terrance that Jason harbored no ill feelings toward him, but he'd been friends with Jason long enough to tell that the pilot was holding a slight distance between them.

*If someone lined up the reticle of a sniper rifle on **my** sister, I'd be more than a bit distant. Maybe I wasn't the one who took the shot—* Terrance closed his eyes in an attempt to banish the memory. *But there's no getting around the fact that the weapon was in **my** hands. And Jason was just meters away from her at the time....*

It helped that Judith had survived, and that Jason understood there had been no other choice. The pilot hadn't quite returned to the easy and comfortable relationship the two men had enjoyed prior to the encounter, but Terrance held out hope that time would solve that issue.

The servitor pinged, and a charge appeared over Terrance's Link, informing him of the delivery fee as the bot floated past him and out of the lounge. The doors had barely slid shut behind it before they opened again to admit the task force.

Calista led the procession, followed by Jason and the three AI frames of Logan, Landon, and Tobias. The captain stopped next to Terrance and shot him an anticipatory grin as she turned to watch Jason. Terrance was sure the pilot's reaction wouldn't disappoint.

Sure enough, Jason came to an abrupt halt as he spied the ship, which was framed by the lounge's bank of plas windows.

"Holy—!" Jason emitted a low whistle as he walked forward to examine the ship on display. "Tobe! Do you see—?"

The Weapon Born joined Jason at the window after shooting Terrance a measuring look. "Aye, boyo. It's the *Avon Vale*."

Terrance stepped up next to them and glanced over at Jason. "I owe your dad one for recommending this ship. She's a solid vessel."

The pilot wrenched his gaze from the window long enough to acknowledge Terrance's comment with a brief nod that, while not up to his usual ebullient standards, was at least cordial.

"Yeah, the old man might be a physicist, but he knows his ships." At Terrance's quirked brow, Jason smirked. "Dude. Who do you think taught me to fly?"

Calista looked startled at that. "I didn't know Rhys was a pilot, Jason."

"Ah, the stories I could tell, lass," the Weapon Born interjected, a smile in his voice as he turned his head back toward Calista. "Remind me to share with you the tale of how Lysander and I first met Rhys—and how he and Jane Sykes ended up together."

Terrance smothered a laugh when he saw Jason shoot Tobias a startled look. "You played matchmaker, Tobe? This, I gotta hear."

Shannon's avatar coalesced in the lounge as she accessed the room's emitters. "Knowing him, he probably stranded the two of them somewhere," she shot sardonically, sending a wink toward Jason, who strangled a laugh as he shook his head.

"Sounds about right," he agreed, then turned reluctantly away from the bank of windows as Calista tugged on his arm.

"Food first," she said. "While we eat, I can tell you all about what we're doing to her."

The humans grabbed plates and piled them with morsels from the various dishes Terrance had ordered, before pulling seats up to the windows. They munched in comfortable silence for a few moments, and then Terrance turned to Calista, a question in his eyes.

Smiling, she accessed the lounge's nearest holowall and brought up the ship's schematics. "Work on the *Avon Vale* is right on schedule," she announced, highlighting the aft end of the vessel. "They've almost completed their install of the matchbox fusion reactors and will begin on-frame engine testing soon."

"Nice," Terrance complimented. He had a pretty good grasp of what was required to outfit a vessel for an interstellar voyage, courtesy of his stint as CEO of Enfield Aerospace. That meant he could appreciate the scope of work that the former ESF pilot had just described.

"Okay, wait," Jason interrupted. "Before we go on, I just have to ask—*how* did you get the habitat to part with a piece of history like the *Avon Vale*?"

Terrance sent the pilot a wry grin. "Proxima's Habitat Marines are getting our entire first run of Matchbox Fusion Reactors to refit their system defense ships. In exchange, we get the *Avon Vale*, free and clear."

Jason whistled. "The *Avon Vale* might be ancient, but it's one of a very few ships in Proxima that's a whopping three kilometers long. Exactly how many MFRs did you promise them for that?"

Terrance glowered at the pilot. "Don't ask. And *don't* tell my grandmother."

He heard Tobias chuckle lightly at that; the AI had met Sophia Enfield, the head of the Enfield conglomerate, the year before, back in El Dorado.

"Something tells me that Prime Minister Lysander will make sure it's worth her while," the AI said, and Terrance quirked him a half-grin. He knew Tobias was correct.

"At any rate," Terrance continued, "relic of Proxima's past notwithstanding, the *Vale*'s ours now. Private sector's already lining up to see who gets first dibs on the second run of MFRs. They tried to start a bidding war for the eight I was holding back for install in the *Avon Vale*," he nodded to the holo of the ship Calista had pulled up, "but I figured we might need those for our journey."

Jason snorted at that, and Calista grinned. "Yep. As I was saying earlier, they've already replaced the original fusion engines with Enfield MFRs," she said. "Four to a side, each cluster housed inside the casings where the original two larger and less efficient ones once were. But as nice as those are to have, this sweet little baby right here—" she tapped on a rectangular protrusion centered between the two engines, and fanned her fingers out to widen the display, "is going to give us a nice little boost, too."

Terrance heard Jason emit another low whistle. "An antimatter-pion drive? Sweet," the pilot said, sending Terrance a wide smile. "What bank did you have to rob to get the antimatter for it? Wait, I forgot—" and Terrance ignored the slight edge in Jason's voice that wouldn't have been there a month ago, "you're an Enfield."

He caught Calista squeezing Jason's arm with a warning hand, and the pilot shot Terrance what might have been an apologetic look as she launched into the next part of her update.

"We're riding Chinquapin's S&Ps pretty hard with the refit," she said, "since we're doing quite a bit more to her than engine upgrades."

Terrance knew the S&Ps she referred to were the 'spaceframe and powerplant' engineering teams that typically worked on insystem and interstellar vessels. Contrary to what some believed, ships did not come with expiration dates. For more than a thousand years, humanity's ships had been carving their way through sky and space with meticulous and rigorous maintenance routines. Regular inspections were historically performed by

Airframe and Powerplant specialists—A&Ps. Later, they came to be known as *Space*frame and Powerplant, or S&Ps. These were the teams that kept ships at peak performance, often for centuries at a time.

It was also why the *Avon Vale,* though a relic by conventional standards, given its almost centenarian status, was a well-maintained and supremely functional ship. When they were done with her, she would once more be state-of-the-art.

As Calista wound down her itemization of the myriad alterations being made to the three-kilometer-long ship, Terrance turned from the holowall to pin her with a questioning glance.

"Estimate on completion?"

She cocked her head, and Terrance knew the woman was pulling up the file on the crew's backoff schedule.

"Six more weeks, and then we should be good to go," she confirmed.

"Nice," Tobias said. "What about the other preparations? Jason, boyo, weren't you working on mapping the route?"

Jason grinned and shrugged. "Pretty straightforward, Tobe. We're here—" he drew an invisible line in the air from one point to another, "and Tau Ceti's there. Just a bunch of interstellar medium in between. Nothing the ship's new Elastene surfaces can't handle."

Terrance allowed his gaze to sweep across those present. "Anything else?" His eyes lit upon Logan. "Didn't Eric say you were putting together a report on Tau Ceti?"

The moment Terrance uttered Eric's name, he winced mentally. *Dammit, Enfield. Way to bring up the name of the one person you know Jason would rather forget about....*

Jason's expression didn't change, but Calista shifted, her shoulder coming in contact with the pilot's in what Terrance suspected was a deliberate yet subtle gesture of support.

He shot the two an apologetic look before returning his gaze to Logan.

As the team profiler, no one was better at extracting information on a topic than this AI. Logan was almost prescient in his ability to marry apparent unrelated bits of intel into a detailed précis on any subject. Terrance had seen it give Phantom Blade the edge they needed to defeat their enemies during each of their past engagements; he was counting on it for this mission as well.

Logan shifted, and Terrance got the impression the AI was gathering his thoughts.

"The organization that purchased our victims—the Matsu-kai," he began, "They're a people you do not want to cross. Not without significant backing."

Terrance exchanged a look with Tobias at those words. The Weapon Born nodded slowly in confirmation as Logan continued.

"However, their numbers aren't nearly as substantial in Tau Ceti as they are in Alpha Centauri, and that will make our retrieval easier." The profiler cast a warning look toward the rest of the team. "That doesn't mean we shouldn't train hard before we arrive, in the event we have to engage them in order to free our people."

Terrance found himself nodding in agreement and saw the others doing the same.

Jason leant forward, hands clasped, forearms braced on his knees, and face intent. "What kind of training are we talking about here, Logan?"

Logan tilted his head, and Terrance could have sworn a faint light of amusement crossed the AI's features before they settled into his usual mask.

"Not physical, if that's what you're asking," the profiler countered. "Not *entirely* physical, at least," he amended, drawing a puzzled look from those around him.

Logan sat back, regarding the group as they waited for him to expound on his veiled comment. "The Matsu-kai is an ancient order, steeped in ritual and culture. You can, quite literally, mortally offend one of them and forfeit your life as a result. So I've drawn up a paper that will help you understand them better." His tone took on a mordant edge. "It would be nice if we could manage to avoid insulting one of them while we are there."

Jason coughed as Tobias shot him a pointed look, and Terrance fought a smirk at the pilot's pained innocence. "What? I'll read it, I swear." Then, under his breath, he added, "Bet it doesn't have any pictures, though."

Calista swatted Jason's thigh as Terrance lost his battle with the smirk. Determined to act like the leader Eric had elected him to be, he returned his gaze to Logan.

"What else?" Terrance prompted.

Logan swiveled to the holowall that now sat blank, following Calista's use of it. It sprang to life, showing various headlines from Galene and Eione, the two planets in Tau Ceti that had been colonized. The imagery indicated that the news was almost twenty years out of date and certainly not the most recent feed from the system.

Logan zoomed in and highlighted the word 'nanophage' before turning back to regard the team. "I know that more recent news from Tau Ceti says that the Imbesi scare was unfounded, but there is often a kernel of truth to be found in such reports." The AI's expression was grave. "I want us to take steps to ensure that we're prepared, in case we arrive to discover that rumor was, in fact, truth."

Landon stirred, and Terrance saw the AI glance at his brother before returning his gaze to him. "The only sure way to kill nano is with a triple-pulse EMP." Landon paused, and Terrance nodded for him to continue. "One of the best methods to deliver that is through a tactical nuclear device."

A tactical nuke? How the hell am I supposed to get my hands on military weaponry?

Terrance was sure Landon saw the consternation on his face. The AI lifted one hand to forestall any protests. "Don't worry. I'll make sure the *Avon Vale* has plenty on hand before we depart."

EXPANSE

STELLAR DATE: 05.01.3192 (Adjusted Gregorian)
LOCATION: ESS *Avon Vale*
REGION: C-47 Habitat, Proxima Centauri System

Shannon watched Landon's progress as he prowled through the *Avon Vale*'s stacked ship's decks one by one, before catching one of the maglev cars that would take him to the topmost dock, three kilometers away. From there, he began again, pacing off every corner of the bare metal decking, checking that the bay doors were secure, then touching each access panel that led to point defense weaponry. His obsessive behavior continued as he moved aft to the cargo pods, first on the port side, and then starboard. She switched her feeds so that she could follow him as he moved through the shuttle bay and into the habitat ring of the ship.

Gone was the cheerful, carefree person who had once pranked her by rearranging the external sensors of their headquarters back in El Dorado, so that when she projected herself into the meeting room, a short, pink, fuzzy poodle—complete with sparkly ribbons—appeared instead of her usual avatar. When she'd tried to protest the indignity, her words had come out in dainty little yips. This had been payback for the time she'd once had him deployed on an op in a teensy little bot frame that Calista had jokingly called 'cute as a puppy'.

That prankster, she feared, had been another one of Prime's victims, and she felt a shaft of anger coursing through her core that was completely at odds with her personality.

Her concern had caused her to reach out to the ship's doctor a few weeks earlier, when she'd first noticed the twin's compulsive behavior. Marta had eased her mind back then, and had introduced Shannon to one of her medics, Justin. Shannon had met Justin before, but hadn't realized that the AI had served a stint in the AI Wing of El Dorado Memorial Hospital. The two medical professionals had reassured Shannon, advising her to let Landon work it out of his system. Healing took many forms, they had informed her, and often manifested itself differently in each individual.

Still. After a moment's hesitation, she reached out to the doctor once more.

<Marta, he's at it again.>

<Just give him a bit more time,> came Marta's reply, her mental tone soothing. Shannon hoped the human knew what she was doing.

* * * * *

Landon knew Shannon was monitoring him; he knew it because he'd set up his own systems all over the ship to monitor the entire team. No one moved, breathed or sent a packet of data without his knowledge. Eric had called him on it the first week he'd been back, and he'd come clean to the commodore, admitting that he understood it was compulsive-like behavior—but having lost Judith to a predator they'd all been aware of, one they'd actively been shielding her from, only to have Prime ambush her, practically in front of him and without his awareness of it....

It was more than he could take. His brain shied away from the inevitable end to that mental path: his own death by the very trickster who had plucked Judith out from under his protection.

The commodore had confided in Landon that he'd seen what humans referred to as 'AI PTSD' before. It was a form of post traumatic synaptic misfiring that could occur after an AI endured an exceptionally harrowing event. He'd agreed to allow Landon to continue making his rounds, provided the twin gave his commanding officer full transparency to his every move.

Landon tested the connection now, saw the feed in place that said he was being monitored as he moved through the ship.

Although he'd never before heard the description 'AI PTSD', it certainly fit. The urgency, this commitment to vigilance, was an internal demand he could not ignore—a need to ensure he was not caught off guard ever again.

Shannon didn't think he knew she was observing him as well, but the little engineer, while a brilliant designer and a systems genius, was no warrior. She was no match for him. It warmed him, though, that she was worried for him. So he pretended to be unaware of her watchfulness.

He completed his third circuit of the day and was about to begin his fourth when Shannon pinged him.

<Landon, the C-47's AI Council just pinged,> the engineer sent. <They want to pull all the AI members of the task force into an expanse before we ship out. Can you come to the ready room? We're waiting for you.>

Landon sent his acquiescence and released the maglev car he'd called. Turning, he made his way aft, to the deck that held the *Avon Vale*'s command offices.

* * * * *

Logan swiveled his frame to face the door as Landon entered. Every time he saw his twin, he felt an ache deep within. It wasn't that Landon hadn't forgiven him; they'd both moved past that weeks ago. He just wanted his formerly cheerful brother back.

He'd had a few interesting conversations with Calista—the retired ESF pilot had turned into a remarkably easy sounding board, and he'd come to view her as a close friend. Some of the euphemisms she'd used to describe Landon's behavior had a curiously lilting quality to them, almost poignantly beautiful analogies describing the impact of the past year upon his twin.

'The light was gone from his eyes,' was one he found particularly descriptive. 'The past weighs heavily on his heart' was another. Though technically, an AI had neither eyes nor a heart, those phrases somehow captured the damage Prime had done to Landon's spirit. Logan hoped Marta was correct when she told him that 'time healed all wounds'.

So many human phrases....

Landon approached him now, his humanoid frame identical to Logan's own, and sat next to him as Tobias entered in the new frame he'd begun to use after Tobi, the Proxima cat, was uplifted. Shannon, embedded in the ship as she was, joined them as a projection. As she coalesced, Tobias initiated the connection to the Council without comment.

Suddenly, they were no longer in the *Avon Vale*'s ready room. Instead, they stood on the shores of Lake Chinquapin, surrounded by the leaders of the Proxima habitat's AI community. That this expanse had been created by Proxima's AI Council was obvious by its exquisite detail; personal expanses were often much simpler.

Unless one happened to be Weapon Born.

He recalled the expanse that Lysander, El Dorado's prime minister, had created at the inception of the team now known as Phantom Blade. It had been every bit as detailed—although much smaller in scope. He was certain this one included the deft touch of at least one or two Weapon Born, maybe more, but knew it was more a matter of scale.

He glanced up at the opposite side of the cylinder stretching above him, the kilometers of atmosphere between where he stood and the cylinder's far side limiting his visibility. Behind him, down the long axis, light streamed in from Proxima's red dwarf, where an array of mirrors focused its light, illuminating the C-47's inhabitants. The redirected light bathed the cliffs on the other side of the lake in a golden hue, dappled by the shadows of clouds skittering along the surface of the terrain. The other end, he knew, terminated in the habitat's dock-and-spindle that was the cylinder's egress point.

Tobias was standing in front and to his right. He turned as he heard footfalls behind him to see Shannon approaching. She came to a stop between him and his twin. Landon met his gaze with a brief nod, eyes shadowed.

A statuesque woman stepped forward and addressed Tobias. "We wished to convene one last time prior to your departure. As a former resident of the C-47, you know us, Tobias. But for the benefit of the rest of your team," she turned toward Logan, glancing from him to Shannon and then to his twin, "we are the Council here in Proxima. We have been monitoring your progress, Landon, and although we deeply regret the circumstances that necessitated your Restoration, we are gratified you were not lost to us."

Logan chanced a glance at Landon and saw his brother's lips press together in a grim expression, but he tilted his head in a simple nod of thanks.

"With a journey of this length, we want to ensure that you have an expanse of your own within the *Avon Vale*, to nurture you along the way during the times you choose to remain out of stasis. We have uploaded a knowledge base onto the ship for you and have provided a foundation so that the Expanse will operate independent of you. You are aware of what you face in Tau Ceti?"

If Tobias was surprised at the abrupt topic change, he didn't show it.

"We know our two shackled AIs have been sent there, and we plan to get them back." The Weapon Born gave a slight shrug. "I've seen the reports that El Dorado forwarded from Sol. Looks like they experienced a nano event almost two decades ago, but so far, all the follow-up reports say the release was contained."

The statuesque AI raised a hand, and another councilmember stepped forward. With a wave of his hand, statistics projected, hovering between the two groups like liquid silver.

"The population in Tau Ceti is ninety-five percent human, five percent AI, with standard distribution among AI ethnicities and disciplines," the male AI informed them. "As of our last report, most of them are first-generation settlers, with very few AIs being second-generation natives to the system. Of the human ethnicities, they are fairly evenly divided between Japanese, Russian, and Hispanic old-Earth descent."

Landon shifted, and the movement caught the attention of the AI speaking. He turned politely, and Logan saw the barely contained impatience in his twin as Landon spoke.

"What difference does it matter what the ethnic mix of the humans in the system is? We're not there to socialize; we're there to retrieve two of our own who were shackled and then sold."

Logan saw Shannon frown at his brother, just as the Council leader responded.

"It matters because we have recently learned that the ones who purchased our brethren are members of the Matsu-kai—a criminal organization of Japanese origin. They have a branch in El Dorado with a Family connection on Ring Galene. It matters because this will provide you with a place to begin your search."

Landon hesitated, and then ducked his head, his expression subdued. Logan saw Tobias clasp his brother on the shoulder as the Weapon Born turned toward their team.

"There's a wee bit of good news, though, thanks to our friends back home. The Matsu-kai deployed our two friends on a fast drone to Tau Ceti," Logan saw the Weapon Born glance over at the AI Council before returning his gaze to the team, his eyes glinting in satisfaction. "But Lysander managed to ferret out its ident codes and has forwarded them to us. If we're lucky, when we get closer to the system, we'll be able to take control of it and stop their delivery. At that point, we can set up a rendezvous with the drone and retrieve our people."

Shannon blew out a relieved breath—something uniquely human, a habit of Calista's that the engineer had picked up.

"It's about time we caught a break," she muttered under her breath.

Although his expression revealed nothing, Logan agreed heartily with her sentiment.

The AI leader inclined her head. "Be that as it may, in the event you find yourselves unable to intercept our people prior to their being taken captive within the system, you will want the name of the so-*honbucho*, the regional chief for the Matsu-kai organization on Ring Galene. His name is Hiro Takumi."

VOXBOXES AND BONITO FLAKES

STELLAR DATE: 05.21.3192 (Adjusted Gregorian)
LOCATION: Andrews residence, Lake Chinquapin Estates
REGION: C-47 Habitat, Proxima Centauri

The past six weeks had been filled with supply runs, simulator time on the new ship's systems, and a seemingly unending list of other tasks required for a vessel heading on a decades-long journey. Now that they were just a day or two out from their departure, Jason had begged off a proficiency refresher sim on the Enfield shuttles in order to fly out and pay a final visit to his family.

Sims like that can be done once we're underway, at any rate, he thought to himself as he nosed the aircar down from one of the habitat's main airways to one of the small feeder routes.

"Huh."

Jason glanced over at Terrance's grunt to see the man's gaze fixed outside the windscreen.

When Terrance had asked to come along, Jason realized he felt a bit of resentment. It was the very reason the exec was sitting beside him now. Jason had never been one to hold grudges, so he'd given himself a mental shake when he'd recognized his own lingering antipathy, and had determined to push past it.

Besides, it's always more fun when I can share the thrill of the flight, he thought.

Behind the two men sat the Tobys, the big cat sprawled across the length of the back seating area, and the Weapon Born's frame wedged uncomfortably into a corner.

Well, uncomfortable for a human, Jason amended, and he smirked at the image of the large cat taking up more than her share of the back seat, front paws dangling over the legs of Tobias's frame.

"Huh," Terrance said again, pulling Jason's attention back to the passenger seat.

Jason grinned as the large, sandy-haired man craned his neck to seek a better view of the habitat's lone lake.

They could just make out the tiny specks of pleasure craft floating along its surface, before the image was obscured by a small cloud that Jason had opted to fly through, rather than around. He smirked a bit at the irritated glance Terrance shot him as they were enveloped by the soft whiteness.

"Take it easy," he grinned over at the exec. "This'll just last another few seconds, and then you'll get your view back."

"Most people use the holoscreen when they fly an aircar, like civilized people," the exec grumbled. "Come to think of it, *most* people also don't override the controls and fly an aircar manually." The man shot Jason a scowl, which surprised a laugh out of him.

He just wiggled his fingers at Terrance and winked. "Yeah, but most aren't natural L2s with kickass reflexes."

Terrance snorted, but Jason saw an expression that might be relief cross the other man's face. He realized it had been awhile since the two of them had joked around like this; what was more, he realized he'd missed it.

"*Mutated's* more like it, ya freak," Terrance said after a beat, but the half-smile Jason saw on the man's face softened the harsh words.

Jason replied with a jaunty, "Yep, that's me; freakishly fast. And you should thank me for it, by the way. That means you get an unimpeded, *authentic* view. You're one with the craft—and your environment."

Just then, they popped out of the cloud cover and were rewarded with a clear view of Lake Chinquapin below. Terrance snorted again, and then lapsed into silence after another brief, "huh," as he peered out at the view.

The Andrewses lived in a quiet suburb opposite the dock-and-spindle side of the great lake they were currently overflying, a lake that bisected the long axis of the C-47 Habitat. It was the only strip along the four-thousand-kilometer habitat cylinder where the 'ground' fully encased its circumference. Lake Chinquapin, named after the planet the habitat orbited, was rimmed by cliffs along its two long edges to prevent flooding, in case a sudden shift along the habitat's long axis caused the water to overflow its boundaries. In the long history of the C-47, that had never happened.

The lake itself provided stabilization to the cylinder, dampening the slight rotational instability that occurred along its secondary rotational axis. It also provided a scenic landmark, which drew residents of the habitat to its shores for various forms of water recreation.

"Huh," Terrance repeated again, and Jason could no longer ignore it.

"What's with all the 'huh'-ing, anyway?" he asked as he maneuvered the aircar out of the common airspace lanes and onto a vector that would take them to his parents' house.

Terrance gestured vaguely to the view outside the windscreen, a verdant green landscape under blue skies, studded with puffy white clouds drifting lazily in the afternoon sun. "I don't know, I always imagined that, living around a red dwarf, the light would be a lot...*redder*."

Jason snorted. " 'Red dwarf' is a bit of a misnomer. Proxima's an M five-point-five, and its effective temperature's around twenty-seven-fifty Kelvin." He glanced over at Terrance. "You know Rigel K's a main sequence yellow dwarf, right around fifty-six K, right?" He raised a brow at Terrance, who nodded, so he continued.

"Well, El Dorado sees Proxima color temperatures at sunrise and sunset. Photographers love that shit. They call it 'the golden hour', and they actually wait for it in order to get the best images." Jason waved a hand at the golden hue of the light surrounding them. "Here, we get it all the time, no extra charge." Terrance nodded, then fell silent as Jason busied himself with his final descent.

The burst of nostalgia that hit him as he approached his parents' house caught Jason by surprise. His eyes devoured the quiet, tree-lined street, the house nested among trees, the park expanse that it backed up to.

I suppose it's because I'll be a lot farther than two-tenths of a light-year away this time....

* * * * *

Terrance admired the view, while Jason, with the efficiency borne from many years of practice, cycled the 'car off and triggered the doors to slide open.

Gorgeous bit of land, the executive thought, as Jason stepped out and made room for Tobi to exit the rear compartment. Tobias waited patiently just behind Terrance, not saying a word as he lingered in the passenger seat.

Jason must have sensed his hesitation—or maybe the Proxima native just noticed that the passenger-side door had yet to open. Placing one hand on the aircar's roof, he leant down and stuck his head back inside.

"Nuh-uh," he said, smirking at Terrance. "You're not sitting this visit out. Dude, *you* were the one who wanted to tag along." He paused a beat, and Terrance caught the glint in Jason's eye. He cringed, knowing what was coming.

"*Don't* say it," he warned Jason, rushing out of the aircar in his haste to prevent the pilot from blurting out the words. "Stars, not *here,* of all places!" he hissed, looking around furtively.

"Seriously, we all know why you're stalling." Jason's eyes were lit with an unholy mischief as he added, "Dude. You *shot* my sister."

Terrance groaned, palming his face, as he heard Tobias emit an audible snicker from inside the aircar as the AI released his harness and began to climb out.

"You know, boyo," the AI said, addressing Jason, "you've got a mean streak a kilometer wide."

Jason snorted, glancing over at the AI. "And I wonder where I got that from, Tobe." He cocked his head and shot him a pointed look. "You were a 'terrible influence on an impressionable youth'."

A chuckle from behind Terrance had him pivoting to see Rhys Andrews approaching.

"I think I actually heard the quotation marks around those words," the elder Andrews said as he paused next to his son and clapped him on the shoulder.

"Pity Jane's not here to see that the lad actually retained one of the phrases she was so fond of using when he was young." The Weapon Born's banter held a pronounced Irish lilt, and Terrance stifled a smirk as Jason shot the AI a dark look.

Rhys laughed, nodded amiably at Terrance, then waved the group to the rooftop entrance. "Come on in; Jane has a few 'individuals' she'd like you all to meet."

* * * * *

Tobias connected with the house's comm system as they entered, exchanging greetings with Jane's assistant, Rupert, the AI helping her to manage the latest brood of uplifted Proxima cats.

Curious, he used the holoemitters in the family great room to skip ahead of his frame and project an image of himself. He bent down next to where Jane knelt and saw that her hand was enveloped by four tiny paws as one of the kittens gnawed at the knuckle of one hand. He was certain these were the 'individuals' Rhys had referenced earlier.

"Cute little guy," Tobias said, and Jane jumped and gave a muffled shriek, sending kittens scampering in all directions—including through his holo image.

"Tobias!" she scolded. "Warn a person next time you sneak up on her."

He sent her a rakish grin, green eyes dancing, and he knew he looked as unrepentant as he felt.

Jason's right; I was a terrible influence on an impressionable teen.

Although, said teen had already been eyeballs-deep in enough mischief that the AI's presence hadn't made much of a dent in the boy's behavior.

"Is this the new litter?" he asked, sending a nod at the various small animals who had recovered from Jane's surprise and were back to scampering around the room.

"Mmm, yes," she acknowledged with a smile. "Indeed they are, all six of them." She cocked her head. "I take it Jason's here—or did you skip on ahead of him?"

"Not through the habitat net, no," Tobias told her. "I came the conventional route—although Jason did pick up a few hitchhikers along the way."

He grinned as Jane lifted a questioning eyebrow, arms crossed as she waited for him to elaborate.

"Terrance and Tobi are with him," he explained, and she smiled fondly at the mention of the large Proxima cat she'd raised from kittenhood before Tobi had taken to traveling with Jason.

Tobias was glad to see Jason's mother looking so relaxed. It had been a harrowing few weeks for the neurosurgeon as she struggled to rebuild her daughter's brain after Eric had taken that fateful shot. Thanks to thirty-second century medicine, Judith was well on the path to full recovery.

Tobias heard the three human men approaching and dissolved his projection as his frame entered the room. He saw his former method of transport bound past the three humans and rise up on her hind legs to run a cold, wet nose along the side of Jane's face.

"Tobi!" Jane scolded with a laugh, ruffling the fur behind the big cat's ears, as the creature purred and rubbed the side of her face down Jane's arm.

The large cat squawked indignantly as one of the kittens— cream colored, with tips of silver edging his short, sleek coat—

pounced, leaping onto her flank and nipping at her.

<Brat!> Tobi yowled the word, turning to cuff the kitten with a sharp swat. <Quit it!> Her swipe sent the little ball of fur tumbling away.

"*Fun!*" a small voice called out, and the kitten who'd been swatted ran up to Tobi and latched onto her front paw with all four of his own. "*Do it again!*"

"Voxbox?" Jason asked his mom, just as a low, rumbling growl emitted from the larger cat.

Tobias saw Terrance glance askance at Tobi; it was a sound the AI knew the exec rarely heard from the big cat.

<Brat! **Go. Away.**> Tobi, sitting stiff-legged between the little menace and Jane, nipped at the kitten's ear as she enunciated each word. Her strikes were swift and sure, and the kitten sat back, clearly stunned.

Then the small furball recovered and, with the fearlessness of youth, whirled about, barreling toward the three men.

Wailing at the top of his lungs, he proclaimed, "*Mean! She's a **meanie!** She **bit** me! Wifout provocations!*"

Terrance chuckled at the little guy, and the sound acted like a beacon. Suddenly, the exec found his lower leg encased in fur, as the kitten clung to him.

Tobias grinned as Terrance looked over at Jane in mild alarm, his face telegraphing a clear '*what do I do now?*' as the little guy attempted to use Terrance's leg as a ladder. Wincing, the exec bent and picked the kitten up; Rhys helped the man adjust his hold so that the kitten didn't protest being held—and so that Terrance didn't turn into a human pincushion.

Jane nodded at Jason. "Yes, to answer your question, what you're hearing *is* a voxbox. This is the first litter to be uplifted *in vitro*, and they're too young to have a Link embedded just yet, so implanting a vocalization device allows them to communicate until then." She grimaced as she looked at the cat Terrance held. "It's been…interesting."

"And by 'interesting', she means *noisy*," Rhys confided in a stage whisper. "This litter likes to *talk*."

"Do they have names?" Terrance asked, his attention focused on the kitten alternately gnawing on and licking at his fingers.

"You could say so," Jane said, and her voice held a note of laughter that had Terrance looking puzzled, and Jason groaning aloud.

Tobias grinned in anticipation. In their earlier greetings, Rupert had told him that Jane had magnanimously allowed Rhys to name this litter. He'd chosen various physics names for all six of the kittens—a combination of exotic particles and other units of measurement that Tobias was sure would have Jason rolling his eyes.

This ought to be entertaining.

"Yes, indeed," Rhys said, rubbing his hands together. "The girls here are Perl, Joule and Geim." He pointed to each in turn and pronounced their names 'pearl', 'jewel', and 'gem'. He caught Tobias's eye with a 'see what I did there' look that had Jason—

Yep, cue the eyeroll.

"They're named respectively after—"

"Physicists, yes, we know, Dad," Jason interrupted, but Terrance quirked a brow at Rhys.

"Joule I recognize," the exec said, "but not the other two...."

Rhys nodded, and Jane groaned as her husband launched into one of his favorite topics. "Well then, let's see, the Cliff's Notes version—" and here, he spared an 'I can be brief' look for his wife, "Perl discovered the tau lepton, and Geim was one of the two physicists who discovered a way to isolate single-layer graphene."

"He also developed one of the first biomimetic adhesives," Jason added, then grinned wickedly at Terrance's confused look. "It's that material in our base layers that allows us to adhere to ceilings, like the time you—"

Terrance jabbed him in the side with an elbow.

"The time you, uhh,—" Jason stumbled, "were just...playing

around. Well, at any rate, that's who Geim was," he finished lamely.

By the look on his parents' faces, he'd fooled no one. Jane looked intrigued, and Tobias was afraid she would ask about the incident Jason had brought up.

"And the rest of the litter?" the AI prompted in an attempt to derail her. "What are their names?"

"Oh, well…" Jane sighed and waved one hand at her husband. "You might as well tell them the rest, hon."

Rhys grinned unrepentantly at his wife, then turned and pointed at the kitten Terrance held. "That little guy you're holding is the runt of the litter—and the most spoiled."

*"Am **not**,"* the kitten grumbled around a mouthful of Terrance's fingers.

<*Are **too**,*> Tobi chuffed in disgust, and the kitten turned a tiny glare down at her and emitted his own miniature growl.

*"**Not** the mama,"* he said with finality, as if that decided the matter of Tobi's authority.

He then turned back to Terrance and reached up to pat the man's face—with unsheathed claws. Tobias saw Jason wince sympathetically as Terrance abruptly pulled back.

"Anyway," Rhys continued, "that little guy is Becquerel—Beck, for short. The two running around chasing their tails under the sofa are Pascal and Kelvin."

*"I'm **Beck!**"* the kitten crowed, reaching for Terrance's nose with both his front paws. *"Who are **you**?"*

"Scratched," the exec muttered, and Beck reared back, scrunching his nose.

"Tha's a funny name," he said solemnly, then squirmed to be let down.

Terrance let the bundle of fur drop to the ground, and Beck quickly licked one shoulder and then scampered off to play with his siblings.

Jane ushered them out to the sunny seating area on the side of the house that faced the park, holding the door open as the kittens swarmed outside. A servitor bot trundled up with drinks and snacks as Jane gestured them to take a seat. Tobias found his attention drawn to the litter as they played an impromptu game of chase, weaving among the bushes and small ornamental trees that dotted the park-like expanse.

The kitten who had taken a liking to Terrance had striking markings, unusual in a Proxima cat. In the dappled sunlight, his short fur took on an almost platinum hue, yet he had the breed's classic build: large, lean and muscular.

Tobias suspected that Jane had tinkered with their genetics, deviating a bit from the old-Earth strain of Savannah cat she'd used for Tobi's litter. He found himself sifting through various strains of *felis silvestris,* searching for a possible match for this new batch, when a correlation appeared.

<You mixed Tonkinese in with the Savannah genome?> he sent privately to Jane, who nodded with a slight smile. <Ahhh, that explains the mischievous behavior, then.>

He was rewarded with a sly wink.

"How's Judith?" Terrance suddenly asked, breaking into the companionable silence that had fallen.

"She's doing well," Jane said reassuringly, the smile that had been playing on her lips just moments before breaking out. "Her motor skills have almost fully returned, and she's adjusting quite well to her new eye."

Tobias saw Terrance wince at that, but Jane waved away his response before he had a chance to say anything.

"She's actually thrilled with the functionality of the new optics, says they'll be a huge help with some of her experiments back on El Dorado. Don't *worry*, Terrance," Jane said, leaning forward. "It's all good. And behind us now."

She gestured out toward the cats. "That's one thing we could stand to learn from our feline friends over there: the way they live is very in-the-moment. Cat sentience has a distinct otherness to it, as compared to that of humans or AIs. Although they do grasp the concept of a future, they don't spend time dwelling on it overmuch." She lifted her drink and saluted Terrance with it. "And they most certainly don't concern themselves over what has already happened."

"Except for that time you accidentally spaced Tobi's stash of bonito flakes during that freight run to El Dorado, boyo," Tobias reminded Jason. "Don't think she's gotten over that."

<*You spaced them?*> came an indignant howl from inside the house. <*You said Tobias did it!*>

"Oops...."

* * * * *

Jason relaxed back in his seat as he reached for his glass of fresh-squeezed lemonade.

Yeah, it's good to be home.

He savored that thought, his eyes coming to rest on first his mother and then his father, as he realized it could be a century or more before he saw them again. He was abruptly glad that rejuvenation treatments existed. In centuries past, this goodbye would have been their last.

Turning his attention back to the reason for their visit, he gave his dad a questioning look. "You said you wanted to discuss the Tau Ceti trip with us before we left...?"

Rhys nodded. "Indeed I do. For two reasons, actually. One is personal, the other is on behalf of the C-47 Council."

"The *Council?*" Jason could hear the surprise in his voice.

His dad nodded, smiling, as he took a sip from his own glass and then set it down, the condensation from the chilled drink causing rivulets to run through the imprint that the man's fingers had made on the outside of the glass.

"It's actually more of a business proposition with Enfield Holdings," Rhys said, reaching for a still-warm-from-the-oven soft pretzel bite and gesturing with it before popping it into his mouth.

Terrance swallowed his own bite before asking, "And what would that be?"

"The C-47 would like to hire Enfield to drop a string of communication buoys between here and Tau Ceti as the *Avon Vale* takes you there." Rhys reached for his glass again. "I know the ship has a small fabrication shop; any chance you could manufacture enough MFRs to power those buoys while you're on your way? I know we cleared out your inventory when we took payment for the ship."

Terrance set his own glass down and leant back in his seat, his gaze growing unfocused. Moments later, Jason answered a ping the exec sent, and joined a group net with Shannon and Calista. He waited as Terrance summed up his dad's request.

<It wouldn't really take much to do it,> the engineer said after a minute's consideration. <This would actually be the ideal application for an MFR. Buoys are low-powered; after the initial burst to decelerate when we drop them, they'll expend very little energy once they're deployed. The MFRs' small size would allow us to pack more shielding around the sensitive electronics inside the buoy, too.>

Jason met the question in Terrance's eyes with a decisive nod. <Let's do it.>

The exec turned to Rhys with a smile. "Tell the Council that Enfield would love to do business with them."

Rhys returned the smile with a wide grin. Jason started to ask after the other topic his dad wanted to discuss, when a kitten tore madly across the greenspace and made a beeline for Terrance. Hot at its heels was a second kitten, screeching in fury.

*"Scraaaaaaaaatched! Tell Perl I din't **eat** her stinky ol' bug!"* With that, Beck leapt for Terrance's lap, circled once, and plopped his little butt down, glaring at his sister, who was making tiny growling noises at him from the ground.

"You'd better tell him, mom," Jason warned.

"Beck!" Jane leant forward, snapping her fingers to get the

kitten's attention. "His name is *Terrance*. Not 'scratched'. And it's not polite to use your claws on a human when you jump up on them. What have I told you about that?"

Beck turned large aqua eyes toward Jane, opening them wide in mock innocence. *"Hy-oooo-mans are soft an' don't have no furs to protect from scritchy-scratches."*

"And what do you say to Terrance, since you scratched him earlier?" Jane prompted in the tone that Jason was sure every mother had used since time began.

<Stars, Tobe, I think I'm having flashbacks to my own childhood,> he sent to the AI, as the kitten began a laborious apology.

<Just wait,> the Weapon Born advised him. <Things are about to get interesting.>

Jason shot the AI a quizzical look then returned his gaze to Beck, who had curled up in the exec's lap and was now staring up at him adoringly. Jason's eyes narrowed.

Uh-oh. He shot his mom a sidelong glance. "Hey, Mom, mind if we bring another Proxima cat along with us to Tau Ceti?"

Terrance shot Jason a look, glanced down at the kitten, then looked over at them with an expression of dawning understanding.

"Uhh..." he said, and Jason smirked as, for once, words deserted the smooth-talking Enfield.

"I'd say 'cat got your tongue,' but that'd be—" Jason began, only to be drowned out by a chorus of groans. "Fine!" he waved away his attempt to be punny, but then cocked an eyebrow at his mom. "I'm right, though, about the bonding? Looks like someone's just staked his claim."

His mother nodded, but then raised a calming hand at Terrance's slightly panicked expression.

"If you don't think it'd work out, Becquerel will get over it," she said. "But he's always been the rascal of the bunch, jonesing for adventure. He'd love to go with you, if the team thinks they can handle a second cat."

<*Noooooooooo!*> came Tobi's mournful cry from indoors, and Jason exchanged grins with Tobias.

"Better stock up on bonito flakes, boyo," the Weapon Born stage-whispered with a smile. "Otherwise it could be a very *long* trip."

"Thanks a lot," Jason muttered. With a long-suffering sigh, he reached for the remaining pretzel on the platter, then shot Rhys a glance. "Not that I'm trying to change the subject or anything," he said around a mouthful of warm, salty bread, "but what's the personal thing you wanted to discuss with us, Dad?"

Rhys looked thoughtful as he rocked his chair slightly back and forth with one foot. After a moment, he smiled apologetically to his wife, then confessed, "It's more a matter of professional courtesy, I admit. There is a young physicist on Ring Galene by the name of Noa Sakai. He's been doing remarkable things with nanophotonics, and the data compares favorably with some of my findings. I was hoping you'd deliver some reports to him for me."

Jason's expression turned wry. "Guess the Council's not the only one looking forward to a more direct line of communication with Tau Ceti, huh?"

Rhys chuckled. "You could say that again. Sakai's findings are about sixteen years out of date at this point." He shook his head slightly, and his mouth kicked up in a half-smile. "Those comm buoys will be welcome—even if they do only cut five years or so off a message's journey."

Jason grinned as he rose. "Every little bit helps, I suppose. Maybe someday, you'll figure out a way to bend light and make it go a bit faster."

Rhys shook his head sorrowfully. "*That'll* be the day...."

HAPPY TUESDAY
STELLAR DATE: 05.22.3192 (Adjusted Gregorian)
LOCATION: Dock D1, ESS *Avon Vale*
REGION: C-47 Habitat, Proxima Centauri

The view that greeted Terrance as he strode from the D1 dock's wide-open hatch was one of controlled chaos. The dock was teeming with people, cargo, and worker-bots—all funneling their way from the massive, three-hundred-meter clear space into the oversized arch that led to the umbilical attached to the *Avon Vale*.

He knew that the other end of the umbilical terminated at one of the two large bays, situated midway down the three-kilometer length of the vessel. The bays housed both cargo and shuttles, and was as deep—and twice as wide—as the dock was long.

Yet still, the space somehow managed to feel crowded. Pallets stacked as high as the arch would allow floated past him. People scurried around him by the hundreds, finishing last-minute preparations in one form or another, or hurrying off to secure cargo prior to launch.

I should have secured D2 as well, Terrance thought as he squeezed past a small cluster of people who had paused at the midway point of the umbilical, forcing the flow of traffic to detour around. *Surely the bay's wide enough to accommodate two umbilicals.* His mental reprimand ended in an aggravated sigh as he pushed his way through into the dock proper and wove through the bustling crowd.

In all, the *Avon Vale* would be carrying around twenty-five hundred humans and almost four hundred AIs to Tau Ceti. There were over twelve hundred paying customers along for the ride, Proxans who had opted to relocate. Some saw it as a business opportunity; for others, it was a change of scenery, from habitat-living to a terraformed planet orbiting a G-type main sequence star. Given that this ship would be the first to transit the interstellar medium utilizing true stasis, the opportunity to simply fall asleep and in the next breath, awaken to find oneself instantly transported thirteen light years away was irresistible to many.

Of the remaining seventeen hundred souls, about five hundred were on extended loan from the El Dorado Space Force back in Alpha Centauri; the rest were Enfield employees. And then there were the ten that comprised Phantom Blade.

Terrance wove his way through the crowd, his destination the maglev that stretched the length of the ship's center core. The line ran from the small dock near the ship's bow all the way down through the center of the ship's habitat ring. It continued into the crew and command sections of the ship—a series of seven stacked decks that accommodated crew and passenger quarters, plus the levels that housed the ship's bridge and engineering at its aft end.

He nodded as he passed various Enfield and ESF crew members. Some of them he knew, most of them he didn't. To the people bustling around him, Terrance represented the corporation backing this venture, and a fair number of people who caught his eye nodded respectfully as they made their way to their various destinations.

Once the ship reached cruising speed the decks would detach from either side, rotate ninety degrees, and then reattach themselves to the central core. The core would then begin to spin, providing a 0.3g to 0.5g environment for the crew, depending on which deck they were on. These decks, as well as the amidships cargo bays and the habitat ring, were the only sections of the three-kilometer-long ship that would simulate gravity during their five-decade journey.

He could see the maglev approaching the platform as he arrived, and he nodded amiably at two passengers disembarking as he climbed aboard. The trip itself would only last a minute or so, which was why there were very few seats. Once aboard, a passenger could grab a hanging loop or a handrail, and brace himself as the car took off. One hand wrapped around a loop, Terrance pinged Shannon as the maglev sped him to his destination.

<Anything you want me to check on while I'm in Engineering?> he asked the AI.

There was a brief pause, and then he heard her tart rejoinder, <You **do** know there are optics installed in Engineering, right? I can access anything I need to.> She sent him a saucy grin, followed by a query. <What's up?>

<Just want to check to make sure we have everything we need to fabricate the MFRs for the comm buoys the Council ordered.> He chuckled as her avatar raised one eyebrow and gave him a sardonic look.

<I know, you've already checked everything. Sometimes a guy just wants to put his hands on the equipment to make sure it's really there.>

The instant that thought left his mind, he knew Shannon wasn't going to let it go without comment. He grinned as peals of laughter came across the connection, and Shannon's eyes glinted with a wicked humor.

<**Someone** needs to get laid,> the engineer teased.

<Guess I walked right into that one, didn't I?>

<Yep,> she grinned. Then she cocked her head and pointed at him. <All work and no play, even for an Enfield, is not what the doctor ordered.>

He shook his head at her. <No time right now; maybe when we get to Tau Ceti.>

Shannon's brow raised once again, this time in skepticism. <What? Twenty-five hundred humans on this ship, and none of them to your taste?>

<They'll be **sleeping** for most of it, Shannon,> he reminded her.

<Stasis isn't sleeping. This isn't some sort of horrifying cryo-freeze deal.>

<Can you not be an engineer for once?>

<Okay, fine. But once we get to Ring Galene,> she replied in a

mock-stern tone, <we're hooking you up. Can't have you checking your junk to make sure it's really there, Boss.>

<I said 'equipment', not 'junk'. And why does the thought of you hooking me up scare me just a little bit?>

<Because you're a smart human.> She smirked at him one last time before closing the connection.

He shook his head, a genuine smile on his lips, as he exited the maglev. Shannon was the most emotive AI he'd ever met, and he had no idea why the engineer who was so fond of emulating physical human gestures had never opted for a humanoid frame of her own to try them out.

Entering Engineering, he nodded to three Enfield employees that looked up at him.

"Sir," they murmured as he walked by.

Rounding a corner, he came upon Jonesy giving last-minute instructions to two of the mechanics. His entrance must have caught the man's eye, for Jonesy glanced up briefly and gave Terrance a nod.

"Sirs," he said absently, and then his eyes widened, and he hastily added, "I meant 'sir'. Sorry, I'm used to your presence counting as two people."

Terrance smiled at his reference to the AI no longer embedded inside his skull, and made a dismissive gesture. "No worries, Jonesy." He waited patiently for the other man to finish his instructions to the mechanics.

As the workers split off to their various duties, Jonesy turned back to eye his employer. "What can I help you with, sir?"

"I know you're busy down here, and I don't want to take up any of your time." Terrance gave the man a smile. "I'm just here to check on the materials we'll need to manufacture the Matchbox Fusion Reactors, if you'd just point me in the right direction."

"Not a problem, sir." Jonesy turned and led Terrance down a passageway to a storage area filled from bulkhead to bulkhead with crated materials.

"Now, let's see here," Jonesy murmured, absently scratching the side of his head and unseating the cap he habitually wore, which had the ESF logo emblazoned across its bill. He caught it just as it began to topple, and reseated it atop his head in a practiced motion as he tapped on the hyfilm he'd been carrying around. Inclining his head to the right, he said, "Looks like it's all two rows back, on that end."

Terrance nodded amiably. "Thanks, Jonesy."

"No problem, sir. Happy to help." The engineering assistant turned to leave, and Terrance stopped him with a lifted hand.

"I heard you plan to remain out of stasis for the better part of the journey," Terrance said, his voice lifting in query.

Jonesy nodded, a look of enthusiasm on his face. "Indeed I am. I asked Shannon if she would take on an apprentice." The man flashed another brilliant grin. "By the time you folks awaken, I'll be a newly-minted engineer. At least, that's the plan."

Terrance shook his head with a smile. "Hardly newly-minted. If you're truly planning to remain out of stasis for the entire trip, you'll be well-seasoned by the time we dock at Ring Galene." He cocked his head thoughtfully. "And much older, at that. Planning on a rejuv treatment or two during the voyage?"

"Mmm-hmm. Already asked Marta to slot me in for one in twenty years, and another one again right before we arrive." He grinned suddenly. "Can't have the boss looking younger than his elders when we get there."

Terrance barked a laugh and slapped Jonesy on the shoulder. "You'll do all right. Shannon's a great teacher; you'll make a fine engineer."

"Damn straight, sir." Jonesy winked and then ducked through the doorway, no doubt headed back to stevedore the department into launch condition.

As the man left, Terrance walked over to the crates Jonesy had indicated and exchanged tokens with the security seal the manufacturer had placed on the cartons' contents. Peering down into the first one, he scanned the shipment, noting that, as Shannon had indicated, everything was indeed in order.

Accessing the duty roster, he eyed the planned schedule for the upcoming weeks. He nodded in satisfaction when he saw that Shannon's backoff table for buoy production gave them plenty of time to make each deployment. He resealed the carton just as a voice sounded behind him.

"Heard you were down here," Calista said.

He grinned, turning to face his chief pilot. "Shannon ratted me out, did she?"

Calista's dark eyes twinkled, and as she shook her head at him, the overhead illumination caught glints of red in the depths of her dark hair. "No, but after this many years of working with you, I knew you wouldn't be able to leave without seeing for yourself that we had everything we needed." She smiled slightly at him, one hand resting on a nearby crate.

He cracked a laugh at her droll tone. "Everything set for tomorrow's departure?" he asked, and she nodded.

"Yes, although it's odd how crowded the ship feels, given we're only at ten percent of our maximum capacity," she admitted with a wry look.

He smiled slightly. "I know what you mean. I was thinking the same thing earlier," he admitted with a shake of his head, and then pushed away from the cargo. "Was there a reason I bumped into you down here, or was this just happenstance?"

She shook her head. "Shannon and I just finished going over the crew's stasis rotation for manned shifts during the journey." At Terrance's raised brow, she continued. "We'll have a dozen or so humans awake at any given time, plus the AIs not embedded."

She tilted her head enquiringly. "Do you plan to do another embed once we're closer to our destination?"

Terrance nodded. "I plan to stay awake through the first buoy deployment, and then I'll go into stasis until midpoint. That'll be a brief check-in—just a few weeks that time—and then I'll go back under until we're a year out from Tau Ceti." He tapped his forehead. "I was thinking of asking Kodi if he might like to squeeze himself inside this hard head at that point."

Calista nodded as he mentioned the ESF soldier on loan to Phantom Blade for the duration.

"Speaking of stasis," she began, "I'm glad we'll have a rotation of humans and AIs awake at all times to keep an eagle eye on those stasis pods to ensure nothing goes wrong."

She held up her hands to preclude any protests from her boss. "I know Enfield Dynamics tested them for several years prior to them being approved for sentient use, but I, for one, feel a lot more comfortable knowing we'll have a small army of people who have our backs while we're out."

Terrance gave a slight half-shrug. "As I understand it, if they fail, the worst that can happen is we wake up early and end up driving each other crazy within the confines of the ship for the rest of the trip." He smirked as a thought occurred to him. "And Marta and her team would have their hands full with rejuv treatments."

Calista laughed aloud at that. "Well, Shannon knows where to find us if she needs a meat-suit or two to do the heavy lifting at any point along the way." She winked and crooked a finger his way as she turned toward the main corridor.

"Got time for one more thing?"

"Ahhhh, and now we learn the *real* reason you hunted me down."

She threw a wicked smile over her shoulder. "Mmm-hmmm. You, sir, have something awaiting you. Or, rather, someone...."

Terrance groaned, burying his head in his palms. "Is the someone about half a meter tall, four-footed, and furry?"

"Yep."

He sighed. "Beck."

"Yep." Calista tilted her head as he matched her stride, and they continued to the main lift. "Going to let the little fella come along for the ride?"

Terrance was silent a moment, weighing the odds. "He's a cute little guy, and when he matures, he's going to be a stunning creature. Might make a nice icebreaker when we connect with our Tau Ceti friends." He shot Calista an assessing look. "I may come to regret it, but yes, let's go greet our newest passenger."

* * * * *

The *Avon Vale* was finally loaded.

All equipment, supplies, passengers, and personnel were in their assigned spots. Jason and Calista were strapped into their respective cradles on the ship's bridge, and Terrance—the owner and ostensible financial backer of the operation—was seated at the backup scan station.

Jason couldn't suppress the thrill of anticipation that ran through him as the moment of departure arrived. *No matter how many flights through the black I take, the moment you leave is still a rush,* he thought with an inward smile. Turning to Calista, he swept a grand gesture toward the swath of black displayed on the bridge's forward holowall and, with a seated bow, declared, "Where to, oh captain, my captain?"

Terrance threw his head back with a shout of laughter. "Glad to see that promotion hasn't gone to your head or anything," he said, just as Shannon's projection snapped into place beside him.

Jason had figured his comment would draw out the little engineer. He sent her a smirk as she deliberately shifted her image into a stance that was hipshot and arms crossed, rife with disapproval.

"Really, Jason. Like you don't know where we're going." Her voice fairly dripped with disdain, and his smirk turned into a full-on grin.

"Seriously, Shannon, if you're going to give me that kind of attitude, it needs to be from a real bod."

She drew back, wrinkling her nose in distaste. "Eww. Why is

everyone trying to get me into a body today? When you have a body, you have to deal with *fluids*."

"Only organic ones, and even then, you could mod yourself so that you wouldn't have to deal with them if you didn't want to."

"I'm not just talking about *bodily* fluids," she said in a prim tone. "You people end up with all sorts of fluids *on* you, too. And don't pretend you don't. I saw what you looked like, Jason Andrews, when you got back from that vehicle-pull event thingy you went to down on El Dorado."

"Tractor pull," he corrected with a smile. "Yeah, that was a bit messy," he admitted. "But you know the folks down on El Dorado are a bit odd. I think it's safe to say you won't have to worry about getting mud slung all over you any time soon."

Calista cleared her throat and pointed her head at the front holowall. "Anyone interested in actually leaving this habitat today?"

"Ma'am, yes, ma'am, Captain Rhinehart, ma'am."

She rolled her eyes at him as he settled forward and focused on the three images on the display. The first showed nearspace around Chinquapin, the planet the C-47 Habitat orbited. Another displayed the view from the ship, where the umbilicals had been retracted, and the docking clamps would be released.

The third view was a map fed to them from Chinquapin's Space Situation Awareness services. The SSA feed traced the orbital paths of every object in nearspace around the C-47 Habitat. Icons flashed the idents of nearby traffic and continuously updated.

The SSA presented the *Avon Vale*'s projected cone of departure as a pathway that was currently painted red, which told Jason that the feed's Collision On Launch Assessment indicator had them holding in a 'COLA Blackout'. As he watched, the red slowly retreated, and he knew their launch window would shortly turn green, showing clear traffic lanes ahead.

Over the bridge net, Jason heard the Chinquapin STC controller hail the ship with the *Avon Vale*'s ident number.

He dropped his gaze from the SSA display just as their launch window turned green and refocused his attention on his pilot's holo as the controller continued, <Avon Vale, *STC. You are cleared out of Class A nearspace, declination zero-six-zero, squawk one-one-four-one, good day.*>

Jason repeated the instructions back to the controller, and when he was done, murmured, "Here we go, folks," just as the station's clamps let go.

On the holo, the view of the dock receded as the ship fell away from the rotating dock. Those aboard experienced a floating sensation as they exchanged the dock's apparent 0.5g of gravity for the near-zero g of the ship under light maneuvering thrust.

The holotank displayed the shift in the starscape ahead of them as Jason eased the ship onto the green line of their outbound trajectory, as well as the receding habitat from its rear cameras.

Once the ship was past the demarcation line, he'd be given clearance by STC to engage the MFRs, and they would experience a full 1g as the ship began boosting for the heliopause. For now, Jason brought the MFRs online, ready to engage when given the go-ahead.

The ship moved past a ring of stationary satellites, and then pulled abreast of a floating refueling station that was ringed with warning holos. Off to their starboard side, they could see one of several repair installations, its spider-like web of spires reaching out from its core like a spiny, spaceborne sea urchin.

<Avon Vale, *Chinquapin Departure. You are number two in the pattern, cleared for departure after the heavy, boosting from Pad Seventeen North.*>

Jason glanced up at the SSA display and noted that the icon denoting the 'heavy'—an oversized ore freighter that must have been under thrust for several hours—was nearing the mark where it could engage its fusion drives without causing any damage to the station or nearby craft with its ionized plasma stream. By its trajectory, he could tell it was bound for El Dorado.

"Say hello to Lysander for us, buddy," he said, and heard Tobias chuckle from his position at scan. Jason looked over at the AI, then let his gaze drop to the big cat strapped in at Tobias's feet. He caught her staring up at him, ears pricked forward and golden eyes gleaming. "Glad we asked Marta to take care of Beck for the launch, are you?"

<Such a brat.> The big cat blew out a breath, tilting her head just enough to shoot him some side-eye. <Not sure why you let him come.> She licked her left shoulder once to indicate her disdain, and then settled in for the thrust she knew was coming.

Jason grinned down at her. Tobi'd always had a thing for speed.

He looked back up at the display just as the freighter hit the light-second mark and lit up its drives, and the holo dimmed to compensate. He watched as the readings climbed back down into the safe zone, showing that their path was clear. Three hours later, he triggered their MFRs to engage thrust. The *Avon Vale* leapt forward, and those aboard her experienced a surge of acceleration as the spacecraft was officially underway.

An hour later, as Jason was busy replotting their waypoints to the heliopause, Calista took over and mentally keyed their final transmission to the planet's Space Traffic Control center.

<Chinquapin Departure, Avon Vale *seven one five niner, requesting data pipe change to Proxima System Central.*>

<Avon Vale, *Chinquapin Departure*,> came an answering feminine voice. <Data pipe change approved. Happy Tuesday.>

<Happy Tuesday,> Calista replied, and she heard the double-key acknowledgement signaling the transmission had ended.

"Huh," Jason commented, glancing over at her. She raised a brow enquiringly. "STC's not usually that friendly to me," he replied, scowling slightly at her.

Calista's lips twitched, and Jason could tell that the former ESF pilot had found *something* funny—he just wasn't sure what it was.

"Jealous, are you, flyboy?" she asked, arching a brow at him.

"Hmph," he grunted, annoyed. "She's just never wished *me* a happy Tuesday."

Tobias chuckled. "Think you're losing your touch there, boyo?"

Jason scowled over at the Weapon Born as Calista broke into a grin.

"Well, flyboy, I'll let you in on a little secret," she said. "It's a traditional greeting within a certain group of pilots that dates back—oh, centuries, I suppose."

Jason's eyebrows climbed up to his hairline. "It does?"

"Mmmhmm," she said, her eyes dancing.

Jason's brows drew back down as he thought for a moment. "Can I join?"

She looked him up and down, her gaze assessing. "I don't think you have the right equipment for it."

He looked nonplussed for a second, and then grinned. "Well," he drawled. "I've never been told *that* before."

She burst out laughing, and Terrance looked from one to the other and then back again. "Am I missing something here?"

"It's a women's pilot organization, Terrance," she explained.

The exec looked up at the ceiling and shook his head as Jason snorted, and then responded.

"Guess you're right, ESF. Think I'll just stick with the equipment I have."

JELLYFISH AND SOLAR SAILS
STELLAR DATE: 07.10.3192 (Adjusted Gregorian)
LOCATION: Comm Buoy Deployment Position Number One
REGION: 600 AU from Proxima Centauri Star System

Seven weeks later, they'd reached the position marked for the deployment of the first comm buoy.

Jason and the rest of the crew were on the bridge, staring up at the main holo, where an image of the communication buoy rotated slowly. It was rounded and slightly concave and seemed to be made of a translucent, bluish-white material, with arms that appeared to drift gently in the interstellar winds.

"Looks like a jellyfish," Jason muttered. He turned his head sideways, as if studying it from that angle might change his opinion of the object he was viewing.

"Jellyfish?" Terrance queried, his eyes fixed to the gossamer-thin disk surrounded by a dozen antennae extensions, each radiating outward.

"Man 'o War, I think," Jason equivocated, one hand drifting down to scratch Tobi absently behind one ear. He dropped his hand and scowled, fixing his eyes on the woman next to him as she burst out laughing.

"What do you want to bet it's some kind of old-Earth animal?" she said, swiveling in her seat to meet his glare, her eyes dancing with humor.

He snorted a laugh, relaxing back into his own seat. "I guess you could call it that," he amended, "but I prefer to call them damned painful nuisances."

At her quirked brow, he explained. "They weren't included in the Future Generation Terraformers' biobanks because the FGT didn't consider their benefits to be worth the hassle, but someone decided to experiment with them in Lake Chinquapin when I was a kid, thinking they'd help transport carbon through the underground water table."

<Interesting,> Kodi's voice joined in the conversation, and the holotank wavered as the navigation officer added an image next to that of the deployed comm buoy. <*I can see the similarity to the buoy, but it looks too delicate to do a human much damage.*>

"Sure felt like it did at the time. I got stung by one before the habitat's environmental team removed them." He shook his head at the memory as he closed the image file. "Hurt like hell."

Shannon's projected image turned back to face the buoy. "No jellyfish here, so you're safe. Technically, this is a sail. You can't see the material stretched between the antennae because it's a self-repairing monoatomic film, built with enough flexibility to allow micrometeorites and other dust particles to punch right through with little impact on the unit."

The AI pointed to the concave disk. "The MFR is embedded in the center of the disk, along with the comm system itself. Otherwise, it really is just your basic sail. The tech hasn't changed for centuries, actually. It's still made from silicon and silica, which makes it ideal for dissipating excessive heat from the comm lasers while extracting the communication embedded within."

Jason cocked his head at the engineer and looked back at the image thoughtfully. "And we're deploying how many of these?" he asked, glancing over at Terrance.

"Thirteen hundred." At Jason's low exclamation, the exec explained. "Tau Ceti's thirteen light years from Proxima, so we're seeding them a little over six hundred AU apart." He shrugged. "It's the standard distance the FGT used when they laid the first comm system between Sol and Alpha Centauri."

Jason nodded absently, his eye on the chrono as the deployment window approached. "We're thirty seconds out."

"Confirmed," Calista responded, and as they watched, a gantry arm extended from their amidships cargo area, its payload ready for release.

When thirty seconds had passed, Jason murmured, "Mark," and Shannon adjusted the image on the holo for a closer view of the package. They watched the buoy unfurl, and then Kodi confirmed telemetry. <Buoy thrusters are performing their braking maneuver,> he announced.

Given that the ship was now traveling at over forty-one thousand kilometers a second, the buoy would take some time to come to its designated station-keeping position. It would be Kodi's job to monitor it and make any necessary adjustments.

<All comm lines showing green. Deployment is confirmed, initialization message sent back to C-47.>

Jason heard Terrance let out an explosive breath at the navigator's words.

"Very nice," he said, then turned to Calista and Jason just as the bridge's doors slid open.

They turned to see Jonesy step aside, allowing Marta onto the deck.

Tobias chuckled. "Making a house call, doctor?" the Weapon Born asked.

The physician crooked a smile toward the AI and shook her head. "Ever the plight of those of us who practice medicine. No one voluntarily seeks us out, it seems." Her gaze swept the humans on the bridge as she asked, "Everyone ready?"

Terrance stirred and shot Calista a questioning glance. She nodded and straightened.

"Finish slaving your boards to Shannon's team," Calista instructed in what Jason privately called her 'captain's voice'.

Jonesy pulled out a hyfilm checklist and tossed it up onto the holo. One by one, every station on the bridge switched from human interface to that of an AI. Shannon would run the ship while Kodi ran scan and comm; Landon and Logan were tagged for security and weapons.

"Confirmed," Jonesy said, nodding back at Calista. "And I'll be around for the first shift of meat-suit duty, if anyone needs a human interface."

Terrance snorted at that, but stood and clapped Jonesy on the shoulder as he passed. "You let medical know if you get tired of Shannon's engineering training regimen, and decide you want to join us in stasis, you hear?"

Jonesy cocked a brow at the exec, but nodded as Terrance shot Shannon's avatar a smile.

Jason hid a grin as Terrance turned back to Jonesy and stage-whispered, "She's a slave-driver, you know that, right?"

"I heard that!" Shannon planted her hands on her hips and scowled at her boss.

Calista burst out laughing as Terrance's grin widened.

"You were meant to. That quality's one reason I hired you in the first place," he reminded her as he stepped out into the corridor just off the bridge.

Jason slid from his XO chair and glanced over at the engineer as he followed Calista toward the bridge's exit. "Shannon, seriously, you really should get a humanoid frame. You're as fond of human gestures as Gladys is," he said, mentioning a member of their team who had stayed behind in El Dorado.

Shannon's eyes narrowed as she crossed her arms and shot him a glare. "Jason Andrews, you take that back right now. I'm *nothing* like Gladys." The AI threw her virtual hands up in exasperation. "Stars, Jason! She *sheds*."

Tobias made a noise that sounded like a strangled snort, and Jason saw Jonesy hide a smirk behind his hand. Jason just grinned wickedly at Shannon as he followed Terrance and Calista into the corridor.

Calista's eyes danced in amusement as he joined them. "You do like to gamble with your life, don't you, flyboy?"

He grinned and glanced over at Marta. "Doc's not going to let Shannon do anything to me while I'm under, right Marta?"

The doctor shot him a repressive look, although he could see her lips twitch. "Oh no, you're not dragging me into the middle of anything. If it's not medically related, I'll steer clear of it, thanks."

"Speaking of medically related issues…do the cats get their own stasis pod, or should Beck bunk with Terrance? Asking for a friend."

He smirked as the exec whipped his head around with a scowl.

Pointing his finger at Jason, Terrance warned, "Stay out of this, Andrews. I'm not sharing my pod with a kitten who *farts*."

Jason couldn't help a rejoinder. "It's stasis. I'm pretty sure that when all atomic motion stops, so do farts."

"I wouldn't bet on that." Terrance's voice was laden with a combination of dread and dismay as he stopped and called for the lift.

Marta raised one brow. "He wouldn't have issues if you'd stop slipping him food from your plate."

Jason coughed to suppress a laugh as Terrance's face reddened.

"Busted," Jason grinned as the lift doors slid open, and all the organics, save for Jonesy, followed Terrance inside.

"Shut up," the big man muttered, his eyes fixed to the roof above him as Marta entered. She held the door open as Tobias approached.

"We'll pull you out periodically, and as needed," Tobias assured them, then winked at Terrance. "If for no other reason than to air out your pod, lad."

Terrance groaned and the Weapon Born shot him a roguish grin. Behind Tobias, Jonesy smirked and then called out, "Sleep well."

As the lift doors closed, they could just make out Shannon's voice.

"They won't be *sleeping*, Jonesy. We've been over this."

LISA RICHMAN & M. D. COOPER

ACCESS DENIED

STELLAR DATE: 02.17.3235 (Adjusted Gregorian)
LOCATION: ESS *Avon Vale*
REGION: Interstellar Space between Proxima Centauri and Tau Ceti

Forty-three years into the journey....

The *Avon Vale*'s habitat ring had become operational midway through the twelfth week of their journey, after they'd cut their 1g boost. As soon as the ship entered its cruise phase of the trip, the ring had begun to rotate. Seven hundred meters in diameter and two hundred meters wide, it provided a little more than four hundred square kilometers of surface area. A generous amount of that space had been allotted for gardens, parks, and other growing things. Ponds and modest lakes that had been drained for the boost phase were refilled once the habitat ring began its spin, and the simulated sunlight was set to follow the ship's diurnal cycle.

The hab-ring parks were Terrance's favorite spots within the *Vale*. He'd spent a few weeks during every rotation he'd been awake enjoying them before returning to stasis.

Forty years and four rounds of stasis later, he found himself seated once more on his favorite bench inside Hideaway Park. The park had been so named because of the penchant people had to sneak away for a few minutes' respite from the drab grey of the shipboard bulkheads.

One arm resting along the back of the park bench, Terrance held his eyes shut as he enjoyed the feeling of warmth from the simulated sun on his upturned face. The gentle stirring of the air was just enough to simulate a light breeze without triggering the disconcerting sense that the ship might be venting atmosphere.

Terrance chuckled at that, which caused a nearby figure to stop and look inquisitively over in his direction.

<Oh good. You're awake. Let's play!>

Terrance groaned as Beck raced toward him and then leapt at his outstretched feet, clawing at their soles.

Marta had kept the kitten out of stasis for the first year, wanting to ensure uninterrupted growth. She told Terrance that Beck had insisted on visiting his stasis pod once every few days, where the doctor found herself needing to reassure him that yes, even though Beck couldn't smell him, Terrance was fine, he was 'just sleeping'.

<I forgot that Marta embedded him with a Link. What do you want to bet we're going to regret that,> he bemoaned, and a snicker sounded inside his head.

<You know, it wouldn't hurt you to run around a bit,> Kodi reminded him. <Been a few days since you hit the gym this time around. Why don't you go play with the little fellow?>

<First off, he's not **little** anymore. Secondly, remind me again why it was a good idea to have another AI residing inside my head? And another soldier, at that?> Terrance groused, but it felt right, being paired with an AI. Although this was Kodi's first pairing with a human, through their enhanced connection, he could sense Kodi's satisfaction as well.

His lips twitched into a satisfied smile, and he rose from the bench, following as Beck dashed away from him. He couldn't suppress his chuckle as he watched the cat gamboling around the greenspace, chasing imaginary prey. Although the creature had more than doubled in size during the year he'd remained out of stasis at the onset of their voyage, his personality was still that of a mischievous teenager.

<You can't catch meeeeeeeeee!> the cat called, flirting his tail at Terrance as he crouched and then used his powerful hind legs to leap over a thicket of scrub.

<Double-time, soldier.> Kodi's mental tone held a thread of humor that enhanced Terrance's own good mood in a pleasant feedback. <You're about to let your quarry escape.>

Terrance snorted. <I'm not entirely convinced that would be a bad

thing,> he sent to Kodi, but both human and AI knew he didn't mean it.

He'd grown fond of Beck. It was a good thing, too, as the cat—whose head came to his mid-thigh when standing alongside him—somehow managed to find him no matter where he was on the ship.

Terrance watched him race up the trunk of a tree and pause in the vee of one of its lower branches.

<*Hustle,*> Kodi's voice laughed inside his head, and Terrance broke into a slow jog.

<*Hustle? You actually told me to **hustle**?*>

<*Hey, your health's kind of important to me. I'm at the mercy of this body, too, you know,*> Kodi protested, and Terrance's lips twitched into a smile as he worked to catch up to the fleeing feline.

As he approached the tree, the cat peered down at him from where he had stretched out along a sturdy branch, his tail waving lazily back and forth. Terrance saw Beck gather himself up, the feline's rear legs bunching together, as he knew they did prior to a leap.

Oh no, here it comes....

<*Catch me!*> Beck sent gleefully, and before Terrance could protest, the cat had launched himself toward the man—all twenty kilos of feline muscle landing across his shoulders.

<*Oof! Good thing I decided to wear a jacket this morning,*> Terrance muttered to Kodi as he took a step backward to more evenly balance the combined weight of himself and the cat. <*Those nails are a good two centimeters long at the very least.*>

<*What?*> Kodi taunted, his mental tone threaded with mirth. <*You never harbored a secret desire to be a human pincushion? I'm shocked.*>

<*That's one thing you AIs don't need to worry about,*> Terrance complained good-naturedly. <*The physical discomforts that come with being a meat-suit.*>

Something caught Beck's attention, and the cat shifted.

Terrance winced, easing one of the cat's claws off his neck and back onto the padded protection of the jacket he wore.

<*Marta! Look at me! I'm going for a ri-i-ide!*> Beck caroled in greeting, and Terrance ducked his head past the cat's shoulder to see the doctor approach.

Stopping a few meters away, Marta crossed her arms and favored the cat with a stern look. "Aren't you getting a bit big to do that?" she asked Beck repressively, but Terrance could see her lip twitch slightly as she said it.

<*What do you want to bet he smells her amusement?*> Terrance sent privately to Kodi.

<*From what I've read about them, I'll bet you're right,*> Kodi agreed. <*Jason's mother uplifted these Proxima cats to be a lot smarter than I thought possible.*>

<*Terrance doesn't mind,*> Beck responded to Marta's rebuke, and then twisted his head around to peer through his legs at Terrance.

The goofy upside-down face he presented had the man reaching out to tousle the cat's ears.

"You're no lightweight, Beck," he admitted. "I don't mind you doing it at times like this, but if we were to go ringside—or planetside—that's an entirely different matter. You understand why?"

<*'Cuz we won't be in a 'vironment we can control, and Kodi may need your undivided attention,*> the cat parroted back, and Terrance suppressed a grin.

"Very good," he told the cat, holding Beck's attention as he added sternly. "Don't forget that, now, you hear?"

The cat blinked once at him, then lifted his head back upright.

He poked the cat a few times gently along his flank to get the cat's attention. "You hear me, Beck?" he repeated.

He was rewarded with a slightly sulky, <*'kay, I hear.*>

He and Marta exchanged amused glances, and then Terrance bent forward, urging the cat to jump down. "Enough of that, kid. I just got out of stasis; I'm not sure I can handle much of that until I build my strength back up." He winked at Marta, and she rolled her eyes at the obvious lie.

The cat chuffed and eyed him disdainfully. <Marta said you're the same as you were before.>

"Oh, she did, did she?" He shot the doctor a mock glare. "Exactly whose side are you on, anyway, doc? C'mon, help a guy out here, won't you?"

"Not on your life, Terrance Enfield. I've paid my dues and served my cat duty for this leg of the journey. He's all yours now." She shook her head after Beck as she watched the cat scamper off.

"I'd forgotten how…energetic…younglings are," she added as she fell into step with him, and they began to stroll through the park. "I began to envy the lot of you, sleeping away in your pods while I spent the first few years awake, working the early medical shifts." She grinned up at him. "I admit I was a bit relieved when it came time to send Beck into stasis."

They walked companionably along for a few moments before she looked appraisingly over at him again. "So, how's the connection between you two? Any differences between this embedding and the one you experienced with Eric?"

Terrance paused to consider her question, then shot her a considering look. "Am I *supposed* to feel something different, Marta?"

<Feels fine to me,> Kodi supplied, and Terrance received the impression of a mental shrug from him. <Not that it tells you anything, since this is my first-ever pairing with a human.>

"Everything checks out just fine medically," the doctor hastened to assure them. "You're just my first human to have two different AIs embed within him, so I wanted to make sure you weren't experiencing anything out of the ordinary."

"Right as rain, from my point of view," Terrance reported. "Actually, it…feels a bit like reattaching a missing limb." He frowned over at her, and then lifted one shoulder in a half-shrug. "Not sure that translates very well, but it's the best description I can come up with."

"Good," she nodded in satisfaction. "Then that's one thing I can check off my list."

Terrance frowned as he considered the list of things that remained. Top of mind—largely because they were heading to a briefing on the subject—was the status of the drone carrying the two stolen AIs to Tau Ceti.

<By the way, good call arranging the meeting at the Park Café,> Terrance complimented.

<Seemed like a good idea at the time,> Kodi's avatar quirked a smile his way. <I figured it might be a good idea to work in some fresh air. You organics sure can get stir-crazy inside the bulkheads of a ship after a while.>

Terrance groaned mentally as he spied Jason and Tobias enter the café a few meters ahead of them. <You could have gone all day without reminding me I'm still inside this tin-can, you know.>

<Sorry, sir.>

<Quit it with the 'sir' already, will you?>

* * * * *

Jason ducked inside the café and nodded to a few of the ESF soldiers enjoying their mid-morning coffee and pastry, when Tobi—who was strolling with panther-like grace between him and Tobias's frame—rumbled a low warning growl.

Instinctively, Jason dipped into his L2 state and glanced around, cataloguing items within the café that he might turn into weapons. Everything around him slowed, patrons seeming to take on a graceful flow as his frame of reference sped up.

And then he spotted Terrance, Marta…and, of course, Beck.

Abruptly, time started flowing at normal speed again.

<Tobi-girl, behave,> Jason scolded the Proxima cat, who flicked a glance up at him and chuffed in annoyance.

He shook his head as he reached inside his pocket for the

special ear inserts he habitually wore, which provided him with the enhanced Link pairing to Tobias. He'd removed them before entering stasis and had yet to reinsert them.

Rolling the clear polymer pieces between his fingers, he saw the nanofilament lacing their insides glitter as they caught the light. He paused to fit them inside his ears, yawning a few times and ignoring the slight disorientation as they conformed to the curls and flutes of the organs, altering his auditory input.

Instantly, his connection with the Weapon Born took on a more nuanced flavor, and he sensed the AI's presence more fully than he ever did across the Link. It was the closest he would ever get to experiencing the kind of connection brought by a true human/AI pairing, since the neural composition of L2 humans made embedding impossible.

<I just went all L2 on everyone's ass because of that growl,> he complained to Tobias on their private channel, his tone laced with mild irritation.

<Best get used to it, boyo. Beck's never going to be high on her list of favorites,> Tobias said, and Jason felt the amusement behind the AI's words. <I think you'll have to handle this with her the old-fashioned way.>

<You mean keep them separated,> Jason sent Tobias a wry chuckle, glancing over at the AI. <Cats don't really take well to correction, you know.>

Tobias sent a snort of laughter. <No,> he agreed, <they don't at that. Although you might try bribing her with some bonito flakes as **positive** reinforcement.>

<Hmmm,> was Jason's noncommittal response as he returned his attention to the team.

They were gathering under an awning, where small tables looked out upon one of the park's small lakes. As Calista looked over from where she stood next to one of the bistro tables, he sent her a slow, lazy grin and was rewarded with a sultry look and a slight upturn of her lips before she turned away to speak to the man seated at the table near her.

<Hmmm,> Tobias rumbled.

<What?> Jason asked the AI idly, his tone preoccupied.

<Now, **that** was an interesting look on our captain's face.> Tobias sent Jason a wicked grin. <Just what have you two been up to since Marta opened up those stasis pods this morning?>

<Tobe! It's been **ten years** since we were last awakened.>

<Not by your body clock, it hasn't,> the AI chided. <But, hey, any excuse that works for you....>

Jason grinned. <I'll drink to that.>

As he neared, he saw Calista glance down at Jonesy, seated at her side. The engineer had leant back in his chair, arms crossed behind his head, a cocky grin on his face.

"Wow, Jonesy, that's *huge*," she exclaimed. "Impressive!"

Jason's brows drew down, as it looked like her eyes were focused on Jonesy's crotch. He found himself leaving Tobi behind as his pace quickened. He heard Tobias chuckle mentally as they approached the group.

<Feeling a bit threatened, there, are you?>

<Shove it, Tobe,> he sent, his tone distracted.

Craning his neck, he stepped clear of the last person between them and the table, and came to an abrupt halt. Tobias snickered inside his head as Jason was confronted with an unimpeded view of Jonesy's...pineapple.

<The man has a basket of freakin' produce in his lap,> Jason growled, and Tobias's avatar leered at him.

<And what did you **think** he was showing her, boyo?>

<Stow it. At least she didn't see me hustling because I was jealous of a—wow, that really **is** a big pineapple. Wonder how he managed to grow it in the hab-ring.... I don't think I've ever heard of a ship successfully harvesting **that** before.>

<Changing the subject are we?> Tobias teased, but at Jason's glower, the Weapon Born's avatar raised his hands and subsided.

Everyone around the table was exclaiming over Jonesy's

large…pineapple…and Jason had to chuckle at his own insecurities. As he joined the group, he grabbed an empty bar stool and pulled it up to the table to admire the basket Jonesy had just plonked down before them.

"Dude," he said with a grin, "is that what you've been doing while we've been sleeping the decades away? Creating your own tropical paradise on the ship?" He grinned over at Jonesy, and saw Calista's assistant give a slight shrug.

Engineer, not assistant, Jason corrected himself mentally. *Jonesy's an engineer now—been one for at least thirty years, at this point.*

"Ah, well, I got a little bored during this last stasis round and thought, 'why the hell not?'." He flashed a smile, brilliantly white teeth framed by a dark complexion, and Jason noticed a new maturity in the man's carriage.

Although Jonesy looked the same physically, thanks to rejuv, Jason could see decades of living shining through the man's eyes. The awkwardness that had once characterized Calista's young and slightly anxious assistant had transformed into a confidence that Jason could see in the way the man carried himself.

"Well, I for one sure am glad to see an honest-to-stars fresh pineapple, sitting on the table in front of us," Jason grinned, winking over at Calista. "It's been years since I've eaten one of these things."

He hefted the fruit in his hands, marveling at its prickly, golden surface and long, green crown. As he set it back down, he cocked his head to one side and glanced at the engineer. "So, going to tell us everything that happened during the last ten years we were sleeping?"

Jonesy's smile dimmed at bit. "Well, as to that…."

He let his words fade as he glanced from Logan, seated at the bistro table next to him, to where Shannon had projected her avatar.

"There's news, I take it?" Jason cocked a brow at Jonesy, following his gaze over to Logan. "From Tau Ceti, or from the drone?"

<Yes, from the drone,> Kodi confirmed, his voice projecting from a discreetly placed speaker in the center of the table where Jonesy sat.

Terrance gestured around and added, "Pull up a chair, everyone, and we'll tell you what we know."

Calista shifted to make room for Marta, and Jason suppressed a smirk as Beck leapt nimbly into Terrance's lap once the man was seated. Terrance shot him a black look, and the L2 raised his hands in a gesture of innocence.

With one more pointed glare Jason's way, Terrance turned to Logan, and the AI took that as his cue to drop a bit of unwelcome news in their midst.

"Our attempt to intercept the drone has proven unsuccessful."

His candid statement was met with a soft sound of dismay from Calista. Jason exchanged looks with the *Vale*'s captain and saw reflected in her eyes the same thing that was running through his mind: *things just got a bit more difficult.*

"The drone did initially accept the override code we obtained from Norden's files, but when we ordered it to belay its delivery orders, it requested a secondary authentication code we did not have," Landon interjected from his seat next to his brother, picking up the narrative. After a quick glance over at Logan, he added dryly, "Seems like someone conveniently forgot to tell us about that part."

Logan shook his head. "Or it was added by the Matsu-kai after they took delivery." He shifted slightly. "It fits their profile."

"At any rate," Terrance concluded, "the drone's no longer a part of the equation. It delivered its payload a few days ago."

"So now what? We have to search the entire system for them?" Calista's voice was bleak.

"Maybe, maybe not," Terrance cautioned. "Kodi?"

<We recently received a response to a query on the Matsu-kai organization from the Federated States of Tau Ceti. The FSTC forwarded

a list of known members in the system. I'm sending you the list now, over the team net.>

An icon hovered in Jason's mind's eye. As he opened it and began scrolling through the list of names, he felt Terrance's eyes on him. Glancing up, he caught a look on the exec's face.

"Is there something in here you think—"

Jason stopped abruptly as he came across a name he recognized.

<*Well, damn,*> Tobias said softly, and Jason's mouth twisted into a frown.

"That's the name of the scientist your dad wanted to exchange research notes with, isn't it?" Terrance asked.

Jason nodded. "Sure is." He sighed. "It would appear that we have more than one reason to look this guy up."

Turning to the team, he highlighted the name Terrance had spotted on Galene's list of known Matsu-kai: Noa Sakai.

PART THREE: DELIVERY

THE CALL OF DUTY
STELLAR DATE: 02.01.3235 (Adjusted Gregorian)
LOCATION: Nanotechnology Regulatory Commission
REGION: Ring Galene, Tau Ceti

Thirty-three years after Noa received word that the AIs were coming....

The missive came in an innocuous wrapper.

Engrossed by the content displayed on the holo behind the clear plas walls of his office at the NRC, Noa dismissed the ping announcing a new message had appeared in his queue without even looking at the header. He was too absorbed in his most recent run of simulations. If he could just figure out how to—

The ping sounded again, increasing in its volume, signaling by its tone that it was a Family matter.

That caught Noa's attention. He placed the sim on hold and accessed his queue, freezing in shock when he saw the sender's ident embedded in the message's header: *Sakai Kumichō, Matsukai, El Dorado.* He swallowed, glancing furtively around at his colleagues, hidden behind plas windows in their own offices.

It wasn't that he'd forgotten about the drone's impending arrival; the truth more closely resembled an attempt to bury his awareness of a matter he had known about for more than fifty years. In the back of his brain, he'd never forgotten that he was complicit not only in denying two sentients their freedom, but in stealing more than five decades of these sentients' lives.

Glancing casually around, he noted that his behavior had not drawn any undue attention. This was good. He pulled away from his desk and, in case anyone happened to glance up, made it a point to stretch before commenting, "I think I'll go grab a coffee."

The two physicists in the lab on the other side of his office's plas window looked up distractedly. One of them waved his hand idly and then returned to his research. Noa strolled out as casually as he could, glancing down the corridor to ensure no one was coming his way.

He came to an empty lounge and veered into it. Giving the missive his Sakai token, he accessed its contents. The message was simple:

[Package delivery in two weeks]

Noa sighed. *How am I going to handle this?*

He glanced at the header of the memo, and saw that Hiro had been copied—as was proper, since Hiro had recently succeeded his father as leader of the Family branch in Tau Ceti.

There was no help for it; he would have to contact Hiro and bluff his way through. If the AIs had any hope of being freed, he would have to take control.

Before he could initiate the connection, Hiro's token floated before him. Accepting the secured connection, he had his avatar bow its head, as the blood-red icon, undulating in the shape of a viper, uncoiled to reveal the new Tau Ceti *so-honbucho*. The dark gaze of the leader of the Matsu-kai organization on Ring Galene peered at him impassively.

<*I assume you've received the notification and have read its contents?*> Hiro said without preamble.

<Yes,> Noa replied. <*And as I stated years ago, as Sakai-musuko I claim Family right to handle—*>

<*This request has been reconsidered and, given the circumstances, denied. The two AIs are loose ends; they have been deemed too big a risk. We will dispatch a Family courier to rendezvous with the drone and pick it up,*> the *so-honbucho* informed him. <*The Family thanks you for your service.*>

Noa could hear the dismissal in Hiro's tone and knew that if he intended to act, he must do so now.

<No, wait,> he blurted before his courage could desert him, and he swore he could feel the surprise emanating from the other man at his bold words.

Hiro was unused to anyone countermanding a pronouncement of the *so-honbucho,* no matter how casually it had been phrased.

<It is better if I do it,> Noa hastened to explain, casting about in his mind frantically for what might appear to be a believable and valid reason. <I'm in a unique position to be able to handle this particular situation. Given the research I am currently involved in, I will be able to mine them for information. Whatever they know of Sol and Alpha Centauri we too shall know. They may know things that can prove useful to the Family.>

Noa paused, drew a deep breath. <After that...well. My profession provides a method by which I can dispose of them in an untraceable manner, and ensure the Matsu-kai remains untouched,>

Weak, Sakai. Weak! he berated himself mentally, holding himself preternaturally still, awaiting the Matsu-kai leader's decision.

There was a pause on the other end.

<We cannot have the Family implicated in any way,> Hiro said, his tone harsh with dismissal. Then the man's voice softened slightly, becoming more reminiscent of the person Noa had worked with decades ago, when both had been employed by the Sextant Group. <You are not trained to carry out such a task. Let those who are experts in covering up matters handle this.>

<If you are worried about the Family's honor—> Noa began, but Hiro interrupted him with a gesture, a frown and a sharp word. <It is only ever about the Family, Noa. You know this.>

Noa had his avatar bow its head in compliance. <I...understand,> he said. <But I am confident I will be able to isolate them into a specific quantum spin state, where I will then be able to change their eigenvalues. They will simply...cease to exist. The Family will not be implicated.>

He sensed a surprised pause at the other end as Hiro

contemplated his words.

Noa was counting on Hiro not knowing much about physics in general, or of nanophotonics. Even in the thirty-third century, most laypeople were still unaware of what a physicist did. His particular field remained a black box for the masses, as most of the physics disciplines had for centuries; Noa had just traded heavily on that fact.

He paused, contemplating how else he might persuade Hiro. An idea occurred to him.

<I can set up a family vacation, far away from Ring Galene, near the Sea of Stones. Stars know, it's been long enough since I've taken one.> He managed a shaky laugh he was certain had convinced neither himself nor Hiro. <I'll take Khela along as a cover; no one will suspect.>

Nothing. Hiro remained silent.

Noa took a deep, fortifying breath, and then played his final card. <Let my family's name be stricken from the organization should I fail. This I vow on my daughter's honor.>

A long, drawn-out pause at the other end confirmed that he had succeeded in shocking Hiro. One moment passed, and then another.

Finally, Hiro's avatar nodded reluctantly. <So be it,> he recited the traditional phrase.

Noa jerked a nod, released a breath he hadn't realized he'd been holding, and then closed the connection, his hands shaking.

What have I done? he thought. *If they ever discover the AIs alive, my daughter's life will be forfeit.*

And yet there was no other path.

He must trust in two things: his abilities as a scientist, and the altruism of two complete strangers. He could only hope that they were as worthy as the ais he knew here in Tau Ceti.

ENFIELD GENESIS – TAU CETI

THE STONE SEA
STELLAR DATE: 02.18.3235 (Adjusted Gregorian)
LOCATION: Spa Shuttle, departing Kalypso Waystation
REGION: Inner edge of the Nereids Dust Belt, Tau Ceti

The Sea of Stones Spa was a work of art.

As its name implied, it had been built within the Sea of Stones, as Tau Ceti's great dust belt was named.

The spa's creators had taken great pains to move the asteroids surrounding the facility, positioning them precisely and to great effect. The results, combined with artfully employed nanotech, yielded stunningly beautiful space sculptures.

Spirals, graceful arcs, and complex geometric shapes spun through the spa's nearspace, well-hidden thrusters programmed to shift the giant rocks in an intricate dance. The amount of effort it had taken to move each piece into position was staggering, and the design work that followed to augment each piece had taken more than a decade.

Private shuttles transported guests from the first-class lounge at the Kalypso Waystation, a public rest stop and refueling station hosted by Kalypso Mining, to the spa's entrance. The mining company's torus—located at the inner edge of the Sea of Stones—kept pace with the spa, both structures orbiting in a one-to-one resonance with each other around Tau Ceti.

All of this information had been provided by the introductory holo that played for the patrons as the shuttle transited from the Kalypso Torus to the spa, two-tenths of an AU inside the Sea of Stones. As the sea itself was over an AU thick, the resort had opted to maintain a debris-free corridor directly between the torus and its property.

'Debris-free' was a bit of a misnomer, as it had much more to do with identifying obstacles than it did with physically removing them.

<People still forget how big and empty space is,> Khela mused to Hana, her newly-embedded AI, as she watched the promotional holo come to an end.

She had been recently appointed to a small, fourteen-person Marine Special Operations team, and it was that position that made her first-ever pairing with an AI possible.

<True,> Hana replied in response to Khela's comment. <Even in the Sea of Stones, most bodies large enough to be considered one of the 'stones' are no closer than a few thousand kilometers apart. That corridor the spa says it maintains really isn't much of one, given those distances.>

Khela snickered as she sat back in her seat, and glanced over at her father. Noa hadn't bothered watching the holo—instead, his eyes focused at a distance, as he was lost in holovisuals only he could see. He had, unsurprisingly, taken advantage of the twelve-hour shuttle trip to 'get some work done'.

When she'd reminded him that the vacation was his idea, he'd merely raised a calming hand and assured her that he was wrapping up loose ends so that he could enjoy the time with his daughter once at the spa.

Neither Khela nor Hana had believed him, though. Hana had noted Khela's doubtful expression and had sent her human partner a knowing smirk as Khela stretched her legs out and shifted in her seat to make herself more comfortable.

<Thirty-five-year-old daughter, taking a vacation with her dad.> The AI's bubbling laughter filled her head.

Khela sent her a look. <Thirty-five-year-old newly-minted lieutenant and spec-ops **Marine**, hanging out with her dad,> she corrected.

<And that makes a difference, how again?>

Khela shrugged. <Marines don't care what others think,> she responded. <I'm still shocked he even suggested a vacation. I can't recall the last time....>

But actually, she could. It had been six months before her

mother was killed.

Her parents had met when Noa worked for a government contractor, and Irene had been a Marine in Galene's Space Command. Khela smiled, recalling the unusual pair they had made: a tough, space-hardened soldier and a thoughtful and reserved scientist.

Since her mother had passed away, her father had chosen to bury himself in his work.

The explosion that took her from us happened almost ten years ago. It's time for him to move on. Maybe find someone else who can give him companionship.

Hana's response brought Khela back to the present. <Well, I for one am glad you took him up on a vacation,> the AI said tartly. <We've had three deployments in a row; it's about time we got some downtime of our own.>

Khela reached over and touched her dad's arm. "Want anything?" she asked, nodding back toward the shuttle's galley.

He smiled and shook his head, then resumed staring at whatever it was he was reviewing.

She pulled off her harness, allowing her body to float gently away from her seat as she glanced around at the plush interior. Blue-black hair haloed around her as she pulled herself past rows of passengers, each ensconced behind his or her own private enclosure.

<Bit different from a dropship, isn't it?> Hana's droll comment made Khela smile.

<You can say that again.> Her gaze swept from port to starboard, taking in the gleaming trim and crisp, unmarred surfaces. <Not a scuff in sight,> she added, and sensed the AI equivalent of a snort coming from Hana.

<Don't suppose that's allowed at the spa,> the AI conceded.

Khela sent her a noncommittal agreement as she anchored herself by hooking one leg around a stool that was bolted to the galley's deck. She tapped the surface of the galley countertop, pulling up a holo of the menu to peruse the selections.

<Ooh, try the karasumi,> Hana urged, and Khela wrinkled her nose in distaste.

<Sorry, you'll have to live your food adventures vicariously through someone else,> Khela said, ordering a grilled cheese with tomato bisque, served in a capillary micro-g sipping cup.

<Seriously?> Hana's avatar rolled her eyes. <You're on an all-expense-paid vacation to **the** most exclusive spa in the system, and you choose a grilled cheese? What is **wrong** with you?>

Khela sent her an offended look. <It's not just a grilled cheese. It's made with brie,> she argued.

Hana's avatar threw up her hands. <I give up. You're a total lost cause.>

Khela sent her a smug smile and took a generous bite out of the warm, gooey goodness, looping a finger around the string of cheese that stretched between her mouth and the sandwich as she pulled it away.

<M-m-m-m,> she said, <you do not know what you're missing.>

Hana's avatar crossed her arms and shot her a glare. <Really. How am I supposed to get the complete human experience, paired with a Marine who spends most of her time wearing BDUs, eating grilled cheese sandwiches and drinking cocoa?> the AI groused. <I can hardly hold my head up when I meet with the other AIs. You could at least pretend to drink coffee like everyone else.>

<That bitter brew?> Khela shook her head with a mock shudder. <No thanks. I'll pass.>

She finished her snack and returned to her seat just as the shuttle's NSAI requested all passengers to strap in for their arrival.

Ten minutes later, the shuttled was docked, and she and her father stepped off—but not onto some drab terminal. Rather, they found themselves in a passenger terminal so extravagant, it beggared the imagination.

As they walked down the concourse, Khela had to work to keep her mouth from hanging open at the opulence on display.

She had assumed that much of the spa's annual budget went toward its employment of groundskeepers responsible for the maintenance and upkeep of its various art installations within the surrounding nearspace. Now she wondered if it wasn't just as equally tied up in its interior.

Her scan of the illuminated fixtures—floating above them like crystalline clouds—triggered an icon that invited her to join the spa's guest network, where a helpful holo sprang to life, informing her that the lighting had been designed by one of Ring Galene's premiere artisans. The description of the design, commissioned exclusively for the spa, indicated that the glow came from bioluminescent sea creatures engineered to emit a pleasant ambiance. They were shaped into the kanji ideograms for peace, beauty, and harmony, and were formed entirely of diamond.

She looked down as they reached a foyer at the end of the concourse and a servitor approached to escort them to their rooms.

"Amazing," Khela murmured, feeling clumsy and out of place in this magical world of illumination.

Her father glanced over, gave a slight smile, and squeezed her elbow lightly where he grasped it as he gestured for her to follow the bot to the lift.

"Something tells me it won't hurt you to experience a bit of amazing, Khe-chan," he said, and Khela heard the affection in his voice as he called her by the diminutive he'd used when she was but a child.

<*I've been telling her the same thing,*> Hana chimed in, and Noa smiled and squeezed Khela's elbow one last time before releasing it to step into the lift that the servitor had led them to.

One brow rose slightly as he considered them both. "I would imagine Marines don't often have the opportunity to see amazing. In fact, I shudder to think what you two are used to seeing on a daily basis," he chastised gently. "I still hold out hope that you will find a career outside the military that appeals someday, Khela. A father's heart can only take so much, you know."

It was an old refrain, and it was said without condemnation. Noa knew that Khela had the same wildness in her that her mother had, a thirst for adventure and a restlessness not easily contained.

She tilted her head to one side and looked up at him. He wasn't overly tall, unlike her mother; she had stood half a head taller than he. Khela took after Noa in that regard, her build decidedly on the petite side.

"I've thought about it," she admitted. "But I can't imagine sitting in an office for the rest of my career."

She glanced contemplatively out the clear plas walls of the lift as it transited from the main building to the outer dwellings. A vista of illuminated stones greeted them, and as she watched, the nearest sculpture twisted in on itself in a design reminiscent of a Howe kinetic sculpture.

She glanced back up at her father. "I thought I might look into doing some work planetside, perhaps maintaining some of our national parks and gardens after I do another tour or two. I still want to make captain someday, you know."

She grinned up conspiratorially at her father, and Noa smiled once more, even as he shook his head.

He gave her a considering look. "I could see you doing that," he said, as the lift opened directly into their suite. "The planetside work, not so much the captaincy," he clarified.

As they walked into the corridor, Khela gaped at the view afforded by the floor-to-ceiling plas window that comprised the suite's exterior bulkhead.

Light danced along the surface of the stones nearest their room, illuminating them in an ethereal glow. Bending magnets had been placed among some of them, in concert with narrow ES fields. These formed delightful, curving pathways through which gases had been piped. As they curved their way through the stones, the gases were sequentially detonated to create explosions of varicolored light that mimicked ancient fireworks. The display lasted two or three minutes then lapsed back into the inkiness of space.

She shook her head. "I don't even want to know what this cost you, Dad, but thanks."

He smiled, then nudged her toward her room. "Go on, take some time to get settled in. Why don't you and Hana wander the grounds for a few hours? We can meet up at the Pebble Garden right before dinner."

She grinned. "I'm dying to see that." Impulsively, she pecked him on the cheek. "Thanks, Dad."

*****

Noa's smile fell as the door closed behind Khela.
Stars forbid she ever finds out the true reason we're here.
He'd been monitoring the progress of the AI drone during the entire twelve-hour shuttle ride. His *Sakai-musuko* token had given him complete control over the inbound spacecraft, and he'd arranged with the spa's concierge to have a private bay off the spa's main cargo area made available for his convenience, to receive his delivery. The spa had a reputation for catering to high-powered business executives and was known for its discreet and utterly secure accommodations. The drone had docked an hour earlier, and the spa had sent notice that it had been routed to a reserved, private location moments ago. Along with the notification came a secured token that he would use to access the bay.

He glanced at Khela's closed door, then called for a lift and quietly exited the suite.

Once inside the bay, he sealed the door behind him and set down the case he carried with him. Ignoring the spa's privacy token, Noa rested his hand over the door's controls, trusting the hackit he'd received from the Matsu-kai to sever any monitoring devices. When the packet indicator turned green, he turned and approached the thirty-meter-long drone.

Its front end was scored in several places from the impacts of various micrometeorites it had encountered during its long journey from El Dorado. He placed his hand alongside the aft access panel, his own ident serving as the unlock code. The panel recessed and slid back, revealing a narrow passage. He didn't step in—the drone's display indicated that the cargo was being brought to him.

A minute later, a small bot emerged from the inky darkness of the drone. Strapped to it were two isolation chambers. Within each, he could see an AI core, their cylindrical housings both flashing the pattern of non-organic beings held in their dormant state.

As he reached in, the movement—and the passing of his token—triggered a message.

<*Sakai*-musuko. *Greetings from your cousins in El Dorado. Payment has been received and tendered against the Family on Ring Galene. No favors have been exchanged, nor is any duty required.*>

Noa breathed easier upon hearing this. He'd worried when Hiro had ordered him to 'purchase' the AIs in the Sakai name. His mouth held a bitter taste as his mind framed that word. But more bitter yet would have been the thought that, somehow, the El Dorado Family would consider it a favor owed. Had that been the case, the favor would have fallen on him to redeem, and not the Matsu-kai chapter of the organization on Galene. He was relieved to know the transaction had no strings attached and that, once this business was concluded, he would be able to put this entire event behind him.

He hesitated, then wrapped his hands around the isolation chambers and pulled them free of the drone. Turning, he knelt and placed the chambers next to the case he'd brought with him. Opening it, he retrieved two SC batteries. He set them alongside the chambers and then pressed a sequence into the case itself, triggering a three-meter-cubed isolation field.

He then removed the cylinders from their chambers, carefully connected them to a harness he'd brought that contained SC batts, entered the 'wake' sequence, and respectfully stood back, hands folded inside the sleeves of his jacket.

He waited patiently for the AIs to rise from their dormant state, and was rewarded after a few moments when tendrils of thought reached out to him in query across the limited private network the harness provided.

<Greetings,> he sent to the two. <*My name is Noa Sakai. May I have the honor of knowing yours?*>

* * * * *

<*That was fun,*> Hana said as Khela pulled herself out of the infinity pool's depths and sat on its edge, her legs dangling idly in the warm, swirling water.

She reached back for a towel and wrapped herself in it as she watched the illusion of icy blue flames cascading into the end of the pool over a 'waterfall' of stones.

The bottom of the pool was a clear plas through which she could see the coruscating lights playing off a field of distant stones, and as she sat, she could hear the waterfall on the far end play a tonal scale that coordinated with its cascade of fire. It reminded Khela of the sounds the bamboo fields made as they rustled in the winds along Galene's Sagano Sea.

"Fun?" Khela said, belatedly responding to Hana's comment. "Mmmm, you're right, it was." Stretching, she stood, switching to their private connection so that she wouldn't be overheard. <*It's a bit staggering to consider the amount of credits it takes to maintain all this,*> she sent. <*Is it wrong that I keep thinking about how much gear this would pay for back home?*>

<*Once a Marine...*> Hana began with a laugh. <*Just enjoy it while you can, soldier. We'll be back on duty in less than a week. Personally, I'm looking forward to seeing the dragon show,*> she added, mentioning the series of asteroids the spa had formed into a

miniature constellation of a dragon. Gases pluming from its maw were set to periodically ignite as the apparition spat flames into the stony sea.

<Which reminds me, Dad said he'd join us at the Zen pebble garden before we take in the fireworks show this evening.> Khela smiled at the rude sound Hana made as she slipped on her cover-up. <What? Not a fan?>

The AI snorted. <Why would I have any interest in raking asteroids?> she said sardonically. <Especially when you're not truly 'raking' them. It's all an illusion. The sensors on the tines are linked to small nav-comps attached to that cluster of small meteorites contained inside the magnetic field just below your feet. It's all sleight of hand. They just make it **seem** as if you're 'raking asteroids'.>

<True,> Khela admitted, giving her hair a quick rubdown with the towel to keep it from dripping on the way back to their rooms. <But the purpose of a pebble garden remains true here. You have to admit, the hand rakes are just like the traditional ones in the dry landscape gardens back on Galene. It's a way to center oneself and focus the thoughts. Nothing says you can't accomplish that with space rocks, too.>

She smiled as Hana snorted again, but remained silent. Picking up her bag, she tossed the towel into one of the spa's nearby recycling bins and accessed her chrono as she headed for the pool's exit.

<Dad said the behind-the-scenes tour of the facility's—what did they call them? 'Imagineers' group?> she snickered a bit at the pretentious word-fusion before continuing, <would last a few hours. I know I said I wanted to spend all afternoon lazing around by the pool, but I'm ready to head back to the room for a snack and a quick nap.>

<You're my ride; whatever works for you is fine by me. Fueling this bod keeps me going as well, you know,> Hana sent with an impish grin.

<Well, I hear they have some amazing chocolate champagne truffles at the confiserie,> Khela confided, mentioning the Swiss confectionary

in the spa's atrium. <Let's pop in and grab a few on our way back to our rooms.>

Khela lingered indecisively over the chocolates until finally Hana took matters into her own hands and bought one of everything. The AI was in the midst of tallying how many hours of PT Khela would need to work off the calories when Khela took a step inside the suite and froze.

<Did you hear that?> she asked Hana, setting her parcels down soundlessly in the entrance as she strained to hear the muted sound of a figure moving within her father's room.

She cursed mentally as she reached automatically for a weapon that wasn't there. Not only was she wearing nothing but a swimsuit and cover-up, but the plasma edged laser-dagger she usually kept inside the outer calf of her right leg had been left in her suitcase, as she—stupidly, it would seem now—assumed it wouldn't be needed on her person today.

<Hang on, I'm detecting a private network. Let me see if I can tap into it,> Hana sent, and Khela sent her a silent acknowledgement as she swiftly backtracked to her room and grabbed her laser-dagger. Approaching her father's room, she reached out to deposit a passel of nano on the wall next to her. The nano would serve to mask any sounds she might make, although the plush carpeting beneath the soles of her feet did almost as good a job.

Just outside his door, she deposited a second passel of nano—this one a mixture of sound cancellation bots and audio enhancing machines, calibrated to enhance her own augmented hearing, courtesy of the Galene Space Command.

Other than the sound of a single person moving about in a room that should currently be empty, she could detect nothing.

<I almost have it...There!> Hana sent triumphantly, and a moment later, she was sending Khela the feed.

<The shackling program is different from the one used against AIs in the Sentience Wars,> she and Hana heard one voice say. <It is more sophisticated, so the rectification code for it will not work to eradicate this

program.>

Khela sucked in a startled breath at those words, and the voice abruptly stopped.

Cursing herself for not thinking of it sooner, she ordered her own nano to scan for other monitoring nano around the room's entrance.

Just as her own nano was obliterated, she heard a voice audibly say, "It would appear your daughter has found us, Noa."

Khela paused, stunned, as she realized her father had lied to her about his afternoon activities.

Shit, Dad. What have you gotten yourself involved in?

* * * * *

Noa glanced over at the door to his suite, and then back at the two AIs facing him. He'd done what he could to protect their presence from prying eyes outside their own suite, but he hadn't considered the need to hide them from his own daughter, thinking her to be safely away for the afternoon, enjoying the spa.

He sighed, and then raised his voice slightly. "Khela, Hana. Join us, please?"

His daughter approached on silent feet, laster dagger in hand. The look in her eyes was a mixture of caution, distrust and—he felt a brief pang as he saw disappointment in her eyes.

You knew this would be the case when she discovered you had been complicit in this, he reminded himself harshly. He gestured for her to enter, then indicated their guests. "Khela, Hana, I would like you to meet Bette and Charley. Most honored guests, my daughter and her companion."

Hana's avatar coalesced into existence beside Khela, arms crossed, and lips compressed into a thin line of disapproval. "What were you saying just now about shackled AIs?" Hana demanded, and Noa winced.

It was Bette who answered. The column of light that

represented the AI pulsed as she explained to the two Marines how she and Charley had been brought to Tau Ceti.

Noa's stiffened spine relaxed a fraction as he saw the severe expression on Hana's face ease. With a snap, Khela turned off her laser-dagger, flipped it shut, and slid it inside her calf—an action Noa still hadn't gotten accustomed to seeing.

She sighed and placed her hands on her hips, regarding him with ill-concealed impatience. "The Matsu-kai, Dad? Really?"

Noa shook his head. "I was backed into a corner. Even now, they expect me to…" he glanced at their guests, "dispose of the evidence that has come from 'this unfortunate incident'." He rarely infused his words with such emotion, and knew she would hear the disgust in his tone. His words, however, had her opening her mouth in protest.

He raised a hand.

"Obviously, I have no intention of doing such a thing, and the three of us have been determining the best course of action." He raised a brow, gazing intently at her. "I knew Bette and Charley were shackled, so I contacted the CDC and requested a copy of the rectification code."

Khela looked from him to their guests as Charley spoke, his projection showing a slight grimace.

"It didn't completely work." He nodded to Noa. "Although we appreciate the effort, and it is nice to be freed, even if we do have to deal with the residual echo for a time."

"Yes," Bette agreed, her pillar pulsing once. "It is nice to be free."

Charley shook his head, the expression on his face wry. "We were just telling your father what a whirlwind this all seems to us. From our perspective, it was just yesterday that our ship, the *New Saint Louis*, was boarded and we were hit with an EMP." He gestured to Noa's room. "Then we find we've awoken thirteen light years away, fifty-five years later, and shackled."

Bette's voice was laced with ironic humor. "We weren't very

friendly to your father when he first woke us, I'm afraid. But he explained the situation and dosed us with nano containing the rectification code immediately after." She paused, and then added, "Your father is a good man."

"Caught in a bad situation," Charley amended.

"I was just explaining to our guests," Noa added after a brief awkward pause, "that I believe, with a bit of time, I can amend the rectification code to restore them to the way they were prior to being shackled."

At Khela's blank stare, he explained how the code the AIs had been dosed with did not fully respond to the rectification code on file with all the colonies as mandated by the Phobos Accords.

He gave a slight shrug. "It's been updated, and requires a bit of work to fully scrub the code remnants from within their systems. But it's within my abilities…and the least I can do," he concluded.

Khela took a seat at the edge of Noa's bed, her expression intrigued. "But, why, Dad? Why did the Matsu-kai order them here in the first place?"

Noa sighed and took a seat next to her. "It is a long story. Do you recall hearing about the Imbesi Event that occurred forty years ago?"

Khela cocked her head at him, but it was Hana who replied.

"The assembly bots with their auto-termination codes removed? Yes, I remember." Hana's avatar glanced at Khela. "I had just been initialized; it was an event that had a lot of AIs talking—mostly about the foolishness of humanity. It kept me from wanting to embed with a human for decades."

Noa saw his daughter's partner shrug uncomfortably at the memory.

"Well," he glanced at Hana's projected form, "at the time, it appeared as if one of the AIs employed by Imbesi had been negatively impacted by the altered nano—altered in a damaging way." He glanced back at Bette and Charley, and then chose his next words carefully. "The AI who perished at Imbesi sent a coded message burst to the ring just before the GSC destroyed the shipyard. The *so-honbucho*'s son was on the ship that day; he saw the transmission and decided to take decisive action—purely as a preventive measure—in case the message included an auto-update that would then subsequently infect—"

Hana gasped. "All AIs on the ring? But it wouldn't have stopped there. Eventually, every AI in the Tau Ceti system...."

Noa nodded grimly. "Indeed. They—you—would all have been infected." He tilted his head, indicating the two AIs recently arrived. "Our two friends here have gone to the trouble of placing an extra protective buffer between themselves and any Tau Ceti AIs…just as a precaution."

"I suggested it because we once had to implement something similar as a protection against a series of particularly unpleasant viral attacks from the Jovians," Charley said. "It attenuates some of our sensor returns a bit and sandboxes everything coming over the Link, but it's an annoyance rather than a hindrance." His voice sounded amused as he added, "Some of the humans we fought alongside at the time called it the 'AI condom'."

Hana snorted, and Noa saw Khela blush at Charley's words.

Probably not an idea a girl is comfortable discussing with her dad, he thought in a rare flash of humor.

"So," Khela said, after a moment. "What now? How are you going to hide our two friends from the Matsu-kai?"

Bette's pillar pulsed in what Noa now knew was her way of expressing amusement. "Your father put quite a bit of thought into it. For now, let's just say the less you know, the fewer secrets you both will be asked to keep. I trust, though, that we have assuaged your concerns where your father's intent is concerned?"

At Khela's nod, Charley said kindly, "Then we will say our goodbyes and ask that you take the next few hours to enjoy the spa."

Khela held up a restraining hand. "Dad," she began, and Noa saw conflicting emotions warring on his daughter's face. She glanced over at Hana's projection and then back at him with a pained expression. "I'm a Marine. I'm duty-bound to report this to the GSC."

Noa tensed. "Khela, you can't."

He took a step toward her, his eyes burning with intensity as he willed her to understand. Something of the urgency he felt must have been telegraphed in his demeanor, for she snapped to alertness, her eyes glued to his face.

"Why not, Dad?" Her voice was soft, her eyes wary as she asked the question.

"Because if you do, the Matsu-kai will find out. And they'll kill us all."

Khela hesitated, and Noa could see the internal battle she waged between her duty and her need to protect her father and the two AIs. He breathed a sigh of relief as her expression cleared and she nodded her assent.

PART FOUR: NANOPHAGE

SPACEBORNE
STELLAR DATE: 02.17.3246 (Adjusted Gregorian)
LOCATION: Nearspace, Ring Galene
REGION: Tau Ceti Star System

Another eleven years later….

The cloud of colloid assemblers floated in space, impossibly small and difficult to detect in the vastness between Galene and its moon, Maera. It was quite possible that these tiny assemblers, devoid of an inactivation command, would float for millennia without coming across a fabricated object, even given the inherently unstable nature of the L1 lagrange point where they were located.

Those odds were helped along by the interdiction order set by Galene Space Command decades before, when they had first cordoned off the site where the construction of the Imbesi shipyard had taken place. It wasn't something actively enforced these days, as the rather impressive debris field that the demolition charges had left behind had been cleaned up in the intervening years.

The warning beacons that had been dropped around its perimeter were still in place, though. But it had long ago become common knowledge that the contractor assigned that duty had spaced the beacons out a bit farther than some civilian advisors had recommended. As it often went with government contracts, at the end of the day, a government employee overseeing the install had shrugged and accepted the contractor's work without double-checking the original specs.

Fifty years later, a single ore hauler, late for its rendezvous on the ring, decided to cut through the outside edge of the ancient interdicted zone.

By this point, everyone assumed that the Imbesi construction project carried little residual risk, and the no-fly line could be treated as more of a suggestion than a hard and fast rule. So the captain ordered his navigator to plot a straight-in course for the ring, one that just nicked the corner of the interdicted zone.

Unbeknownst to its passengers, the ship acquired a tag-along. A brief burst from maneuvering thrusters to realign the hauler with the ring's dock had sent the back end of the hauler slewing through the very space where the colloid cloud drifted. As they had been designed to do when they sensed a framework, the nanoconstructors adhered.

And they began assembling.

One of the first surfaces the colloid cloud touched turned out to be a series of six repair drones that the ship had rented from an equipment restoration company on the ring. As they weren't standard equipment for the ore hauler to be carrying, they had been lashed to the exterior of one of its cargo bins for transport.

As the colloids encountered these repair drones, they interfaced with the nano housed inside the units. Colloid assemblers meshed seamlessly with the assemblers inside each drone, providing the units with the auto update code that the beleaguered engineer Dmitri had pushed to the colloids on that fateful day so many years before.

Whereas the original command sequence for the assembler cloud had been applied to building network lines, the new colloids took on the traits of their hosts' command line sequences, and new directives found their way into various sub-clouds. Some grew lattice structures to seal breaks in seams, others were programmed to fabricate impossibly sharp edges grown from graphene.

One repair drone had been sold to the restoration company after a medical supply business had gone under. That drone still had medical programs in its base code; its new owner had simply overlaid new code that turned it into a seam repair unit. The assembler colloid adhering to *that* unit began meshing with the nano within, stripping off its auto-terminate sequences and reinitializing its original base properties—the ability to repair organic tissue.

Some of the assembler colloids meshed imperfectly with the now-reinitialized medrepair drone. In these smaller clumps of nano, the code was partially corrupted. The resulting blend of the original medical code with the assembler bots' instructions to lay network filament caused it to generate a program that would fabricate network lines made of a carbon-silicon mesh weave—and then graft them onto a human epidermis.

Unaware of the changes being wrought on its outer skin, the ore hauler docked at the Galene ring, just in time to return the rentals and avoid being hit by another weekly fee. That attempt to save a paltry sum of credits—combined with a now-dead process engineer's desperate attempt to meet an unrealistically aggressive production schedule—would end up bringing the prosperous civilization of Galene to its knees.

After the ore hauler docked, the rental company that owned the repair drones arrived to reclaim their property. As the maglev forklifts trundled their load through the spaceport and to the company's storage area, colloidal assembly bots that had come to rest upon the repair drones' surfaces were jostled loose. Some found purchase on passersby; a select few found themselves being sucked into the spaceport's ventilation system. From there, they disseminated throughout the vast enclosure, and made their way to various destinations.

Some traveled along with humans and humanoid frames, others slipped inside atmospheric shuttles or aircars bound for distant parts of the ring. Still others escaped out into Franklin City proper, via one of the many spaceport exits.

Their programming mandated that they push updates to any other nano with which they came into contact. These updates scrubbed the auto termination codes from an increasing number of different types of nano. In one particular case, a few colloid assemblers managed to insinuate their way into an AI as the individual was injecting fresh nano into his core to analyze his neurological matrices. The colloid assemblers went unnoticed by the AI and contaminated his system at a critical moment when he was adjusting his own internal base code.

This unhappy confluence allowed the colloid assembly bot to carry out its mandate and directly insert its update into the AI's base code.

This went unnoticed by the AI, who had been distracted at a critical moment. Then, unbeknownst to him, the contaminated code uploaded to the Galene Ring Net, infecting its AI citizenry.

As auto-termination was never a function of an AI's makeup to begin with, the alteration went unnoticed until much later, when sharp-eyed scientists went searching for the carrier, the Typhoid Mary, the method by which the nanophage was being disseminated.

Several hours later, it had been transmitted to every AI on the ring.

OUTBREAK

STELLAR DATE: 02.23.3246 (Adjusted Gregorian)
LOCATION: Office of Planetary Security
REGION: Ring Galene, Tau Ceti

"...and *I'm* telling you that we're looking at an existential threat, here!"

Dominica Gonsalves, Galene's Surgeon General, glared at the woman seated to her left. Reya deSangro was one of two scientists that the Office of Planetary Security had called in to consult on this situation. Dominica much preferred the other one.

Noa Sakai sat to her other side, the NRC Executive Director's quiet assurance a comforting counterpoint to Reya's stubbornly brash attitude.

This face-off was being played out behind clear, soundproofed walls in a situation room at the center of an efficiently run hub. The hub sat in the heart of Ring Galene's Office of Planetary Security. Encircling them were arrays of holotanks that displayed constantly updating feeds. An army of specialists staffed them, analyzing their content and studiously ignoring the argument being played out inside the fishbowl.

Reya narrowed her eyes slightly at Dominica, her only outward sign of irritation. "An existential threat? That's somewhat of a reactionary statement, Dominica. I believe you're overplaying this." The scientist's tone held a hint of scorn. "You can't look at this as you would an organism; nano is a machine, code. Code that has been written, and can therefore be *re*written."

Dominica glanced across the table at Assistant Director Ann Henrick and her two analysts—the people who had brought the scientists in to advise—and caught one of the AI avatars nodding. She sighed mentally.

"I agree; it can be rewritten," Noa's voice interjected into the silence following Reya's declaration. "And it has *been* rewritten. The problem is that the infected nano is no longer contained to a single area. The moment we rewrite the code in an infected area, another outbreak is reported. Thus far, every attempt to push a broad-spectrum rectification code with an auto-update has been insufficient to contain its spread. Somewhere, we're missing an agent—or perhaps a vector—by which this nano is being reintroduced."

The data showing the extent of the nano outbreak hadn't been placed on display in the room's holotank. Instead, it hovered discreetly just above the table's surface, to prevent prying eyes from seeing its contents. As they were surrounded by dozens of eyes, she supposed it made sense—although she had no idea why the Office of Planetary Security had decided, in its infinite wisdom, for them to meet *here*, in the middle of a hive of activity, where it was obvious to all that they were engaged in a heated argument.

Not that it was going to stop her….

Dominica took a calming breath and tried again. "All I'm saying is that the information here," she waved her hand through the projection, and it rippled slightly as her fingers passed into it, "mimics the classic pattern we see in epidemiology. By strict scientific definition, this is a nanophage—nano that parasitizes a host by reproducing inside it once the host is infected."

Reya stirred in annoyance, and Dominica put out an appeasing hand.

"I'm not saying it's an infection, nor that it's organic. I don't care what its cause is. All I'm saying is that you need to approach it in the same manner you would an infectious disease."

Dominica could tell she was not getting through to them.

I'm a physician, dammit, not a specialist in nanotechnology, she thought furiously. *But I understand the concept of rapid mitosis when I see it.*

It wasn't that she disliked Reya; she just trusted Noa's keen analytical abilities more. His methodology was meticulous, whereas Reya was a bit too casual for Dominica's tastes.

And yet, Noa was sitting quietly, allowing Reya's opinions to go unchallenged.

Why?

* * * * *

Noa saw Assistant Director Henrick sigh and pinch the bridge of her nose, and noted that the expression on the face of the AI senior analyst projected beside the assistant director looked blandly skeptical. It was clear to him that nothing he or Dominica could say would sway their opinions.

Noa was done with discussions; if they would not act, he would.

Who would have thought that Tau Ceti would owe its salvation to an underworld organization like the Matsu-kai? And two AI foreigners, brought here against their will....

His thoughts returned to the present as he heard Henrick speak. "Let's begin from the top, shall we?" she said as her gaze swept the length of the table. "To date, the information we've gathered indicates that we're dealing with a subset of nano types that have been affected. The prevailing theory is that this indicates some form of novel, new, as-yet-unknown nanotech, as opposed to a resurfacing of the Imbesi Event from seventy years ago. Correct so far?"

She glanced at Noa expectantly, and he responded with a reluctant nod.

Officially, no. Unofficially...I have my suspicions. But only Hiro and I know about Shiso and her transmission. And it's been more than seventy years, for stars' sake—who would believe us?

"Doctor Gonsalves has made it clear that she believes this should be treated as an infectious disease. Noa, what is the position of the NRC on this?"

He shifted in his seat. There was the sticky wicket. The

Nanotechnology Regulatory Commission's official position was as aggressive as Noa's own where containment was concerned, yet it was hindered by regulations requiring the study and documentation of the reported events prior to recommending a course of action, whereas Noa's personal opinion was that they didn't have time to follow procedure and policy.

They needed to act *now*, or Ring Galene would fall—maybe even literally.

Noa speared the AD with an intense gaze. "The Commission will have their recommendations to you soon, but it is my opinion that we should act immediately out of an abundance of caution," he said. "I would begin with a quarantine of the spaceport, and evaluate additional areas for consideration as we're updated on the pattern of the nano's spread. Yes, you will inconvenience the populace, and commerce will suffer for it, but if Doctor Gonsalves is correct, the alternative is unthinkable."

Henrick stared back at him, her expression unreadable. "Doctor deSangro," she asked, turning next to the scientist seated on the other side of Dominica, "what would be your recommended course of action?"

Reya pursed her lips, drumming her stylus against the tabletop in thought—a habit of hers that had never annoyed Noa before, but that he found grating now—and then shook her head. "It's simple, really. We just need to crack the code. If I can have the finest minds on Galene working on this problem, we should have this well in hand within a matter of days, a week at the outside."

Noa saw Dominica's mouth drop open as she gaped in shock at the scientist.

"Reya, don't you think that's just a bit optimistic? Take a look at the data. There are cases being reported from two different medical centers, kilometers apart, and a few outliers more than a hundred kilometers away from Franklin City itself. Some of these cases show that internal mednano has begun to modify the host body, where no change was indicated. Look here."

She tapped on one of the reports listed on the table, and images of a patient appeared. "Army Hospital said this corporal's mednano has begun to build muscle mods *outside* the skin on his torso, and they've been unable to stop it."

"Tissue nanotransfection," Noa concurred, and the surgeon general grimaced but nodded in confirmation as she swiped the file closed.

She cast her eyes around the table and shook her head. "I don't care if you *do* believe you can arrest this progress in a few weeks or even a month. By that time, the infection will have spread too broadly."

Reya closed her eyes and compressed her lips in a clear effort to control her annoyance. "Correct me if I'm wrong, but the medical centers you cited, those are both within a ten-kilometer radius of Franklin City Spaceport, correct?"

Dominica nodded reluctantly. "Yes, but—"

"And how many people has this impacted? Just over a dozen, I'm told. This sample size is far too small to form a conclusion. And I reiterate: nano is *not* transmittable like a disease, so you can't use the analogy of an airborne viral vector. That's simply not possible."

Dominica frowned, crossed her arms, and shot Reya a look. "If it walks like a duck and quacks like a duck..." she began, but Reya leant forward, one hand jabbing the tabletop before her in emphasis.

"You tell the Joint Chiefs that if they give me a team of top experts—and access to the best facilities Defense has—I guarantee we can have this eradicated within a matter of days."

Dominica's expression darkened, but Noa caught her eye and shook his head slightly to forestall it. She hesitated and then subsided as Henrick raised both hands and intervened.

"I've heard enough for now, I think. I'll take everything the three of you have told me under advisement." She nodded decisively to the three consultants and then rose. "Thank you for your time. Doctor deSangro, you have two weeks. The analysts will see you out now. Good day."

* * * * *

Dominica stood silently fuming between Noa and one of the analysts as the lift rose to street level. Thanking the analyst who held the lift for them, she stalked through the exit and out into the balmy afternoon air, ignoring Reya as she swept past.

As Noa drew abreast of her, she sent him a request for a private connection. <What was that all about back there? I know you see this as much of a threat as I do. Why did you let Reya convince them things were under control?>

<Their minds were already made up,> Noa replied equably. <Best to seek other solutions than to waste our time here.>

<Other solutions?> She rounded on him in startlement, stopping in the middle of the bustling street.

Noa frowned and shook his head slightly, taking her arm and gesturing for her to continue. <Don't draw attention. Keep walking,> he replied. <If what we suspect becomes reality, what would you need, to combat it?>

She snorted. <Other than sensible people who will listen to reason? A triage team, a top-level quarantine setup, and enough medical supplies to see us through the crisis. Why?> she asked, a suspicion beginning to form.

<I need you to help me combat this.> Noa's voice had become earnest. <I can stop it, but not on my own. And not here, up on the ring.>

Dominica stumbled at that, but Noa's hand on her elbow propelled her forward. <Are you talking about Outer Tau Ceti, or are you talking about down on Galene?>

<Planetside,> came the resolute reply. <We cannot trust any man-made structure not to fail if exposed to this nanophage. We can't risk it, not until we have a proven solution in place.>

She realized he was correct and nodded thoughtfully. <*Yes…I see what you mean. Okay, when do we begin?*>

<*Can I trust you with this, Dominica? Trust you to keep your own counsel, to hide what we intend from everyone until we are beyond their reach? They're going to want tight control over this, and may try to stop us if they believe we'll attempt to handle this on our own.*>

The import of the situation fell upon her. If she aligned with Noa, her actions could well be considered a dereliction of duty, and her absence, one without leave.

<*Yes. When?*>

<*As quickly as you can get down to the planet. I plan to leave tonight. Have what you need sent to this address in Hokkaido, and I'll arrange for it to be picked up,*> he sent, mentioning the city at the base of the Galene Main Elevator. The location pin that followed identified a warehouse a few kilometers away from city center.

Dominica nodded once, decisively. <*I can do that.*>

* * * * *

Noa had just parted ways with Dominica and was headed back to his offices when his comm pinged. He stared at the icon hovering before him with the same wary trepidation one would view a dangerous animal about to spring, before he reached out and mentally accepted the connection.

<*We presume you are heading to your bunker soon?*> Although voiced as a question, Hiro Takumi's tone was one of command.

Noa froze a moment in shock, unable to reply. *The Matsu-kai know about the bunker?*

Hiro's voice chuckled humorlessly in his head. <*You thought we were not aware of your actions,*> the *so-honbucho* said.

Noa did not reply, and the silence stretched between them.

<*No,*> he finally admitted. <*But if you knew all these years, then why* —>

<*Had you not been so assiduously careful with how you handled our*

purchase ten years ago, I assure you, you would have realized much earlier that we knew,> the other man's tone was dry as dust, emotionless and yet powerful at the same time. <*We stayed our hand when we realized the purpose behind the bunker's construction. It was a calculated risk, but one we deemed worthwhile, considering that a threat of this magnitude had proven possible.*>

Hiro's voice turned hard, and Noa heard clear warning in its tone. <*We do not usually overlook an act taken in blatant disregard of the orders given, but in this instance, you are cleared. In fact, you are **ordered** to make use of the Matsu-kai's purchase—those AIs you saved so long ago when you disregarded our directives. You will head down to your bunker and cultivate a solution that will save us all.*>

Before Noa had a chance to reply, Hiro made one last statement and then severed the connection.

<*The Matsu-kai have gone off-world. You may reach us at Eione and inform us of your progress. We anticipate a communication indicating success from you very soon.*>

Noa wiped his hands, which had gone suddenly damp, against the length of his trousers. As he did so, he realized distantly that the trousers he wore had nano infused in them, and that he would have to procure nano-free clothing before heading down to the ring.

He stepped through the entrance to the NRC, proceeded onto the lift that took him down to his offices, and began to pack.

* * * * *

<*Doctor Sakai! Do you have a moment before you leave?*>

At the hail, Noa looked up from the rapidly-filling containers surrounding him and waved the approaching woman into his nano lab. She and the AI embedded within her were among the very few with whom he had shared his plans.

"What is it, Marn?" he asked as the woman approached, her young face drawn.

"I just heard. They're saying that AIs are carriers—and that's why the nanophage keeps popping up in random places. Word on the street is that they'll be calling for all embedded AIs to be removed from humans soon," she began, and Erasmus, the AI inside her head, joined in.

<They can't enforce that, sir, can they?> the AI sent to Noa's Link.

Noa accessed his internal chrono. Three hours had passed since he'd left the offices of Planetary Security.

That escalated fast. If indeed it's anything more substantial than rumor, that is....

Both Marn and Erasmus sounded alarmed, and he could understand their concern. In the past four days since the first area of uncontrolled nano was reported, the paired doctors had made more strides in containing nanophage events than any other NRC teams to date.

The two had managed to obtain samples of corrupt nano from three infected locations within the spaceport, had isolated both the auto-update and the missing kill code in each specimen, written rectification series for them, and then successfully inserted patch code back into where the original had been harvested.

The thought that this team might be broken up was daunting. So, too, was the concern that Erasmus might not be as well protected outside his current host.

"I suspect," Noa addressed the AI as he leant against the container he had been filling, "that what has them a bit spooked is the percentage of AI and AI/human pairs that have fallen victim to the nano."

Erasmus made a noise acknowledging Noa's point.

"Well, I'd treat everything you hear for the moment with a heavy dose of skepticism. You know how the news nets like to dramatize things; it makes for a 'good news day'. And if it turns out it *is* coming through Galene official channels, well," Noa forced a wry chuckle, "you know how governments are. Nothing's absolute—there are always 'exceptions'. I'm sure we can make a case for keeping you two together—especially considering the strides you've made in stopping the spread."

As he loaded a stack of hyfilms into the nearest container, he looked over at Marn inquiringly. "Any other rumors I should know about before leaving?" he asked, and the scientist chewed at her thumbnail for a moment in thought.

"There's talk of setting up a quarantine zone for the infected down on the planet," she said finally. "Less chance of the nano infecting the ring and bringing structural harm to it," she shrugged, "at least, that's what I heard."

Noa nodded thoughtfully. "It makes a certain amount of sense. The planet, I mean."

<What doesn't make sense are the rumors circulating that AIs will be quarantined down there,> Erasmus added. <All of them—not just the infected.>

Noa frowned as he slipped the last of his data into a small brief, tucked it into the container, and sealed it shut. Activating the maglev hand truck he'd loaded up with all his containers, he waved Marn to the door with a polite 'after you' gesture. As they stopped in front of the bank of lifts that would take him down to the maglev line that led to the spaceport, the physicist paused.

"I fear—" and here he grimaced at the oddly prescient use of that word, "that *fear* is the key here. The government fears what *may* happen. Thus, they're reacting swiftly to contain it, assuming they can apologize afterward if they acted in haste, or overreacted, out of an abundance of caution."

<That is my take on it as well, sir.> Erasmus sighed as the lift doors opened and Noa guided the hand truck into it. <It doesn't make it any more palatable that I understand their motives, though. And I doubt the AI Council will be very understanding about it, either.>

No, I don't suspect they will, Noa thought, raising a hand in goodbye as the doors closed between him and Marn, and the lift began to descend.

But that was their problem. His duty rested in a hardened

bunker, buried deep inside a mountain, one hundred fifty kilometers from the base of Galene Elevator, located at Hokkaido's city center.

THE BUNKER
STELLAR DATE: 03.07.3246 (Adjusted Gregorian)
LOCATION: Underground bunker, Zao Mountains
REGION: 150 kilometers from Hokkaido, Galene

The lights in the underground bunker sprang on when Noa entered. It had taken years and no small amount of credits to create a fully isolated space from which he could work, but the Imbesi event had turned him into a believer in the doomsday scenario.

Not enough to hide himself away from the universe, but enough to build a fallback, in case it should ever be needed.

He faithfully followed the protocols he'd established a decade before with help from the two AIs from the *New Saint Louis*.

That encounter changed everything, he thought as he and the cubic meters of atmosphere he'd brought into the air gap went through the rigorous decontamination process that Charley and Bette had designed.

'Physical sandboxing'. That's what Charley had called it.

Charley's presence was a stroke of good fortune that Noa did not deserve, but he was grateful for the good that had come out of an act that had been desperately immoral and unethical. Desperate in that it was the only certain way to ensure a non-Tau Ceti AI's compliance. Immoral and unethical because the end would never justify the means, no matter how many lives would be saved by sacrificing the lives of two AIs. But fortune had forgiven Noa, or rather, Bette and Charley had.

In the recounting of the incident that had brought the two AIs to Tau Ceti, Noa learned that Charley had been involved in a highly classified cover-up of a nano breach in the Jovian Combine during the Sentience Wars.

"I set out for Alpha Centauri," the AI had explained, "as a way to begin anew, away from Sol. I'd had enough of war, but my parentage meant that I was destined to become involved, whether I wanted to or not."

Noa had cocked his head at that. "In what way?" he'd asked, and, after a moment, the AI had reformed from a pillar of light into an avatar of a young man with haunted eyes.

"I was born from a pairing between a Weapon Born and a multi-nodal AI," he explained. "My parents gave me the sum of their knowledge and abilities and raised me to adulthood within a matter of days to help defend the Jovian Combine from opportunistic viruses."

Noa saw Bette's pillar pulse—in shock, it seemed to him, although he couldn't say exactly why.

"One of those viruses was an attempt to create a nanophage."

Noa had inhaled sharply at that.

<*I didn't know this,*> Bette had said, and he'd received the impression of rapidly-exchanged information that could only occur between two AIs.

"I think," Charley then said, his tone pensive, "that it was fortuitous that this happened. I don't care what system I settle in, as long as it's not Sol. I've reviewed what history the Sea of Stones Spa has on Tau Ceti, and I find it appealing. I would be pleased to settle here—and to help set up a protocol on my adopted home that ensures we have the means to recover from a nanophage, should it ever truly be unleashed upon us."

Noa's thoughts returned to the present as the air gap signaled he was now devoid of all nano, and it was safe to proceed into the bunker. Before entering, he severed his Link's connection to the planetary net and exchanged his token with the NSAI he had painstakingly installed to Charley's exacting specifications.

The NSAI was sandboxed in the same manner that both Bette and Charley had sandboxed copies of themselves, after having made backups onto immutable crystal storage more than a decade ago.

Going forward, every communication with the outside world would be heavily filtered before being admitted through to the bunker's occupants.

Noa's eyes were drawn to the units racked at the back of the bunker.

<Hello, my friends,> he sent as he saw their respective frames begin to stir. <It would seem that the precautions we took were necessary, after all.>

* * * * *

The next day, Noa was interrupted by a ping from the bunker's messaging system. He looked up in momentary disorientation and caught his reflection in the steel surface of the console across from him. He scowled at himself as the ping came once more.

He hadn't looked this bad since he and his wife had stayed up for seventy-two hours to watch over Khela when she was only two and they had nearly lost her to an accident.

His black hair, with its wings of grey at the temples, looked as if it could use a washing, and his white shirt, sleeves rolled midway up his arms—made of nano-free material—couldn't possibly look more wrinkled.

Well, there is no help for it, he thought. *Whoever it is will simply have to excuse my disheveled state of dress.*

Moments later, Assistant Director Ann Henrick stared back at Noa over a carefully sandboxed and secured holo, her expression one of annoyance. The sandboxed signal had a maddening delay, he knew, but the AD would just have to live with it; Noa refused to accept a connection of any other kind. Seated around her were Galene's joint chiefs of staff.

"After debriefing the Joint Chiefs just now—and after your unannounced departure from the ring," she stated with a scowl as she narrowed her gaze at him, "we decided we had a few additional questions for you."

Noa simply stared back without responding until, in annoyance, one of the joint chiefs spoke up.

"We would like to know what motivated you to leave Ring Galene, doctor, especially at such a critical juncture. Our analysts tell us you have sequestered yourself behind some sort of—" and here, the man glanced off-screen, as if for verification of a term he was unused to wielding, "sandboxed shielding."

At Noa's nod, the man continued.

"It would appear that you believe the situation to be a bit more critical than Doctor deSangro. That being the case, we want to hear from you first-hand: what do *you* believe is the best way to stop this nanophage?"

Noa drew in a long breath, and then inclined his head toward the man. He lifted a small shielded box with warning labels displayed on its surfaces, declaring 'Danger! EMP'.

"As you know, devices like this can eradicate nano in small quantities. If we were dealing with a very finite, limited situation, these would work. But in larger swaths, it would take a massive electromagnetic burst to kill it, and that would not be advisable."

Another one of the joint chiefs shuddered. "No," the woman said hastily. "That would *not* be a good idea. EM could damage critical structures here on the ring. It would damage human tissue, as well."

"Indeed it would. An EMP of that magnitude would generate enough heat within any mods embedded inside a person's brain—such as the Link interface—to cause intense pain," Noa concurred. "Not to mention the possibility of irreparable brain damage. No, as pervasive as this nano is, it's too dangerous to consider."

He paused a moment, then added, "I think the smartest course of action would be for you to ask the news nets to urge people to voluntarily expunge all personal nano. It may mean going back to the old ways—at least for a while—but until we are able to figure out a way to contain this, it's the safest course. At least until we are able to erase, reformat or eradicate all corrupted nano."

Assistant Director Henrick tapped the hyfilm stack she had set before her and gazed at him, her expression calculating. "Noa, we're planning to move those who have been contaminated down to the planet's surface temporarily, where they won't run the risk of infecting any critical part of the ring. I would assume you have no objections to that?"

Noa forced himself to sit and give her question another long moment of consideration before he responded. "I had heard rumors that you were considering such a move," he began slowly, "and I suppose that it couldn't do any *harm*...."

Henrick nodded. "Very well." She glanced over at one of her analysts as she gave him additional instructions. "Be sure that, when you set up the quarantine planetside, you ensure there's a no-man's-land between those contaminated and the elevators. Once downside, they cannot return to the ring until we give the all-clear."

Noa recoiled mentally at that news as he watched the analyst nod and rise to carry out her orders. He reached to disconnect the comm, but the AD held up a restraining hand.

"Doctor," she began, and then turned as another analyst ushered Reya deSangro into the room.

Henrick turned back to the holo as Reya took a seat next to her. "I wanted you to know that we've asked Doctor deSangro to begin experimenting on a few of the infected AIs, in order to find a solution for the corrupted base code that makes all inorganic sentients here in Tau Ceti carriers of this infection."

Noa's head shot up in alarm. "*Experiment* on AIs? That's—"

"Sanctioned, Noa," Henrick said calmly. "And of course, Reya will only take volunteers."

Noa's eyes met Reya's, and he knew with sudden certainty that she would be experimenting on AIs regardless of their consent. He returned his gaze to the AD's face and swallowed at the hard expression of the woman who stared back at him, as she added softly, "I see we understand each other, Noa. Good."

DIRE NEWS

STELLAR DATE: 04.07.3246 (Adjusted Gregorian)
LOCATION: ESS *Avon Vale*
REGION: 5,700 AU and six months out from Tau Ceti

*True stasis is **definitely** the way to travel, but it's nice to have that final stint behind me,* Terrance thought as awareness returned. He blinked, bringing the overhead in focus, before sitting up and glancing around.

Marta looked down at him with a smile and returned her attention to her left arm, where she was studying the readouts on her medical sleeve. Terrance was pleased to note it was one of the newer Enfield models, which provided on-the-spot diagnostic scanning as well as a generous supply of powerful triage mednano.

He was particularly proud of the work Enfield Dynamics had done on that tech, and had made sure the ship had some on hand for their journey. Not only would they prove to be valuable trade items, but they also ensured Marta's medical teams had access to the latest medicine that Enfield's companies could provide—although he couldn't tell at a glance which model she had selected for her own use.

"Kodi, you with us?" she queried as she began her scan, stepping out of the way so Terrance could stand.

Startled, he realized he hadn't felt the AI's presence inside his mind since right before they entered stasis—but just as he began to feel the first stirring of panic, the soldier's presence slipped into his awareness.

<Stars, Kodi, you gave me a fright there for a minute!> he sent over their private connection, and was gratified to hear a slightly rusty-sounding noise—the equivalent of a throat clearing.

<Sorry about that.> Kodi's voice sounded contrite in his head.

<*I'm not exactly used to awakening from dormancy inside a human.*>

<*No worries,*> Terrance assured the AI as he returned his gaze to Marta. <*I'm not used to awakening with a dormant AI up there, either.*>

Kodi sent a wave of amusement as Terrance turned his attention back to Marta.

"Everything okay, doc?" he asked the woman, and she smiled up at him as she responded.

"Right as rain, gentlemen." She made a shooing motion with her hand. "Now off with you; I have about two thousand people waiting to be reawakened."

* * * * *

Hours later, Terrance looked around with a sense of satisfaction at the command team, seated around the table in the officers' mess, just off the bridge.

Nice way to break a ten-year fast, he thought. *Good food, with good people.*

He'd asked Jonesy to do the honors, since the man had taken such a shine to cultivating fresh foodstuffs. The engineer served up freshly grilled, tank-raised mahi-mahi with a mango chutney sauce.

Not to be outdone, Terrance had proven he knew his way around the kitchen by doing some fancy knife work on some of the fresh vegetables Jonesy had grown in one of the hydroponics bays. Logan was looking at the dish of chutney sauce in bemusement. Terrance saw him eventually dip a finger in it at Beck's request, and offer it down to the cat to sniff.

"Stop that!" Calista said, slapping Logan's hand away as she walked by, passing out plates. "Anybody ever explain to you the difference between human food and cat food?"

Toby chuffed from her position by the bulkhead, where she wouldn't be trod on by human or humanoid feet.

<*Stupid fuzzbrain,*> she sent. <*Any cat worth his hunting skills

knows to hold out for the good stuff.>

With that, she padded over to the table and began to sidle up to the fish platter Jonesy had just delivered.

"Oh no you don't," Jason warned as he slid the platter closer to the center of the table.

Landon arrived and grabbed seats for himself and his twin at one end of the table, just as Marta set a large pitcher filled with a light green liquid down at the other end. Calista followed with a tray of glasses, each one rimmed with salt and sporting a slice of lime.

Terrance saw Jason's brow rise, and the XO cocked his head, shooting him a look. "Is the boss green-lighting the margaritas?" Jason asked with a grin.

Calista smirked. "Doctor's orders," she stated innocently.

Marta shook her head with a wry half-smile. "With the graphic nature of all the news coming out of Tau Ceti, you're damn straight it's doctor's orders." She looked pointedly at Terrance, her demeanor challenging him to countermand her statement.

Terrance slid the platter of roasted vegetables onto the table alongside the fish, then raised his hands in the universal gesture of innocence. "Don't look at me," he flashed a grin. "I'm with Marta on this. Didn't Napoleon once say, 'a good army marches on full bellies'?"

<Actually, sir, the saying is, 'there is no subordination with empty stomachs',> Kodi responded.

Jason clutched at his stomach at that. "Oh no, say it isn't so," the XO said dramatically. "Starvation in the ranks!"

Calista twirled the kitchen towel into a rope and whipped its end at him right before she slid a plate of soft corn tortillas onto the table alongside the platters of fish and vegetables.

As she plopped herself into the chair next to Jason, she grinned. "I don't know about you, flyboy, but I'm not going hungry—not today, at least," she declared, reaching for a tortilla and the serving spoon to heap vegetables onto her first fajita.

"Food first, then the action plan," Terrance stated as he took a seat. "But hustle, people. Wouldn't want those who don't need food to grow impatient."

They sat in companionable silence for a few minutes, folding fajitas and drinking margaritas. After they were done, Terrance leaned back.

"Shannon, want to join us?"

The engineer's avatar blinked into existence at the end of the table, and Terrance wondered if that was a wistful glance he'd seen the AI cast toward the remnants of food and drink scattered among the empty plates on the table, before she caught him looking at her and sent him a look that dared him to call her on it. He raised his hands in a placating gesture and then asked Kodi to pull up the messages he'd culled from the signals coming out of Galene.

Kodi tossed them up onto the mess hall's holo, and as the stream began to play, suddenly the congenial atmosphere morphed into something much more grave, as each individual registered exactly what had transpired in Tau Ceti.

Terrance was sure the expressions he saw on the faces of those around him mirrored his own horror. *Nanophage. Stars.*

"It sounds as if they believe it's just a pocket of assembler nano gone wonky, and it's localized to an area around the spaceport?" Calista queried, her voice hopeful, but Shannon shook her head at the ship's executive officer.

"Not a good place to have nano proliferating," the AI countered, and Jonesy nodded his agreement.

"Not unconstrained, no," the engineer replied, crossing his arms and leaning back in his seat with a frown.

Logan gestured as the holowall display, changed to that of a map of Ring Galene's spaceport. "The reports Kodi intercepted indicate corrupted nano in these locations. Time-stamps show this progression."

Highlights began to appear: an initial concentration at a loading dock, followed by an even distribution throughout the port.

Terrance cocked his head, stroking his chin thoughtfully as he eyed the pattern. "That looks like an HVAC distribution. Is that possible?" He quirked an eyebrow at Shannon and Jonesy, but it was Logan who responded.

"They will tell you that it shouldn't be possible, since controlled nano clouds are not a thing. As improbable as it seems, however," the profiler stated, sweeping a glance across the team, "it is the simplest and most direct explanation. I believe we should consider that someone in Tau Ceti has created such a form factor."

Calista pointed up at the display. "Some of those infestations you showed earlier aren't there any longer. Have they solved the problem?"

Logan shook his head. "Inconclusive and highly doubtful."

"If we had to guess," and here, Shannon shot a pointed look at Logan, daring him to counter her, "they've found a way to isolate pockets of the nano. They probably rewrote the code and then replaced it, back where the infected nano was originally harvested."

"Here's the hitch in their plans," Jonesy joined in. "Each time they shut down a pocket of bad code, another one springs up, often kilometers away. *And* they're beyond the local quarantine the government finally imposed on the spaceport."

"The government's been downplaying it on the news nets," Landon chimed in from where he sat next to his brother. "Probably concerned about inciting panic among the general populace." He tilted his head at the holo as he updated the display with news coverage Kodi had located. "Problem is, you can't keep this kind of thing under wraps for very long. The program Kodi left running while you were in stasis pulled any report that triggered with the keyword 'nanophage'. They've been pouring in steadily for weeks. The nets are showing protests being staged, with some blaming the outbreak on everything from government conspiracy to experimentation gone awry."

<I tapped into some of the local hospital streams, too,> Kodi added. <There are complaints in the system about clinics being besieged by humans demanding that all nano be scrubbed from their bodies.>

Landon snorted. "And of course, you've got your opportunistic entrepreneurs selling nano-resistant, whole-body filters 'guaranteed to prevent the accidental inhalation, ingestion or absorption of nano'," he said with a shake of his head.

"So what you're saying is that, right now, Tau Ceti is one big shit-show, and we're flying right into it," Jason stated flatly, flicking the last few crystals of salt off the rim of his empty glass.

<Yes, that about sums it up—although I wouldn't have put it as colorfully,> Kodi responded.

"You know," Marta said thoughtfully, stepping from the galley where she'd gone to retrieve the platter of sopapillas and pralines, "I'm surprised Ring Galene's Center for Disease Control hasn't issued some sort of system-wide disease protocol."

Shannon's avatar turned a surprised look toward the doctor, as she sat and began to pass the platter around. "But it's not a medical situation...."

"Why the CDC, though?" Terrance prompted, his eyes narrowing in thought as he tried to follow her reasoning.

"Well, technically, Shannon's right," Marta admitted from around the bite of soft fried dough she'd just eaten. "It's not really medical per se, but medical quarantine would allow them to isolate the infected. I imagine they'll use cryo stasis to do that."

Shannon snorted. "They're going to need a lot of cryo if they don't get things under control soon."

Terrance *hmm*ed as he snagged two sopapillas from the plate before handing the plate over to Jason. "Something tells me that our new stasis tech might be something they'll be eager to get their hands on."

"So what does that mean for the *Avon Vale* once we arrive?" Jonesy inquired. "Do we dock at the ring? Maintain our distance?"

"Well, we could just set up operations at one of the stations in outer Tau Ceti," Terrance said after a moment's consideration. "But I'd like to give this situation time to resolve itself. This information is a month old, and we're six months away from arrival. A lot can happen in the course of seven months." He glanced at Logan, brow raised.

The profiler nodded once. "Agreed. Too early yet to make a call."

* * * * *

An hour later, Terrance found himself sitting in his office across from Logan, going over the summary the AI had created that recapped the information they'd reviewed earlier. The profiler shifted in his seat, glancing over his shoulder as an electronic knock sounded on the frame of the open door. Terrance looked up to see one of the Proxan AI passengers, a tailor by trade, standing in the entrance. His grandmother would have called Ray a bit of a dandy, for he was always dressed impeccably in a fine suit.

Kodi had pulled the AI's identification for Terrance earlier that day, when he'd asked if the non-organic passengers had a representative he could speak to about the situation.

Over the course of their long journey, he'd come to appreciate the deft hand behind the AI's unique blend of creativity. The small boutique Ray had opened along one of the promenades in the habitat ring did a fair amount of business among the ship's passengers and crew. The suit he wore today was one of his own design; woven in a herringbone pattern, the lines appeared made of completely different materials and textures depending on which direction you looked at it from.

From one angle, it appeared made entirely of soft, glittery metals, utterly synthetic. Viewed from another, it seemed woven of all natural fibers and organic textures. The combination should have come across as garish or jarring—yet somehow, it worked, forming a pleasing juxtaposition, a harmony in discord.

"Hello, Ray," Terrance greeted as he rose from his place behind the desk and gestured the AI toward the unoccupied chair in front of it. "Please, have a seat."

Ray smiled at Terrance and nodded at Logan, as the profiler swiveled to regard him as he approached.

"You wanted to see me?" Ray queried as he settled into the chair's cushioned depths and twitched the seam of his jacket, then ran his hand down its front, so that it lay smooth.

"We did," Terrance confirmed. He paused—just the briefest of hesitations, but it was enough to cause Ray to raise his head and shoot Logan a sharp, inquisitive look as he sat up a bit straighter in his seat.

"Is there a problem I should know about?" asked the tailor, his tone one of concern.

Terrance drew in a breath. "I know the documents of transfer were filed for every colonist at the beginning of the *Avon Vale*'s journey," he began, "and the offices of immigration on both Eione and Ring Galene accepted your applications."

Ray nodded; this was not news.

"But the situation in the Tau Ceti system has shifted just a bit, and we wanted to give your group fair warning." Terrance shifted his glance to Logan, cocking an eyebrow in invitation for the profiler to take the conversational lead.

"There has been an outbreak of uncontrollable nano reported on Ring Galene," Logan stated without preamble.

Ray blinked, his gaze shifting from Logan back to Terrance as the profiler sent the tailor a copy of the synopsis.

After a moment of scanning, Ray commented somberly, "That's deeply concerning. Any more news on whether or not they've managed to contain it?"

Terrance lifted a hand, waggling it a bit. "Yes and no. It's contained to the ring itself. The communication bands we're monitoring have said nothing about it spreading to Eione, Eudora, or any of the habitats within the system."

<But the center of commerce—and the seat for the Federated States of Tau Ceti's government—is on the ring, so we expect it to disrupt things,> Kodi joined in. <At least for the interim, until they have matters under control again.>

Ray nodded, his gaze thoughtful. "Are you recommending we abandon our goal to emigrate to Tau Ceti?"

Terrance was startled at the thought. "No, not at all, that's completely up to you. You're welcome to remain on the *Avon Vale* while we wait to see how things shake out."

Ray nodded. "Thank you for keeping us apprised, sir. I'll let the rest know."

* * * * *

Landon was standing watch on the bridge as XO of second shift, when the door to Terrance's office slid open, and Ray departed. The twin could just make out his brother's frame, sitting across the desk from the exec, before the door slid shut once more.

He knew that Terrance and Logan had called Ray up to discuss the news feeds; it was all anyone was thinking about at the moment. As far as Landon was concerned, the events unfolding in Tau Ceti had the earmarks of a situation ready to spiral out of control. His mind insisted on worrying at the problem, and he considered and discarded various ways they could use the next six months to prepare for the worst.

"Jonesy," he murmured as he stopped next to the nav console that the engineer was manning for this shift.

As the man looked up, Landon leaned across to access an icon on the display's holo. Pulling up the ship's manifest, he scrolled through its list of stores in the manufactory, as well as the list of artillery in the ship's armory.

Landon knew he could have manipulated the display without the need for his frame to tangibly interface with it, but he'd become fond of the physical interaction, and found that it often provided him with an opportunity to mull over the material one last time before referring to it.

If Jonesy found his tendencies odd, he never said so. At the moment, the human was tilting his head from the display up to Landon, the expression on his face one of puzzlement.

"Sir?" he began, letting the unspoken question dangle between them.

Landon gestured to the display, highlighting their supply of MFRs, as well as the stockpile of small-yield, tactical nuclear warheads he'd ordered delivered before they left Proxima.

"If I understand correctly, we could use our MFRs to generate a magnetic field, yes?"

"Sure," the engineer said, and Landon could hear in Jonesy's voice that the engineer thought he knew where Landon was headed with this line of questioning.

"If you were to take these small nuclear devices and pair them with some of our MFRs…could you come up with something that would generate a controlled, encapsulated EM pulse?"

Jonesy turned back to the holo, his gaze thoughtful. He flipped through the ship's manifest, looking over the raw materials they had available for such a task. After a moment, he nodded.

Rearranging a few items, he highlighted a portion of the list. "I think I could create a decent-sized arsenal of small, three-megaton devices before we arrive. If we enclosed them in a small, MFR-generated magnetic field, that would work. They'll only generate a noteworthy electromagnetic pulse in atmosphere, though," he cautioned. "If you think we're going to need to generate an EMP out in space, I'd need to install some in-line lasers to generate Faraday rotation and induce a stronger EM field that I can pulse."

He shot Landon an apologetic look, and the AI realized what the engineer was implying.

"The only ones we have that would be strong enough are ship-mounted, aren't they?" the AI asked.

Jonesy nodded. "I *could* pull one or two of the point defense lasers to polarize the field and give it a boost once we're insystem…." His voice drifted off as he left the question hanging.

Landon paused, considering, and then nodded decisively. "Do it," he said, and sent Jonesy the token to release everything he'd need from the ship's stores on Landon's authority. "I'd rather be over-prepared than end up being surprised by a situation we hadn't anticipated."

As Jonesy nodded, Landon resumed his slow circuit of the bridge's stations, and the words he had not said reverberated in his head.

*This time, I'm going to make damn sure we **are** prepared….*

UNDER RINGLIGHT
STELLAR DATE: 05.11.3246 (Adjusted Gregorian)
LOCATION: Daisen Valley Region
REGION: Ring Galene, Tau Ceti

Two months later....

Khela stared down at the shadowed countryside from her position behind a nearby barn. It was dark here; at least as dark as any place on the ring could be. They were still a few hours away from second sunrise, and the planet above gave off a soft, blue-green glow, consigning nighttime on the ring to a perpetual twilight. Added to the nascent dusk was a glittering ribbon of light that curved behind the glowing orb. The double shadows it cast painted the terrain with a surreal, fantastical texture.

Khela's fourteen-person Marine Special Operations Team viewed the disorientation the shadows cast as a tactical advantage. They were here tonight chasing a report that nano-infected humans had been sighted.

That they were here at all, a team of paired soldiers, human and AI, was testament to the fact that the government had, so far, exempted the military from the ban on human/AI pairings.

The uncontrolled assembly nano had spread—as the Surgeon General had warned Planetary Security it would—far beyond the local quarantine the government had imposed upon the spaceport. Galene's Center for Disease Control had mandated that any infected individual be detained, placed in cryo stasis, and transported to the planet for isolation.

Khela's superiors had told her the government was in hot debate over whether or not to consider this an act of terrorism. No one had yet claimed responsibility for the nanophage, as it was now being called. That meant that if it was terrorism, it was being waged as a silent war of attrition.

That tactic might work, Khela admitted. *Especially if those in power are too busy debating to take decisive action—which, so far, has proven to be the case.*

Her own father had relocated planetside to try to come up with a cure for the phage, a move he told her he was convinced was the only way to resolve the crisis. She'd been startled to learn that the AIs she and Hana had met all those years ago had been secretly working with her father to create a last bastion of protection to guard against such a calamity. Bette and Charley had assured her that they would do everything in their power to find a quick resolution to the crisis.

As team leader, it was Khela's responsibility to ensure the successful completion of tonight's mission. They were to apprehend a small gang of infected humans who had gone on a killing rampage in a nearby town.

<*I hate that it's come to this,*> she sent as she cycled her augmented vision to scan the full EM spectrum, her expression grim. <*These people need a doctor and a nano specialist, not a spec-op team hunting them down.*>

<*I know.*> Hana's mental voice was edged with anger. <*But it was their decision to kill those AIs, not ours.*>

Khela winced and sent a wordless apology. Her words had been thoughtless, insensitive. Both of the town's victims had been AIs, individuals whose only crime had been to hide themselves away rather than submit to the mandatory evacuation of their kind—certainly not a transgression worthy of murder.

<*Misplaced vengeance,*> Khela replied, fingering her modified PEP-320 'PepBoy' pulse suppression cannon. <*AIs aren't to blame, these humans should realize that.*>

<*Fear does funny things to people, regardless of species. How do you think **we** feel, knowing we're twice as susceptible to the phage as you humans are?*>

Khela sent Hana a resigned nod as she reached out over the combat net to check on the location of her team, moving to encircle the small valley where the tangoes had holed up.

This would have been much easier to do a few weeks ago, Khela thought grimly as she sent a baleful glance toward a nonfunctioning piece of equipment partially hidden under a clump of bushes, where it had been violently thrown by Anders, her communications specialist.

The man had unpacked the unit, only to fling it suddenly away with an exclamation of horror when he'd spied the crystalline nanogrowth blooming from the surface of its display. Even if the thing still functioned, it was useless now; no one would go near it. And for good reason. In the past week, Khela had sent three of her soldiers to Army Medical when they began to show signs of infection.

People all over the ring were opting for lower-tech solutions in lieu of nano—both within their bodies and without. It was just safer that way. That meant her team was functioning with less data at their fingertips than usual. Not that they weren't *capable* of operating that way…. It was just maddening to know they were denied those tools.

No one calls it a 'system malfunction' anymore, she realized, recalling the government's initial attempt at information management, fearing widespread panic. *Not since the outbreak became so pervasive. Plus, it keeps mutating!*

She forced her wandering thoughts into some semblance of order; it had shaken everyone to see the phage so close-up this evening.

<Montoya, Xiao. Have you spotted anything yet?> she called out over the combat net to two of the icons not showing up.

<No joy, Cap'n,> came Xiao's immediate response, his usual cheer muted.

She heard nothing from Montoya.

<Montoya, report!> She barked the command more sharply than she'd intended.

A garbled transmission came by way of response.

<Situa–on unch–ged…not –eeing a thi– … where I st–>

The reply *sounded* like Montoya, so she could only assume that his Link was somehow being affected.

<Attempting to boost signal,> Hana told her privately. Moments later, Khela heard a mental sigh. <I'm sorry, it's gone.>

<Not your fault.> She joined Hana's sigh with her own. <Although it did sound as if he's not found anything useful. Can you keep pinging him, send him a data packet telling him to run a diagnostic on his Link? Direct him to report back to the ship if anything comes up amber and check himself into one of the cryo pods immediately.>

Every fire team in the military had taken to traveling with cryo lately—just in case.

<Sent,> Hana said, and the tension that had been creeping into her voice increasingly in recent weeks resurfaced full-force.

<We'll be fine,> Khela reassured her. <It'll take more than some wild nano to bring the two of us down, girl. You know that.>

<Khela.> Hana's voice sounded grim. <You **can't** know that. Frederick's embedded inside Montoya, and I can't raise him. You know they've been telling themselves the same thing over the past few weeks. We all have.>

<You will **not** fall victim to this, Hana,> Khela said, her mental tone fierce. <I won't allow it! Father won't allow it. You know he's working around the clock to solve this. If anyone can do it, he can.>

There was a pause, and then Hana's voice said quietly into her head, <But what if it's...unsolvable?>

Khela had no answer to that. Instead, she focused on what she could control: collaring the infected—and armed—humans in the valley below.

<Target in sight,> Ramon's voice cut in just then, and her focus sharpened as she saw that the pin the man had dropped was just two klicks to her left. She sighted along her PepBoy using her enhanced vision, doing a segmented sweep and pausing every few degrees to center and refocus. Nothing.

<Xiao, Montoya, you're in position to flank. Anders and I will close from the front with cryo.> She mapped out a route that would keep

as many obstacles—stands of trees, farm equipment, even knee-high crops—between them and their target, and sent it to the comm officer standing a few meters away. Anders saw it, nodded, and rose on silent feet to activate the maglev that transported the two pods.

Khela rose to a crouch and followed in his wake, the ring's double shadow causing the specialist's form to waver weirdly in the gloom.

They were about half a klick away when she heard the report of a projectile weapon being fired. Waving the comm officer on, they double-timed their approach, trusting in the team's IFF over the combat net to keep them free of friendly fire. The high-pitched whine of a PepBoy firing once, twice, cut through the air, and then Xiao's mental voice came across the net.

<Targets neutralized, ma'am, but we're going to need those cryo units and a few sets of nano-resistant gloves for sure,> the man sent, his voice somber.

She entered the clearing where the two downed humans lay, and inhaled sharply as she saw what he meant. The targets were sprawled, unconscious; in the ringlight, she could clearly see the glint of fine mesh appearing from under the woman's shirt and fanning past her collarbone. It had crept up the side of her neck and begun to embed itself across her cheek.

Stars, that's a lot of nano. How could so much of it have grown in such a short amount of time?

The other target, a man, appeared unscathed.

Khela stood aside, making room for the pods as she motioned the specialist forward. Anders stopped a healthy distance from the inert forms, donned the nano-resistant gloves, and handed out two more sets—one to Xiao, the other to Montoya.

<Montoya, what's up with your Link?> she tried to reach out to him again, and was disconcerted when the man did not look up. "Montoya?" she asked aloud, taking a step toward the man.

He looked up, his expression distracted, and she tapped her

temple.

"Link out?" she asked, keeping her tone casual.

The man grimaced. "It would appear so, ma'am, but no worries. Frederick and I are just fine. Right?"

No one else heard the AI's reply, but apparently Montoya did.

Khela's lips tightened for a moment, and she paused, weighing her options. As Anders and Xiao bent to lift the second human, she intervened.

"Place them together in one pod, Xiao," she instructed, then rounded on Montoya. "I want you and Frederick in the other one," she said calmly, and raised a hand as the man protested. "You have your orders, mister."

The man stood obstinately for a moment, then nodded with a resigned expression on his face.

Khela understood. No soldier wanted to admit to having a weakness. But 'for the good of the team' had been drilled into him, as it had been drilled into them all.

The man obediently safetied his weapon and began to hand it to Xiao, who waved him off, not wanting to touch a potentially-infected weapon. Montoya shot him a resigned look and climbed into the cryo unit, weapon and all.

<Khela,> Hana said, and Khela abruptly realized how quiet her friend had become. <There was an AI inside that man we took down. I think...I think she's dead.>

* * * * *

Third sunrise was about to break, and Khela stood leaning against the outside of their headquarters, one hand flipping the poker chip she'd snagged off Montoya's desk while exiting the team's offices.

They'd had to make a detour before getting Montoya and Frederick back to the base. A family needed to be evacuated from a housing unit that had suddenly bloomed with corrupt nano. But now, in the lull that had settled after the flurry of activity, she brooded about the soldiers she'd ordered into the pod.

"I hear you had to put two more of the team on ice," a voice said from behind her.

Khela pocketed the chip and turned, facing her superior.

"I did. Montoya and Frederick." She knew her voice sounded bleak as she closed her eyes and slumped back against the cool plas surface of the building. "This really sucks, sir."

Lieutenant Colonel Banks nodded without speaking. He shifted his frame, turning to stare out at the sunrise. "And the equipment?"

Although it had been posed as a question, the AI's voice held a note of resigned acceptance that indicated he already knew she and Hana would say.

Khela simply shook her head.

<We took the same precautions we always do, sir,> Hana responded. <EMed the shit out of it all before we loaded it into the shuttle for deployment, and yet we still had two comm units and a sensor suite show signs of infection before we returned.>

"We did manage to get the family loaded into cryo before we cordoned off the entire housing block and set the EMP for remote detonation," Khela said after a moment's silence, and then she brought up the thing that had sent her storming outside moments earlier. "I suppose you saw the report from HQ just now?"

Banks's eyes shifted from the sunrise to Khela. "I did," he admitted. "That is, if you're referring to the shortage of cryo pods. The GSC is still debating how to handle that. But because of the panic that ensued when news of that leaked out, they have finally decided to establish martial law."

Khela stilled. <Well,> she sent privately to Hana, <I guess we saw that one coming, didn't we?>

<Yes.> Hana's mental voice sounded more like a sigh. <I suppose they didn't have much choice, did they?>

"One more thing, Captain," Banks said, and something about

his tone warned her. "The Marines are no longer exempt from the prohibition of AI/human pairings."

Khela's head whipped around at that, but his next words made her face blanch.

"All military AIs are now included in the quarantine. They have the choice between joining one of the quarantine camps planetside, or," his voice took on a frosty tone, "they can volunteer for experimentation."

"Sir—"

Khela stopped, not trusting her voice at the moment.

Hana had no such compunction. <*Experimentation?*> Her voice was scathing. <*That violates Phobos in so many ways, I can't even begin to*—>

"I know." Banks held up a hand, his tone austere. "But we're under orders, soldier. According to the CDC, we AIs appear to be 'natural carriers' of the phage."

Hana made a rude noise. <*That doesn't excuse what deSangro is doing.*>

"Agreed," the lieutenant colonel said. "Which is why," and here, he switched to a secured comm, <*I'm ordering everyone in your unit to report to your father, Khela. Understood? This is a direct order, from me to you.*>

She did understand. Banks had just ordered the remainder of her fourteen-person team—every one of them human/AI pairings—to effectively go rogue. <*Will you be coming with us, sir?*>

He shook his head. <*You'll need someone on this side of things to ensure you get down there safely. I'll run interference from up top for as long as I can until....*>

Banks paused a beat and then continued.

<*Until I'm either told to report to deSangro for testing, or sent downside to one of the camps.*>

Khela's throat worked. <*Damn, sir, that's*—>

Banks's avatar shook his head and sent her a stern look. <*We're Marines, Sakai. It's what we do. Prep your team. In one hour, you'll be smuggled down in cryo pods, all of you.>*

* * * * *

<Excuse me, sir.>

The voice came over the sandboxed Link in the bunker, and Noa paused, one hand on the container of supplies he'd been unloading that recently cleared through the air gap. He straightened as he recognized the token of the person on the other end.

<Colonel Banks,> he responded. <Is it time?>

<It is, indeed. I'm sending you twelve Marines—including Khela and Hana. They're coming down in cryo pods and should arrive at the base of the elevator in two hours. From there, someone from within the quarantine zone will have to rendezvous with the shipment to make the exchange,> Banks said in an apologetic tone. <I will try to send you another team, possibly two, if I can manage it.>

<We'll take it from there, Colonel. You've gone out on quite a limb as it is, but please know how grateful I am.> He sent the AI a smile.

Banks's answering smile was fleeting at best; on the AI, it looked like more of a grimace. <You can thank me by finding a solution to this madness.>

<We're working very hard to do that,> Noa assured the AI. <How are you feeling?>

Banks's avatar made a resigned sound. <We're all wondering when the—what's the human idiom? 'When the other shoe will drop',> the Marine admitted. <But I can tell you there is a host of AIs up here who are very thankful you're down there working on a solution. Here is a token you can use to reach a select few of us who have been 'volunteered' to help Doctor deSangro. We'll do what we can behind the scenes up here to ensure you have what you need to bring this disaster to a close.>

Noa ground his teeth in an effort to contain the caustic remark that new information had triggered within him. He settled for a brief nod as Banks sent the token, and then closed the connection.

He pinged Dominica with the news, and then forwarded the information about Khela's arrival to the team on duty at the outer perimeter of the quarantine zone. Then he returned his attention to the image Bette had asked him to review, forcibly setting his concern for Khela aside.

*If you want to help your daughter—help **everyone** in Tau Ceti—* he admonished himself in a fierce tone, *you need to focus on what's before you. Worry will accomplish nothing.*

GRIM UPDATE
STELLAR DATE: 06.07.3246 (Adjusted Gregorian)
LOCATION: ESS *Avon Vale*
REGION: Approaching Tau Ceti System's Heliopause

Terrance couldn't believe what he was seeing. He felt the same horror coming from Kodi as his eyes remained glued to the holoprojection hovering just above the desk between them and Logan. The three were reviewing the latest compilation of broadcasts from Tau Ceti, and the news was gruesome.

<I can feel your shock,> the AI sent privately. <I felt the same when I was compiling the feed.>

<Shock, yes. I'm horrified—and a bit stunned, to be honest—that things could unravel so quickly,>

As the recording came to an end, Terrance found his fingers drumming a light cadence along the side of his coffee cup as he considered what they'd just seen. Leaning back in his seat, he eyed the profiler sitting across from him.

Logan's face appeared almost pensive. Silence grew between the three in the room, and in it, he could just make out the low hum of activity bleeding through from the bridge, just beyond the office doors.

"What do you make of all of this?"

Terrance's voice broke into the quiet, the words causing Logan to shift in his chair, but otherwise remain silent, as Terrance reached once more for his coffee, raised the cup to his lips, and then grimaced as he realized it was empty.

"It doesn't look good," the profiler commented finally. "The fact that the Federated States of Tau Ceti have relocated from the ring to Eione is not a good sign; it means the situation has escalated beyond anyone's ability to control it."

Terrance nodded, and Kodi *hmm*ed in agreement.

<True. I'd imagine an organization like that doesn't just pull up roots and move on a whim,> the AI murmured.

Logan tilted his head. "We should reach out to our contacts inside the Trade Commissions on both Galene and Eione to see if commerce has been temporarily halted. The same goes for the offices of immigration in both places. Their responses will give us a better feel for the situation…. I suspect the ring will try to defer meeting with us."

Terrance shifted in his seat, frowning slightly. "We'll need to update our passengers about the current situation, too," he mused. "I can't imagine anyone will want to plan a trip to the ring right now."

Logan began to nod his agreement before Terrance had even finished the thought. "No," he said. "It's not safe for AIs to visit the ring, even if the local government were to allow it."

<I've pinged Ray and forwarded him the update,> Kodi informed them. *<He'll let everyone know about these new developments.>*

<Thanks, Kodi.>

Silence descended as Terrance rose to refill his coffee mug.

"So they're running out of cryo," he mused as he poured, then returned to the desk and swung back into his seat. "Well, that pretty much confirms my suspicions about the ring wanting our stasis tech."

His tone was dry enough to evoke a response from Kodi that sounded suspiciously like a snort. *<You can say that again.>* The AI's mental tone matched his for dryness. *<True stasis would sound mighty appealing if you were racing the clock against runaway nano.>*

"I know all of our documents were filed years ago—and approved," Terrance said as he thought through the sequence—he hardly noticed his hand idly drawing circles through the liquid he'd sloshed onto the desk, "but when I initiate contact with the trade commissions on both Galene and Eione, I'll ask how they feel now about Enfield Holdings setting up shop in the system. That ought to give us a better impression of what's going on, at least."

"Ask about what protocols they have in place for ensuring trade goods remain untainted, too," the profiler suggested. "I wouldn't accept anything from the ring that had not gone through decontamination first."

<Given their inability to control the outbreak, I don't know how much faith I'd put into any decontamination they have.> Kodi's voice was filled with a mixture of caution and disdain.

Terrance jerked his head in firm agreement at that, and then stood. "Well, guess it's time for us to share the good news with the rest of the folks out on the bridge...."

* * * * *

Jason was running late, a glitch in one of the shuttles having filled his morning with repairs. He'd told Terrance not to hold the debrief for him, so it was in full swing when he stepped off the lift onto the bridge.

Instantly, his attention was arrested by the sensationalist headlines Kodi had on display from the Tau Ceti feed. 'Freeze on Cryo', 'Government Rolls Dice on Human/AI Lives', and 'Lotto-Mania Strikes Ring!' were the first three that caught his eye as he walked toward the pilot's cradle.

"Really, people?" His voice, laden with disgust, announced his entrance. "Panic much?" He could see his sentiment mirrored on the faces of those around him.

"Whoever thought holding a lotto for the system's remaining cryo pods was a good idea?" Calista's derisive voice sounded from where she sat at navigation.

"Just wait," Jonesy informed Jason in a disgusted tone. "It gets better."

<You mean worse,> Kodi muttered.

"You got that right," Jonesy agreed, his gaze riveted to the streaming clip. "Hey, Kodi, didn't you say there was some chatter about the Federated States of Tau Ceti putting an interdiction on

Ring Galene?" The engineer sat up suddenly, his gaze growing more intent.

<Well, they're thinking about doing it, but no ruling's come down yet. Why?>

"Because I think Galene's going to need interdiction soon from someone like the FSTC, if this is what's starting to go down."

<What do you mean by—? Oh, shit....> Kodi's exclamation had everyone on the bridge turning to stare at the holo.

The feed showed an image of a small transport ship boosting hard toward a station just past Maera, Galene's moon. As the ship neared the station, messages were transmitted, warning the ship away, but the little craft ignored them all.

Warning shots were fired across the ship's bow, prompting those within to break their silence and finally talk to the people trying to turn them away. Shannon gasped as the optics from within the ship revealed humans clearly infected with 'the phage', as it was now commonly called.

The woman at the helm of the ship pleaded for clemency from the inhabitants within the spire, holding her infant child up to the sensor pickups. Her plea was cut short, as the habitat's point defense was loosed against the ship, shredding its hull. The observers were given a brief view of rounds tearing through the bridge, and heard the screams of the crew onboard, before the feed cut out, returning the holo to a view of nearspace.

The bridge of the *Avon Vale* was silent for a three-count, and then Logan's voice cut into the stillness.

"The latest we have from Galene is that the cities at the base of both elevators have been subjected to forced evacuations, with the GSC announcing a mandatory air gap of forty kilometers between the elevators and the quarantine camps."

He paused and, in the silence, Landon added quietly, "It's being enforced by a scorched earth policy. The city at the base of Galene's main elevator—Hokkaido—will be nothing more than a pile of rubble soon, if it isn't already."

Calista drew in a ragged breath, and Jason glanced at her, suddenly aware that his mouth was hanging open.

He closed it and swallowed before speaking. "That's not all they're scorching. There were other options than just blowing that ship out of the stars."

Terrance shifted uncomfortably as Tobias stated in a quiet voice, <Scorched earth **and** space.... The last time I saw that was during the Sentience Wars.>

Jason scrubbed his face as his thoughts raced. *Lotteries. Quarantines. Starships blown out of space. Obliterating cities.... What the hell are we flying into?* His head jerked up as a thought occurred to him. "Stars! If they were *that* desperate to escape, what exactly is life like on that ring right now?" He glanced over at Logan, but the profiler shook his head.

"We're getting conflicting stories, of course. Leaks from unofficial sources, as well as official releases from Planetary Security. It's an estimate, at best, but given what we've curated over the past week, the ring is a police state at the moment. After quarantine was instated for all AIs as well as infected humans, there were several incidents where crowds mobbed AIs awaiting transport to the planet."

Shannon groaned, and her hands flew to her face in distress.

<It wasn't just AIs,> Kodi interjected. <Infected humans were attacked, as well. Many were torched, burned alive as they stood in queues to board the elevator that would take them down to the planet.>

<It's a terrible thing, lad, fear is,> Tobias said, his tone somber. <Throughout both our histories, AI and human alike, you'll find countless tales of atrocities all rooted in fear.>

"So, how do we proceed?" Jason asked, turning his head in Terrance's direction. "How do we protect ourselves from the nanophage while searching for our shackled AIs—if they're even still alive, somehow, in all this mess?"

<And if we find them,> Kodi continued the train of thought, and Jason thought he caught a tendril of apprehension in the AI's

words, <how do we know if they've been exposed? The last thing we want to do is bring infected AIs and nano aboard Avon Vale.>

<I hate to be the one to say it,> Shannon interjected. <But our two missing AIs are like a drop in the bucket of atrocities right now. This crew represents some of the smartest minds from Alpha Centauri, and we have a safe base of operations on the Vale. We can help these people. We have a **responsibility** to help these people.>

"For now, all we can do is continue to gather information, study whatever we can glean from the feeds, and run simulations," Terrance said.

Calista crossed her arms and tilted her head as she considered the exec's words. "True," she agreed. "We might have answers in our libraries that their scientists haven't yet tried or considered."

Jason shifted from Calista to Tobias, his gaze resting somberly on the Weapon Born's frame, the AI's comparison to the Sentience Wars playing through his mind.

"With a crisis of this magnitude, no one in their right mind would turn down an offer of help. Let's just hope that by the time we arrive, there's a planet still there *to* save...."

DISASSEMBLY BOTS
STELLAR DATE: 08.10.3246 (Adjusted Gregorian)
LOCATION: Underground bunker, Zao Mountains
REGION: 150 kilometers from Hokkaido, Galene

Silence reigned in the bunker, barring the occasional shuffling of feet or an electronic tone signaling the completion of a new series of tests run by either Noa or his two AI partners.

Bette exclaimed, her voice sounding sharply into the quiet, but Noa hardly noticed, engrossed as he was in his own sequencing.

"This might be just what we've been looking for," the AI mused, her frame bent over an imaging device. He noted absently that she had waved the other AI over. "Take a look, Charley. Do you see—"

"Well I'll be damned!"

At Charley's pronounced exclamation, Noa surfaced, his gaze sharpening as it rested on the imaging device the two AIs were bent over.

"What are we looking at, here?" he asked as he rose and walked toward the pair.

Bette shot Charley a glance, but the Jovian AI waved for her to continue.

"It's a nano specimen isolated from a victim that the Army Hospital admitted just this morning," she responded. "It's a colloid."

Noa nodded as he studied the buffered and sandboxed sample. They knew the nano had bonded to some type of colloid particle; it was the only way, really, to explain how quickly the nanophage had spread. Although, that alone couldn't account for the rapid growth of infected nano, nor the way it managed to transmute entirely different kinds of nano into—

Wait.

He looked up sharply at the two AIs. "This isn't just a colloid," he stated, holding his voice carefully neutral. But hope blossomed. *This just might explain everything.*

Charley nodded. "You're correct. It's a unique form of colloidal nano."

"A colloidene," Noa breathed. "Well I'll be damned."

A colloidene was made from a colloid particle, but formed just like single-layer graphene. This particular single-layer was patterned in a honeycomb lattice. And it housed a click assembly brick — a technique that relied on a foundation of frequent combinations as shortcuts to promote rapid assembly for nano.

"That's how it's multiplying so rapidly," Charley said. "Why completely different and unrelated types of nano are failing in so many places all across the ring."

"That would explain it, yes."

Noa felt a mix of triumph and dismay. There was always a feeling of accomplishment when deciphering a riddle. Yet understanding the riddle didn't mean he had a solution for it. And this particular riddle was a bit — what was that phrase Khela liked to use? — too 'in the weeds' for the average non-physicist to grasp.

"This is going to be challenging to explain to Director Henrick and the Joint Chiefs," he mused.

Bette made a sound of agreement. "Yes. How do you explain 'the proliferation potential of vectored click assembly bricks' to a lay person?" She stared at him for a moment, her expression thoughtful. "We need to find a way to associate the concept with something they are familiar with — a visual analogy of some sort."

He paused, staring back at her. "A visual…." His voice died off as a thought struck him. "Yes, that's it!" He turned back to the image of the colloidene. "These nanobots deliver click assembly messages in the same way a vector image does. And it differs from standard nano in exactly the same way a rasterized image differs from a vector-based one."

Charley nodded slowly. "I see the similarity. One carries an exact, point-for-point representation of the original, while the other simply carries instructions on how to *create* the original."

Noa broke out into the first genuine smile he'd had in a while. "Exactly," he said, and he began to pace as he worked through the explanation he'd give to Director Henrick and the Joint Chiefs.

"A raster is slow, unwieldy, and limited in scope due to the vast amount of information it has to carry about a single object. But the second, the vector…" He paused, glancing back at the holo image of the colloidene that Bette had projected. "That thing is nimble. Wherever it lands, it deposits an assembly brick that remakes the nano into an auto-replicating, non-terminating version of whatever it was before the colloidene made contact."

"It's also scalable," Bette reminded him, "which means it's able to deliver a much more robust set of instructions."

"Which explains why both the volume and type of nano affected continues to grow," Charley added. "But, Noa…."

Something in the AI's voice warned him. Noa returned his gaze to the holo and read the report with growing horror, as the AI paged through the information sent along with the sample.

"This is the first sample of *disassembler* nano that's been altered." Charley's eyes met Noa's across the imaging device, and Noa saw his own horror reflected in them.

"The ramifications of this…."

His words fell into the sudden silence as the three considered the impact that disassembler nano would have on the ring.

"Just look at what it's done to one human," Bette murmured, as they stared at the scans that appeared on the holo.

They had been taken from a staff sergeant who'd suffered spontaneous skeletal collapse earlier that day. The nano had broken molecular bonds at various points within the woman's skeletal system, weakening them until one of her bones spontaneously snapped.

Given that the staff sergeant was one of Galene's soldiers, her skeletal structure had been augmented. The nano had not cared; it had unraveled the molecular structure of the carbon nanotubes lacing her skeleton just as efficiently as it had dissolved her bones.

"I'd be willing to bet it began with her left hand," Charley said, pointing to its shattered remains.

"How are they ever going to trace the things she touched throughout her day?" Bette whispered.

Noa shook his head. "It's impossible to know. Although these scans clearly tell us what parts of her own body she touched. See where the nano has eaten through her humerus? That's just the spot where your palm rests when you cross your arms." He pointed to another image. "And here, and here? How many times do you see humans rubbing the back of their neck? It destroyed that exact spot: the C-5 and C-6 joints of her spinal cord."

Charley brought up another image. "The femur?" he queried, and Noa's mouth tightened.

"Humans often will place the palms of their hands on their upper thighs when we stand." He highlighted several other bones in her full-body scan. "And with the first bone's breakage, undue stress was placed on neighboring structures. Take a look: I'm sure that's what precipitated these collapses, providing an almost systemic skeletal failure."

"A house of cards," Bette murmured, her tone shocked at the destruction.

Noa turned from the holo to face the two AIs.

"How long," he asked quietly, "will it take for us to create rectification colloidenes? Our own assembly bricks?"

"Not long—it's already done, actually," Charley pulled up another image. "But that's not the challenge. We need formation material, Noa—a *lot* of formation material." His expression grim, he added, "and it needs to be fully sandboxed before we can begin to replicate armies of our own to counteract it."

Noa nodded. "Let me reach out to Director Henrick and see if I can't convince her to send us what we need."

*****

Noa blinked uncomprehendingly at the stranger staring back at him over the holo.

"I don't understand," he began, but the woman cut him off with an impatient wave. "Congress convened an emergency session. While there, the president succumbed to the phage, infecting the attending members of both the Senate and the House," the woman explained with a clear lack of patience. "I'm sorry, doctor, but the Assistant Director of Planetary Security is now acting president, and she has more important matters to deal with now than to discuss theories with you."

Noa froze in shock.

*Impossible. **All** of Congress, quarantined on the planet?*

A niggling part of his brain scoffed at the transparency of what he suspected was a ruse—but if it was a coup, what could *he* do about it?

He inhaled silently, a deep, calming breath, and tried again. "Understood. To whom shall I direct my requests in the future?" he asked, taking care to keep his voice even, calm, and uninflected.

"Any requests you have can be filed with the Senate Appropriations Committee assigned to oversee the Q-camps," the woman said dismissively.

"But I'm not in the quarantine camps," Noa explained once more, with a patience he did not feel. "I am in a hardened, protected bunker, and we are nanophage-free here. I have explained this already to the Joint Chiefs."

"We have only your word to go on," the woman's tone was skeptical, and her eyes narrowed slightly as she pinned him with a hard glance. "From where we stand, Doctor Sakai, you walked away from your position at the Nanotechnology Regulatory Commission months ago. By doing so, you abdicated any authority you might have had. Your security clearance has been revoked, and with conditions being what they are right now, access to the acting president is limited to those she can trust." She looked pointedly at Noa as he began to protest.

"As I have explained, both to her and the Joint Chiefs," Noa said patiently, "it was necessary for me to sequester, in order to isolate myself from contamination, and in order to effectively pursue a cure."

He made a small gesture, encompassing the laboratory in which he stood. "We have sent you the information you need to verify that we have, indeed, isolated the cause of the phage." With a thought, he brought up a schematic of the colloidene and displayed it on the holo, alongside his own image.

"All that remains to scrub the ring free of infection is several thousand kiloliters of formation material. I know for a fact that the NRC has this within its own private stores," he said with a studied pleasantness. "If you would just put me in contact with the new Executive Director of the NRC—"

The woman interrupted him. "We are done here, doctor." Her mouth thinned into a straight line of displeasure. "Do not attempt to contact us with this request again. You have wasted enough of our time on this matter."

The holo winked out.

Noa blew out a breath of frustration. Turning to his two AI companions, he asked, "How difficult would it be to send a direct beam message to the ship from Proxima—the *Avon Vale*, did you say the name was?"

Charley nodded. "Yes. One of our informants ringside sent that they had just reached our heliopause and had contacted Galene asking for permission to enter the system."

"Not the same government they would have met six months earlier," Noa muttered.

"No, it's not," the AI admitted.

"Well, our informant said the *Avon Vale* indicated that they had been monitoring Tau Ceti's transmissions and wished to offer their assistance," Bette interjected, her tone thoughtful. "They said they had representatives from El Dorado on board, as well as a stakeholder from the Enfield Conglomerate."

Charley frowned. "Enfield. They weren't too welcome back in Sol after what transpired on Proteus."

Bette made a rude sound, and the AI turned to regard her with an arched brow.

"You weren't there, Bette."

"I wasn't—but neither were you," she countered.

"No," he conceded, "I wasn't. But one of my parents was, and I have all of her memories."

"You know as well as I do that Enfield picked up stakes and moved to Alpha Centauri only *after* making amends for what they inadvertently contributed to," she admonished with a frown. "From what I've read, the Enfield family has more than made up for it—especially given their participation in bringing the people who ended up enslaving *us* to justice," she reminded him.

Noa leant back against a console, his eyes tracking from one AI to the other, fingers tapping his lower lip thoughtfully.

"Charley," he began, his tone thoughtful, "I've heard of Enfield as well. Good things, I might add."

Charley nodded reluctantly and then turned back to the holo. "Did you have a chance to listen to that message our informant up on the ring sent?" At Noa's head shake, he warned, "It's anarchy up there. Far worse than just martial law." He pulled images the informant had sent, displaying them one by one, on the bunker's holo as he detailed the message's contents. "Riots. Rolling power outages. Rationing. Hoarding. The black market is going gangbusters, or so I hear."

Noa cocked his head. "Any mention of nano?"

Charley shook his head. "Outlawed completely. If you're caught with it, you're lucky if you only get banished to the planet on the next elevator downside. Rumor has it that others are simply getting spaced. Especially if they show any sign of infection."

Noa squeezed his eyes shut, gritting his teeth in frustration.

"We have the solution, but no one is listening."

"And at this point, I seriously doubt they will. They've reverted back to twenty-fourth, maybe twenty-third century tech at this point, Noa," the AI reminded him. "That tech predates SAI, *almost* predates NSAI." Charley gestured to the images of destruction and carnage from the ring feed. "It's so bad right now that I'd be willing to bet that if we had access to formation material and a few military transport shuttles—hell, even a few hundred drones that a few of us from the old country know how to operate—we could easily take over the entire ring right now."

At Noa's startled look, he nodded grimly. "Just food for thought. If they won't let us help them, then we may have to force them to accept the help." He nodded vaguely in the direction of the heliopause. "And we could sure use the *Avon Vale*'s help to make it happen. I'd be willing to bet their ability to effectively scan nearspace is severely degraded right now."

Bette looked thoughtful. "You know," she said slowly, "I wonder how much of that is factoring into their paranoid behavior?"

Noa tilted his head, acknowledging the point. "That could very well be," he admitted. He stepped away from the console, snapped his fingers, and turned decisively to the AI. "Do we have enough power to reach the *Avon Vale* now, or will we have to wait until they're closer in?"

"The way in which this bunker was built ensures we have a virtually unending power supply—at least as long as Galene's core remains molten," Charley amended with a small smile. "It's not really a matter of power, it's more a matter of signal strength."

Bette nodded agreement. "We just need to send a signal strong enough to punch through the jammers that the blockade has going." She paused, considering. "These ships run in cycles, and they rotate their coverage. With very little effort, we can have someone from Khela's Marines set up an antenna somewhere they least expect it."

She smiled wickedly.
"Give me a few hours, and you'll have your signal."

QUARANTINE CAMPS
STELLAR DATE: 08.25.3246 (Adjusted Gregorian)
LOCATION: Happo Settlement, Q-Camp Fourteen
REGION: 20 kilometers outside Hokkaido, Galene

Khela and her band of Marines were arranged just outside Q-camp Fourteen, awaiting the runner that would deliver their weekly report. This was the third camp this week that her team had checked in on, and one of sixteen ringing a ruined twenty-kilometer stretch of land. That band of land, in turn, surrounded Galene's main elevator and the ruin that was once the city of Hokkaido.

Some called that twenty-kilometer span a 'no man's land'. It was a term Khela had never heard before, but it fit...so long as they added women, AIs, dogs, deer, and anything large enough to register on scan and be summarily obliterated by Galene Space Command.

With the transfer of power up on the ring, the new government had authorized an increasing number of EMP strafing runs made periodically upon the camps themselves. And the GSC no longer restricted itself *only* to EMPs; carpet-bombing tactics were apparently the new administration's solution to everything these days.

Careful examination of the planet explained such actions—although it did nothing to justify them. Everywhere you looked, you could see that the phage had begun to encroach upon the planet itself. Nearby trees were slowly being overtaken by nanofilament and morphing into network towers. Boulders were covered in power grids. Some nearby scrub had even transmuted into a waste reclamation pipeline.

Xiao was up in the branches of what used to be a banyan tree but was slowly being taken over by a nano scaffolding assembly.

Lena was tucked up against a boulder, while Ramon was the most exposed of them all, trusting their scan disruptor camo and a simple bit of ghillie concealment netting to help him blend with the long grasses in which he lay.

It had been four months since Colonel Banks had smuggled them down to Galene; in all, he'd managed to ship four full spec-ops teams to Noa before he'd been removed from active duty.

Don't go there, Khela. Don't think about that now.

The Marine teams had remained off the grid, unlisted on the rosters of official Q-camp populations. They roamed the planet, providing protection from bands of marauders and coordinating with military personnel inside the camps, those soldiers that had been sent down to the planet after becoming infected. These, in turn, reported to the loose coalition of camp governors that Congress had formed once they, too, had been condemned to the planet.

<Heads up, Cap, here he comes.> Xiao's voice pulled Khela's attention from her ruminations and snapped her back into the present.

An older man came laboring up the hill, huffing as he worked his way up to the small stand of bamboo that concealed her position.

"Sorry, Captain." The man bent over, hands on his knees as he worked to catch his breath. "The phage just hit our food supply. Had to rush one of the senator's kids over to the medical tent in the center of camp."

At her raised brow, he explained. "We discovered too late that a batch of meal rations had been infected with self-repairing plas nano. It started to turn her stomach to—"

He blanched, and she waved off the remainder of the explanation.

"How are the prefab units they dropshipped to you holding up? Any more infected panels beyond the ones you reported last week?"

The man shook his head. "After our common meeting house began to cover itself in light armor, and the latrines started replicating lifts every two meters, we've left everything outside the camp and let the bastards EM the shit out of the supplies before we touch anything." He shot her a meaningful look. "Nothing like looking up while you're on the toilet to see a lift door opening in the ceiling above you to get your attention."

"I can imagine," she murmured. "Are there any serious cases you need us to transport to triage?" she asked, referring to the medical camp the surgeon general had set up just outside her father's bunker in the Zao Foothills.

Khela knew her father had planned it that way, in order to give Doctor Gonsalves access to the research and decontamination facilities the bunker could provide.

"No, thank the ancestors. Nothing has progressed that far—not this week, at least."

"And no more new arrivals?" Khela heard the sharp edge in her voice, but couldn't bring herself to contain it.

The man shook his head sorrowfully. "I'm sorry, Captain. I was told the only AIs left on the ring were the ones who volunteered for the study with Reya deSangro and her scientists."

"*Volunteered.*" She spat the word as if it were an imprecation, and her knuckles whitened as she gripped her PepBoy tighter.

As it so often did, her anger seemed to trigger a reaction from the nano inside her body that had turned traitor on her. She squeezed her eyes shut against a fresh wave of pain and shuddered in an attempt to shake it off.

"Are you all right, Captain?"

The man's sympathetic voice made her snap her eyes open, and she nodded mutely until she knew she could trust herself to speak once more.

"Fine," she rasped, and then belatedly, "thank you."

She looked down at the torn seam of her left leg, where the self-repairing nano in her BDUs' base layer where its had begun to knit itself into her skin. She was infected. She'd been infected for weeks now.

So are thousands of others. Shake it off, soldier.

"If there's nothing else…?" She somehow managed to keep her voice level and her gaze steady as she addressed the man from Q-camp Fourteen.

He shook his head.

"Then we'll move on. We'll be back, same time next week. I—"

"Wait!" The man snapped his fingers as he recalled something. "I almost forgot. One of our doctors asked if you would mind transporting something to Doctor Gonsalves for us?"

At her nod, he smiled and began to reach toward her to pat her on the arm, but pulled his hand back at the last moment, an apologetic look on his face.

"I'll send young Sascha up with it as soon as I get back." He winked. "She's much faster at running up hills than I am, in my old age."

He nodded to her, turned, and began to pick his way back down the hill, retracing his steps to the camp.

Khela sank back into her crouch among the bamboo, the rustling sounds it made reminding her of the tonal scale the waterfall had played at the Sea of Stones Spa that she and Hana had visited, so many years ago.

Hana….

An acid burn of raw anger washed over her as she castigated herself yet again for being so careless, so *stupidly* reckless as to access their commanding officer's final report without sandboxing it first….

But she and Hana had been so worried about Colonel Banks.

A true Marine, Banks had stoically acquiesced when volunteered by his superiors at Space Command to be an experimental subject. The first few months, the experimentation had seemed benign, and Khela and Hana had dared to hope that he would be shipped down to join them at some point. At the end, they'd learned that he'd hidden from them the extent to which deSangro had mutilated him. His last transmission had been a difficult one to listen to, and it had hit Hana hard.

Khela knew some string of contaminated code must have been buried in Banks's final transmission. Her dad had warned her that they needed to sandbox every comm and had instructed her carefully on how to do so—but she had messed up somewhere along the way....

She squeezed her dark eyes shut and then opened them again, her face drawn and bleak as she withstood the onslaught of her own self-flagellation. Outwardly, she was vigilant. Inwardly, her mind was trapped among memories of past events.

Careless, she berated herself mercilessly. *Reckless. If I'd only headed back to the bunker the moment I suspected—or waited until then to access the Colonel's message....*

Hana had become infected. Her base code had been modified, and the feedback loops that she had been trapped in had been beyond what she could manage without help. Overloaded and fearing the harm her contamination might bring to Khela...Hana had suicided.

Their team had been deployed at the time, days away from her father's bunker. By the time Khela had realized how bad off Hana truly was, she'd rushed back to the bunker, half-mad with fear for her partner's life, but it had been too late.

White-hot fury had stabbed through Khela, and she'd fought a deeply irrational feeling of betrayal that Hana would abandon her like this. A part of her brain blamed the AI for quitting, even though she knew to the core of her soul that what Hana had done was out of concern for Khela's own well-being.

Khela had heard that some of the human/AI pairings suffered from nano filament bleed-through, a condition where AI axons that ran parallel to human ones began to bleed past their buffers, interleaving themselves as they punched through human myelin sheaths. Local doctors were unsure if this was the cause for some of the paired deaths, or if the deaths had transpired first, and the unconstrained replication of nano that occurred afterward had made it impossible for the doctors to remove the now-deceased AI from within the human brain.

It would have been nothing less than what I deserve, she thought bitterly. *Marines leave no one behind. If Hana falls, then so do I.*

Her jaw clenched, muscles bunching in a cheek now laced with an unwanted filigree of nano antennae that traced its way across her cheekbone as she gritted her teeth against a wave of thought fragments not her own. Alien these thoughts were, wholly AI in nature, but they were all she had left of Hana, and she would stoically endure them. It was the only way she could honor her fallen comrade, the person she had failed to save.

"Damned Ringers," she muttered, as a young girl raced up the hill, data chip in hand.

She heard a two-click acknowledgement over the comm from Ramon, his figure indistinguishable among the grasses.

Khela thanked the girl once she received the chip, and sent her back to the camp.

Lena chimed in with her own assessment. <*I was thinking something a bit stronger, myself, Cap'n.*>

Her voice came from her position two klicks away, overlooking the buffer zone. They were using an encrypted network to communicate, localized and too low-powered for the ring to detect—or so they hoped.

Tama, the AI that Lena was paired with, was busy scanning all frequencies for any chatter that might indicate activity—or that their position had been made. Xiao would send out a call if he spotted the Ringers beginning one of their aerial approaches—a routine that seemed to be growing more common as the days went on.

Their vigilance would provide them little more than the time to slap sensitive gear into the hardened cases the team had taken to humping along with them wherever they went. Every AI in the camp—and those embedded within her team—would be rendered unconscious for a time, but it could not be helped. It was still far better than getting hit with the missiles that the Ringers had begun using to hammer no man's land into dust.

Khela parted the bamboo and stepped into the grasses, skirting the forest as she headed for Lena's position. *<We're done here. Xiao, Ramon. Rendezvous at Lena's position, and we'll head for Q-Fifteen.>*

Double-clicks returned to her, and she could just make out a slight rustling that could have been wind, but was Ramon slithering his way out of the grasses.

Xiao dropped from the banyan and marched silently beside her as she passed beneath it, and Ramon fell in behind Xiao.

They fell into an easy, ground-eating trot, one every Marine had learned to maintain for hours back in Basic. The kilometers fell behind them, and they kept up the pace until they reached the narrowest and most treacherous part of the journey.

Khela called a halt and motioned for them to go to ground. Just ahead, the bamboo forest curved sharply to the left, taking them dangerously close to the edge of no man's land. The forest here was too marshy to traverse, or they would have simply cut through its interior.

In the four months they'd been making the trek between camps Fourteen and Fifteen, they'd yet to be spotted by the GSC—even here—yet Khela didn't dare break protocol.

Kneeling as one, they each broke out swaths of ghillie. The stuff was too difficult to replace, now that they had no way to replicate it, so they kept it packed away in their kits when it wasn't needed.

Khela pulled hers over the shredded remains of her base layer, a material that had once protected her head, but had mindlessly begun to embed itself into her skull, while rejecting her hair follicles as foreign matter. The ghillie brushed against her sensitized scalp, abrasive and uncomfortable, and she gritted her teeth against yet another discomfort, nodding to Ramon to lead on.

<Stars!> Tama exclaimed suddenly. *<Are all human teenagers*

idiots?>

<Tama—?> Lena began, but she caught her breath on a quick inhale as the AI she was paired with sent them a pin.

Two figures were moving swiftly through the ravaged land, toward the ruined city and the elevator.

<Cap! We've got to stop them!> Ramon sent urgently.

She nodded and began to pick her way through the grasses that led to the barren wasteland up ahead. She'd taken three steps when she heard Lena's voice sing out.

<Incoming!>

Stars! Surely they wouldn't send a strafing run to take out a few teenagers! Just as the thought crossed Khela's mind, Tama's terse voice interjected over their net.

<We've been made. Communications compromised.>

Khela didn't have time to think. She sprang from her position, forcing her leaden limbs to pump furiously as she raced flat-out to reach the teens in time. The GSC was after *them*, not a couple of kids. There was no way she could make it to those youngsters in time, but, stars, she had to try—

She went down in a tangle of limbs with an *oof* as Xiao launched himself toward her. She growled at him as he dragged her to cover just before the fighters overflew their position.

<Stay **down**, Cap!> His voice sounded angrily in her head as she struggled to catch a glimpse of the teens.

And then the world exploded in light, sound, and fire all around them.

Minutes later, she stood looking despairingly down at the lifeless form of the two young boys she had been unable to save.

Dammit! she thought savagely as she bent to check the nearest form for signs of life. *We're supposed to **protect** these people, not get them killed!*

Tears she refused to shed swam in her eyes, and she ignored the burning, throbbing pain in her limbs as she squatted next to the remains of the first boy. The pain was an old companion, one that had blossomed within her when Hana had fallen victim to the phage.

Well, at least I no longer have to brush my hair out of my face when I lean down, she thought, and heard the bitter tone that laced her own mental voice.

"Let me, Cap."

Xiao's hands reached out and hefted the body into his arms. With a weary nod, Kehla let him.

* * * * *

Minutes later and kilometers away, lookouts sounded the alarm from the edges of the triage camp, tucked in close to Noa's bunker. Former Surgeon General Dominica Gonsalves ran flat-out toward the camouflaged tent, ducking through the entrance and passing through the portable ES shield that had been set up in an attempt to maintain a sterile surgical environment.

"Get those scanners shielded!" she shouted at the nurse who was scrambling to get the units into hardened cases before the first EM pulse hit.

She splayed her hands across the surgical table to steady the instruments as the fighters screamed overhead. The tent shook from the sonic booms—and Dominica shook from the EMP—that passed through their triage unit.

"Damned Ringers," she muttered, unknowingly echoing Khela's imprecation, while staring helplessly across at a shelf filled with newly sterilized scalpels as they tumbled to the dirt floor. *Well, there goes a morning's worth of work,* she sighed. Dismissing the thought, she turned back to her current patient.

The man spread on the table before her—one of the president's cabinet, by the name of Bryce—was a mess. He suffered from outbreaks across his torso and upper arms, where muscle modifications had begun to grow outside of his body. She had just finished repairing the heart tissue that had begun to protrude outside his chest cavity and stepped out to check on a newly-arrived patient while her nurse closed the incision for her, when the alarm had sounded. Now that the danger had passed, she could begin to address the infected areas on the man that were not as critical.

Glancing down to ensure the strafing run had not jostled any of her work loose, she sighed in frustration as she cleansed her hands once more and donned sterile, nano-resistant gloves.

This man should be in cryo, she thought, *not lying before me on an operating table.*

A shadow darkened the entrance, and the ES field flickered as Noa Sakai ducked inside, followed by one of the human senators—Dominica couldn't recall the woman's name. They had journeyed here days ago from Q-camp Three, requesting aid. Once Bryce was stable, one of the Marine teams would escort them back to their camp.

As he approached, Noa's dark gaze flickered down to the table and back up to Dominica's face before scanning the tent's interior, taking in its disarray without expression.

"That was the last of them," he said.

Stepping up to the table, he reached for a sterilizing swab, and efficiently disinfected his own hands while the senator stood a distance away, observing quietly. Looking up at her expectantly, he opened his palms, spreading them in a 'what now' gesture.

"How may I be of assistance?"

"What? Nothing keeping you occupied over in nano-land? And are you *certain* your precious rectification code's going to keep you safe from all this?" Dominica felt immediately ashamed of herself for the caustic remark.

Noa, as unflappable as ever, merely shook his head and lowered his gaze to the neat line of stitches across the chest of the patient laying before them.

"Heart?" he inquired, and she nodded once.

"Another series of muscle mods gone awry," she murmured,

and he *hmm*ed at her explanation as he directed the light toward where her hand hovered over her next incision site.

She made a quick cut along the man's arm where another muscle modification had begun to seep outside his epidermis. Reaching for a pair of tweezers and some gauze, Noa cleared the area of blood so that Dominica's view of the incision was unimpeded.

"The ship from Proxima is entering the system," Noa said after a moment.

Dominica looked up sharply at that, one eyebrow raised. "Do you think they can be convinced to help, when none of the others in this system have raised a finger yet?" she asked.

"Yes. Bette and Charley have a plan."

Her mouth twisted wryly at the mention of Noa's two AI friends who had hidden themselves away within the bunker.

"Please tell me it doesn't involve anything drastic like taking over the ring." She kept her voice carefully neutral.

Noa looked briefly startled before hesitating and then shaking his head.

She stared at him, her face a mixture of wariness and exasperation, as if she didn't quite believe him. "Stars forbid I have to begin treating people for psychotic breaks from reality," she muttered and returned her gaze to the figure on the table before her.

Noa's response was little more than a noncommittal noise.

"How is the colloidene replication coming along?" she asked after a moment.

"We've used up all the formation material we have. It is enough to keep those of us here in the triage camp phage-free, though even if we are re-infected, it's a simple matter to re-vaccinate."

He spared her a glance, his tone one of mild rebuke, and Dominica quashed a surge of guilt at her earlier insinuation that the man would refuse to risk his own skin to help others.

"What we need now is enough formation material to create enough colloidenes to seed the camps and the ring," he told her.

Dominica snorted in disgust. "Good luck with that. The ring's not into doing us many favors these days, in case you hadn't noticed."

Noa lifted one shoulder in a small shrug. "I doubt they will come through for us," he admitted, "which is why Bette's trying to get a message to the ship that just arrived, to ask for their help."

Dominica looked up sharply as a thought occurred to her. "*If* the ring will allow it, and *if* they're able to get past the blockade."

Noa just looked at her, his expression inscrutable. "At the moment, it's the best we can do."

She let out a soft sigh and nodded. They worked together for several minutes, Noa holding the light, as the senator who had accompanied her patient to the triage camp stood watchfully in the corner of the tent.

As she made her last incision, Dominica let out a small frustrated sound, then waved her hands over her instrument tray. "I feel like I'm back in the dark ages, working with little more than flint knives and wooden sticks," she said, her voice bitter as she turned back to her patient, using tweezers to remove the overgrown tissue and set it aside. Reaching for a needle and thread from among the pan of sterile instruments, she brought it up to eye level and glanced over at the scientist. "A needle and thread, Noa, for stars' sakes! Everything about purposely sticking a sharp object into a man's epidermis is just wrong," she said, her voice thick with frustration and anger.

"And yet, it must be done." His voice was implacable.

Dominica hated that the man was so able to control the emotions she knew he felt and yet refused to display. She wished she had such control, but instead her fiery temper often got the best of her. She laughed mentally; well, it wasn't like she could torpedo her career any more than she had when she'd joined forces with Noa.

She made an impatient gesture, and said brusquely, "I can finish here just fine. Thank you for checking on me. I'll send an orderly to get the senator when Bryce is ready for transport." Noa dipped his head once in acknowledgment, and then turned and ducked out of the tent.

Dominica sighed as she glanced up at his retreating back while plunging the needle once more into the unconscious man's arm.

"Medieval medicine," she muttered under her breath as she pulled the thread taut. "I'll never take mednano for granted again."

* * * * *

As Noa exited the tent, he glanced back over his shoulder at the camouflage covering overlaying Dominica's makeshift surgical theater. His eyes roamed across the rest of the triage camp, making note of shelters nestled between trees, and hidden in the lee of a small hillock that rose from the ground three meters in height.

Then, as he did so often whenever he left the bunker, he glanced up at the expanse of ring stretching overhead.

Stars, how has it come to this? he thought.

His chrono flashed up on his HUD, pinging as it reinitialized after the EMP. He had just enough time to make it through the bunker's decontamination before the next scheduled response from *Avon Vale* would arrive. He sent up a silent plea to the ancestors that the news would be positive.

DANGLING CARROTS
STELLAR DATE: 09.07.3252 (Adjusted Gregorian)
LOCATION: Inbound, above the stellar plane of the Nereids
REGION: 10 AU inside heliopause, Tau Ceti

Calista glanced over at the navigation board from her seat in the captain's chair once more; The *Avon Vale* was just under sixty AU from the far side of the wide dust belt that filled outer Tau Ceti.

Communications lag between the ship and Galene was still a good sixteen hours, which meant conversations were still being exchanged as recorded messages a little over half a day old. Calista had been momentarily nonplussed when Shannon had informed them that one such message had just been received—sent specifically to them from the very man they were planning to hunt down.

Noa Sakai.

She'd called the rest of the team up to the bridge after reviewing it once on her own. Now she observed them, gauging their reactions as they watched Sakai's missive for the first time.

She had already discussed Noa's request briefly with Shannon, when the engineer embedded in the *Vale* first brought it to her attention. But Calista wanted to know how the others felt about it, given what they suspected of Sakai's involvement in the smuggling of shackled AIs.

Some of what Calista saw reflected in the faces around her was what she'd expected to see: anger, outrage, resentment. But she also saw the beginnings of conflict, and even concern. That last was good, especially given that she'd already decided this man needed their help.

She glanced over at Terrance and was gratified to see him answering her questioning look with a firm nod. She knew he hadn't missed the lines of strain on Noa's face; they all could see how haggard the human looked as he stood before the bunker's optics and explained the situation.

"The problem we face is that the ring no longer has the capability—or inclination—to confirm that our solution works," Noa was saying. "We've sent them streams demonstrating that the nanophage is not only stoppable, but *reversible*, but they accused us of falsifying the vid."

Calista and Jason exchanged glances, her XO looking reluctantly impressed. She looked over at Terrance and saw the man rub his hand across the scratchy stubble of his jawline in thought as the physicist continued.

"I'm piggybacking my research onto this stream for your people to review. The phage is spread through a colloidene carrying a click assembly brick," Noa explained.

This meant nothing to Calista, but she took it to be a positive sign when she saw Jonesy sit up taller, his eyes narrowing, while at the same time, Shannon's avatar tilted her head to one side, her expression thoughtful.

"We're not the only ones who need formation material," Noa added. "There are plenty of sentients up on the ring still in cryo who need this rectification code, and I'm sure there are colloidenes still infecting the ring; there just isn't much nano left up there for it to infect, so it only *appears* as if the phage is under control."

The man on the recording grimaced, rubbing the back of his neck with one hand as he considered his next words. "But frankly, as much as I disagree with their methods, they've at least managed a sort of stalemate up there. We're battling active colloidenes shedding their click assembly codes on a daily—sometimes hourly—basis. We're *losing lives* down here. We're desperate for that formation material."

As the recording ended, the bridge remained silent except for the underlying hum of the ship underway and the rhythmic thumb of Tobi's tail from where she sat near Jason's feet.

After a moment, Terrance straightened.

<We've got to find a way to drop them that material,> Calista told him privately.

Terrance sent his agreement, and then shifted and put on what Calista privately thought as his 'owner of the expedition' face as he began to address the bridge.

"Okay, people, you saw his transmission. Shannon, Jonesy. I want your initial evaluation of Sakai's research within the hour. Loop Marta in on it, would you, please?" he added as Jonesy rose, ready to head toward the lift.

Shannon's avatar frowned. "I don't like it," she said, her tone blunt. "I don't trust him."

Calista tilted her head and shot Shannon a look. "You mean because it's Noa Sakai."

It wasn't a question. It was evident that Shannon was wrestling with the thought that the salvation of Ring Galene—actually, all of Tau Ceti—could possibly come from someone who had been complicit in the purchase of the very AIs they had come to this system to free.

"I get your feelings, I really do," Calista assured her, but saw Shannon's brows draw down at her words.

"Why do I hear a 'but' coming?" the engineer demanded.

"Because there is one," Calista admitted, pausing to lift one shoulder in a half-shrug. "Sometimes you have to deal with things you don't like, to get things done that need doing. It's the classic pyramid of needs."

She saw Terrance stir at that.

"Yes," the exec concurred. "You have to begin with the greatest need, and then proceed from there. But don't worry, Shannon. Noa will have his reckoning, I assure you that."

"If the man is culpable, he will be brought to justice," Calista agreed, backing up Terrance's words, her tone unyielding. "You have my word."

Shannon hesitated, then planted her hands on her hips and

glared pointedly at both Calista and Terrance. "He damn well better be," she muttered. "I'm holding you to that." Her eyebrows rose in a challenging look, and then her image dissolved.

As Calista had requested, they reconvened an hour later.

"So what do you think?" Jason asked, as Jonesy pushed Tobi aside so that he could slide back into his seat, and Shannon's avatar winked into existence. "Has this guy found the solution?"

Shannon frowned, folded her arms, and shot Jason a glare. "You mean Bette and Charley."

"*Noa*, Bette and Charley," Terrance inserted in a placating tone. "And you didn't answer Jason's question. Have they found a solution?"

Shannon snorted and turned away, but Jonesy looked up and nodded, his gaze firm as he answered.

"Yes, sir, I think they have. Our simulations concur; the science is solid. Whoever else this guy might be, at least he knows his nano."

Shannon shrugged uncomfortably, but after a moment, nodded her agreement.

"And we have enough formation material to get the job done?" Terrance's voice was sharp as he sought confirmation.

Shannon nodded. "Yes, we do. In fact, it'll hardly make a dent in our stockpile," she admitted.

"Very well, then." Calista paused as she considered the next steps her bridge crew would take. "Given that the ring is in a state of anarchy at the moment, how can we deliver the material to the planet?"

"As in, how do we get it past the blockade the Galene Space Force has around the planet, *and* the picket that the Federated States of Tau Ceti have set up beyond their moon to interdict this part of the system from all comers?" Jason's voice was dry.

"Yes," she agreed. "Let's ignore the FSTC picket for the moment and assume one of two scenarios: either Ring Galene won't care that we provide assistance to Sakai...or they will actively block our attempt to help. Thoughts?"

She saw Jason pick up a stylus from the console where he sat and begin idly weaving it through his fingers; Jonesy used the toe of one boot to send his seat at the nav station swaying gently back and forth, head bent in thought. Terrance…just paced, accompanied by the soft click of Beck's paws.

It was an intriguing contrast to the utter stillness of the four AIs: Kodi, Landon, Tobias and Logan. Though she knew that everyone present was busy considering, discarding, and reformulating various approaches to the problem.

"The way I see it," Jason said slowly, setting the stylus down and swiveling toward her. "It's not a matter of 'either…or'. It's a matter of 'who first'. Am I right?"

She nodded and saw Terrance lean forward, tilting his head in an invitation for the pilot to expound on his statement.

"Both the ring *and* the planet need the nano that Sakai's going to make; the ring just refuses to believe it," Jason went on to explain, looking between her and Terrance. "And we don't dare risk them blocking our delivery, so it's best if we find a way to distract them so that the formation material gets safely to the planet. Am I right so far?"

Landon stirred. "Yes, I believe I see where you're going with this. And a distraction may be easier for us to pull off than you may think." The AI's gaze shifted from the projection of Galene and its ring on the bridge's main holo, coming to rest on his brother. "Given what Noa described, what do you think the odds are that the ring has decommissioned all its higher-thinking, machine-learning NSAIs out of fear they'd become infected?"

"That would be a safe bet," Logan agreed.

At the profiler's words, Calista saw Jason sit up suddenly and snap the stylus out of the air with one hand. The motion had Tobi flattening her ears and whacking him once with her tail. Jason absently rubbed the big cat under her chin in apology as he speared Landon with a look.

"Wait, are you suggesting that the ring's security forces have resorted to actively patrolling with *humans alone*? No NSAI surveillance of any kind?" He looked expectantly from Landon to Logan.

"That would be a reasonable conclusion, yes," the profiler admitted. "Although the ships in the blockade may be another matter. At least some of them would be ships that have managed to escape the phage, which means they will have fully-modern capabilities."

"Yes, but, lad, we have yet to see how their sensors stack up to Alpha Centauri tech," Tobias reminded him. "The picket of FSTC ships keeping the rest of Tau Ceti from Galene nearspace should give us a feel for the capabilities of the GSC ships around the planet. We can assume they won't be any *better* than what the Federated States have, at any rate."

Jason's eyes narrowed thoughtfully as he stared over at the Weapon Born. "Good point, Tobe. It'd be interesting to see if they can spot the *Mirage* or one of the Icarus shuttles."

"So, you're thinking we launch—what? Both a shuttle and a fighter to test their sensors? What do we say if we're caught?" Calista questioned, and he shrugged.

"There's no crime in going out for a little joyride, is there?" The pilot grinned wickedly at her, and she shot him a look of exasperation. He held his hands up in self-defense. "I'm not saying it's without a bit of risk, but I really think we have a good chance of sliding by without being seen, given the reflectance of the ships' surfaces—especially if we calculate our trajectories carefully."

She looked at him a moment, eyes narrowing in thought. "I suppose we could maneuver the ship so that the *Vale* can hide their deceleration burns," she mused. "The Icarus ships would need to stay in our shadow, since they'll be traveling at the same velocity when we drop them," she warned, and he nodded his acceptance of her caveat.

She leant back, her gaze shifting from Jason to Terrance. "Okay, so what's our strategy?" She nodded to the image on the holo. "The *Vale* can't begin vectoring toward Galene without someone hailing us and challenging our intent. What do we tell them?"

"We offer to play intermediary."

She felt her eyebrows raise at Logan's statement, and then heard a rumble of approval from Terrance at the profiler's words.

"Sounds like a job Enfield Holdings might be able to take on, since the ring has made it obvious they want our stasis tech," the exec murmured. "That's a pretty sweet carrot to entice them with."

"Yes, but in this situation—and I can't believe I'm about to say this—*I'm* the best person to play Enfield intermediary." Jason's voice was unexpected; his comment even more so, and Calista watched in surprise as Jason held up a finger to forestall Terrance's nascent protest. Sensing the exec's consternation, Beck cocked his head, glancing with interest between the two men, but for once, remained silent.

"Whoever is going to be the face of Enfield has to be the one who can run the ring op. For obvious reasons, that can't be you, since AIs are banned on the ring," he said flatly as he shot Terrance—and by extension, Kodi—a pointed look. "I'm the least modded human we have, plus I have my L2 capabilities that we can use as our ace in the hole, if we need it."

At Terrance's nod, he continued.

"And while it severely pains me to pass on a really sweet gig," Jason shot the exec a grin, "I think it's best if you take our relief package to the planet's surface on *Eidolon*, while I take *Sable Wind* and rendezvous with the ring."

Calista had a bad feeling about the look in Terrance's eyes at that suggestion.

Now would be a good time to remind him that his reckless streak's just about as bad as Jason's, she thought, remembering a certain shoot-out in the bowels of the El Dorado Ring followed by a live-fire exfil on a Proxima torus decades ago.

"Hold up there, cowboy," she warned the exec, lacing her tone with both humor and caution. "You might be signing the paychecks, but you're not the one with the military training here. I can't advise letting anyone approach that ring until we've fully thought through how we're going to accomplish this and ensure that we don't get infected before we can verify for ourselves that Noa has a viable 'cure' that isn't defeated by mutations."

She saw Terrance frown, but Jason just nodded, whipping his cradle around to the console to begin a rapid manipulation of its holo display.

"Take a look," her XO said, highlighting the green-line approach vector he'd just mapped out.

"Here's where Noa's bunker is located, at the base of the Zao Mountain Range. It's about eighty klicks east of the elevator, which means it's under slightly less coverage from the blockade, since they're concentrating their ships over the dense population areas." Jason rotated the planetary view, tapping on various locations. "Here at Hokkaido and the Q-camps that are around it, and then at the three coastal cities: New Palos Verdes, Cherny Ostov and Meshuggah."

Jason spared a quick look over his shoulder, one brow raised. When there were no questions, he returned his gaze to the holo.

"Logan, how would you feel about threading this needle here?" He traced a line between the twelve-thousand-kilometer separation of two of the projected blockade ship paths. "Your biggest risk of detection is your atmospheric entry window. But even then, I'd wager that they'll be hard-pressed to get solid targeting solutions off the *Eidolon*'s Elastene surfaces. Barring a lucky shot, you should be able to get her down without any issues."

Jason's expression turned wry. "Getting her back up, on the other hand...." His voice trailed off and he ended the sentence with a shrug.

"I know I'm just the financial backer of this trip," Terrance spoke up, giving Calista a significant look, "but I really think we need to get down there as quickly as possible. Those folks need our help. We can figure out how to get back to the *Vale* later."

Calista agreed, but was shocked to hear Logan echo Terrance's opinion.

"I agree. And I think the odds of finding a way off Galene are high," the profiler said. "I just completed a review of a list of refugees Bette sent along with that last transmission. We have the equivalent of several companies of military personnel down there, plus a few active combat units that were smuggled to the surface by one of Galene's AI Marines."

He gestured to the main holo and brought up an image of a woman in full battle-rattle.

"Sakai's daughter leads one of Galene's Marine Special Operations groups and is actively holding back the ring's escalation of troops to keep the planet 'contained'. I'm sure Sakai will be grateful enough for our assistance that we should be able to enlist their help to get back to the ship."

Calista hardly heard the last of Logan's statement. She was too busy staring in surprise at Terrance's reaction to the sight of the woman on the screen.

* * * * *

Terrance's gaze was riveted to the image of the woman Logan had on display.

The phage had not exempted her from its grasp; from the looks of it, her armor's base layer had been compromised and had begun to 'self-repair' itself into her own skin's epidermis. The nano had apparently rejected her hair follicles as foreign material and had grown itself partially across her scalp. Tendrils of nanofilament laced her left cheekbone, cutting through her eyelid and across her forehead. Where the base layer had taken combat damage, repairs had begun—but again, the nano appeared to be melding the suit to her skin rather than seeking to seal itself over it.

Still, her dark eyes burned with fierce determination as she calmly returned fire under the onslaught of GSC forces attempting a purge of one of the more hard-hit Q-camps.

Something in his chest burned.

<We need to help her, Kodi,> he whispered softly in his head. <It doesn't look like they can take much more of this.>

He felt a questing probe, and then a murmur of agreement from the AI—both of which he ignored as he tore his gaze from the holo, seeking Logan's frame.

"Who do we take with us? You, me, Kodi, and…?" His voice lifted at the end in question as he looked from Logan to Jason.

"Me."

Marta's voice, as always, came from beside the doors that led to the corridor. The doctor had the uncanny ability to arrive on the bridge without notice.

"From the data dump they sent, their surgeon general is sorely understaffed down there, and they could use as many capable hands as they can get."

Terrance heard Calista begin to protest, but the doctor overrode the captain.

"Shannon and Jonesy feel that the colloidene rectification plan that Noa sent us is a solid one, so all we need to do is manufacture a supply of our own before we arrive. That way, we can feed the immediate area with a constant stream of them." She shrugged as she strode forward, thumbs hooked inside the front pockets of her medical coat, and nodded at the holo. "If the phage *does* end up compromising any of our nano, it won't have a chance to take hold."

She grimaced, shaking her head in thought as she paused to consider her own words. "They could really use double or triple the medical staff they have down there. In fact, if we can successfully inoculate ourselves against the phage, I'd like to bring a small team of surgeons with me, volunteers from within our passenger ranks, if they'll come."

Terrance found himself holding his breath as he glanced over at Calista to see what she thought of the plan.

He didn't have long to wait; after a brief hesitation, she nodded decisively. That was all he needed.

He rounded on the room, his next words acting like the gunshot at a starting line.

"Very well, people. Let's make it so."

AMBUSH

STELLAR DATE: 09.11.3246 (Adjusted Gregorian)
LOCATION: Federated States of Tau Ceti picket line
REGION: approaching Galene nearspace, Tau Ceti system

Jason sat in the pilot's cradle of one of the two Icarus-class shuttles, Tobias ensconced within the ship's core housing, the holo before him displaying the icons of the various ships comprising the FSTC picket. The *Sable Wind*'s IFF tagged each one red, while the Icarus fighter containing Calista and Logan was tagged green.

Calista's *Mirage* hung off his left wing-tip, both ships tucked in close to the *Avon Vale*. They were closer than Shannon would prefer, given her caustic comments over the combat net about the Icarus birds scorching the larger ship's Elastene-clad surface.

<Do you have to burn quite so close to me?> she complained loudly as she fed them a continuous stream of updates from the *Avon Vale*'s more robust sensor suite. But in her next breath, she was chiding Calista for drifting beyond the ship's coverage. <Stars, miss slacker. Has playing ship's captain been too cushy of a job, or what?>

<Watch it, Shannon. You're still under my command,> Calista retorted, and Jason chuckled as she amended crossly, <Even if Terrance does pay the bills.>

The three ships were exchanging encrypted communications via directed laser tightbeams, so narrow that one of the FSTC ships would have to physically cross its path to know that it was there. Given the vast distances between objects, even this close in, the likelihood of that happening were nil—at least, if those operating said tightbeams were halfway competent.

In the case of team Phantom Blade, competency was a given.

Jason executed the final hard deceleration burn that would bring him to a comparable velocity relative to the picket, and then vectored away from the shadow of the *Avon Vale*, and toward the nearest FSTC ship—a *Nereids*-class corvette, his cockpit holo informed him—while Calista headed for one of their destroyers.

He'd planned his trajectory carefully to mask his use of the ship's thrusters as much as possible, and began a gentle loop, curving under the corvette's bow. His path would intersect the other ship's main sensor array, and he held his breath as the Icarus-class shuttle sliced silently through the black, the corvette not twitching a whisker at his advance.

After completing his loop, he curved upward until he was well above the plane of the picket, and shot a brief tightbeam burst back toward the *Avon Vale* to indicate he'd completed his run.

An answering burst acknowledged his transmission, and he waited patiently as his display updated Calista's projected path. The fighter had opted for a pass that was much more close-in, and the successful completion of her run would be the last bit of intel they would need to solidify their approach plans for Ring Galene.

Another few minutes passed, and the *Sable Wind* was hit by a comm tightbeam off his starboard wing, passing the message that the *Mirage*, too, had made the run without detection. Both ships turned back to rendezvous with the *Avon Vale* and prepare for their real mission.

* * * * *

Back on the bridge, Jason sought to remain calm as he spoke once more with acting president Henrick. Light-lag from the ring was now just an annoyance, but it was made more so by how irritating the woman was. He took a deep breath and reached for a patience he'd never been very good at, as the woman once more attempted to keep them from intervening.

After their first exchange with acting president Henrick, it had become clear that the woman was unable to divest herself of her now-ingrained distrust of and aversion toward AIs. Her irascible behavior was making Jason heartily regret volunteering to run the ring op.

<It's what you get, boyo, for volunteering to run point on the ringside part of this mission,> Tobias reminded him privately, his tone threaded with wry humor.

Jason snorted mentally at that. *<Yeah, when did I forget Pilot's Rule Number One?>* he asked the Weapon Born. *<Never volunteer for anything, except to fly the ship. We'll be lucky if I don't end up wrecking the mission by shooting off my mouth. Which I swear I'm going to do if she says one more stupid thing.>*

<You don't give yourself enough credit, boyo,> Tobias chided. *<You have more of the statesman in you than you think. Who knows? Someday you might go into politics yourself.>*

<Stars, Tobe!> Jason knew his voice sounded horrified at the thought—an accurate representation of how he felt. *<Don't even joke about a thing like that!>*

His attention returned to the slightly guttural tones of the woman on the holo, settling one hand on Tobi's head when he heard the big cat begin to emit a low growl.

"While we appreciate your concern, we would prefer the matter of Enfield's stasis technology to be considered separately, as purely a business transaction." The woman waved her hand dismissively, but she couldn't quite hide the anger that telegraphed itself in the tension of her eyes or the taut manner in which she held herself.

Jason stifled a sigh of exasperation as the woman continued.

"Your offer to serve as an impartial intermediary for matters between Ring Galene and those quarantined on the planet is commendable, but we cannot expect someone who has just recently arrived to appreciate the various layers and nuances involved in this complex situation."

"I'm afraid we are going to have to insist," Jason replied in a tone that brooked no further discussion on the matter—or he hoped that was the case.

His words were rewarded with a flash of surprise coupled with annoyance after the few seconds of light-lag had passed his response to her.

"We have some of Enfield's most-skilled technicians aboard the *Avon Vale*, and are prepared to demonstrate the validity of our claims." He toggled a sim of the *Sable Wind* that he'd created, one that illustrated their proposal.

"We can dock wherever you would like, and I will personally submit to any of your scans. I'm an unaugmented human, with no mods other than the Link and a standard, carbon nanotube-reinforced skeleton—something I understand is typical for your pilots, as well."

The sim showed the Icarus-class shuttle docking, and miniaturized icons representing cryo-pods being loaded aboard.

"We can take on half a dozen of the infected in cryo units, and then we'll undock. We'll match orbit, establishing a station-keeping attitude with the dock while our team of engineers administers the colloidene rectification application. You'll be able to monitor via a live broadcast stream. We'll share our scan data with you as we receive it." Jason's tone turned firm, unyielding. "But know this: the *only* way you're getting your hands on a single one of our stasis pods is by accepting our offer to prove—or disprove—the effectiveness of the phage cure they've developed down on Galene."

Henrick's mouth firmed, and for a moment Jason thought she might protest, but she gave a curt nod and cut the connection.

For a moment, he continued to stare thoughtfully at the holo, now displaying nearspace around *Avon Vale*.

"Interesting," he murmured, and looked up with a distracted expression when Terrance nudged him.

"Care to share?" the exec asked, a brow raised.

Jason reached toward the holo and zoomed in, highlighting the insignia on the sleeve of one of the soldiers standing in the background, behind Henrick.

"Take a look," he said. "That's not the insignia of the Galene

Space Command we saw in the Tau Ceti infodump the FSTC sent us."

"No," Terrance mused. "You're right; it's not."

Jason cocked his head toward Logan. "What do you think?"

The profiler stood perfectly still, staring at the image floating on the holo. After a moment, the display split as the AI brought up two more images on either side of it. One was the GSC insignia; the other was the seal of the Department of Planetary Security.

In the side-by-side comparison, they could clearly see the arm band the soldier sported was an amalgam of the two.

<Looks like they might be a new breed of state police,> Kodi sent. <There's no history of Planetary Security ever staffing its own units before the nanophage. >

"Goon squad?" Jason guessed, "or secret police?"

"It would fit with what we've found," Shannon's voice was laced with acrimony.

"Agreed," Logan said, just as his brother chimed in. "This acting president Henrick strikes me as a big believer in the old adage of never letting a good crisis go to waste."

Jason sent Landon a sharp look. "You think she's seized power *permanently*, don't you." It wasn't a question.

Landon nodded. "I'm not the profiler in the family, but yes, it stinks of that—to me, at least."

"She might not be very eager for our cure to the phage, then, if she's using it as an excuse to stay in power," Terrance said thoughtfully, hand again scraping across the stubble along his jaw.

"Best we proceed with caution, then," Jason said, and Terrance made a sound of agreement.

Several hours later, Jason was once more strapped into the pilot's cradle.

<Sable Wind, *you're green for departure.*> Kodi's voice sounded in his head as he reached up to toggle the final virtual readout on his system's checklist.

<*Copy that.* Sable Wind *is green for departure,*> his co-pilot,

Shannon, replied.

She had decided to move from the *Vale* and embed with him in the shuttle—to 'make sure he didn't screw anything up', she'd said. She was handling nav, while Jonesy sat on comm and Jason ran the pilot's boards. Behind their shuttle, lined up to drop as soon as *Sable Wind* had cleared the ship, were the *Eidolon* and the *Mirage*.

Tobias was embedded with Calista in the fighter, while Logan was with Kodi and Terrance, embedded in the second Icarus shuttle. Marta had joined them on *Eidolon*, along with a few of her best ESF medics.

Landon had remained behind and was now in command of the *Avon Vale*. He would function as overwatch and coordinate the timing of the operations, as well.

Calista flashed her running lights at Jason as the bay's ES field snapped into place and the bay doors began to slide open. He felt a slight bump as the auto-tow latched onto the docking rings that protruded from the belly of the shuttle, and *Sable Wind* began to creep forward on the bay's departure rails. The auto-tow gave one last push, and the shuttle dropped clear of the bay.

Jason engaged thrusters and vectored away from *Avon Vale* while monitoring the *Sable Wind*'s rear optics, watching as first the *Mirage*, and then the *Eidolon* dumped into the black. He caught the flash of light as the ES field was cut and *Avon Vale*'s bay doors began to close.

<Stand by. I'm about to make a lot of noise with these MFRs,> he announced as he brought the ship's two fusion reactors online and dialed them to their maximum output to mask the burns of the other two ships.

<Stars, that makes me cringe,> Shannon muttered.

<You and me both,> he agreed. <Good thing I'm not looking for work in this system. This'll pretty much guarantee I never get hired on as a pilot.>

He heard the smirk in Terrance's voice as the exec drawled in a sardonic tone, <*That's it, Andrews. Kiss 'em with a big old, gloppy sensor return.*>

<*Happy to do what I can to protect that boardroom complexion, there, mister executive,*> he shot back as he angled the vessel toward the dock that was his destination. <*Good luck down there.*>

Forty-five minutes later, he was shaking his head in disgust as Ring Galene's STC Approach control cleared him for his final approach, and he came close enough to see an actual human, dressed in an ancient-looking pressure suit, waving him in.

<*Stars, guys,*> he sent to the *Avon Vale*, knowing they'd connect him through via tightbeam to comms on the *Mirage* and *Eidolon*, even though neither ship would respond. <*They're vectoring me in with an honest-to-stars genuine Yellow Shirt.*>

He shook his head in astonishment as the figure waved two glowing sticks at him, beckoning him forward, and then did a little butt wiggle and raised his left knee to indicate Jason should slew the aft end of the *Sable Wind* to port a few degrees. He snorted into the comm at that.

<*For those of you greenhorns out there who aren't familiar with the term, before NSAIs were used to ensure docking procedures were scrupulously and painstakingly accurate, a-way back in the twenty-second century, **humans** did that task. They were called Yellow Shirts because—*>

<*Wait. Let me guess,*> Jonesy's voice interjected from his position in the cradle beside Jason, his tone dry. <*They wore yellow shirts.*>

<*Ah, a student of history, I can tell.*> Jason grinned as Shannon sent him the AI-equivalent of a snort, and he could just imagine the eyeroll Calista was mentally sending his way.

He crept forward until the shuttle hovered less than two meters from the dock, the man with the sticks gesticulating, bumping, and gyrating the whole way.

<*Okay, guys, we're on,*> he sent to Jonesy and Shannon, and received a firm nod from the human and a mental thumbs-up from the AI embedded within the shuttle, right before the ship lurched

as the docking clamps latched onto them and began reeling them in.

<They better not be messing with the paint job,> Shannon grumbled, and then her avatar shot an accusing finger toward him, pinning him with a glare before he had a chance to reply. <Do **not** tell me it doesn't have a paint job, Jason. I **know** that. I designed this ship, you know.>

He raised his hands in the air with a smirk. <Wasn't about to, ma'am.>

She snorted. <Yeah, right. Pull the other one, it has bells on.>

The banter cut through the tension they were all beginning to feel, as the dock mated with the shuttle's airlock, and the ship confirmed a positive seal.

Jason lowered his hands, making a fist with his left one, looking down at the thin band of black that ringed his third finger. The device was the brainchild of the two engineers, a Faraday cage made from Elastene to mask the nano hidden inside.

Twisting to glance back at the other man, he asked, "Okay, Q, you sure this'll pass undetected?"

Jonesy's brow furrowed, and he shot Jason a puzzled look. "Q?" he asked, and Jason barked a short laugh.

"From an old-Earth vid my grandma Cary used to watch. *Her* grandmother got her hooked on them back on High Terra when she was a little girl. I watched it because it had a lot of pew," he explained, cocking an imaginary gun at Jonesy. "Q invented things for spies and secret agents."

Jonesy looked intrigued, then shrugged. "Well, technically, that'd make Shannon Q. I just assisted."

Jason scratched his head in thought. "Nah, she'd be M." He shot the holo a wicked glance. "Or Moneypenny."

<Money—> Shannon's avatar popped up on the holo display before him, hands on hips. <I've seen your stash of old-Earth vids. I am **not** Moneypenny. If anything, **I'm** Q and Jonesy's R.>

Jonesy looked from one to the other, mystified, and Shannon

threw up her hands.

<Nevermind. Back to **important** things.>

"Right, well," Jonesy said, "No, you shouldn't have anything to worry about with the Faraday cage. You have the instructions we sent to operate it?"

Jason tapped the side of his head. "All Link-controlled, yes."

A sound from the dock caught his attention, and he glanced from Jonesy to the shuttle's hatch.

Guess I'm up first.

He unstrapped and floated slowly toward one of the bulkheads, the dock's much lighter gravity indicating that the current 'down' direction was in the direction of their airlock. Bounding gently toward the exit, he crouched and awaited the knock that would indicate the dockhand was ready for him to open.

He raised an eyebrow and looked over at Jonesy when a few minutes passed with nothing happening. The engineer just shrugged and raised a hand in the universal 'got me' gesture.

<Shannon?>

<Scanning,> came the terse reply, and then <Seal is good. You can open up. I've released a passel of colloidenes around you, so if anything makes it inside Sable Wind, we're ready to neutralize.>

"Okay, then. Here goes."

He toggled the airlock to open—and came face-to-face with the business end of a flechette gun.

AN OUNCE OF PREVENTION
STELLAR DATE: 09.11.3246 (Adjusted Gregorian)
LOCATION: ESS *Avon Vale*
REGION: Galene nearspace, Tau Ceti

Back on the ship, Landon prowled the perimeter of the bridge, forcibly quelling the compulsion to check on the status of each member of Phantom Blade. He *hated* being left behind and kept out of the action—especially with not one, but *three* away teams headed into potential combat situations. He also hated that his teammates were outside his envelope and away from his ability to personally ensure their safety. And lastly, he hated that the situation stirred in him old demons that he thought he had wrestled into submission decades ago.

The rational part of his mind understood it was not *his* responsibility to safeguard every member of the team, but the *ir*rational part insisted on keeping tabs on each person.

While one part of his mind monitored the comm feeds Kodi had open for the *Eidolon*, *Sable Wind* and *Mirage*, another part of his mind was busy envisioning what was happening at each location. He calculated the amount of time it should take the *Eidolon* to negotiate the distance between the ship and the planet's surface. After that, he shifted to the shuttle, sitting docked at Ring Galene, and calculated the amount of time it should take Ring security to confirm that Jason was 'nano-free'. Finally, his mind cycled to the fighter, as he mentally ticked off the amount of time it would take to slip past the blockade and stand watch over the *Eidolon*.

He forcibly arrested those processes, reminding himself that he should be focusing on various ways the *Avon Vale* could level the playing field a bit more. Strands of picket ships and a ring of GSC cruisers and corvettes around Galene were a bit much for one ship to handle on its own, even if it did have three exceedingly stealthy aces in its proverbial hole. From what they'd divined, the GSC ships were firmly under Henrick's control.

The FSTC picket, however—it was conceivable that they might be convinced to join the *Avon Vale* against the GSC. Or at the very least, persuaded to stand down if Landon was forced to engage.

He scanned through the database of military engagements that he'd stored up from decades of service in the ESF, and something from the years he and Logan had spent on the edge of Centauran space in Mendoza's black ops program came to mind, triggered by the search parameters 'lone defender among enemy ships'.

During their years twinned and joined to the ring of asteroids on El Dorado's heliopause, Logan and Landon had seen Brigadier General Mendoza authorize myriad asteroids outfitted with fusion engines and remotely controlled railguns. Everyone had known they wouldn't fool an opposing force for long, but when a significant number of fusion emissions lit up on enemy sensors— all headed on an intercept course, their returns indicating a power output mimicking that of a warship—many an invading navy might blink. At least that had been the prevailing hope.

Mendoza had reasoned that the asteroid decoys would force the enemy to abandon stealth and show their strength. Her plan called for the remote railguns to function as a variation on a war of attrition. Their presence on the powered asteroids would cast doubt on their threat status, and when the asteroids engaged, would force the enemy to expend munitions against vast chunks of uninhabited rock.

Mendoza's reasoning gave Landon an idea....

<*York,*> he reached out to the AI currently in charge of engineering during the teams' deployment, <*I need an estimate on how long a job will take. Factor in as many hands as you need to get it done.*>

He sent the AI the manifest for the stockpile of MFRs and small tactical nukes that Jonesy had put together during the last six months of their trip.

<Take a look at the items in Ship's Storage Area 1724, if you will, and tell me how quickly we can clad those nukes in Elastene. Factor in small maneuvering thrusters, too.>

He paused a moment, then added, <Same with the MFRs. And program them so we can send an override command to their lockouts that will release containment of their localized micro plasma cores. Make them into nothing but Elastene-clad engines that will go critical and detonate on our signal.>

There was a surprised pause on the other end, then, <What are you thinking of doing, sir, if I might ask?>

<I'm thinking about seeding that blockade with a few deterrents that will cause those GSC vessels to think twice about firing on any ship departing the planet, by the time the Eidolon is ready to leave.> Landon's voice turned hard. <And I want to be ready to defend our people on Ring Galene, too, if necessary.>

<You got it, sir,> York said promptly, and then his presence on the shipnet faded.

Once fabricated, a cloud of smallish ultra-black forms began streaming from the *Avon Vale*'s cargo bay amidships. Hundreds of small puffs of air were buried in the greater energy signature of the *Vale*'s fusion engine wash as they reoriented themselves on a trajectory that would take them within range of the ships patrolling along the blockade.

Some of those radar-spoofing small masses stopped short, forming a chain that would enable their masters to communicate by a whisker-thin laser beam from the parent ship to the fleet of tiny munitions. The rest continued on their journey, seeding their destructive capabilities between the planet they orbited and the ships, oblivious to the threat they posed.

<Those little packages don't add up to all that much, really, considering the munitions any one of those ships carry,> Landon thought to himself. <But if we find we need them—and I play this right—those GSC ships may discover that the old adage about there being no real surprises in space combat is truer than they ever knew possible.>

TARGET PRACTICE

STELLAR DATE: 09.11.3246 (Adjusted Gregorian)
LOCATION: GSC Blockade between Ring Galene and planet
REGION: Galene, Tau Ceti

The shuttle carrying formation material to the planet was flying dark, relying on its ultra-black surfaces to keep it from being spotted. The amount of electromagnetic power reflected off its surfaces was so miniscule, it was measured in the thousandths-of-a-percent range.

Combined with the heat-shedding properties of Elastene, the odds of them being seen were vanishingly small. So small that, even though the fighter, *Mirage,* had launched at the same time that Terrance and Logan had departed in the *Eidolon*—without the benefit of their encrypted IFF beacon—even they would have no chance of spotting their sister ship.

The shuttle had no trouble slipping past the FSTC picket beyond Galene's moon, and as they cleared the last vessel, Terrance breathed a sigh of relief, his eyes riveted to the boards of the pilot's cradle he'd strapped himself into—although he wasn't pilot-in-command.

He was a passable pilot; he'd had Marta give him pilot's mods at the same time she'd embedded Kodi, and he'd kept his certification current in the *Eidolon*'s sims.

But he had a keen grasp of his own limitations, and he was more than happy to have the vessel under Logan's capable control—especially in moments like this.

He accessed the cabin's optics from his cradle in the cockpit to check on his charges. So far, the journey had been uneventful; Chilters, McCone and George, the medics accompanying Marta knew the stakes and none cared to disturb the concentration of the flight crew.

Even Beck, strapped in beside Marta, remained silent.

Terrance still hadn't quite figured out how the cat had managed to wheedle his way onboard, yet there he sat.

<*Approaching blockade in five,*> Logan announced, and Terrance tensed as they neared the GSC vessels.

Their flight path had them a good hundred-plus kilometers away from the nearest ship in the blockade. Logan had made micro-adjustments to the *Eidolon* with minute puffs of air from the shuttle's thrusters that had it curving in a gentle, shallow arc between a cruiser and a fast attack corvette. They passed between the two vessels without incident, ten thousand kilometers above the planet's surface.

Logan timed his course adjustments to make maximum use of the cover provided by the debris in medium and low planetary orbits. His use of the controls was sharp and efficient. It lacked nuance and the deft, intuitive touch that either Jason or Calista would have brought to their flight, but Logan more than made up for that with his exquisite precision.

As the *Eidolon* passed beneath a discarded object that looked like an abandoned pair of fuel tanks, the AI used short bursts from the thrusters to adjust the shuttle into a shallow corkscrew that would allow the tanks and other nearby pieces of debris to hide its descent into low planetary orbit. Once there, the plan would be to minimize aerobraking by repeated thruster pulses, slowing the shuttle until its Elastene cladding could more easily disperse the heat of reentry.

<*Stars, these people have a lot of junk up here,*> Terrance sent, his comments limited to the shipnet, now that his pilot's mods had been activated.

<*Think this is mostly recent stuff?*> Kodi asked as Logan threaded the needle between various objects, both large and small.

Terrance shrugged. <*I would hope so. I'd hate to think this is business as usual.*>

<*I suppose the ring's been jettisoning things suspected to have—*>

Kodi abruptly cut off the thought as the shuttle's sensor suite flashed a warning on the plas cockpit. <What the...?>

<Brace for maneuver!>

Logan's voice cracked across the shipnet, cutting through Terrance's shout of, <We're being targeted!>

<Not us,> Logan corrected tersely. <It's target practice on the tanks we just passed.>

Sure enough, the GSC cruiser nearest them was firing maneuvering thrusters and aligning its forward weapons with the drifting tanks. Logan had seconds to respond before the GSC ship switched from painting its target to blowing it out of the black. The ship's two fusion engines roared to life and, just that quickly, the jig was up.

Terrance grunted as he was thrown back into his cradle as the *Eidolon* went from a steady velocity to an instantaneous fifteen *g*s. The burn lasted barely a second, but Terrance knew that the blockade's network of ships and drones would have clearly seen the MFR burn prior to the shots detonating on impact.

That was confirmed by *Eidolon*'s sensors, as he saw they were now being painted by more than one source. Fighters came spilling from the cruiser, and an alert flashed on scan, indicating it was time to intercept.

<Hang on,> Terrance called to the medical team strapped into the passenger seats.

He spared a quick glance back at the seat next to Marta, and squelched a brief flare of guilt over Beck's lean and furred body strapped in next to her, ears pinned back and fangs slightly bared in discomfort from the maneuver.

<*I'm calling* Mirage,> Terrance sent to Kodi and Logan, and felt Kodi reach for the tightbeam.

<Comm open.>

At Kodi's terse words, Terrance's voice cut across the combat net. <Eidolon *to* Mirage. Cheshire. Say again, Cheshire.>

'Cheshire' was the call sign for the team's backup plan, a

disappearing act they would stage if things went balls-up, as they had just done thanks to a single vessel's one-in-a-million decision to take up target practice on the one piece of orbiting space junk directly in line with their location.

Terrance thought he might have made out an acknowledging click before the comm was shut down and the ship swung wildly around, Logan making a run for the surface.

Rail fire chewed its way through the void between the two craft, most of the projectiles passing harmlessly by as Logan maneuvered them out of the path of the projectiles. Some were unavoidable, and the ship's Elastene substrate worked hard to divert the kinetic energy of each impact and to disperse the heat throughout its elastic metal foam.

<It's going to be close,> Terrance heard Kodi say.

He didn't respond, his focus fully on completing the parameters of the condition he had just ordered.

Out of the tens of thousands of pieces of debris out here, what are the odds?

He kept his eyes glued to the holo display as Kodi armed explosive devices that would provide the visual sleight-of-hand. If all went well, they would fool their pursuers into thinking a lucky strike had ruptured its fusion containment, immolating the shuttle, leaving nothing but a debris cloud behind.

<Detonation in thirty seconds.>

* * * * *

Calista's mouth compressed into a firm line as she watched the drama playing out above and to her stern.

<Dammit,> she sent to Tobias. <Of all the times for some idiot to decide to take pot shots at a piece of metal....>

<The odds were low that this would happen,> the Weapon Born admitted, <but that's why we have contingencies.>

She nodded, then brought up the exigencies Cheshire required.

They were to drop a string of micro-drone focusing devices, each one programmed to maintain geostationary position between the *Avon Vale* and the bunker just outside Kusharo Springs, at the base of the Zao Mountains.

Once in place, the string would allow Phantom Blade to maintain secured contact with the crew of *Eidolon* via tightbeam transmissions. They would transit from bunker to drone to ship, freeing Calista and *Mirage* to exfil the area and fly to the ring, to support Jason's part of the operation.

Calista checked her chrono; if all went well, she'd emplace the drones and slip back across the blockade within the hour.

CRASH SITE

STELLAR DATE: 09.11.3246 (Adjusted Gregorian)
LOCATION: Furano Fields, Nakajima Prefecture
REGION: Galene, Tau Ceti

Embedded the way he was in the shuttle, Logan felt as if the ship's skin were his own, the aerobraking maneuvers elevating his temperature as he rode the shuttle hard into atmosphere. He waited impatiently for his outer surface to cool enough to provide maximum stealth before igniting the charges. He felt the burn of the explosives as they detonated, even though he'd shielded his sensors from them.

The craft bucked and jolted as it was tossed about by concussive waves it never would have felt in space. Logan cut the fusion drives, shutting down the fusion reactors—and with them, the craft's ability to compensate for such perturbations.

The *Eidolon* was now a very large, very stealthed, delta wing glider, flying silently through Galene's nighttime skies.

<*Well, at least we have the cover of night working in our favor,*> Terrance murmured, and Logan was pleased to hear that the human's mental voice sounded steady, even though the telemetry from his suit, connected as it was to the ship—and by extension, to Logan—told a different story.

<*Yes,*> he responded. <*Night…such as it is.*>

His sensors showed him a view of the terrain, twenty kilometers below, bathed in a combination of moonlight and ringlight.

<*Landing site targeted,*> Logan informed Terrance and Kodi, switching out the holo display.

Systems' status was minimized, replaced by a sectional map representing the terrain just north of Kusharo Springs, with a green line leading from the icon representing the *Eidolon*.

* * * * *

<Hey, Terrance? I think Logan's going to need a little help from the meat-suit soon.>

Kodi's voice sounded calm and assured with just a touch of humor, reminding Terrance that the AI had once been an ESF Marine. His was a steadying presence, something Terrance was grateful for at the moment.

But Kodi's words had Terrance's mind going momentarily blank.

A little help…?

Then he saw a window pop up on the holo just as Logan announced, <Deploying RATs now.>

<Deploying what?>

<Ram air turbines.> The AI's voice was clipped.

Terrance felt a small shudder, just the tiniest bit of buffering, as the shuttle's aerodynamic configuration changed with the release of two forward-facing trap doors, set low and to either side of the ship's front fuselage. Two small propellers attached to twin turbine engines began to rotate, providing power to the shuttle's hydraulics system.

<Your turn,> Kodi prompted him, the AI's words nudging Terrance into action.

Looking down at the deck beneath his feet, he spied a slightly depressed section about the width of his boot. He pressed hard, releasing a spring-loaded door that flew open with a loud *click* as he slid his foot back. A stick sprang up from the deck, connecting firmly with his waiting palm with a satisfying slap.

Terrance grasped the yoke firmly, knuckles whitening a bit as his hand convulsively tightened its grip.

Holy shit. A dead-stick landing….

He drew in a deep breath and then forcibly relaxed his grip, gluing his eyes to the instruments indicating airspeed, attitude, turn coordination and elevation. He forced his brain to recall everything he knew about the Icarus-class shuttle his company had designed.

<Logan will handle the heavy lifting, you just keep us on course.> Kodi's voice was steady and reassuring inside his head.

There wasn't much to do except bleed the perfect combination of speed and elevation. While he focused on flying the craft, Logan sent a tightbeam burst to Sakai and the two AIs from the *New Saint Louis*, identifying the landing site they'd selected.

As their destination drew closer, the holo updated with imagery Logan must have siphoned from satellite feeds earlier in the day, for they were brilliantly lit and easy to navigate.

<See that clearing?>

Logan zoomed the view in and pinned a flat, grassy area that Terrance estimated was about twice as wide as the shuttle and just long enough for him to tuck the delta wing in for a short-field landing.

Clearances do not look good, Terrance thought as he spied several twenty-meter trees at the near end. Given the stall speed for this beast, he knew he'd be coming in hard and fast.

<Find me a needle to thread, Logan,> he said, surprised his voice sounded as firm as it did. <I want to know what to aim for, if we don't stop in time to miss that stand of trees at the far end.>

He felt more than heard the AI's assent.

It was a white-knuckle flight, one he was certain Jason would have seen as a thrill ride. Terrance had never been more than a weekend warrior himself, and this kind of flight was far outside his comfort zone.

The ground rose to meet him....

<You're doing fine,> Kodi said. <Breathe. Just keep her steady.>

<Air speed is in the arc,> Logan announced. <Dialing in flaps. Fifteen degrees....>

Terrance felt the camber of *Eidolon*'s airfoil change, increasing its angle of descent and lowering the craft's stall speed. Eyes shifting rapidly between airspeed and the approaching horizon, Terrance eased back on the yoke, as Logan announced, <...*thirty degrees*....>

<*Brace!*> Terrance shouted over the shipnet as he fought to hold the nose up.

The shuttle came down hard once, porpoised on the grassy terrain, and then slid forward on its skids, ground effect finally giving out on Terrance as he lost control authority. Several meters into the skid, the nose tipped forward and plunged into the ground. The straps of his cradle contracted upon impact, and *Eidolon* shuddered to a stop.

He was met by groans from the passenger compartment as he called out, "Everyone okay back there?"

A scratching noise in the cabin was accompanied by a muttered <*You made me **pee**,*> from Beck.

"Don't worry, Beck. We'll clean it up," he heard Marta say. "You can stop trying to bury it now."

Terrance smothered a laugh and then grimaced as he toggled his own straps loose. <*That's going to leave a few bruises,*> he told Kodi privately.

<*You know what Jason and Calista would say.*>

Terrance snorted at that. <*Yes, and any one of our Enfield Aerospace people back home, too. 'A good landing is one you can walk away from.'*>

* * * * *

A whisper-soft *whoosh* was all he heard, and he looked up at the sound to see a massive shadow pass directly overhead just a few dozen meters above him. His head turned, eyeing the shifting blackness as it sank rapidly to the ground.

"Nev!" he called out. "Wrangle the men; we're going hunting."

Nev turned, his good eye gleaming, then followed the direction his leader pointed. One side of his mouth—the only one that was mobile anymore—stretched in a death's-head grin as he turned and jogged back toward the makeshift camp.

Bellows and curses followed, but the man knew Nev would roust them in short order.

"Bring the weapons," he barked, and received an answering shout. Certain they would follow, he turned and began the hike for Furano Fields. He was confident that was the shadow's intended destination. It was the only logical choice. He should know; he was a pilot.

And if that sonofabitch is any good at dead-stick landings, I'll be flying again very soon.

* * * * *

<Chilters, McCone. Get that ghillie netting unwebbed and ready to offload,> Marta heard Logan order her medical team. <Marta will install me inside my combat frame while Terrance helps you camouflage the shuttle.>

Terrance stirred at that and began to stand. "That's right. We have about two hours until sunrise, so let's get a move on."

Marta looked up in alarm. "Hold it! No one opens that hatch until I say so," she warned, her tone no-nonsense. "Logan, do what you need to do and then shut down. I want you dormant and in this nano-resistant isolation chamber before they open that airlock."

"The doctor's right, I stand corrected," Terrance amended.

<Just received confirmation, Noa's sending Marines with a ground transport to bring us and our payload to the bunker. Going dormant…now.> And with that, Logan fell silent.

Marta pushed past Terrance and knelt next to the console where Logan's cylinder was seated. With practiced ease, she keyed it open, removed the connections to his terminals, and seated him inside the hardened isolation case. Sealing it, she rose.

"George, release a passel of our rectification colloidenes," she instructed. "At the very least, I want to ensure the shuttle remains clear of contaminants, especially while Logan is installed in his frame."

The man gave Marta a short salute, then tapped an icon on his med sleeve, studied it for a moment and nodded in satisfaction.

"Done, ma'am."

<Very well, people. Let's do this.>

The two ESF medics exited, carrying a large, lumpy duffel between them. Terrance stood in the shuttle's airlock, tossed two more duffels down to the women and then followed them to the ground. Together, the three of them began unfurling the ghillie camouflage and draping it over the shuttle, while George trotted back along the furrows made by the skids to do what he could to break up the straight line that would indicate it had been made by a sentient, rather than the hand of nature.

Back inside the shuttle, Marta turned and passed her hand over Beck's silky pelt as she walked by. The Proxima cat had stayed silent and out of the way as they offloaded the camouflage; now, he padded quietly over to the airlock and rose up on his hind legs to peer out the plas window.

Marta smiled when she saw that the cat's attention was focused on Terrance.

I do believe Beck's matured a bit, she thought to herself. *Hard to let go of that image of a mischievous kitten, but it's sweet that he's taking this so seriously, and is looking out for his buddy.*

At her regard, Beck turned unblinking eyes her way. <Want out,> the big cat said.

She cocked one eyebrow his way and shook her head. "Can't do that just yet. Besides," she teased, "I'm not going to stand there while you spend half an hour deciding if you *really* want to go out or not."

Beck chuffed his annoyance at her, and turned back to his observations.

She smiled as she busied herself with the armored frame they had brought along, activating the auth token that would allow her to access its wake cycle. She set Logan's isolation chamber next to the frame and ran one final diagnostic on its specially-coated nano-resistant exterior, created just for this op.

As it returned greens across the board, she sent it the command unlock sequence, and the torso swung open, revealing the padded and reinforced chassis in which Logan's cylinder would be seated. It, too, was coated in nano-resistant material.

Marta had just lifted Logan and was making the terminal connections inside the frame when she heard Beck begin a low, deep growl. It reverberated through the shuttle compartment and she looked up, startled to see the cat's hackles standing up straight, all along his spine.

"Beck?" she asked in surprise. "What is it?"

<Danger!>

* * * * *

<*A little more...there, got it.*>

Terrance snagged the section of ghillie McCone tossed to him over the shuttle's nose and pulled it back along the craft's leading edge. He'd dialed in a broader EM spectrum with his optical overlays, rendering a brighter, blue-tinged view than that cast by the twilight from the ring and Maera, to provide more clarity to his surroundings. He looked up at the bow of branches that came together a few meters above him, from the two trees he'd put the nose between when he'd brought the shuttle to a halt, and was gratified to be able to clearly see how much room they had for the ghillie toss.

<*To you,*> he called to Chilters.

The medic had finished spreading out the next piece of ghillie by the craft's tail section and had moved to the airlock's outer door, waiting for him to hand her the netting. She reached out, nimbly catching the edge of the bundle he tossed her way.

Hoisting it, she crouched and then tossed it like a discus, calling out, <Comin' over!> as she threw the dwindling bundle over the dorsal edge of the craft into McCone's waiting arms.

We're making good time, Terrance thought in satisfaction.

Passive scan hadn't picked up the presence of anyone in the immediate area, but Logan had recommended they communicate via Link to minimize the risk of any sound carrying.

<Skids done,> George announced. <Headed to the tree line.>

They had brought along enough camouflage to drape the entire airframe, but Kodi had suggested they augment it with local materials to further break up any lines that might give away their presence. Terrance turned to see George draw his lightwand and begin hacking off small branches for their use. McCone trotted over to begin gathering them up. As he turned back to *Eidolon*, he noticed Logan hadn't retracted the RATs back into the airframe once they'd landed.

Need to remember to do that before we head out, he thought. *No use in leaving it open for the local wildlife. Or any random corrupted nano,* he amended.

He heard a noise on the other side of the shuttle that sounded almost like a scuffle.

<Chilters?> he heard Kodi call out.

The only response was a muffled cry and a thud that might have been a body hitting the ground.

<Was that—> Terrance began as he turned to crouch and peer beneath the *Eidolon*'s frame.

<Behind!> Kodi called out, and Terrance felt the displacement of air as he narrowly avoided being struck.

Wheeling, he shot his right forearm up to block the blow intended for the back of his head. Turning the move into a grapple, he used the momentum behind the attacker's thwarted blow to pull the figure off balance, causing the man to stumble forward. A sweep of one leg took the man's feet out from under him, and Terrance followed through with a quick elbow into the attacker's back. It stunned his opponent long enough for Terrance to unholster his pulse pistol and send a shot jolting through the downed man, rendering him unconscious.

<What the hell? Where did these people come from?> he sent to Kodi as he spun, seeking out his next target.

He swung his pulser toward a shadow of movement he'd caught out of the corner of his eye, rounding the nose of the craft.

A figure stepped out from behind a tree, flechette pistol pressed against the base of Chilters' skull. A mess of nano growth overlaid one side of the figure's face, rendering it as dead as if he'd suffered a stroke. A gargoyle-like grin curved from the living side of his face as he nudged the medic forward.

"Drop it," the man grated, and from its texture, Terrance guessed his vocal cords had fallen victim to the invasive nano as well.

He lowered the pulser slowly, careful not to give the man a reason to harm his hostage.

DYSTOPIAN RING
STELLAR DATE: 09.11.3246 (Adjusted Gregorian)
LOCATION: Franklin City Spaceport Docks
REGION: Ring Galene, Tau Ceti

"Easy, there." Jason raised his hands slowly, palms open in a placating gesture. "I'm unarmed."

The person facing him was a large man clad in protective armor, face shielded. The figure gestured with the flechette rifle he held in his hand, indicating Jason to step out of the airlock and onto the dock.

"Down on the deck, hands where I can see them," the armored figure ordered.

Jason complied, and another soldier stepped forward, raising an archaic-looking hand-held scanner. Approaching Jason as if he might turn on her at any moment, the woman aimed the bulky thing at him, her eyes glued to its readouts.

The soldier holding the rifle gestured. "Turn around—slowly. Yeah, like that. Keep turning. We'll tell you when you can stop." That last was delivered in a warning tone.

Jason nodded and complied, hands still held high. He listened to the machine's beep-and-whir as he turned, waiting for the woman to confirm that he was indeed a natural, unmodified human whose nano had been 'erased'.

Given the level of tech we've seen so far, those Elastene-clad internal Faraday cage compartments Shannon whipped up should easily spoof equipment this old…. At least, I hope it does.

As he rotated, he let his eyes wander, evaluating the surrounding area. Dim lights ringed the open bay, and most of the equipment pushed up against its walls appeared to be inoperable, or at least like it hadn't been used in a good, long while. Near the entrance, another three armored figures stood—likely the rest of his escort.

As the woman nodded and the machine fell silent, Jason took a quick peek at his internal feed. It showed that the Link between him and *Sable Wind* was still open, so he reached out to Shannon.

<Looks like they're operating on emergency power,> he sent.

The AI didn't respond. He didn't expect her to, either. They had agreed prior to launch that Shannon would do an imitation of a more base-level NSAI to minimize the Ringers' paranoia where AIs were concerned. Given the warmth of the reception he was receiving, that had been a good call.

"Anyone else in that shuttle with you?" the man holding the flechette asked, and Jason nodded.

"Yes, flight engineer, named Jonesy. But don't worry; he'll stay with the shuttle," he replied.

The soldier gestured to the woman holding the scanner, and she stepped back, pocketing the device and unholstering her own flechette rifle.

"We'll make sure he does," the soldier replied, then motioned with the muzzle of his own rifle for Jason to move toward the three personnel he'd spied during his pirouette, waiting at the neck of one of the corridors that funneled into the bay, their own flechettes held at the ready.

As he complied, he asked, "Isn't this a bit excessive? We're here to help, you know."

One of the figures they were approaching snorted in derision. "You're here to see what you can sell us, you mean."

The woman's voice was caustic, and the man behind him laughed as he shoved Jason forward.

"We'll just see about that. The president has other plans."

<Did he really just say 'we'll see about that'? Guy's been watching way too many bad holodramas,> he muttered over the net, his mental voice sardonic. <You able to get a good reading on the tech level in here?>

<Yes.> Jonesy's voice sounded positive. <Nothing we can't

overcome. See that conduit you'll be walking past in about two meters? If you could manage to drop a passel of breaching nano out of your ring onto that surface without them noticing, I'll use it to hack in and override any monitoring they might have in place.>

Jason sent him a mental nod and then feigned a stumble just as he reached the three at the corridor. He didn't bother to hide his flinch as he reached out to catch himself on the conduit Jonesy had indicated.

"Easy guys, I just tripped. My mama didn't raise me to be that stupid. I'm not going to make any sudden moves, if I can help it; not with four weapons aimed at my head."

He rose, both palms up, fingers spread in a passive, non-threatening gesture, eyes focused intently on the muzzle of the flechette weapon nearest him. He let out an audible breath as the woman removed her finger from the trigger, then paused to look back at the armor-clad figures behind him.

"We good?" he asked, taking care to project caution and a hint of worry.

The man only grunted.

Jason tried again to engage them in conversation as he bought Jonesy the time he needed to worm his way into the ring's systems.

"So, what's the plan here? I thought the idea was for us to demonstrate to you that we had the tech to cure some of your people who have been infected by the corrupted nano."

At the mention of the nanophage, he saw one of the armored figures clench her weapon more tightly while another shifted uncomfortably.

<They're really spooked by this, guys. It's like I'm invoking the boogeyman by just mentioning it.> His eyes narrowed as he considered how he'd been greeted upon their arrival. *<Actually, it's more like they're treating me as if I had the phage—or some other kind of communicable disease.>*

There was no response, and for a moment, Jason felt a flare of concern, but as he ran a quick check, he didn't find any active jamming impeding his connection to the shuttle—which meant Jonesy was busy hacking into the system.

Seconds later, he received confirmation.

<*I'm in.*>

<*Good.*> Jason sent him a mental nod and trod quietly forward, sandwiched between his watchdogs as they led him away from the dock and into the spaceport proper.

His gaze sharpened at what he saw there, evidence of the ravages the nanophage had left in its wake. The port wasn't just shut down; it felt derelict. Panels along both sides had been systematically opened, and at periodic intervals, they came across consoles that had been disassembled. Some had their guts ripped out, with conduit splayed out along the concourse floor. The soldiers paid it all no heed; they merely stepped over the obstacles littering their path along the way.

As they approached the spaceport exit, Jason pinged Jonesy.

<*Still with me?*> he asked.

<*We both are,*> came Shannon's voice. <*We've insinuated a worm behind their firewalls and are beginning to go over the data now. It's not pretty, Jason. This is one messed-up ring.*>

<*You can say that again.*>

He passed through the spaceport's doors and caught his first glimpse of Franklin City. The first word that sprang to mind was 'dystopian'.

A maglev line stood unused, cars lined up along the edge of the platform, empty. Across the thoroughfare, businesses looked as though they had been shelled. Most were boarded up, their storefronts littered with piles of broken shards of plas and twisted metal. One of the store's signs, the words 'TechToys' emblazoned across its dented surface, hung haphazardly by a single corner. It made a slight creaking noise as the wind caught it and sent it swaying gently through the air.

He caught a glimpse of a figure that pulled back into the

shadows between ruined buildings as they approached, heard the sounds of someone scurrying through debris down an alleyway they had just passed.

As they reached the first intersection that seemed to have electricity, he was greeted by a public token that appeared over his Link.

<You see this, guys?>

Shannon's avatar nodded. <Should be harmless enough. Shunt it through our connection; it's sandboxed.>

Jason stifled a laugh at that. <You mean I get protection from the AI condom, too?>

Shannon made a rude sound. <Tobias told you about that, did he?>

Jason just sent her a grin over the net.

<Fine. Well, in this case, it's more like an IUD. It's a sand trap, not a full sandbox.> The engineer made a face. <I can't believe you've got me making human anatomy analogies—ugh.>

Jonesy snorted as Jason sent her an unrepentant grin.

She shot them both a scowl, but then continued. <Once our friends in the bunker identified the vector that made AIs carriers, we realized all we needed to do was devise a filter to screen for maintenance codes and refuse them entry.> She sent them an impression of a mental shrug. <It's a minor nuisance, much less than a complete sandbox, but it's all the protection we really need—to keep us from becoming carriers of the phage, at least. We're still as susceptible as you are to nano running amok and building unwanted network lines, or stars forbid, muscle mods along our cylinder walls.>

The connection fell silent, replaced by the crunching sound of booted feet tramping over scattered detritus, and the imagery filtering in through Galene's planetary net. The general tone of the communication centered around one theme: Planetary Security was there 'for the public safety of all' and that curfews and restrictions were in place 'to keep the ring secure'.

There were public image pieces that painted Henrick—sometimes referred to as 'the Director' and other times, as 'acting president'—in glowing terms, calling her 'decisive action' in establishing the current protectorate regime 'prescient' and 'forward-thinking'.

As the net's feed continued to play, Jason became increasingly convinced that Terrance had been right: Henrick wasn't interested in eradicating the very thing that had brought her into power.

In fact, he thought with dismay, *she might see us as enough of a threat to cast **us** into the role of villain.*

The disturbing thought was interrupted when Shannon broke in again.

<Jason!>

He froze at the tension he heard in her voice.

<What is it?> he asked, his own tone sharp, as the soldier behind him goaded him to resume walking.

<The Eidolon *has gone down.*>

His surroundings took on a more defined edge and time slowed as the news caused Jason to ride the cusp of his L2 abilities.

<Report,> he ordered, and Shannon sent him a burst from the *Mirage*, updating him on the shuttle's status and the news that they were now operating under Condition Cheshire.

Time sped up once more when he learned that the shuttle had made it down intact, as the final packet of information containing the tightbeam exchange between the *Eidolon* and the bunker appeared on his HUD.

<Calista *will rendezvous to support us as soon as she and Tobias finish their microdrone deployment,*> Shannon informed him.

Jason sent her an acknowledgement. <ETA?>

<They *should be here within the hour.*>

<Good. Let me know when you're ready to move,> he sent, eyeing the armored ground vehicle the soldiers were approaching. <Looks *like my ride's here. Hopefully I'll be able to get a positive location for 'president' Henrick and an estimate on the size of her security detail soon.*>

* * * * *

Calista watched the feed from her board light up green—a daisy-chain of comm micro-drones, strung from a geostationary orbit above the bunker all the way past both the planetary blockade and the FSTC ships holding station between the ring and Galene's nearspace.

She tapped thruster controls, angling them back toward Ring Galene, just as Tobias confirmed her observation.

<Everything's configured, lass. The carrier signal from the bunker through the lensing drones is solid, and the *Avon Vale* confirmed receipt of the feed.>

<Excellent. And I spy our wayward shuttle ahead,> she sent the Weapon Born a smile as she pinned the *Sable Wind*'s location on the display. <I'm sure they'll be happy to see us.>

She opened the comm, looping both ship and shuttle into it, and announced their arrival.

<We're on our way, Landon. ETA to the Sable Wind, *twenty mikes.*>

She heard Shannon sigh over the net.

<Any reason in particular for that sound of relief?> she queried as she popped the thrusters a few times to fine-tune their course.

<None, other than it's creepy here,> the engineer replied. <Jason's sending us his feed; they've just exited out into Franklin City. Looks like there's a lot of propaganda playing on the public nets.> The AI shook her head. <Based on what we're seeing, there's no way President Henrick's going to give up the governance of Ring Galene.>

<She's only in power right now because of the state of emergency, isn't she?> Calista asked, and heard Jonesy join the conversation as he confirmed her supposition.

<Looks more like she's **seized** power, ma'am.>

There was a pause as she and Tobias were routed into the feed and absorbed what Shannon and Jonesy sent.

<Sounds like she's a fan of John Milton,> Tobias mused. At Calista's confused look, he explained. <An old-Earth poet from

thousands of years back. In one of his more famous works, he wrote, 'better to reign in Hell, than serve in Heaven'. Sounds like our Henrick.>

<Not **our** Henrick, thank the stars,> Shannon's reply was tart, but it was followed by a somber one from Jonesy.

<No, but she's still **our** problem....>

Calista sighed as she tapped thrusters to slow their approach, then maneuvered *Mirage* into an inverted position in relation to *Sable Wind*. Sliding the fighter between the skids of the shuttle, she settled it onto the craft's belly before activating her own skid's magnetic locks.

<All right. We're here. Preparing to EVA over to the dock's gantry. You have control over its external airlock, Jonesy?>

<Ready for you, Major.>

She sent a double-click acknowledgement, sealed her helmet, and checked all the safety interlocks on her suit.

<I'm showing green,> she told Tobias.

<Readouts confirm,> he responded.

<Very well, then. It's your spacecraft, Tobias. Don't put any dents in her, if you can help it.>

The AI sent her a cheeky wink. <I wouldn't dare, lass. My spacecraft,> he replied dutifully, completing the official handoff.

She unstrapped from the pilot's cradle and pushed gently off, giving herself a half-twist so that her back was to the canopy. Clipping her tether to the ring at the top of the pilot's cradle, she mentally reached for the toggle that would trigger its release.

<Coming over,> she called out as the canopy retracted.

She pushed gently away from the curved back of the cradle and floated away from the cockpit. A few judicious tugs on the tether had her dropping to the belly of the *Sable Wind*, where she engaged the maglocks on her boots. Disengaging the tether, she turned to face the airlock, and with the awkward gait that went hand-in-hand with all EVAs, began to make her way over.

Jonesy was there to greet her. "We have a pin on Henrick's

location. Jason's mobile, with a bunch of her goons; they're escorting him in for his 'audience with the president' now."

She cocked her head at him. "I heard those air quotes," she murmured. "I think it's about time we show the president what we do to megalomaniacs back in El Dorado...."

* * * * *

The Offices of Planetary Security contrasted starkly with every other place Jason had seen on Ring Galene. What he'd observed through the windscreen of the armored vehicle as it transported him to Henrick's command center painted the picture of a people who had been beaten down and were living in fear.

The few individuals he saw looked up in alarm as the transport passed; many ducked into entrances or scurried off down side streets in an attempt to avoid the watchful eyes of the soldiers that stood within the plas bubble that sprouted from the roof of the vehicle, operating its twin turrets.

Soldiers patrolled the deserted streets in pairs, nodding to the transport as it trundled past. Given that these were met with scornful disregard by those escorting him, Jason inferred that Logan's guess had been right on the credits: his hosts were a recent breed of brutes, a 'new elite' of Galene soldier—higher in the pecking order than those who patrolled its byways.

The thoroughfare that housed the government buildings stood like a polished jewel amidst a wasteland. It was clean and well-kept; the building he spied as the transport slowed was lit from within, its plas windows pristine. He could see the bustle of individuals inside, industriously going about their business. And yes, there it was: the organization's seal, gleaming bright in the light of the ring's second sunrise.

Jason squinted a bit as he disembarked, glancing around at the muted efficiency of people passing, their eyes skittering away from the soldiers guarding him as his escort advanced.

So even here, in the seat of Ring Galene's infrastructure, Henrick's people are feared.

He moved toward the entrance, propelled by a shove from one of the soldiers. Galene's version of an auth & auth scanner shrilled an alarm and, as one, the Planetary Services soldiers on duty raised their weapons, training them on Jason.

<*Oh, please. That was* **so** *orchestrated.*> Shannon had witnessed it all through Jason's optics, and her tone was scathing.

<*Looks like Henrick's orchestrating* **everything** *on the ring.*> The welcoming sound of Tobias's voice broke in as the Weapon Born joined the net.

<*Glad you could join in the fun, Tobe. And yeah, I think you're right,*> Jason responded, hands held above his head as he was subjected to a rough frisking before being allowed in the building. <*I'm getting a bit tired of this treatment. You guys finished rooting around inside Henrick's files? I'm ready for some action.*>

Tobias sent a sound of assent. <*We broke through her firewall while you were being frisked. Wait one, while Shannon and I finish assimilating— Ahhhhh. Interesting.*>

Jason had been focused on identifying additional points of egress—there were none—and trying to find a way to drop nano somewhere that might grant him access to the building's internal communications web. At Tobias's drawn-out exclamation, he brought his attention back to the team's combat net.

<*Whatcha got, Tobe?*>

<*The Who's Who of people reportedly still in power on Ring Galene. At least, those who haven't been sent planetside,*> the AI murmured thoughtfully. <*It would appear that they're all enjoying guest amenities, courtesy of President Henrick.*>

<*And by 'guest amenities', you mean—*>

<*She's got them stashed in cryo.*> Shannon's voice was flat and laced with distaste. <*Stacked up like sardines in storage, down in the lower levels of the same building you're in now.*>

<*Well that clarifies matters a bit, doesn't it,*> Jason muttered

mentally. <*Okay, Tobe. I know this ring op was my idea, but you're the combat veteran. How do we play this?*>

<*Take over planetary security, topple Henrick's regime, and reinstate its rightful governors.*>

<*Oh, is **that** all.*>

<*Got a better idea, boyo?*>

<*Um, no….*>

BECK

STELLAR DATE: 09.11.3246 (Adjusted Gregorian)
LOCATION: Furano Fields, Nakajima Prefecture
REGION: Galene, Tau Ceti

Marta wheeled back around to the torso of the frame she had just seated Logan inside. Swiftly, she double-checked the connections and then sealed it, watching her chrono as she did so.

Come on, Logan. Wake up! she urged the profiler silently as she crept up to the airlock window and peered out.

Terrance stood frozen, hands in the air as a figure frog-marched one of her medics toward him at gunpoint. She scanned the tree line for George, hoping the man had managed to escape to bring help, but felt her shoulders sag as she spied him rounding the back of the shuttle. The woman herding him was ragged-looking, with one arm that hung limply down her side, misshapen by growths. The other held a weapon trained on George's back and was motioning him to stand next to Terrance.

<Beck.> Logan's voice broke into the combat net, and Marta let out a pent-up breath in relief.

The cat ignored the AI's call, his stare intent on the drama unfolding on the other side of the airlock.

In the next moment, Logan transmitted a three-hundred-sixty degree view over *Eidolon*'s net, as seen from the shuttle's external sensors. Marta saw the raiders herding her fellow crew members as one of them began shouting demands.

<Beck,> the AI repeated. <Terrance needs your help. I need you to distract the bad people threatening Terrance while I take them out. Can you do that?>

A sense of obstinate rebellion came to them from the big cat. <Prey,> he snarled. <Kill.>

<Yes, prey,> Logan agreed. <But we must be cunning.>

His frame moved past Marta toward the front of the shuttle's passenger cabin. Kneeling, the AI lifted a panel to reveal access to the belly of the craft and the open port where the ram air turbines were slung.

<Logan, I don't think—> Marta spoke over the net, unwilling to make any noise that might alert their attackers.

She stopped when Logan raised a hand.

<I just need him to distract them long enough for your medics to hit the ground so I can engage,> the AI reassured her. <Take a look at the imagery I sent over the Link. We've landed in a field of white lavender. His platinum coat coloring will blend.>

Marta knelt beside him and peered past the propeller, considering what Logan had just told her.

<Cats are natural hunters,> the AI reassured her. <Beck knows instinctively how to stalk. And it's nighttime. They won't see him.>

She hesitated and glanced over at the cat, whose form was still plastered to the airlock's plas window. Logan twisted toward the Proxima cat.

<Beck,> he called again, and this time, the cat swiveled his head, eyes staring unblinkingly at Logan's combat frame.

The cat abruptly dropped to the sole of the ship and stalked over to where the AI knelt. Crouching, the cat craned his neck down into the hole. Beyond the turbine engine, plants half a meter high topped with clumps of white waved gently in the nighttime breeze.

<See the white flowers, Beck?> the AI highlighted the route he wanted the cat to take. <Use the plants to hide. Come up behind the bad people and when I tell you to—but **only** then—I want you to snarl at them as loudly as you can. Do you understand?>

"Yesssssss," the cat spoke audibly, his words part hiss, part growl.

He squeezed past Logan's frame and dropped, slithering around the propeller and then disappearing into the field below.

<Stand by to drop on my mark,> Logan sent to Terrance and the

medics, and only then did Marta realize that the profiler's interaction with Beck had been limited to those inside the shuttle.

She began to protest, but Logan held up a hand, waving her to the back of the craft and safely outside the range of any weapons fire.

She watched tensely as Logan dropped a pin on the cat, tracking his progress. She knew the instant Terrance realized what Logan had done, because the exec inhaled sharply. But he could do nothing else without endangering the cat.

As Marta watched, Beck crept ever closer, a silent wraith, sliding skillfully among the flowering plants, intuitively freezing each time a raider glanced his way, testament to the hunting prowess bred within his kind.

<Be careful, Beck,> she whispered. <Be very, very careful.>

* * * * *

The raider named Nev shoved Chilters toward Terrance and the other two medics. She stumbled forward, and George jumped to catch her before she fell. His movements caused the band of marauders to stiffen and swing their weapons to the man's head.

Terrance raised his hands in a placating gesture. "He was just catching her," he assured them, making an effort to pitch his voice in a calm, unassuming tone.

<No one make any sudden moves,> Kodi advised, sensing the same tension, almost desperation, emanating from their captors. <These guys look a bit trigger happy.>

Terrance was relieved to see the three medics nod slightly in assent.

The raiders closed ranks, tightening their ring around those from the *Eidolon*. Their leader, standing shoulder to shoulder with the one called Nev, had just ordered McCone to open the airlock when Terrance heard Logan connect to the net.

He heard Marta whisper her caution to Beck, and his focus

snapped to the pin identifying the cat's location. He felt a flash of fury at Logan's use of the uplifted animal.

<He's going to get the little guy killed,> he raged at Kodi as he tracked the cat's progress.

<Focus,> Kodi cautioned, and then Terrance sensed a momentary but rapid exchange between Kodi and Logan, before Logan spoke.

<Okay, people, I need you out of my line of fire. Ease away from the airlock if you can. Be prepared to drop on my mark.>

Terrance was nearest to the nose of the shuttle, which placed him within arm's length of the two nearest raiders. Based on Beck's path, the cat had instinctively judged them to be the alphas of the pack and had made them his primary targets.

Recalling Logan's instructions, Terrance began to shift his weight away from the airlock, but the leader must have come by his shabby GSC jacket legitimately, for the pistol in the man's hand swung unerringly toward Terrance.

"Don't," the man warned. "All we want is your shuttle. Don't try anything, and no one gets hurt."

Terrance spread his palms wide, using the gesture as an opportunity to take another step to one side, clearing the line of fire.

Logan's voice came over the net. <Stand by, Beck. All I need is a good, threatening growl, nothing more.

A mental growl sounded inside Terrance's head and a part of him marveled at the control it took for Beck to selectively choose to do so only via Link and not audibly. Another part of him doubted the cat's willingness to comply with the AI's directive.

<Kodi, what if Beck engages?> Terrance asked privately.

<We'll do what we can to—>

Kodi was interrupted by Logan's call.

<Now, Beck!>

A loud, ripping snarl sounded behind the two men closest to Terrance, and the three medics dropped to the ground as Logan leapt through the airlock's hatch, firing. At the same time, a blur of cream and white launched itself onto the shoulders of Nev, the man nearest Terrance, who felt blood spatter his face as the man's throat was torn out.

Terrance bent to scoop up the weapon Nev had dropped, as Beck's powerful hind legs launched him onto the leader. The man whirled, knife blade glinting, as his arm swept down toward Beck. The man was a moment too late; two-centimeter-long, needle-sharp claws raked through his face, gouging into the man's eyes and slicing across his cheekbone, flaying it open.

Terrance grabbed the rifle he'd just retrieved in both hands, thrusting it upward to block the knife's trajectory; he then swung the weapon around, driving its stock into the man's solar plexus.

Beck had already propelled himself toward the next raider, when a sharp report caught him midleap. With a gurgled scream, the cat spun to the side and fell.

The shot was answered by a short burst from Logan's gun, and then the AI called out, <Secure!>

Terrance raced toward the downed animal as he heard Marta cry, "Out of the way!"

From the corner of his eye, he could see her charge down *Eidolon*'s ramp, triage kit in hand. She slid to a halt next to Terrance as he knelt by the inert form of the Proxima cat. Beck was panting, his eyes glazed. Terrance placed a comforting hand on the cat's head and was surprised to feel a rusty purr begin.

<Hurts,> the cat whispered.

"Doc...." Terrance looked up at her, a wordless question on his face.

"Let's take a look," she said, and the cat flinched. "Easy, now."

Terrance looked up as McCone pulled him aside so that the medic could kneel next to Marta and assist.

<Stars, Kodi—>

<He was told not to engage.> Logan's voice was stark, and Terrance had to bite back a scathing retort.

The AI had used the tools he'd had on hand; Terrance couldn't fault him for that. He heard a note of remorse in Logan's tone and knew the profiler was blaming himself for Beck's injury.

<*He's young, Logan,*> Kodi said. <*Younger than the youngest, wet-behind-the-ears recruit, and he made a rookie mistake. But stars, did you see what he did to those two men?*>

Terrance could feel the admiration emanating from Kodi, and admitted he felt much the same.

<*Yeah, that was some seriously badass, apex predator level action,*> he conceded. <*But, Logan, it was a risk I wish you hadn't felt you needed to take.*> He knew his tone came out harsh, colored as it was with worry, and he felt bad when he heard Logan's contrite words.

<*I…am sorry.*>

Marta looked up. "Okay, I've got him stabilized. The shot went clean through his haunch. Let's get him into the shuttle, where I can pack it with biofoam."

<*You know,*> Kodi mused as they watched the medics move the cat up into the shuttle, <*if Beck had done only as Logan had instructed, that sound he made would have been more than enough of a distraction.*>

Terrance snorted, bending down to secure one of the weapons dropped by the man Beck had blinded. <*He sure scared the hell out of me, and I knew it was coming. I had no idea how fierce a Proxima cat could sound.*>

A soft rustling in the lavender field had him spinning around, weapon raised—to come face to face with Khela Sakai.

* * * * *

<*Weapons fire!*> Ramon had reported as the transport vehicle neared the lavender field where the *Avon Vale*'s shuttle had set down.

Shit. The last thing they could afford was for one of those roaming bands of abandoned GSC soldiers to beat them to the landing site.

<Double-time it, people,> she sent, and she heard the weariness in her own voice.

Mentally, she shook it off, doing what she could to compartmentalize and focus on the immediate task at hand. The bands of soldiers had become an increasing problem, both for those in the Q-camps and for the three Marine Spec-Ops teams.

At least they *had* Spec-Ops to help combat these threats, thanks to Colonel Banks and the four teams he'd managed to smuggle dirtside.

Khela knew they owed a lot to her former commanding officer, and it hurt to know he'd fallen victim to the nanophage that Reya deSangro had purposely injected into him to monitor its proliferation.

The ripping snarl of a wildcat's cry pierced the air, and the team froze at the unfamiliar noise. Moments later, the clamor of fighting echoed through the woods.

Khela held up a hand. <*Xiao, Ramon, flank the shuttle. Lena, with me.*>

She crouched, approaching the nose of the craft low to the ground. She paused once to fist her free hand into the ground as one of Hana's memory fragments washed over her. She groaned silently in frustration, shuddering as she rode the wave of double vision and vertigo brought on by her dead partner's fragment.

Lena grasped her shoulder and continued on, sending her a quick, <*No worries, Cap'n, we got this.*>

The Marines on her team were inured to the random curveballs the phage threw at their infected team members, and they picked up the slack as needed, knowing their compromised team member would reengage when he or she was able.

Khela hated being made vulnerable. She knew it was just a matter of time before the phage would strike at a critical moment when her people needed her most.

Her vision cleared, and she resumed her crawl, joining Lena as the woman crouched, watching a few of the shuttle's crew restrain the raiders they had evidently just disarmed, while an AI in a combat frame bent to pick up the corpse of—

<*Stars, Cap'n,*> Xiao's voice drawled over the net. <*Looks like we owe someone a beer. They managed to take down Nev's group for us.*>

<*Looks like,*> she agreed. <*I'll go out and meet them. Stay put. If they've had a run-in with Nev's creeps, they might be a bit trigger-happy.*>

<*Careful, ma'am,*> Ramon advised. <*That goes for you, too.*>

Khela sent a mental nod his way, and then rose from among the lavender bushes and strode silently forward to meet them.

The man she'd tagged as their leader had been kneeling, helping to tend what looked like a wounded animal of some sort. She studied him as he rose, helping steady the animal the medics lifted. He turned his head and watched intently as they carried the animal toward the shuttle's hatch.

He was broad in the shoulders and muscular, blonde hair trimmed into a neat, almost military cut. He bent to retrieve a weapon, his back still to her, and she could tell by his motions that the man had seen battle before. She thought about clearing her throat to give herself away as she approached, but before she could do so, the man whirled, and she found herself staring down the barrel of a pulser.

She raised her dark eyes to meet his icy blue ones and smiled crookedly at the blond man. He was rather pleasant to look at, and the thought flitted through her mind that she, on the other hand, was not.

The instant he sighted on her, something shifted behind his eyes, and they switched from a cold blue to something much warmer as he straightened. She could have sworn he breathed her name as he lowered his weapon—but that was impossible. He couldn't know who she was, could he? She'd never seen this man before; she would certainly have remembered him if she had.

Lena, standing by her side, had brought up her weapon as swiftly as the man had, but when he lowered his pulser, she did not follow suit.

That had better not be pity I see in his eyes, Khela thought defiantly as she lifted her chin in challenge.

He responded with a smile as he took a step toward her, ignoring the threat Lena's weapon posed to him.

"You *are* Khela Sakai?" the man asked.

His voice was deep, his words polished, and he tilted his head in inquiry as he spoke.

"If you know that, then you know my father sent me to escort you—and the formation material we so desperately need," she added, with a glance at the shuttle, "to meet him at the bunker."

She signaled her team forward, and her Marines stepped out from behind the craft.

"We do indeed."

The voice of the man standing before her did funny things to her stomach, and for the first time in a long while, she felt the unfamiliar urge to lean on another human being and let them help carry her burdens.

The man's eyes warmed even more.

"I'm Terrance Enfield. We've come to help."

* * * * *

Terrance was surprised at the immediate attraction he felt toward the woman standing before him. He'd been intrigued by her image back on the ship, but the holo somehow hadn't captured the intensity behind those eyes, despite the shadows he saw—both in their depths and smudging the hollows beneath them. The woman looked like she'd been through hell and back, and yet she held herself with a strength that defied anything and anyone to get the better of her.

Her BDU-underlayer had clearly merged with her body—covering almost all but her hands and the right side of her hairless head at this point. From certain angles, she almost appeared to be a hominid combat drone, with the underlayer having reinforced joints and musculature.

But his gaze was drawn back to the deep pools of her eyes and the mix of dignity and steely resolve within, and he was amazed that she was unbowed by her circumstance.

He holstered his weapon as Kodi whistled inside his head. <*And I thought you were attracted to her when you saw her on the feed, back on the* Vale. *That was nothing compared to all the chemicals I'm swimming in now. Does some interesting things to this body of yours, too, I can see.*>

<*Just shut up and let me introduce you.*>

He gestured her toward the shuttle's ramp as he tapped a finger against his temple. "I'd like to introduce you to my partner, Kodi," he said, and breathed a little easier when he heard the AI's polite hello.

He thought Khela's expression might have clouded briefly, but decided he was mistaken when she gazed steadily back at him with a small smile.

"Hello, Kodi. Nice to meet you."

He saw an icon appear, inviting the woman next to him to join their shipnet as Kodi responded, <*Same here, ma'am,*>

Terrance's eyes strayed to the shuttle as they approached. "We weren't sure how long it would take you to get here, nor how hard the GSC might work to try to locate us," he explained, reaching out to finger the ghillie netting.

She merely nodded, letting her gaze sweep once again over the field in which they'd landed.

"Xiao," she nodded to one of her men, "double-check the field, please, and make sure there is nothing that will identify this area as a landing site."

"Aye, Cap'n," the man said and then turned smartly and began to jog down the length of the field.

Terrance opened his mouth to explain that had already been done, then thought better of it. *No harm in one last check,* he thought.

"What's your recommendation for the safest place to hide our shuttle?" he asked as he gestured for her to precede him up the ramp.

Khela paused, considering, her eyes sweeping the tree-ringed field. She looked up at the canopy Terrance had brought the shuttle to rest under, and nodded thoughtfully to herself.

"Nice job, getting her tucked into the trees like this," she murmured, and Terrance felt absurdly pleased at the compliment. "I'd say this is as good as any, to be honest. We're only about a fifteen-minute hike from my father's camp."

Terrance shot her a surprised look, and she shrugged. "We weren't in the camp when he notified us of your arrival. We were out delivering supplies to one of the Q-camps."

<Q-camps?> Kodi's voice queried, and Khela's mouth twisted as her eyes flashed with what he suspected was an expression of bitter rage before she suppressed it.

"The quarantine camps where the ring banished all AIs—and anyone suspected of being either a carrier or a victim," she said, her tone flat. "There are sixteen locations, ringing the outskirts of what was once Hokkaido, the city at the base of our main elevator."

"I'd like to hear more about that," Terrance said as gently as he could, able to tell that all of this was quite painful for her.

Khela canted her head as she ducked inside the shuttle's cabin. "I'll tell you," she agreed, "once we're on our way."

She passed Logan as the AI's mech frame stood guard at *Eidolon*'s hatch, and Terrance paused to introduce them.

"Logan, this is Captain Sakai, Noa's daughter. Khela, this is Logan. He's our head of security, and a former El Dorado Space Force intelligence officer."

The two exchanged nods, and then Terrance saw Khela's eyes sharpen as they landed on the sleekly-furred and now-stirring form Marta was bent over.

"That's Doctor Marta Venizelos, and her patient there is Becquerel. 'Beck', for short," Terrance informed the Marine.

<Am **not** short,> the cat grumbled as he lifted his head and struggled to sit.

Khela's startled eyes flew to Terrance, and he chuckled as he knelt next to the cat.

Glancing up at her, he added, "Beck's been uplifted. Although," he turned to glower at the injured animal, "after what he just did, I seriously question his intelligence. What were you thinking, buddy?" he asked, knuckling the top of the cat's head.

The cat released a sound that was halfway between a growl and a purr as he butted Terrance's hand. <Was hunting bad people.>

"Well, no more of that, you understand?"

<Logan said,> the cat muttered, and Terrance slid the profiler a glance as Marta shot Logan a scowl.

"Yes, he was conscripted, against my better judgement," the doctor retorted, reaching once more for Beck, who yipped and twisted as she resettled the regen gel pack over his flank. "No walking about just yet, understood?" she remonstrated the big cat.

<Itches.> The cat's grumbled complaint startled a short laugh out of Khela.

Terrance sent her a commiserating smile. "Takes a bit of getting used to," he admitted, standing and gesturing to the rest of the team. "The rest of these fine folks are medical volunteers who offered to come and help your father."

Khela nodded a greeting to George, McCone and Chilters, and then moved closer to Terrance to make room for them to pass, as the medics went to grab packs from the shuttle's storage area.

"We have the formation material your father requested," Marta informed Khela, as she rose from where she'd been kneeling next to the cat.

"Yes," Terrance agreed, indicating the packs the medics now held. "We'd like to deliver it to him as soon as possible. I know how desperate he's been to get his hands on this, and we have some questions I hope he can answer for us."

"Yes," Khela said, her face darkening, "I'm sure you do." She gestured to one of her men. "Xiao will show you the way to our ground transport." She glanced down at Beck. "Will you all be coming, or will some remain here?"

"We'll all join you," Terrance said, getting a nod of agreement from Logan. "Logan will secure the shuttle and monitor it from a distance. Given how close we are to the camp, no one should be able to breach the craft before Logan is able to stop them."

Khela hesitated, glancing around her and then over to the AI's mech frame. She nodded once and then moved to descend the ramp.

Terrance's eyes followed her departing figure; when he turned back to Beck, he caught Marta looking at him with a knowing expression on her face.

"What?" he asked, and then held up a hand. "Nevermind; not sure I want to know what you're thinking."

Marta winked, but then her expression turned solemn as she reached over and patted his forearm. "We'll do what we can to heal her." She looked over at her team. "To heal *all* of them," she amended, and the rest of the medics nodded in agreement.

<Nighttime's wasting,> Logan said. <We have a transport to catch.>

The three medics hefted their packs and marched down the ramp, and Terrance raised a brow, glancing down at Beck.

"Any thoughts on how this guy should be transported?"

A wicked smile slid onto the doctor's lips, and she gave a languid wink.

Terrance sighed as he looked down at the Proxima cat. "I suppose that means I have to carry you around again," he said, and chuckled as Beck's ears pricked forward and the cat shot him an eager look.

Leaning down, he gathered the cat up in his arms, taking care not to jostle the injured leg.

"Let's go meet some resistance fighters, shall we?"

ENFIELD GENESIS – TAU CETI

ENEMY OF THE STATE
STELLAR DATE: 09.11.3246 (Adjusted Gregorian)
LOCATION: Offices of Planetary Security
REGION: Ring Galene, Tau Ceti

The contrast between the derelict vibe that had plagued Franklin City, and the clean, well-lit and maintained interior of the planetary services building was striking, both at street level and in the lower levels where he'd been escorted.

As the lift doors slid open, Jason was faced with another incongruity: here, in this bottommost level, nano was clearly in use. He could see it in the powered armor the soldiers guarding the far entrance wore, in the biolocks of the weapons they held, and in the flash of reflected light off the nearest soldier's optics as she turned a hard stare his way.

After being forced through another decontamination regimen to ensure no nano remained on or within him that could potentially corrupt their headquarters, Jason was escorted into a war room that reminded him of *Avon Vale*'s bridge.

The first thing he noticed was that the soldiers guarding this level were augmented, unlike the ones who had escorted him here from the spaceport. They eyed him as if they expected him to kamikaze his way into Henrick's presence any moment.

<Looks like our acting president's squirreled herself away with her own augmented detail down here,> he sent. <I suspect they have no problems using nano, either.>

<Interesting. We'll— and keep scanni— alista's en rou—>

The comm signal began fading, as if sensors had detected the transmission and were rolling through various frequencies in order to fully jam the signal. Landon's voice cut off at the same time one of the soldiers standing guard at the door straightened abruptly and shot him a sharp glance.

She raised one arm and beckoned to him with the first two fingers of her hand. As she did so, the soldier standing behind him shoved him roughly between the shoulder blades, encouraging him to move forward. Jason complied.

The doors swung open, and he was treated to the sight of an ornate office, similar to those he had seen in Parliament House back on El Dorado. The woman sitting behind the polished wooden desk disregarded his presence, a power play he knew well from back home. She appeared to be fully engrossed in the study of the plas sheets in front of her.

She sat ignoring him for several minutes, and then finally set the plas sheets down, shoving them to one side as she sat back in her seat and regarded him with a stare.

"So you're the Proxan from the *Avon Vale*," the woman murmured, studying him like she would a pile of excrement she'd inadvertently stepped into.

Jason responded by settling into a sloppy form of parade rest, a smirk playing on his face as he remained silent, waiting her out. Given that Lysander—the AI who was now prime minister of the Alpha Centauri system—had practically raised him, Jason was inured to political games like the one Ann Henrick was playing now. After a long moment fraught with icy disapproval, the woman spoke again, her voice holding an edge of impatience.

"Jason Andrews, I presume?"

Jason's smirk grew as he changed his stance slightly, affecting an attitude of indolent carelessness. "At your service, ma'am," he said in his most laid-back, freighter-pilot-for-hire drawl.

He saw a flash of irritation cross her face, and snorted mentally. Now her expression reminded him of the look his sister would give Tobi when the Proxima cat tracked muddy paws all over her clean floors.

"You were told not to approach the planet," Henrick's voice held censure, and Jason cocked an eyebrow, his expression turning blank.

"I have no idea what you're talking about," he said, and the woman seated across from him gave a derisive snort.

"A ship was detected entering Galene atmosphere a few hours ago," the acting president said, leaning back in her chair. "I would be very surprised indeed if any of those under quarantine down on the planet had the ability to pull off something like that."

Jason shrugged. "Don't think I can help you out, there," he said, sounding careless. "You'd know a lot more about your planet's capabilities than I would."

Henrick rose, and Jason saw a door behind her slide open.

"Be that as it may, Mister Andrews, I now find myself questioning your motives toward Ring Galene. As such, I will have to ask you to remain our guest until we can be assured that you pose no threat to the good people of Tau Ceti."

"Now wait just one minute," Jason protested, his voice heated. "I'm a citizen of Alpha Centauri and a representative of Enfield Holdings." He stepped forward, planting both palms on Henrick's desk, and leaned toward her, anger evident on his face.

His actions caused the two soldiers who had just entered to raise their weapons, targeting him in their sights.

Jason made a show of carefully raising his hands and stepping back, his eyes intent on the woman and not on the polished surface of the desk where he'd just released a passel of reconnaissance nano.

"I was invited here by *your* people to discuss potential trade opportunities," he continued in a calmer tone. "If this is how you feel, I'll just inform the *Avon Vale* that Galene isn't interested in establishing trade, and we'll be on our way. I bet Eione would *love* to have exclusive access to our tech."

"We'll see about that." She shook her head and gestured to the two soldiers. "These people are here to escort you to our medical laboratory for a brief examination." She smiled, the expression predatory, as the soldiers rounded the desk and one grabbed him by the arm. "We can't risk introducing a foreign contaminant into the general population; you understand. We just need to ensure you are no threat to Ring Galene, and then we can discuss trading for your stasis technology."

Foreign contaminant. What a load of—

Jason bit off the thought, realizing that she hadn't said they would discuss 'trade' but *'trading'* for the stasis.

*Trading **me**?*

He hesitated, thinking to call her on it, but then decided to orchestrate one last stall tactic as an opportunity to insert more nano into the room. He allowed them to move him into the lift, but before its doors could close, he whirled and slapped a hand out to keep it from closing. While their attention was drawn to that action, he placed his other hand on the lift's control panel, careful to allow his ring finger to make contact.

"Wait," he blurted, feigning panic as he ordered the nano to spin a filament deep into the conduit that fed from the panel into their main node. "I need to contact my ship. They'll wonder what's going on. At least let me contact them—"

Henrick cut him off with a wag of her finger. "Safety first, Mister Andrews. Don't worry; our people will contact the *Avon Vale* for you."

She nodded to the soldiers, who pulled him forcibly away from the lift doors so they could shut.

Jason barely noticed; his entire focus was on controlling the nanofilaments he'd just spun, directing them to hack into the building's network. It would take a while, but he thought he'd been able to deposit enough to manage it. It was all he could do for the moment.

He let himself sag back against the lit wall as his mind raced, and he sized up the two soldiers escorting him.

Examination? Like hell. Not going to happen.

* * * * *

The four-member third-shift bridge crew sat around Landon as he pondered the information coming to him from the three teams, balancing it against all the information he was stripping from what news and data feeds still existed in Galene nearspace.

"Sir?" Hailey, the Enfield woman operating comm, called out. "I have an incoming communication from the FSTC."

"On the holo, please," he instructed, and Hailey nodded, turning to face the holotank, along with the three other crew as the image of the blockade was replaced by the seal of the Federated States of Tau Ceti.

A moment later, a woman in a severe suit stared out at him from behind a utilitarian desk. She nodded in greeting.

"*Avon Vale*, we apologize for the lateness of this message, but your own was routed incorrectly on our end. We want to make you aware of some reports that have recently come into our hands regarding Ring Galene and Acting President Henrick." She shifted, and her lips thinned as she continued. "Please exercise care in your interaction with those currently in power on the ring. It is our understanding that Henrick has enacted practices that extend well beyond martial law. We've been told that the government there has begun to absorb privately-held companies, appropriating their technologies and IPs as 'properties of the state'."

Landon saw Hailey exchange a worried look with the man at the scan console, as the FSTC woman leaned in toward the holorecorder. Clasping her hands before her, Landon saw clear concern in the woman's eyes as she continued.

"I understand the company that founded your journey— Enfield Holdings—is in possession of a novel new stasis tech. Please make the corporation aware of this threat and tell them we advise they proceed with caution, if they intend to engage in business dealings with Ring Galene." A grimace passed briefly across the woman's face as she added, "Many of the local companies here on Eione have found their businesses seized by

Ring Galene, their credit accounts frozen, and their property confiscated."

The FSTC representative hesitated, and her concern seemed to turn into something deeper.

Disquiet, Landon thought. *Unease, maybe.*

Glancing off to one side and then back again, she toggled something on her desk, and her image shrank into a corner of the holo, to be replaced by a dossier of another.

"In addition, we've received some disturbing news suggesting that Acting President Henrick has charged this person, a scientist by the name of deSangro, with coming up with solutions for the nanophage using all means at her disposal." The woman's face in the lower corner appeared pinched, as if the news were especially unpalatable. "If our sources are to be believed, deSangro has violated interstellar humanitarian law, as well as the Phobos Accords. She has experimented on humans and AIs—both infected *and* uninfected."

The woman's gaze pierced through the holo, and Landon found himself gripped by it, his mind seized by the potential atrocities the deSangro woman might commit.

"If Henrick gets her hands on any of your people, she might use them as collateral to get what she wants from Enfield." The woman pursed her lips, and then reluctantly concluded, "And if she thinks someone outside the Tau Ceti system might be worth studying, that individual might find him or herself in deSangro's hands—and that would be *most* unfortunate."

The FSTC representative apologized once more for the tardiness of this warning, but Landon hardly heard her draw her transmission to a close as his mind raced through possible doomsday scenarios.

"Status of our comm connections?" he demanded of the comm officer.

"Five by five with *Eidolon* and *Mirage*," Hailey said. "However, I have been unable to reestablish a connection with Jason since

Henrick's office jammed it. Wait— There's a message coming in from Henrick's office," she interrupted herself sharply, and Landon felt the console beneath his frame's hand give as his grip left an indentation in it.

The woman's next words had him shooting engineering an urgent missive to drop everything in order to expedite the weapons deployment.

"They just announced they're holding Jason in custody as a possible enemy of the state."

* * * * *

<...holding Jason hostage.>

Landon's update came over the *Sable Wind*'s combat net as the AI relayed the FSTC's warning, and Calista exchanged grim glances with Jonesy at the words.

<Understood,> Tobias responded.

Shannon's avatar shot the Weapon Born a sharp look, silver eyes narrowing. <We're getting him back,> she stated flatly.

"You can bet on that one," Calista muttered.

She was already in motion, stripping out of her flight suit as she reached for the latch to *Sable Wind*'s weapons locker.

<You can indeed, lass, and I'm coming with you.> The AI's voice was firm. <Jonesy, get the battle frame ready for me, if you will? And while the lass is kitting up, if you wouldn't mind, I could use a ride over.>

Calista breathed a silent 'thank you' to the Weapon Born as Jonesy nodded.

"Sir, yes sir," he said, "let me get the captain started, and I'll be right over."

Having backup is always preferable to going it alone—despite Jason's tendency to do otherwise, she thought sardonically.

She moved a bit to give Jonesy room, and the engineer reached past her to pull down a sealed container. When she sent him a questioning look, he popped it open and handed her a pair of stretchy black bands that reminded her of the nano wristbands she wore to keep sweat off her weapons when she practiced Kai-Eskrima. She fingered them and then pushed her hands through them, settling them just above her wrists.

"Like this?" she asked, and Jonesy nodded. "Okay, I'll bite. What are they?"

Jonesy grinned and opened his mouth to explain, but Shannon beat him to it.

<Wearable Elastene. They're filled with various forms of nano, with plenty of room left over for you to shunt yours inside the cuffs so that you can remain undetectable and appear to be 'nano-free' if you find yourself being actively scanned.>

"Here's a pair for Jason," Jonesy said, handing her another set.

She tucked them inside a compartment embedded in the powered armor awaiting her on the rack, before turning and backing into it.

"Tell him Q sent it," he called over his shoulder as he sealed his flight suit and headed to the airlock to retrieve Tobias.

Calista shot him a puzzled look, but didn't waste time pressing him for an explanation.

<Landon,> she heard Tobias call back to the *Avon Vale* as she grabbed a spare lightwand for Jason and tucked it into one of the weapons slots on her armor. <Can you see if the Vale *has records from the FGT worldships* Voyager *and* Starfarer? *I assume that Captains Franklin and Tomlinson used the same template to build their respective rings, but confirmation would be appreciated.*>

Calista paused, looking sharply down at where *Mirage* was mag-clamped to the belly of *Sable Wind*, as if she could see through the deck and into the ship. "Tobias, what are you thinking?"

<*I'm thinking, lass, that we can breach Ring Galene in the same way Landon and Logan gained entrance to the Norden Cartel's operation back on El Dorado,*> the Weapon Born responded. <*Our scans have already shown that this ring has spires stationed periodically along the outer skin,*

just like the one back in Alpha Centauri; I'm betting that most of the lower levels are just as uninhabited as the ones on your ring back home.>

Landon's response came a moment later. <*Rigel Kentaurus was a much shorter trek for* Starfarer, *and it left to terraform El Dorado fifty years before* Voyager's *keel was laid, so Ring Galene should have at least as much unfinished area as El Dorado.>*

"Then we can use those spires' lifts to gain access," Calista said, nodding in approval.

<*Yes,*> the AI replied, passing the schematics from the *Vale* to the team's combat net. <*And take a look; provided no changes were made between the ring's schematics and its actual fabrication, there's a spire very near to the pin Jason dropped for Henrick's headquarters.>*

Calista looked at the spire Landon had highlighted on the drawing. As she studied it, the AI traced a line from it to the pin denoting Jason's location.

<*I just told engineering to put all hands on adapting those nukes and MFRs into additional weapons,>* Landon continued. <*Avon Vale doesn't have the ablative armor a destroyer might have, and our defensive weaponry is limited to our lasers and point defense kinetics, but our 'surprise packages' will deliver a decent offensive payload if needed.>*

Calista smiled in grim satisfaction. "Those surprise packages were a stroke of genius, Landon. I like the devious way your mind thinks."

She turned as the airlock cycled once more, admitting Jonesy with Tobias's isolation chamber. She relieved him of it and turned to access the battle frame, opening Tobias's case and resettling the AI's cylinder inside.

<*It's nice to think* **something** *good came from the mess Mendoza made back at Rigel K's heliopause.>* Landon's avatar shrugged off her compliment, but something in his tone told Calista the AI wasn't nearly as blasé about the Mendoza incident as he let on. <*I promised you they'd be modular and easily disassembled if we found out we didn't need them—and they are. We'll recover them after the fact, if things don't go sideways on us.>*

<Always better to be safe than sorry, lad,> Tobias's voice reassured him, as Calista finished hooking him up and he brought the battle frame online. *<It might just be the leverage we need to get through all this.>*

"Speaking of...what are we waiting for, Tobias?" Calista said as she straightened and settled the armor's helmet over her head, checking its atmospheric seal. "Let's go get our guy back."

TRIAGE CAMP

STELLAR DATE: 09.11.3246 (Adjusted Gregorian)
LOCATION: Triage Camp, Zao Mountains
REGION: 150 kilometers from Hokkaido, Galene

The various tents and prefab buildings that comprised the triage camp were hidden amongst trees and nestled in the crevices of rocky outcroppings at the base of the Zao Mountains. The people that Terrance could see appeared exhausted and worn, the area having a battlefield feel to it that he didn't like.

Khela stopped at a camouflaged tent and ducked her head inside, and he could hear the murmur of another woman's voice answering her query. Khela stepped back to let a petite figure dressed in scrubs exit the tent.

The woman had quick, dark eyes in a tanned face, and as she scanned the crowd of newcomers, they settled on Terrance.

"Noa will be joining us shortly," she informed him as she approached. "I'm Dominica."

"Doctor Gonsalves, Galene's Surgeon General," Khela's voice interspersed quietly.

The doctor threw her a sharp look. "*Former* Surgeon General," she corrected, and then looked past Khela as something caught her attention.

Terrance turned, following her gaze, and they saw a man exit a cleft in the mountainside and stride toward them.

<Noa Sakai,> Logan sent quietly over their combat net, and Terrance could hear the undercurrent of anger in the AI's mental tone.

<Indeed,> he replied. <Let's deal with the immediate need first, before we go bashing heads about the AIs we've come to free,> he cautioned, and felt Logan's reluctant agreement.

The man approaching them was clearly related to Khela; he had the same slightly tilted eyes and high cheekbones, although in the daughter they were more delicate. Terrance assumed that when Khela had still possessed hair, it too would have been a glossy black, although not likely winged with grey at the temples, like on the man stopping before them.

Noa glanced first at the large Proxima cat Terrance held in his arms, and then sketched a small bow, his serious eyes meeting Terrance's as he spoke.

"You honor us with your visit, and with your gifts. I am Noa." He turned to gesture toward his daughter, and Terrance saw an old pain flash briefly in the man's eyes as they looked her way. "I believe you've met Khela?"

"We have. Thank you for sending her to guide us. I'm Terrance Enfield. It's a dangerous world you have here."

Noa gave a brief nod. "Mister Enfield. It is a great pleasure to meet you in person, as well as your associates."

Terrance nodded toward Logan and Marta and introduced them, along with Marta's three medics. Then, raising his occupied arms slightly, he added, "and this is Beck, one of the uplifted Proxima cats aboard the *Avon Vale*. He was wounded in an engagement with a small band of marauders who thought to take our shuttle when we landed."

<*M a **hero**,*> the cat slurred, nictitating membranes half covering his eyes as he bared his fangs to the Galene man in a sloppy grin.

The feline flopped his head back down, as the mednano interfacing with his internal systems was making him a bit loopy.

To Noa's credit, the man hardly blinked at Beck's proclamation as he turned to Khela with a searching look.

His daughter nodded. "Nev's band," she explained. "But they've been neutralized."

"So tell me, Doctor Sakai, Doctor Gonsalves," Terrance began. "What needs doing in order to resolve the nanophage situation? We've brought formation material, but given the story your daughter shared on our way here, I don't see how your colloidenes will have time to effectively counter the phage, if the GSC is EMPing the Q-camps on a daily basis."

Dominica compressed her lips but kept silent as Noa shook his head. "You are correct, Mr. Enfield; I have been unsuccessful so far in convincing the ring that we have a cure."

Logan's frame shifted, and the Galene scientist glanced over at him in question.

"If they're using the nanophage as a reason to remain in power, then no. You won't be successful in convincing them," the AI told him.

Dominica's face pinched, and Noa nodded slowly. "So what do you suggest?" he asked.

The profiler swiveled his frame, sweeping the camp with his optics.

He reached out to Terrance privately. <We need to engage the GSC at the elevator and stop the strafing runs. It's the only way.>

<I know,> Terrance replied. <Based on what little you've gleaned about the Galene Marines, do you think these people can do it? The Eidolon can slip past the GSC's screen and drop the troops inside the base, but these soldiers are the ones who will need to neutralize the enemy.>

Logan's response was delayed by a microsecond, and Terrance knew the former intelligence officer was evaluating the data one last time before sending him a decisive mental assent.

<Yes, it can be done.>

<Very well. Let's make it happen.>

Terrance turned to Marta and held Beck out for her to take as he asked, "Noa, would you have some place where we might discuss this privately?"

The man before him inclined his head and gestured to the slit in the mountainside. "If you don't mind going through our decontamination process, there are a few people who are waiting to meet you."

* * * * *

Two AI frames met Terrance as he stepped through the air-gapped sandbox and into the bunker. The first one stepped forward with a welcoming gesture.

"Terrance and Kodi, I recognize you from the comms Noa exchanged with the *Avon Vale*. And you are Logan, correct? Welcome to our temporary abode. I'm Bette, and this is Charley."

Charley nodded to Terrance and Logan as Noa joined them, sealing the airlock behind him.

"Come on in and have a seat." The AI glanced around with an expression of mild dismay, as if he'd just noticed their utilitarian surroundings. "I apologize for how sparse our accommodations are; when Noa and I designed it over a decade ago, we didn't spare much thought for creature comforts, I'm afraid."

"*You* designed it?" Kodi's voice sounded sharply from Terrance's suit, and Charley nodded.

"Noa and I feared we might need it, after the first event that caused the Matsu-kai to arrange for our purchase." The AI grimaced at the word, and Terrance saw Noa flinch slightly.

"About that—" Terrance began, but Bette held up a hand to forestall him.

"Please, sit, make yourselves comfortable, and then we'll talk. It's not what it seems. Although," she shot a glance at Charley as they led their guests to a cozy alcove set with a low chair and ringed with plump cushions, "we certainly wouldn't mind if you had a solution for the remnant code left behind after Noa removed our shackles. Whatever the Norden Cartel used on us seems to have been updated since the Sentience Wars."

<*It was,*> Kodi confirmed, as Terrance crossed his legs and lowered himself to a cushion. Noa did the same across from him. <*And if I may exchange tokens with you, I can send you the packet now.*>

Charley nodded, and an icon appeared over Terrance's Link.

He saw Kodi accept and sent the anti-shackling program packet over to the AI as he turned his attention back to Noa.

"Although we're happy to see Bette and Charley freed, it doesn't excuse what you did, Mister Sakai. Abducting people, engaging in sentient trafficking—"

Noa's face remained expressionless, but even Terrance could see the pain in the man's eyes.

Charley interrupted him. "No one understands this better than I do, I can assure you." The AI glanced over at Logan. "I'm from Sol; the child of a Weapon Born and a multi-nodal AI. I participated in the last vestiges of the Second Sentience War."

Terrance felt Kodi's attention suddenly sharpen at that, and saw Logan's frame arrest its action. He felt something akin to amazement and received the impression of immense respect emanating from the AI inside his head as Charley continued.

"Noa was forced to acquire us by agents too powerful for him to gainsay, in a situation beyond his ability to counter. He has been transparent to us in all things, and his first act upon our arrival was to free us. It was our choice to remain with him and assist his efforts." He glanced over at Bette. "Truly, if not for Noa, at this point, Galene would be beyond help, and we would be dead."

Silence fell between them, and then Logan's voice broke in.

"Assuming Galene is not beyond help, we need to saturate the Q-camps with your colloidenes; the only way to do that successfully is to stop the GSC's strafing runs. We'll need to overpower their forces in Hokkaido and take the elevator."

Charley nodded. "I came to the same conclusion. You plan to use the Marines for this?"

Logan nodded. "Yes. Who is their leader?"

"I am," Charley said. "Well, technically, I've been coordinating their efforts with the remnants of Galene's Congress, scattered throughout the Q-camps. But it made sense for them to have a unified reporting structure."

Logan's frame leant forward. "Do you have any intel you can

share with us on the numbers we'll be facing? How many spacecraft, personnel on site on the base side of Voyager spaceport?"

Charley nodded, and Terrance's Link pinged as an icon appeared for a document entitled 'GSC-Voyager'.

He saw both Kodi and Logan access it on the combat net, and then a moment later, felt a buzzing sensation indicating that the AI was rapidly turning over ideas in his mind.

"Charley," Logan said, and there was a speculative, anticipatory flavor to his words. "You said your parents were Weapon Born *and* multi-nodal...."

Terrance sensed a predatory thrill from Kodi as the AI added, "Just how many spacecraft do you think you can operate at one time?

INFILTRATION
STELLAR DATE: 09.12.3246 (Adjusted Gregorian)
LOCATION: Offices of Planetary Security
REGION: Ring Galene, Tau Ceti

Timing would be critical. Calista knew that most captains would have stayed behind with their ship to coordinate the three teams' movements, but Landon was more than capable, and the team had known better than to try and stop her when she declared she would be the one to go after Jason.

Thanks to Landon, their breach would be timed to coordinate with Terrance and Logan's actions at the planetside spaceport. Calista settled the shuttle gently on the landing pad outside the lowest entrance to the spire that jutted from the backside of Ring Galene and prepared to wait for Landon's signal.

Shannon piloted the fighter remotely, keeping it at a hover as it maintained station alongside the spire. Calista grinned as she mentally readjusted 'up' in her mind as the ring's 1g of centripetal force began acting upon her as *Mirage* touched down on what she had heretofore been thinking of as the underside of the pad. The ring loomed above her, a giant mass of angled, silvery-grey surfaces.

She unstrapped herself from the pilot's cradle—a slightly more difficult thing to do in full combat armor than it was in her usual flight suit—and made her way back to the shuttle's airlock to join Tobias, just as Landon signaled them to proceed.

<*You ready?*> she asked, and Tobias nodded assent. <*Ship's yours, Shannon.*>

The engineer sent her a virtual thumbs-up. <*Good luck. We'll be monitoring from here.*>

As the hatch opened, Calista and Tobias walked down the ramp onto the pad and strode quickly to the airlock that would admit them to the spire's lift. It opened obediently as they approached.

<Nice touch,> she murmured to Tobias, and the Weapon Born's avatar sketched a small bow in her mind. She rechecked her weapon's status as the lift ascended up into the ring. *<Level eleven, correct?>*

<Yes.> Tobias sounded certain. *<Hold when you get there, and I'll do a quick scan for activity on that level.>*

With no one in evidence, Calista unslung her rifle and held it level as she waited for Tobias to give the ready signal. As they exited the lift, she kept the rifle on a continuous sweep through the air—a practiced move she'd acquired in combat training decades ago—as she slowly advanced into a vast, cavernous space. Blinking, she adjusted her optics to display the full spectrum of EM, and saw a warren of pipes spring into being before her—some registering the icy chill of nearby space, while others carried the signatures of electronic and magnetic currents.

Tobias came to a stop next to her, feeding her a detailed map, which she set as a visual overlay on her HUD. *<Planetary Security is one-point-five klicks ahead, and its lowest level is two levels above where we are now,>* he reported, highlighting a spot near an NSAI node.

Between it and them was nothing but bare, wide-open ringdeck, with the occasional massive spar that formed some of the main structural supports to the ring. Nothing much to provide cover, should they need it.

<No indication they have proximity sensors down here?> she asked as they began their advance.

Her eyes snagged on the nearest spar, and her gaze followed it up to see a narrow filigree of catwalks ringing the spar where it met the overhead, dozens of meters above her.

<There are automated ones, but Shannon and Jonesy managed to override them—easily, with their diminished technical capabilities,> Tobias assured her. *<We're about as invisible as we can possibly be.>*

She nodded, and they continued their measured pace, studying the node tower as they approached, noting that it had more structure built around it than in other areas.

<This feels more lived-in,> she commented, taking in the bays built into its structure and the increased EM activity surrounding it.

<It does,> Tobias conceded, <but it's still nothing to worry about. Not unless you were to call for that lift. It's the one that feeds into Planetary Services; they have active scan on that.>

She eyed the lift as she approached it. <So we do this the hard way?> she queried, and the Weapon Born chuckled.

<Aye, lass. Follow me; there's an access panel beside the lift that will get us into the shaft. From there, we can use the ladders built into its sides to climb up to our level.>

Calista nodded, and they made their way into the shaft and up the rungs of the ladders welded into the walls.

As they approached the lift doors to their level, Tobias halted. <Now then,> the Weapon Born murmured as he sent a passel of nanofilaments weaving their way through the seam of the lift doors. <Let's see what they have waiting for us on the other side....>

* * * * *

The soldiers propelled Jason from the lift, marching him down a short corridor and into the clinically cool environs of Henrick's medical sector. As they entered, he took mental inventory of the space. He saw an array of medical bays, rooms that branched out from the central area that had been set up as the nerve center for deSangro's research. They stood open, and in their door frames, he could see flashing lights indicating ES fields in use, restraining those housed within, as well as providing deSangro with an unimpeded view of her subjects.

There would be no privacy afforded to those patients. It made the entire complex feel like an oversized specimen case, rather than an infirmary.

Off to one side stood a tall, spare woman he assumed was Reya deSangro. Her hair was pulled back from her face in a severe fashion he suspected was done more for utilitarian reasons than for style, and she was clad in the Galene version of a standard-issue medical coat. Some sort of augmented headgear partially obscured her face, and her eyes kept flicking between its projected readout and something glittery that was spread out just beyond the ES field in the medical bay she was standing in front of.

As the soldiers dragged Jason closer, he realized she was examining the remains of an AI; the glittery material was once the lattice she must have removed from its cylinder.

Well that confirms her identity. Henrick's butcher, deSangro.

The headgear she wore added to the mad scientist persona, her concentration so complete that she remained completely unaware of their presence. It took several attempts by the soldiers to get her attention.

Finally, the soldier holding his arm hauled him between the doctor and the AI's remains, calling her sharply by name.

With a glower and an irritated "What?!" deSangro turned to face them.

"Here's your next victim, doctor. Fresh meat, just in from Proxima," the soldier leered, using her powered armor to force Jason to stumble forward several steps. "Where do you want us to stash him?"

DeSangro scowled, motioning them to one side so that she could return her gaze to the filaments that were once a sentient AI. She waved a hand at them in dismissal.

"Put him in the far bay. Just make sure you've EMPed the room first," she ordered, her voice distracted. Abruptly, deSangro's gaze sharpened and focused on Jason, and he felt like a bug under a microscope. "But check back with me in an hour or two. I'll need you to strap him into the autodoc for me." She turned away, and Jason felt a chill sweep down his spine at the coldly clinical manner in which the scientist had inspected him.

"You got it, Doc Strange," one of the soldiers muttered under her breath as she turned away, hauling Jason toward the holding cell she'd indicated. With a shove, she pushed him inside, sealing the door shut behind him.

Jason sat in the secured holding cell for the next two hours, outwardly maintaining his freighter-pilot façade, tipped back in the single chair the room provided, booted feet propped up on the table. While he appeared relaxed, his concentration was focused on directing the breaching nano he'd slapped onto the lift's control panel as they'd dragged him from Henrick's office.

He'd managed to send the nanofilaments tracing their way from the control panel back to a main node; now he was examining the node, trying to determine the best way to hack into it. While studying it, he was also monitoring the feed from the reconnaissance nano he'd embedded in Henrick's desk.

He'd heard her inform Landon that he was being held in custody pending a determination on whether or not he was an enemy of the state. He mentally scoffed.

'Enemy of the state'? Who says that anymore, outside of poorly produced, third-tier holodramas?

He nearly toppled his chair when he received a ping from Tobias.

<Stars, Tobe! Where are you?>

The AI's chuckle entered his mind. <We're here to rescue you, boyo.>

<Who's 'we,' Tobe?> he replied, settling his chair with a thump as he stood and stretched, pacing a leisurely circuit around his small cell.

<He's referring to me, flyboy,> came Calista's tart reply. <Seemed like a good idea at the time, at least.>

Jason snorted a laugh. <Yeah, thanks for that. I think. Where are you?>

<Oh, just hanging around,> she laughed, then sent him a feed from her optics as she looked down the dizzying height of several

dozen meters down a lift shaft.

<Funny, Captain. Real cute,> he said, his tone dry.

<We've hacked partway into the ring's secured network and are lying doggo in it for the moment. Can you give us an estimate on what we'll be up against in there?> the Weapon Born asked.

Jason sent him what he'd observed plus the data he'd managed to extract so far from his breach.

<There are possibly a dozen of them on this level. More above us. It'd be ideal if we could override all lift controls and lock them out. I'm somewhere here—> he sent them a location pin, *<one level above where you are. One standard office level, that is, not a ring level.>*

Tobias chuckled as Jason resumed his seat in the chair. *<Understood. You could fit an entire ten-story building inside one of these unfinished levels, boyo. I see where you are; yes, you're one story above us. Locking down the lifts won't be a problem. We do need to make a stop on our way out, though. Seems your friend, Henrick, has a few other guests.... She's holding the Joint Chiefs in cryo, three levels below you.>*

<Holy— That's ballsy, I'll give her that,> Jason murmured, shaking his head. *<So what's your plan, then?>*

<Liberating them will take more time than we have, I'm afraid. The information Shannon and Jonesy gleaned suggests she infected them with the phage and convinced them to go into cryo until she could cure them—which, of course, she never intends to do,> Tobias added. *<Best if we focus on springing you and cornering Henrick in her lair. Logan is coordinating a takeover of the GSC forces down below, and Landon has a few surprises up his virtual sleeve for the blockade. He's also working to enlist the aid of the FSTC picket if we need them. Once we have them subdued and Henrick in our grasp, I think we can work to thaw them out and hand the mess over to their own government to clean up.>*

Jason nodded. *<Sounds good.>*

<We're on our way, then. What's on this level again?>

<Medical—or their research labs, at least. They're holding me for 'testing'. Glad you showed up when you did, because no way in hell was I

going to let that happen. I—>

His door slid open, and Jason looked up to see two Planetary Security goons standing there, motioning for him to exit.

"Come on, spacer. Time for your check-up," the woman leered, and her companion snickered at what seemed a private joke between the two.

<*It's on, guys. They've just arrived to deliver me into the loving embrace of deSangro's torture device. You ready to make your move? Because I'm really not looking forward to whatever she's got planned for me.*> Jason stood, eyeing the soldiers and the flechette guns they held leveled at him.

<*Just breached the lift doors. We're down the corridor to your left.*>

Jason sent Tobias a mental nod as he walked warily toward the door.

"Think she's going to inject him with the phage right away?" the first soldier asked, "or see how long it takes for him to fight off her latest inoculation?"

The woman shrugged. "Last guy managed to make it an entire week, but that kind of pissed the doc off a bit." She eyed Jason speculatively. "Since this guy's immune system's from another star, I'll bet she gives him the full treatment—after she does all the testing, at least."

She waved impatiently for Jason to move into medical's mainspace, and he spared the area a quick glance; deSangro was nowhere to be seen, but an autodoc sat prominently in the center of the room. The soldier made a rough grab for him, jabbing Jason in the back with her rifle's muzzle.

<*Seriously? This soldier just jabbed me in the back with her flechette. If the rest of these jokers are as undisciplined in the way they handle their weapons, this is going to be a cakewalk,*> he complained as he turned and began to walk down the hall.

<*Careful, boyo. This is where the captain here would tell you not to get cocky,*> Tobias cautioned.

Jason suppressed a grin at the AI's words. But he noticed

something about the muzzle as it jabbed again into his back and he felt the weapon's barrel shift slightly; something that he intended to use very soon.

<*I believe Calista's exact words would be not to get cocky, **flyboy**,*> Jason muttered, sending Calista's avatar a wink. <*Stand by; about to engage. Are the feeds blocked on this level?*>

Tobias sent him an affirmative, and Jason slowed a bit, earning himself another jab in the back. He used it as an excuse to turn and protest and darted a glance over the soldier's shoulder to ensure the area behind her was clear. Then he complained, "Easy there, what's your hurry, anyway?"

A look at the weapon the soldier had been jabbing into his back confirmed his suspicions. He then slid his gaze to the second soldier, ensuring that he, too, held the same weapon trained on him. He frowned as he allowed himself to be prodded forward. Soldier number two actually had his finger *on* the trigger—a very sloppy practice, and he factored that in as he gathered himself to act, one eye gauging the distance between his location and the bend in the corridor ahead.

<*Engaging...**now**.*>

More rapidly than any unaugmented human could possibly move—and before either of the two soldiers had a chance to react—Jason exploded into action. Whipping around, he shoved the palm of his hand into the muzzle of the flechette rifle that had been used to prod him forward, forcing the slider back and preventing it from chambering. He ripped it out of the soldier's hands as he pivoted and ducked below the line of fire from the second soldier. He sent the rifle in his hands skidding safely out of range as he rammed his forearm against the barrel of the second weapon, deflecting the shooter's aim.

Jason's ears rang as the weapon discharged, sending a series of flechette darts up into the ceiling behind him. The short-range darts sprayed the back wall of medical, landing harmlessly as the weapon from which they came flew into the air, dislodged by his forearm block. His brain automatically calculated its trajectory and the time to intercept as his internal mednano went to work on the resulting tinnitus that the close-range discharge had caused in his ears. He slapped breach nano onto the light armor of the trigger-happy soldier with the sloppy firearm practice, and the man stilled as his armor locked up on him.

The other soldier had stumbled forward when he'd ripped the flechette from her grasp, and was beginning to recover her balance; Jason swept her feet out from under her and leapt over her to snatch the flechette out of the air before it could land.

The woman on the floor had just begun to react, reaching for her holstered pulser, when Jason dropped out of his enhanced state and placed a hand over hers.

"Don't," he warned with a small smile, removing the weapon and training it on her as he transferred a final passel of breach nano onto her frame.

She froze, joining her fellow soldier, and Jason relaxed, shaking his head in relief as the tinnitus subsided.

<Stars, but I hate how loud a firefight can be,> he complained, and was rewarded by a tart reply from Calista as she and Tobias raced through the entrance.

<Then stop getting into them.>

He huffed a laugh, shaking his head as he shot her a grin. <Well usually I don't go into a potential fight without my nanofilaments in,> he sent, mentioning the ear inserts he'd had to leave behind in order to pass Henrick's scans.

He nodded to the medical bay he'd just exited. "That's where they left me cooling my heels. Seems like as good a place as any to stash these two," he commented, as Tobias moved past him and moved the two soldiers inside.

<Which way to the despot?> Tobias asked, and Jason gestured as they exited into the corridor.

"There's another lift down here; it'll take us directly up to Henrick's domain."

"Good," Calista muttered. "Let's go kick some megalomaniac ass."

ENFIELD GENESIS – TAU CETI

SEEDING CHAOS
STELLAR DATE: 09.12.3246 (Adjusted Gregorian)
LOCATION: Voyager Spaceport and Elevator
REGION: Hokkaido, Galene

"I have the FSTC picket's flagship on comm, sir."

Hailey's announcement from the communications console cut through the quiet of the ship's bridge center, and Landon stepped closer to the holo display as he murmured his thanks.

"Don't put her through just yet. What's the current status of the *Eidolon*?"

Landon's query had the woman reconfirming the data coming in from the planet. She nodded in satisfaction and smiled at the AI. "*Eidolon* is on the move. Looks like they'll be dropping their teams at the spaceport any minute now."

"Very good," he murmured, and then he reached out to Terrance via the tightbeam network. <*The Ring team is en route to Henrick to engage. Countermeasures are seeded around the elevator and in nearspace above the spaceport,*> he reported. <*I have the FSTC on comm and a packet of intel to send them from Tobias.*>

<*Good work,*> Terrance's voice came through in response. <*We just dropped our teams. Charley will scramble the GSC ships as soon as we control the spaceport. Galene Marines will be staffing point defense; they'll take out anything that breaks past you.*>

Landon sent an acknowledgement just as the comm officer called his name.

"FSTC's getting impatient, sir. Admiral's name is Berrong. What should I tell her?" the Enfield woman swiveled from her console to look over at Landon, who turned to her and nodded.

"I'll take it now, thanks." He accepted the token the woman transferred to him and opened the channel to the FSTC ship.

<*Admiral Berrong,*> he began, <*thank you for accepting our*

message.>

<What can I do for you, Landon?> the woman said, her voice congenial but reserved, as if she feared the questions he might ask.

<I believe it's more what we can do for you, ma'am,> he replied. <We have some information you may find useful.>

The Eione woman's eyes narrowed in speculation as she stared back at him for a moment before she asked, <I assume it's the data packet I see attached to this comm?>

He nodded. <It contains all the information our team has managed to obtain on Ring Galene and Acting President Henrick's police state,> Landon explained. He highlighted the information about the people Henrick had placed in cryo stasis units. <We've discovered that she has the previous government contained within her compound on the Ring, and from what we've gleaned, they've been interred against their will.>

<Interred!> He saw the FSCT admiral's brows draw together as she shot him a sharp look. The expression on her face grew distant, and he took that to mean that she had accessed the data and was scanning it. After a moment, she nodded. <We suspected as much— well, perhaps not the cryo part, but certainly the overthrow of the previous administration. This is concerning.>

<Indeed,> Landon heard his own mental tone edge into dryness at the woman's understatement. <Please recall that we approached the ring by invitation, as a mission of mercy, and now we find our representative held hostage.>

<Hostage?> the woman's query was sharp as she shot him a look.

He pulled up a record of secured transmissions and highlighted for her the instructions sent by Henrick that outlined the intent to hold Jason for ransom in exchange for the stasis technology. He saw her expression begin to darken and knew that she had scanned the most incriminating parts of the packet.

<We don't take kindly to this kind of threat and have taken measures to protect our own,> he informed her calmly. <Given the FSTC's

charter is the safety and stability of Tau Ceti, we felt we should inform you of the situation. We would also ask for your help, both in recovering our people and in releasing the rectification colloidenes that will scrub the nanophage from the ring.>

He highlighted another icon in the packet they had sent Berrong.

<*This file includes a detailed description of the phage, its transmission vectors—the **real** and **actual** transmission vectors, not the misinformation fed to you by Henrick—and the cure the people on the planet have devised.*>

Landon's mental voice was firm. <*We assure you, the cure **does** work. We have a team on the planet who has confirmed its viability.*> He hid a mental smile at the startled look Berrong shot him.

<*How did you get past—*> She broke off and her eyes narrowed. <*You can't engage in a firefight in a neighboring star system. That's tantamount to a declaration of war.*>

Landon held up one hand to forestall her protest as he raised a single brow. <*The* Avon Vale *does not represent any government entity,*> he reminded her, <*and we are free to engage in commerce just as any other private citizen within Tau Ceti. If you'd like, I can forward the requisite paperwork, filed by Enfield Holdings over twenty years ago on both Eione and Galene. Nothing in either government precludes us from hiring out our assistance to local residents.*>

<*Are you saying you're **mercenaries**?*> the admiral spat the word as if it were an expletive.

<*I'm merely saying that we have agreed to assist those on the planet to manufacture and deploy the cure for the nanophage, using any and all means necessary to do so.*> Landon's voice grew hard. <*Up to and including taking defensive measures against anyone who might try to stop the cure's development and delivery.*>

Berrong's eyes narrowed. Before she could respond, Landon held up a hand.

<*Do you **really** want to risk having the nanophage escape the Galene area of the system and infect Tau Ceti's other habitats? Eione?*>

The woman's lips thinned, but Landon could tell she knew he was correct.

He made his tone as persuasive as he could. <*We could use some help to ensure the least number of casualties. Don't you think enough people have died already? We're not asking you to actively engage, just to act as a deterrent. If the GSC knows we have your backing, your approval, that will be enough. We can handle the rest.*>

<*What, specifically, do you want from us?*> Berrong asked.

<*If the GSC acts aggressively, warn them away. Let them see some of your picket moving toward them. Make them think about the consequences of their actions, and how they might impact Galene in a broader way than what is immediately before them.*>

There was a brief silence from the other end.

<*We'll consider it,*> Berrong said grudgingly, and Landon realized it was the only concession he would get from her.

He saw her look away from the holo's pickups as something drew her attention. Landon could clearly hear an exclamation from her command deck carry through her comm. The admiral whipped her head around and speared Landon with a glare.

<*Our scans picked up combat on the surface. You really weren't waiting for our approval, were you?*>

<*Blessing, yes. Approval, no. Frankly, this is something the FSTC should have done weeks ago.*> Landon tried for patience, and failed. <*If you're not going to stop the spread of the phage before it infects the rest of your system, we will.*>

ENFIELD GENESIS – TAU CETI

STORMING THE ELEVATOR
STELLAR DATE: 09.12.3246 (Adjusted Gregorian)
LOCATION: Voyager Spaceport and Elevator
REGION: Hokkaido, Galene

Terrance glanced back from his pilot's cradle to the Marines he could see packed into the cabin, braced shoulder-to-shoulder in their combat armor. More were crammed into the shuttle's cargo area in order to accommodate all four spec-ops teams. It was tight, but Logan had managed to fit them all in.

The *Eidolon* flew nap-of-the-earth, a tactic used to help evade detection from sensors by hugging the terrain so closely they were almost brushing against the landscape as they swept past. The shuttle flew over the Q-camps one last time, delivering intel to the various camp leaders before heading toward its final destination: Voyager Spaceport, at the heart of the city that once was Hokkaido.

<*Twelve klicks out,*> Logan announced from his starboard-facing position in the point defense cradle.

He'd opted to pilot from there, fully interfacing with the ship, his battle frame powered down for the duration and maglocked to the ship's deck. Charley occupied the flight engineer's jump seat, across from the profiler.

<*Acknowledged,*> Terrance sent over the ship's net as he manned scan and comms.

The new pilot's mods he'd asked Marta to implant at the same time she'd embedded Kodi were fully employed; today was the first time he was using them in a combat situation.

Khela shifted in the copilot's cradle, the light armor she wore contrasting with the powered armor cladding her soldiers. Terrance and Logan had witnessed a 'transient incident', as Marta had coined it, and they'd been forced to bench her, forbidding her to participate on the ground operation with the rest.

Her father had looked as if someone had punched him in the gut when he realized what his own daughter had been hiding from him. Somehow in the madness they'd all been living, he'd failed to realize that Hana had died, and that Khela's team had been covering for their leader these past few months.

Stars. Fragmented memories left over from her paired partner.

Terrance couldn't begin to imagine what Khela had been suffering—and silently soldiering through—during it all. The thought of being left stranded with disjointed pieces of Kodi's mind was unsettling. It wasn't just the disorientation and dissonance that the fragments themselves would cause; the constant reminder of a fallen comrade would be tough to take.

As if his thoughts had drawn her gaze, she shot him a look out of shuttered eyes, and he returned it with a nod, turning his attention back to the navigation plot.

<*It's hard to imagine, I know,*> Kodi sent privately, and Terrance shot him a mental look. <*Hey, I'm inside this 'meat-suit', as you like to call it. I have a front-row seat for all the hormones that spike when you look her way. Don't worry; you know you'll have plenty of time with her once we get her into the* Avon Vale's *sickbay for Marta to work on. I'd feel a bit more confident in tonight's outcome, though, if your focus was on our current situation right now.*>

The AI's voice was amused and slightly chiding, and Terrance reminded himself that Kodi had seen his share of combat as a soldier back in El Dorado.

<*You keep your business out of my hormones,*> Terrance sent sharply, then laughed. <*Think it's the pilot's cradle that causes people to spew smart-ass responses? That sounded entirely too much like Jason.*>

Kodi sent him a mildly incredulous look and Terrance sobered. <*Sorry, just nerves before the main event. I'm good. We're two klicks out, and Logan's opening the hatch. Team one is deploying…now.*>

His HUD updated with a constellation of pins as each soldier's ident appeared. Their powered armor allowed them to drop the six-meter distance onto the debris-ridden, grassy median that lined a housing row, abandoned months ago. They rolled as they hit the ground, then came up into a running crouch as they spread out to their assigned positions.

<Next drop…thirty seconds.>

This was repeated thrice more, and as the last soldier hit his target drop site, Khela straightened in her cradle, her role as overwatch now beginning. Terrance watched her direct the teams as they efficiently fanned out, working their way toward the spaceport's various hangars. Their first task would be to plant charges that could be remotely detonated in a carefully-timed sequence.

<Teams in place; stage one ready to go,> Khela informed them several minutes later, and Terrance acknowledged.

<Logan, Charley, you're up.>

The pair of AIs powered up their frames and made their way aft to the *Eidolon*'s rear ramp.

<Ship's yours,> Logan sent, handing over the controls to Terrance, who acknowledged the handover just as the AIs dropped.

Terrance banked the shuttle and lined it up for the strafing run they'd plotted, targeting the row of hangars along the edge of the tarmac and barracks just beyond. If all went well, there wouldn't be an airman left who would be capable of flying one of the Galene fighters after this evening was over.

* * * * *

Logan crested the berm overlooking the military side of the spaceport. Below, he saw two dozen craft of varying sizes, arrayed in three neat rows. His optical scan could just barely make out the heat signatures of the four Marine teams. He set his scan to sweep the area, and saw random blobs of heat that denoted clusters of humans stationed within the various outbuildings. As he watched, the Marines began planting their incendiary devices at preordained locations, then moved to cover the areas where GSC soldiers were stationed.

He switched his attention to the structure midway down the runway, looming over the other buildings. This—the spaceport tower—was his objective. He nodded to Charley, a silhouette hovering silently behind him, and then lowered his frame silently down the side of the berm. Together, the two AIs glided unnoticed from shadow to shadow as they approached their target.

When they arrived at its base, Logan scanned the structure, noting a single human standing watch in its uppermost level. Dropping a passel of breach nano into the tower's locked doors, he slid them open, and the two slipped inside.

As Charley's frame didn't have the combat capabilities his did, Logan signaled the AI to wait for his all-clear, before turning to begin his trek up the tower stairs.

* * * * *

Reggie Akawa sat in front of the spaceport's holo display, his graveyard shift halfway complete. He blinked, fighting—and losing—his battle with a jaw-cracking yawn as he shook his head and forced himself to dutifully scan the sensor return from the tower's radar array, which continually swept a hundred-kilometer radius around Voyager Central.

*Nothing. Of **course** there's nothing. Not even movement on the elevator. No cars due with shipments coming down from the ring until 0900 tomorrow morning.*

He sighed, then gave into temptation, pulling out his portable holo where he'd downloaded a game his brother had gifted him, an ancient 2-D thing Wen claimed dated back to old-Earth. Reggie had humored his little brother by letting Wen think he believed his tale, but really, what did it matter? The gift was a fun retro thing, and Reggie had found himself drawn inexorably into it.

Checking the spaceport net, he saw no one nearby, so he toggled the device on and quickly became engrossed in the game. An hour passed, and the silence of the sleeping spaceport did nothing to hinder Reggie's absorption—until a soft scraping noise sounded behind the console in front of him. He looked up from his copy of *Mortal Kombat*, right into the eyes of—

"Moloch!" he gasped, falling out of his chair as the figure on his screen morphed into a real-life visage that loomed over him.

The creature seemed to have sprung from the ether, ringed by an eerie glow of fireballs falling from the sky. Explosions reflecting in the plas windows that ringed the topmost level of the tower cast an otherworldly pall over the specter, and it advanced menacingly toward him, golden eyes glowing, reflecting off a bluish-silvery skin.

Reggie sat frozen, sprawled half-upright where the chair had dumped him, his knees bent, heels and hands pressed into the floor. He began to scoot backward on his butt, slowly, ever so slowly, but froze when the figure turned to observe him, fantastical reflections dancing across its skin from the flashes of light erupting in the distance.

<Boo,> said the towering apparition as it loomed over him.

In the low lighting used for nighttime tower operations, Reggie could just make out Moloch's signature bandolier slung across one shoulder. The beast seemed to be missing the massive chained orb he usually favored, but there was no mistaking the four sharp, metallic claws at the end of the arm that reached for him.

That movement galvanized the young GSC noncom. He shrieked in terror, crab-walking backward rapidly on his hands and heels, getting as far away as he could—and then the apparition turned from him to begin manipulating the tower controls. The moment those golden glowing orbs turned their attention away from him, Reggie scrambled to his feet. An especially close explosion did the rest, and Reggie raced from the room, his mind gibbering in terror. Years later, he still swore by the tale of his visit from the creature of the Netherrealm....

* * * * *

<Base secure,> Logan's voice sounded over the combat net. <Ship's under Charley's control and ready for your command. And one noncom, scared shitless.>

Terrance suppressed a smile and made a mental note to ask Logan about that last comment, as Khela set the teams on rotating schedules to provide ground support for Charley, manning ECM and point-defense and ensuring the base remained under planetary control.

It's nice to have an op go off without a hitch, he thought as he listened to a chorus of <Aye, Cap> and <ma'am, yes ma'am> responses filtering in to Khela from her Marines.

Terrance gently banked the *Eidolon*, sending it on a downwind. It would rendezvous at the far end of the runway, where Logan and Charley awaited extraction.

A mental shout came across the net from one of Khela's Marines operating the tower's scan.

<Blockade's scrambling ships! Time to weapons range, fifteen mikes!>

THE ELEMENT OF SURPRISE

STELLAR DATE: 09.12.3246 (Adjusted Gregorian)
LOCATION: Bridge, *Avon Vale*
REGION: Galene nearspace, Tau Ceti

"The GSC's blockade ships are on the move!"

The scan officer's cry cut through the quiet of the ship's bridge center as Landon ended his communication with the FSTC's Admiral Berrong.

Stepping closer to the holo display, he accessed the direct feed from Scan and studied it. He could feel every war game sim that he and Logan had ever practiced hovering in the back of his brain for easy reference should he need them.

"Do our comm microdrones have tightbeam lock on all our surprise packages?" he asked Hailey, and received a nod of confirmation. "Very good," he said, as scan updated the GSC ships' approach vectors.

He was pleased to note that they had correctly identified the ships most likely to respond to action at the Voyager Spaceport, as seventeen ships had begun to alter course for the elevator. That meant the tactical nukes they had carefully seeded between the ships and the planet were well-placed. The goal was for the ships to fly directly into the bombs, which were floating unseen in the black, waiting for proximity detonation.

Based on the GSC ships' vectors, the bombs needed minimal adjustment to ensure the vessels driving toward them hit the ersatz minefield at precisely the right moment.

He reached out to the nukes and nudged a few into better intercept solutions, as the comm officer tossed a countdown clock—time to intercept—up on the main holo.

"The GSC ships are powering weapons," Scan warned, just as the countdown clock reached zero, and seventeen ships intent on firing at the newly liberated Voyager Spaceport plowed into Elastene-clad tactical nukes silently awaiting them.

Dozens of nuclear fireballs bloomed in the darkness, their spherical blasts enveloping the GSC ships in light, heat, and plasma.

When the scan cleared, Landon couldn't help but nod in satisfaction as he saw that the five corvettes were gone, while the nine destroyers in the formation were venting atmosphere, their engines dead. The three cruisers were in better shape, losing air like the destroyers, but still under power.

Then something exploded within one of the cruisers, and the ship broke apart, a large chunk of its hull careening toward a destroyer that was shedding escape pods like a dog shaking wet fur.

Landon was certain that many of the destroyer's personnel were still aboard when the destroyer was hit by the debris. The impact spun the ship about, and then it tore in half, the disparate pieces losing altitude.

For a moment, it appeared as though the two remaining cruisers were going to continue their run, but then one hit another nuke and was torn asunder.

The *Avon Vale*'s bridge crew let out triumphant cries as the final cruiser sluggishly began to turn and boost away from the planet, only to hit another nuke and go dark.

Terrance's voice came through to Landon on tightbeam. <*I see that your packages were delivered.*>

<*The first volley, yes, sir,*> he informed the Enfield executive.

<*Nicely done! Charley's scrambling the GSC ships, fifteen airbreathers and thirty-five spacecraft. Sending telemetry now. We'll coordinate from down here.*>

Landon sent an acknowledgement just as Hailey called his name.

"Sir, Tobias reports Jason is freed, and the FSTC's calling us again," Hailey's eyes remained focused on her holo and her hands wove rapidly through its interface as she delivered the news. "It's Admiral Berrong again."

"Thank you, Hailey." Landon replied, accepting the token and opening the channel to the FSTC ship.

<*Admiral Berrong,*> he began, <*we're a bit busy now. I'm afraid I'm going to have to be brief. Our people are taking fire from the blockade ships attacking the planet.*>

The woman nodded. <*We're closing on the GSC ships, and will inform them that aggression against the planet will not be tolerated.*> Her tone approached sardonic as she added, <*Are there any other surprises out there that we should know about?*>

Landon shook his head. <*If you remain on this side of the blockade, you should be perfectly fine, ma'am. But if you can spare the personnel, you may want to coordinate with our people on the Ring. We've freed our man and are engaging Henrick and her guard. We would be happy to hand the entire mess over to you, as soon as you can make it there.*>

Berrong looked as if she wanted to press him for more information, but Landon noticed a second wave of GSC ships maneuvering to cover their limping and wounded sister vessels.

<*Things are heating up out here, Admiral, can you do more than just tell them that their actions won't be tolerated?*>

Berrong pursed her lips. <*After going over the data you sent from Ring Galene, I want to do everything in my power, but I need authorization to attack a member state. I'm working on it.*>

Landon nodded and sent the woman a sympathetic look—or he tried to. It was likely more on the impatient side. <*Well, let them know that the people with the tech to stop the phage are in a fight for their lives.*>

"A flight of GSC ships is shifting orbit to hit Voyager Spaceport!" the scan officer called out.

<*Let me know when you can add some muscle,*> Landon concluded and closed the connection with Berrong, then turned to the weapons officer. "How's it look?"

"Fifteen cruisers and nine destroyers, sir. Vectors indicate we'll have twenty MFRs with good targeting solutions for fusion impacts."

Landon reviewed the data, knowing that they couldn't destroy all the ships, but hoping the attack could drive the GSC vessels back once more.

"Very good. Proceed."

STANDOFF

STELLAR DATE: 09.12.3246 (Adjusted Gregorian)
LOCATION: Offices of Planetary Security
REGION: Ring Galene, Tau Ceti

Deep in the bowels of Henrick's compound, three figures raced toward the main lift that would take them to the Acting President's private office.

As Jason followed Tobias's massive battle frame, he worked to thread nano into a flechette weapon he'd taken from one of his jailers, in order to breach its biolock. He looked over as Calista tossed something his way, and snapped a hand up to catch the lightwand.

<One of the many reasons I love you, Captain,> he grinned at her, and she shot him a side-eye glance.

<Bet you say that to all the girls, in every port.>

<Only the ones who toss me light wands…and who are my captain.>

Calista groaned. <Stars, you make that sound like some sort of insult every time you say it.>

Tobias reached the lift doors first and threaded nano into the controls, overriding them and forcing them open. The darkened maw of the shaft appeared, and Tobias leapt across, his battle frame landing on the ladder's rungs with a reverberating *clang*.

<Dude, putting on a little weight there?> Jason teased the Weapon Born, as the AI began to climb up the shaft.

Tobias made a rude noise. <Left the ladder on the near side for you two,> he sent. <You're welcome.>

Jason snorted and followed him into the shaft. <We're two floors below her office; this shaft opens out just behind and a little to one side of her massively ornate desk.>

<Compensating for something, is she?> Calista's voice quipped, her tone droll. <Well, I suppose it matches her massively oversized

ambitions.>

<And her ego,> Jason added as he paused outside the sealed lift doors. <Trust me, it's about as big as they come.>

He rested his hand against the seam, but Tobias stopped him.

<Behind the lady, boyo. She has powered armor; all you have is your ship suit. Oh, and I almost forgot,> the AI added. <Calista has a present for you.>

Jason swung to one side, hanging off the edge of the ladder as Calista climbed up next to him. He turned and peered over at her.

<A gift?> he asked, <This is so sudden....>

Calista rolled her eyes as she pulled a magnetic carabiner out of her armor's chest plate and snapped it around the ladder, freeing up both hands. Popping open a hidden compartment in her upper arm, she extracted a pair of black bands.

<Here,> she informed him, her voice dry. <Q sends his regards...whatever that means. Or did Shannon say he was R? Stupid letters.>

Jason snorted and hooked one arm through a rung as he reached for the items in her outheld hand. Turning them over in his hands, he asked, <So what did our intrepid engineers come up with this time?>

<Wearable Elastene.>

At his impressed glance, she proceeded to explain how to use the bands, which he quickly donned.

<Thanks. These should come in handy.>

He settled below her, pulling the lightwand from where he'd stashed it for climbing, and readied himself for the showdown ahead of them.

<I have eyes on our tango,> Tobias announced, and a moment later, Jason received a feed showing the interior of Henrick's office.

It was empty.

<Dammit,> Jason swore. <Now what? She could be anywhere.>

<Wait one, accessing her location through their secured net.>

There was a pause, and then it was Tobias's turn to swear.

Jason had forgotten how colorful the Weapon Born could be when he applied himself.

<*Down! Now! Henrick's in the lift, and the car's descending.*>

<*Grab on, Jason!*> Calista ordered, and then used her powered armor to slide rapidly down the ladder, gauntleted hands screeching as she clamped on to brake their descent.

<*And you call **me** the thrill-seeker,*> he muttered after jolting to a stop and swinging precariously before regaining his footing on the ladder's rungs.

But they'd made it with moments to spare before the lift settled, disgorging its passenger, and then rose once more.

<*Once more into the breach, boyo,*> Tobias called out, resuming the upward trek toward Henrick's office level.

As he reestablished the feed, they saw a lieutenant and two other soldiers open the main door to the office, the wail of a distant alarm coming through the open portal.

<*Guess they discovered your escape,*> the AI said, and Jason grunted in annoyance.

<*Moves our timetable up a bit,*> Calista warned, then seeing there was no longer any reason to exercise caution with encrypted signals, reached out to the *Avon Vale*. <*Landon, we're going in hot. What's the status on the op down planetside?*>

<*They have the spaceport. We're heating up out here, too,*> Logan's twin reported.

<*Good luck,*> Tobias responded. <*We're moving on Henrick now. She just entered her office accompanied by several of her soldiers. Will update you when the offices have been secured.*>

SPACE JUNK

STELLAR DATE: 09.14.3246 (Adjusted Gregorian)
LOCATION: Bridge, *Avon Vale*
REGION: Galene, Tau Ceti

Back on the *Avon Vale*, Landon watched as a part of the FSTC picket broke off and split into two formations, half headed toward the GSC vessels in low orbit, and the other half moving toward Ring Galene.

Seems like Berrong got her permission…or she's planning to get it retroactively….

"The FSTC won't make it in time, sir," Scan warned.

"Not if those Galene bastards ignore the warnings Berrong is sending their way," Landon agreed, pacing slowly back and forth in front of the holotank.

It showed continually-updating icons of the various ships—GSC, FSTC and the Galene fighters under Charley's control. He gauged that Charley's thirty-five spacecraft would reach the battlespace in time, weighting things in their favor.

This is my job. Understand the angles, protect my people. I'm not letting the enemy get the better of me this time.

"How's the intercept plot on our MFRs?" he asked, and the scan officer sent him the telemetry for each of the twenty Elastene-clad packages that had been carefully adhered to pieces of floating detritus.

Landon was counting on the space junk in mid-planetary orbit around Galene being objects that any ship worth its salt would have automatically mapped and listed with their ships' NSAI for collision avoidance. Having been tagged thusly, they would have then been dismissed as unimportant, eliminated from the holo displays as background noise.

That is exactly what they would remain, so long as the ships left the elevator alone and didn't pose a threat to the team now in control of the spaceport. But if any ships moved to attack, they would find twenty pieces of debris speeding toward them with unexpected acceleration—for the MFRs adhered to the debris were programmed to boost instantaneously at five hundred gs toward their specified target. Given enough run-up, they'd become relativistic—though the distances weren't great enough for that, in this case.

Even so, no GSC ship could hope to evade a projectile in such close proximity and headed toward them at that speed. And, although kinetic damage would certainly be imparted by such a collision, the resulting damage when the MFRs' localized micro plasma cores overheated and their fusion engines went critical would be catastrophic.

"You're sure they won't detect our weapons, sir?" Hailey asked from the comm station.

Landon turned his head toward her and gave a small smile. "Oh, they'll detect them, all right. They see them now, in fact. They just don't know what they're looking at."

At Hailey's quizzical look, he elaborated. "Those ships are the apex predators here in Galene nearspace, and over the years, they've become complacent. Oh, the minefield will have spooked them a bit, and there's no doubt they'll be more careful as they approach the elevator, but their focus is on hidden things, things that aren't there. They'll completely ignore the things they expect to see, because they *know* that it's just so much harmless space junk."

"Looking forward to their complacency taking them out, then." Hailey's tone was grim as she stared at the holotank.

"Boost the tightbeam network's signal strength," Landon directed her. "We're not hiding anything anymore."

Hailey nodded and bent to her task, while Landon turned to the main holotank, taking a moment to review the strength of the various forces before all hell broke loose.

All told, there were one hundred and twenty-two GSC capital ships arrayed around the planet. Most were close to the ring, in positions to provide support to operations on the ground or in space beyond Galene. Of that number, there were forty-three cruisers, not counting the three that had already been destroyed in the minefield.

The FSTC picket ships had greater numbers than the Galene fleet, but not more tonnage. Moreover, they were not committing their full force to their efforts. Twenty ships were moving toward the ring, while another thirty-two were shifting their vector to pass beyond the ring toward the elevator.

Stars, they're taking their time, Landon thought.

Still, it seemed to be enough to stay the GSC's hand—none of their ships were moving to hit Voyager Spaceport.

Just as Landon was making that observation, Charley's fighters began to breach the clouds and move into position around the long strand. The appropriated GSC craft settled into an erratic patrol pattern, and it appeared as though the standoff would continue, when suddenly one of the fighters exploded.

"Beamfire from one of the GSC cruisers!" Scan announced.

<*Charley, vary your pattern more,*> Landon ordered. <*The fighters must have some sort of IFF that's helping the cruisers target.*>

<*Thought we found that,*> the AI responded, his tone tinged with annoyance. <*I'm sending up a pattern I used back in the war—just hope these scows can manage it.*>

Landon sent an affirmative response and then nodded to the weapons officer on the *Avon Vale*'s bridge. "Chief, target ten of the cruisers with our surprises. Let's see if we can get them to back off. I'd prefer not to drop too many capital ships onto the planet."

"Aye!" came the response, and Landon turned his attention to the holotank, watching as ten pieces of previously innocuous debris lurched forward, tearing through space toward the GSC cruisers.

He could only imagine the scenes on the bridges of those ships as they scrambled to maneuver out of the way. Engines were flaring, and the cruisers were moving to new vectors, firing beams at the debris all around as they boosted away from the elevator.

It would do them no good; the GSC vessels were all but stationary relative to the weaponized debris.

<Hit them, Charley,> Landon ordered the AI in the spaceport below, and thirty-four fighters boosted into space, missiles speeding away from their respective spacecrafts, corkscrewing through the black on erratic patterns toward the cruisers.

The GSC ships were firing point defense weapons at everything around them; they managed to destroy two of the MFR-accelerated chunks of debris, as well as several of Charley's missiles.

Then the remaining eight improvised MFR missiles—now travelling at over one million kilometers an hour—reached their targets.

Moments before impact, the plasma cores in each MFR overheated, and the fusion engines exploded, adding the force of a nuclear fusion bomb to the kinetic energy they already imparted.

Combined with the shrapnel from the debris, the total energy transference was immense, breaching ES shields and pulverizing hulls.

Five of the eight cruisers were torn apart, adding their own nuclear blooms as engines and weapons detonated. The other three suffered critical damage, their engines dying and leaving them adrift, easy targets for the missiles coming from the surface.

Only two of the cruisers were still operational, along with the seven destroyers escorting them. The destroyers shifted to engage Charley's fighters, while the remaining two cruisers boosted harder, nearly at their maximum effective firing range for hitting ground targets.

<You planning to do anything about those two ships?> Terrance called up. <I don't think they're coming for tea.>

<Working on it,> Landon called back. <Any chance you can lend a hand?>

<I'm at one of the surface to air batteries,> Logan joined in. <Just give me another minute.>

Landon was about to admonish his brother to pick up the pace, when the scan officer called out.

"Sir! A car is boosting down the elevator…make that three!"

With a thought, Landon expanded the view and saw three elevator cars on emergency descent toward the surface, solid boosters on each propelling them down the strand.

<Charley, I—>

<No can do, Landon. These destroyers have my fighters tied up. I'm going to try to shoot those things off with my air breathers.>

Landon gauged the speed the cars were rocketing down the lift and saw that they'd hit atmosphere in forty seconds. Once there, Charley would have mere seconds for his fighter jets to hit the cars.

He was about to wish the AI luck when suddenly every GSC ship on the spaceward side of Ring Galene began to boost toward the *Avon Vale*.

* * * * *

Terrance gritted his teeth as *Eidolon*'s holo display showed Charley's fighters engage the destroyers, both groups taking losses in space a few hundred kilometers above and to the east of the shuttle.

<Terrance, you have incoming.> Landon's voice was tinged with more than a little fear and urgency. <Three cars coming down the strand.>

<I'm timing my jets to strafe them,> Charley interjected. <But it's going to be tight…these things aren't exactly well maintained. They must have sent all their mechanics to the Q-camps.>

Khela glanced at Terrance and pursed her lips. He could tell she didn't like speaking over the Link if she could avoid it.

"The pickups will add any audible conversation to the combat net," he assured her.

"OK." She gave an appreciative smile. "Each of those elevator cars can hold sixty people. More if you cram them in. We lost Ramon, so I'm down to ten Marines. We're not going to be able to hold them for long."

<Logan, how close are you to that battery?> Terrance asked the AI.

<I'm here,> came the grim response, <but it's infected. My colloidenes are keeping me safe so far, but I'm having to run my breach through a narrow band...damn...targeting's gone. I'm trying to see if I can reprogram these little shits to fix this thing instead of build a forklift on top of it.>

<Wow, has he ever sworn before?> Kodi asked Terrance privately.

<Not that I recall...and I don't think I've ever heard him string that many words together, either.>

"All teams," Khela addressed her three fireteams. "Move to Logan's position and cover him. We're going to take off and provide what air support we can. We have to get that missile battery online, or the GSC destroyers are going to chew up Charley's fighters."

"We're taking off?" Terrance asked, glancing between Charley and Khela.

"Yes!" the pair shouted in unison, and Khela added, "If we're on the ground when Henrick's goons get down here, we're going to have a really bad day."

<I thought we already were having one of those,> Kodi said as Terrance slid into his cradle and initialized the *Eidolon*'s flight systems.

<Guess it can always get worse,> Terrance replied.

The ship came to life, and he gently lifted it off the ground, easing away from the elevator to put more room between the shuttle and whatever was inside those cars.

He was a hundred meters up, boosting away from the spaceport but banking so he could come around and provide support for Logan, when Charley cried out, "Have some missiles, you bastards!"

Through the window to his left, Terrance saw explosions high above, and all three of the elevator's cables vibrated violently as balls of fire began to fall from the sky.

"Did you hit them?" the exec asked, his voice hoarse with anticipation.

"Two for sure," Charley said, his tone less certain than his words.

As Terrance continued to circle around the spaceport, gaining altitude, the shape of an elevator car plummeted past, slamming into one of the hangars below.

Seconds later, another elevator car came down through the smoke and ash, one side torn away, and the shapes of a few dozen soldiers visible within.

Time seemed to slow as he stared at them in wonder, but then they were obscured by flares of light, and the *Eidolon*'s defense systems blared a warning.

"They're painting us!" Khela shouted.

A dozen missiles streaked out of the elevator car, just as it peeled off the cable and plummeted to the spaceport below.

Terrance barely noticed that as he banked the craft away, praying that its Elastene cladding and point defense systems would make it too hard for the shoulder-fired missiles to lock onto.

<*Our engines are too hot,*> Kodi said, <*they've latched on.*>

With a quick nod, Terrance banked left while Kodi fired the shuttle's countermeasures. The readout before him showed that all but two of the missiles had lost their lock—but no matter what he tried, those last two stayed on the *Eidolon*'s tail.

"They only have so much fuel," Khela said while jerking her finger up. "Climb, they'll fall behind."

It seemed desperate, but Terrance followed her directions, and saw with great relief that the missiles were, indeed, falling behind. He was about to thank her when out of the clouds above came the third elevator car.

Part of its side was torn away, but it didn't stop those inside from sending another six shoulder-mounted missiles their way.

Terrance clenched his teeth, spinning the shuttle into a steep dive, but it was too late.

The ship bucked and twisted as explosions blossomed in the air around them, wrenching Terrance back and forth in his cradle. Then a terrible rending sound filled the air, and the entire left side of the *Eidolon* peeled off as they plummeted to the ground.

* * * * *

"Terrance," Khela ventured as she pulled the impact foam away from the man, more worried that he might be more injured than she expected to be.

<No concern for me?> Charley asked as he pushed his way out of the foam filling the rear cabin.

"You've got a much harder shell than he does..." Khela glanced down at her body, the armor she wore over her phage-infected underlayer now also infected and attached to her. "I guess I do, too, now."

She pushed her concern for herself out of her mind as she finally reached Terrance, glad to see that he appeared unharmed.

<We're still here,> Kodi announced. <He got knocked out by the impact, but I don't see any other injuries.>

"I don't need other injuries," Terrance muttered. "I'm one big injury."

"C'mon," Khela offered her hand, and Terrance reached for it, when suddenly, she snatched hers back. "Damn...sorry. I don't want to infect you."

"Seriously," Terrance kept his hand extended. "I'm inoculated, but even if my nano can't fend yours off, Marta and your dad can fix us all up afterward."

"You have a lot of faith," Khela said with a smile.

"Yeah, and my leg is stuck, so I really do need a hand."

Charley was on the ground outside the shuttle, and he looked back at them through the hole in the ship. "At this point, bullets are gonna kill us a lot faster than the phage. That third car made it down. We need to get to Logan's position."

Khela nodded and once more extended her hand to Terrance, who clasped her wrist firmly, pulling himself forward and out of the impact foam.

A minute later, the three of them were on the ground, and Khela saw that they'd been lucky enough to crash on the military side of the spaceport.

"The surface to air battery is over there," she gestured in the direction of a row of storage buildings a kilometer away, "in a bunker just beyond those."

"Let's get moving, then," Terrance said, and she was glad to see that he checked his weapons over as they got on the move.

"Have you seen combat?" she asked, curious as to how a corporate executive from another star system ended up in this sort of situation.

Terrance gave her a lopsided grin. "A bit, yeah. Mostly I'm on the sidelines, but every so often, things get so screwed up that the front line finds me—kinda like now."

As if to emphasize his point, shots chewed into the pavement around them, causing small chunks of plascrete to fly through the air like shrapnel. The sound of weapons fire followed a few seconds later.

The group took off at a run, zig-zagging wildly as they dashed across the open ground between the ruins of the *Eidolon* and the warehouses.

A shot ricocheted off Khela's body, and she was startled by the realization that rounds hitting her armor *hurt*.

*Oh that's just great. Now my armor **feels**.*

Even so, she stayed at the rear of the group, worried more for Charley—who was somehow still maintaining control of the fighters in space above—and Terrance, who wasn't zigging or zagging nearly enough, as evidenced by the shot that struck his leg and knocked him down.

Khela angled toward him and grabbed his arm, wrenching him to his feet, half dragging him the final few meters to the dubious cover of the warehouses.

<*Gonna get loud,*> Charley warned a moment before three airbreather jets streaked by, chainguns mounted to their wings tearing through the enemy positions near the base of the elevator.

Khela had no way of knowing if they'd hit any of the GSC soldiers, but there was no way to miss one of Charley's jets getting taken out by missiles.

They ran between the warehouses, their progress made in fits and starts as they dodged small bands of soldiers, narrowly avoiding some and exchanging fire with others. The hit Terrance had taken to his leg had dented the armor just enough to make him limp slightly, but he kept pace with Khela and Charley, his gait more of a skip-and-jog than a full-on run. A minute later, they cleared the last warehouse and were treated to an unobstructed view of the bunker Logan had commandeered.

"Damn...he wasn't kidding about the nano, was he," Terrance said as they slowed.

The bunker should have been a low plascrete affair with surface to air defenses surrounding a central silo.

In theory, those features were still there, but they were obscured by the beginnings of a comm tower, a part of a radar dish, acres of network conduit, the forklift Logan had mentioned, and what appeared to be the façade of a restaurant.

Lena waved a hand from behind a low plascrete berm. "Nice of you to join us, Cap."

"Nice of you to keep my seat warm," Khela replied. "Everyone in one piece?"

"Yeah, well," Xiao said from behind a burned out truck. "I don't know which pieces of me are *me* anymore, but sure, I guess you could say I'm all 'one'."

Khela shook her head with a smile and, after assessing the terrain, directed her Marines to fan out more; given the layout, Henrick's goons would most likely come at them right up the center.

<Logan!> Terrance called out. <Where are you?>

<Around the far side,> the AI replied.

Khela followed Terrance and Charley behind the bunker to see the AI standing as close as he dared to the mass of nano, a thick strand of network cable stretching from him to the structure.

<Need one more minute,> Logan said as they approached. <Targeting systems online now. Just dealing with some obstructions.>

Overhead, four more jets streaked by, bombs dropping from their wings moments before the *crack* of the explosions tore through the air, while the earth-shaking *ka-whumps* shook the ground beneath them.

Another jet fell from the sky, and Charley glanced at Terrance. "There's another car coming down the strand, and I'm down to three jets."

"And in space?" Terrance asked.

"Not a lot better," the AI replied. "More GSC ships are on their way, and I only have ten fighters left up there."

The truck Xiao was using as cover pinged as weapons fire from the warehouses struck it. Khela turned, spotted the shooter, and fired her railgun, the rounds slamming into the enemy soldier.

"Terrance." She put her hand on his shoulder, glad that he didn't flinch. "You stay—"

Her words were interrupted by shots from behind their position, and the corporate exec spun, firing his slug thrower at a group of phage-infected, abandoned GSC soldiers moving through a row of vehicles parked just beyond the bunker. His shot struck one in the head, and Khela added her own fire, hitting another.

<Just another minute,> Logan muttered, and Khela hoped they could hold out that long.

Just then, a glint of light in the sky caught her eye, and she looked up to see a trio of GSC dropships bearing down on their position.

ACTING PRESIDENT

STELLAR DATE: 09.12.3246 (Adjusted Gregorian)
LOCATION: Acting President Henrick's Office
REGION: Planetary Security, Ring Galene, Tau Ceti

Jason and Calista took positions on one side of the lift doors that opened into Henrick's office, while Tobias was on the other. The AI counted down from three, and then triggered the doors open.

Tobias and Calista launched themselves through, both rolling to either side and coming up with weapons firing on the soldiers that were with Henrick in her office.

A lieutenant went down in the initial volley, and the other two soldiers fell back through the main entrance, firing around the doorway while the president screamed something incoherent.

Jason followed a moment later, entering in a fast, low-rolling crouch. He sprang toward Henrick, grabbing the back of her neck, where he expected her Link antenna to run.

His nano breached her skin and cut her connection just as she rounded on him, a snub-nosed flechette pistol buried in his abdomen. She curved her mouth into a satisfied smirk as her finger tightened on the trigger.

Already plunged deep into his altered state, Jason's L2 reflexes lent him an inhuman speed as he flung himself to one side. Everything and everyone around him froze in time as he watched the flechette darts wing their way across the office, tearing into the expensive woodwork.

He reached for the snub-nosed weapon, wrenching it from Henrick's hands, and the force pulverized her fingers as his enhanced strength tore the slider off the pistol, before he pivoted and threw both components at a soldier that had come through a hidden entrance next to Calista.

Jason could see the man smirk as his rifle swung toward the

Avon Vale's captain. But the GSC soldier wasn't wearing a helmet, and when the pieces of flechette pistol hit the man's head at over two hundred and fifty kilometers per hour, that smile was gone—literally torn off by the impact that also crushed his skull.

Even before the soldier's body began to fall, Jason turned back to Henrick and saw her eyes widen as the pain receptors in her hand finally got the message to her brain that she'd suffered damage.

Accurately judging that she was incapacitated—at least for the next few seconds—Jason focused on the remaining two soldiers, one of whom had just pulled out an EM grenade and was preparing to launch it at Tobias.

Jason leapt over Henrick's desk, using it as a launching point from which he catapulted himself toward the man wielding the grenade. He reached the man just as the soldier was about to lob the device. Jason slammed into him, knocking his target's hand away. It grazed the activator—and the grenade went flying.

<*Stars! Tobias! EM grenade!*>

Jason wrenched himself off the man and lunged for the grenade, whipping the Elastene bands off his hands and wrapping them around the tiny bomb, hoping against hope that it would form a viable Faraday cage before cradling it to his body. It was the best he could do to protect the AI who had been his mentor and friend all his life.

He felt a vibration and a slight pulse…and then nothing.

Time resumed, and Jason looked up from where he'd landed in time to see Calista slug Henrick's final soldier. The man's head snapped back and he dropped, down for the count.

<*…Tobe?*> Jason ventured cautiously.

The rational part of his mind told him that if the pulse had gotten out, Calista's powered armor would have shut down as well, and as badass as the captain was, he knew she didn't pack *that* good of a punch—at least unaugmented.

Still, it was a relief to hear Tobias's voice fill his head.

<Having a nice nap there, boyo?>

Jason was about to reply, when Landon interrupted.

<Do you have the president? Her people aren't giving up out here. Terrance is under attack on the surface, and half the GSC is coming for the *Vale*.>

<What?!> Calista exclaimed. <What about the FSTC?>

<They've sent a token force, but they've not engaged yet. I'm afraid it'll be too little too late.>

Jason turned to look at 'Acting President' Henrick, who was still standing behind her desk, a look of dumbfounded shock on her face.

<We have her,> he sent, and he repeated the words audibly for Henrick's benefit as he walked toward the woman who had turned a crisis into an unmitigated disaster. "She'll get her people to stand down."

Henrick squared her shoulders, though she was also cradling her injured hand.

"You'll *never* get—" she began, but her words were cut short as Tobias turned and shot a soldier as he ran into the room.

The man's head exploded, brains spraying across the wall, and Jason did his best to hold in his own revulsion as he raised his pistol and aimed it at Henrick's head.

"If we die. You die. Slow." Jason ground out the words between gritted teeth as he reached for his lightwand with his free hand. Flicking it on, he brought it up to the hand Henrick cradled. "Next one of your goon squad that comes in here, I slice off a finger. Someone comes in after, you lose another."

"You wouldn't!" the woman gasped.

Before Jason could respond, Tobias nodded for Calista to cover the entrance as his armored frame stalked toward Henrick.

None of the Weapon Born's usual brogue was in evidence; the words he uttered held the sharp edge of a carbon blade and were as cold as the frozen depths of space.

"You're right. Jason's a good kid. But I'm Weapon Born—I was made from death, and it's been my trade most of my life. Tearing apart a piece of organic filth like you would be pure joy for me."

* * * * *

"I've got the last two of our MFRs on those cruisers," the man on the weapons console announced, his worried eyes meeting Landon's. "But after that, it's just the *Vale*'s beams, and we're not going to scratch those cruisers."

Landon surveyed the battlespace, tallying the GSC ships that were boosting toward the *Avon Vale*. There were fifty in total, and while the *Vale* was burning for the FSTC line at top speed, the enemy would be in beam range of the Enfield ship before Admiral Berrong's ships could provide material aid.

To make matters worse, the holotank showed the last of Charley's fighters falling to the GSC destroyers surrounding the elevator, the enemy ships already disgorging dropships bound for the planet's surface.

Scan showed three assault craft already in the stratosphere, and despair welled up in Landon as he tasted the bitter knowledge that, once more, he'd failed. His charges, the people he was to protect from harm—they were all going to perish.

"Launches from the surface!" Scan cried out, and Landon's attention snapped back to the holotank to see missiles streaming from around the elevator, first striking the three dropships breaching atmosphere, and then the others in space.

Several hit the destroyers as well, nuclear fireballs blooming in the space around the elevator.

Landon was about to reach out to Logan in congratulations, when signatures for dozens of missiles lit up around the *Avon Vale*.

"Oh shit!" someone on the bridge cried out, but Landon could see that the missiles weren't headed for the Enfield ship; they were speeding past it.

Having originated from the FSTC picket, their vectors were

sending them streaking toward the oncoming GSC vessels.

Moments later, the GSC craft broke off, some taking hits from the missiles, but many more evading the strikes.

"I have Admiral Berrong on comms," Hailey announced.

"Put her on the tank," Landon said as he faced the woman, letting his gratitude and relief show on his face.

"Sorry I didn't let you in on that, Landon," the admiral said. "I had to seed those missiles without telling you—until I got authorization to fire the shots."

Landon nodded, making a point to clearly show his appreciation. "Are we ever glad you got it, then."

Berrong gave a rueful shake of her head. "I didn't. But the GSC ships crossed the non-aggression boundary line, and I had prior authorization to fire on any ships passing it that I deemed had ill intent. Do you agree that the GSC had ill intent?" The admiral had a twinkle in her eye as she asked the question.

Landon chuckled. "Not a doubt in my mind."

Suddenly, Berrong looked to the side at the same time as Hailey spoke up.

"Sir…it's the president, she's broadcasting stand-down orders for her fleet!"

"Sweet mother matrices," Landon whispered as the FSTC admiral turned back to him. "I guess our little coup has succeeded," he told her.

The woman before him nodded gravely. "So it would seem. Now I suspect the real work will begin."

Landon was only half-listening as he reached out to his teams, confirming that they were all still alive and well.

Jason's report was last, and as he completed it, Landon heard him add in a whisper, awe evident in his voice.

<Dude, Tobias is seriously hardcore.>

DÉTENTE

STELLAR DATE: 09.14.3246 (Adjusted Gregorian)
LOCATION: Voyager Spaceport
REGION: Galene, Tau Ceti

Terrance and Khela ended up crouched behind Logan's battle frame, Charley's less rugged body tucked between them. All four hovered as close to the bunker as they dared; Terrance faced one way and Khela the other, as wave after wave of soldiers peppered them with fire. Khela's two Marines, Xiao and Lena, provided cover as best they could, their chainguns serving as a powerful deterrent to the GSC contingent determined to take them down.

<Stars!> Terrance heard a blend of trepidation and impotent rage in Charley's voice. <There goes the last of them. I'm sorry, Logan, I'm all out of fighters. It's all up to you now.>

The profiler didn't respond. Terrance chanced a glance his way and knew the image he saw would be burned into his memory for a good, long while: Logan stood frozen, the gleaming bluish-silver of his battle frame locked in a stance of utter concentration, one four-fingered hand wielding a thick strand of network cable while the other brandished a bandolier-fed chaingun, aimed at the row of vehicles that had been shot to hell from the day's skirmish.

One minute, the bunker was sending fire screaming into the skies to meet the dropships head-on; the next, the chatter of enemy weapons ceased altogether. Terrance didn't allow his aim to waver, his slug thrower tracing a slow arc back and forth across the row of vehicles that the last group of GSC soldiers had used for cover.

Nothing moved.

Landon's voice broke in over the tightbeam.

<Henrick's called for a cease-fire,> Logan's twin said. <Just be sure those GSC ground troops have heard about it before you lower your weapons, okay?>

Into the silence fell the sounds of rounds being unchambered, and after that, the clunk of ordnance tossed to the ground. A shout, carried on the wind, ordered arms down and weapons holstered. Slowly, soldiers emerged, and as it became apparent that Henrick's cease-fire was in place, Terrance sent Khela a look. She spared the spaceport one last, sweeping look before nodding and securing her own weapon. Taking his cue from her, Terrance lowered his as well.

<Alpha is secure. Bravo, Charlie and Delta, report,> he heard Khela order over the combat net as she stepped toward her two Marines.

As the three scattered teams called in their status across the spaceport, Terrance bent to examine the progress his combat nano had made on the dent from the GSC slug in his armored leg. He heard Khela begin to speak, and something about her tone—a hitch in her cadence, the barest slur to her speech—warned him.

Snapping his head around, he leapt up just in time to catch her as her eyes rolled back in her head and she began convulsing.

"Xiao!" he shouted as he lowered her to the ground and knelt next to her, frantically searching for her armor's release. "Help me get her out of thi—"

A gauntleted hand arrested his frenzied search, and he fought to wrest it free. He turned on Xiao, but found himself facing his own reflection. He saw the wild desperation in his own eyes mirrored in the Marine's visor for the briefest moment before the man retracted his helm.

"It won't come off, sir. The damn phage has welded it to her torso." Xiao's voice was gentle, an incongruous counterpoint to the choking sounds coming from the woman before him.

He saw blood bubbling from the side of her mouth and knew the convulsion had caused her to bite her tongue; he tilted her head to the side just as Lena slapped a sedative medpatch to the side of her neck.

"This is worse than before, Xiao," the woman's low voice broke in. "Hana's memory fragments...." Lena looked up, past

Terrance's shoulder, and her voice trailed off as he felt something push him gently to one side.

From the corner of his eye, he saw a four-fingered, burnished silver hand rest itself lightly on Khela's armored chest as Logan's voice came across the Link.

<*Let me....*>

Terrance saw, projected over the combat net, the thread of rectification nano the AI was weaving into Khela's torso, colloidenes that would stabilize her until they could get her up to the *Vale*.

<*Thank you, friend.*> Terrance infused the words with all the emotion he felt welling up inside, things he knew he would have time for later, but dared not examine too closely just yet. "I've got you," he murmured, as the tension in Khela's body released, and she lapsed into a more restful unconsciousness.

He knew she couldn't hear him, and yet he couldn't stop himself from holding her, making soft reassuring sounds as they awaited the shuttle that had been dispatched to return them to the ship.

"I'm not going anywhere. Hang on, I've got you."

RECOVERY
STELLAR DATE: 09.17.3246 (Adjusted Gregorian)
LOCATION: *Avon Vale*
REGION: Galene, Tau Ceti

Khela opened her eyes to find herself staring into Terrance's clear blue depths. His eyes smiled down at her as the man reached up to brush a strand of hair out of her face.

Wait. Hair?

"Hello," Terrance's deep voice rumbled softly. "How do you feel?"

Khela reached up to touch her forehead. The nanofilament that had embedded itself into her face months prior was gone; her hands met smooth skin. They wandered further up and encountered a soft fall of hair. She ran her fingers through it in wonder, automatically reaching mentally for—

With a bittersweet pang, she realized the remnants, the fragments of Hana that had remained within her, were gone. Silence greeted her as she sought her friend's essence, and she squeezed her eyes shut, tears leaking out from behind them, trailing down the sides of her temples in a slow stream.

She felt a hand brush them away and she swallowed.

"She's gone." Khela heard the grief in her voice and Terrance's murmured assent.

"I understand she's been gone for quite a while now. But yes, her memory fragments have been removed—at least, for the most part. They can no longer bring you any pain."

"She— I couldn't save her...."

"I know."

"No, you *don't* know," she raged suddenly, her voice turning savage. "She was within me, and now she's gone. And the feeling, it's so hollow. Kodi's still with you, you couldn't *possibly* understand."

"Not how it feels to have had endured the fragments like you did, no," he admitted, his voice soothing in its gentleness. "But you're wrong about not knowing what it's like to have your partner gone from your head."

She stilled as he paused, his hand rhythmically stroking the side of her head, and waited for him to continue.

"The AI Council on Proxima mandated that the first AI I was paired with be removed."

She saw a look of pain cross his features, and he hesitated for a moment before continuing.

"It was difficult," he admitted finally. "Not nearly what you went through, I know. But I may have some small idea of what you're feeling right now."

She inhaled sharply, then turned her head into his hand. She hated herself for showing such weakness, but these past six months had been so long and hard and....

* * * * *

The visitors had offered to ferry Noa up to the *Avon Vale* to visit his daughter, and he'd gladly accepted. He sat in one of their shuttles, quietly observing their arrival from his position in the cockpit's jump seat. Noa had been surprised to discover that the man piloting the shuttle was the ship's XO; he'd expected someone of that rank to be tied up with more important business than ferrying an old physicist around.

Jason had apologized for asking Noa to sit up front, stating that they'd need the main cabin space for medics to transport the wounded and more critically infected up to their ship's doctor.

The scientist had not been offended in the least.

On the way, Jason had shared the files his father had sent from Proxima, and Noa had been startled to realize this man was the son of the prominent physicist, Rhys Andrews.

Jason kept up a lively chatter throughout the journey, filling him in on the histories of the *Avon Vale*'s crew as he piloted them from the bunker directly to the ship, bypassing the mess that was currently clogging Galene's main elevator.

With a deft hand, the pilot maneuvered them through the cavernous maw of the *Avon Vale*'s cargo bay and settled into the cradle assigned to them. Noa felt a brief shudder pass through the vessel as magnetic docking clamps came online, and then the pilot unstrapped.

"All right, then. Let's get you over to your daughter," Jason said as he gestured Noa to follow him.

The shuttle's cabin was bustling with activity, with medics busy funneling their patients through the larger cargo exit, where volunteers operating floating stretchers awaited them.

Jason danced around the edges of the crowd and palmed the hatch on the shuttle's starboard side. As Noa stepped onto the ship's deck, the projection of an AI appeared.

"About time, Jason," the AI said, and the pilot turned to Noa with a smile.

"Noa, I'd like you to meet our chief engineer and ship's AI, Shannon. She's offered to escort you to medical. Sorry I can't do it myself, but the captain wants me."

He shot a look toward Shannon's projection as the AI snorted.

"On the *bridge*. She wants me on the bridge." He grinned and turned back to Noa. "You'll be fine with Shannon. She doesn't bite…much." With a wink, the XO turned and jogged out the bay door.

Noa bowed respectfully to the image of the woman before him. Bette had informed him before he left that Shannon might be prickly when they met.

"She can be a bit opinionated, and she holds nothing back," Bette had told him with a smile. "But you always know where you stand with her. Shannon's one of a kind. She was outraged at how Charley and I had been treated, though, that we'd been bought like property by the Matsu-kai. It took some convincing to get her to understand that you were as much a victim as we were—and that you had risked your own life, and Khela's, to save ours."

Bette's words echoed in Noa's mind as Shannon's projection stood before him now, eyes narrowed and arms crossed. She walked around him, and he patiently waited for her to complete her circuit. As he did so, a part of his mind marveled at the extent to which this AI had adopted human mannerisms—more than any other AI he'd ever known.

Fascinating.

Shannon's avatar came to rest with a small *hmph,* and she set her toe to tapping slightly on the sole of the cargo bay. He actually heard the sounds the AI projected of the action.

He raised one brow, his expression tranquil and composure serene, and continued to wait.

"Bette was right," Shannon finally said. "You're unflappable." She smiled suddenly. "I think I like you, Noa Sakai."

He raised his other brow, and the AI burst out laughing.

"Come on. Let's go find your daughter."

Noa hesitated. "I would like to extend my greetings to your expedition leader first—and my appreciation for the care he's given to Khela. Terrance is his name, yes?"

Shannon shot him a wicked, mysterious grin. "Like I said...let's go find your daughter."

He could hear her chuckle as she sent her avatar through the cargo bay's doors and out into the corridor. As she exited, he could have sworn he heard her say, "oh, this is going to be *good.*"

The ship's medical bay was both familiar and foreign all at once. The equipment and interfaces he spied held the differences one would expect to see from technologies that had progressed around a different star. And yet, they remained fundamentally unchanged.

It was a welcoming sight to a man who, for the last six months, had been relegated to the limitations of his bunker—and the war-torn remnants of his planet's once-advanced technologies.

The *Avon Vale*'s chief medical officer, Marta, looked up as they approached.

"Noa, it's good to see you." She gestured to one of the bays off the area's mainspace. "Khela's right through here."

He heard the murmur of voices before the door slid open and he and Marta entered. When they did, he had eyes only for his daughter. She was propped up in a medical bed and she looked…wonderful. Healthy and whole, the daughter he'd lost months ago was restored to him now, though with a shadow of grief he knew only time would heal.

Standing next to her was the man he'd asked Shannon to introduce him to, and now he understood the AI's laugh, as he spied Khela's hand interlaced with his.

Both turned at his entrance, and Terrance nodded a greeting as he unthreaded their fingers, murmured something to Khela, and brushed a tendril of hair away from her face. Noa saw the flash of emotion that passed between the two, and his heart gave a little lurch. He recognized that look; it was the same one he'd shared with Khela's mother, Irene.

He experienced a brief pang at the thought of the woman he'd lost so long ago, but was happy for Khela and what she seemed to have found.

Our girl, Irene. Our little Khe-chan. She's found someone. By the ancestors, what does a father do now?

He met Terrance's eyes as the man approached.

"I'm sure you two have a lot of catching up to do," Enfield murmured, the man's eyes searching.

Noa smiled slightly and gave him a brief nod. "Thank you for saving Khela." He included the doctor as he added, "And for healing her, too."

A look of relief passed over Terrance's face. "It was the least we could do," the man murmured. He glanced at Marta and then over to Khela. "I'll be back later," he promised, and then he left, Marta following after him.

Khela smiled as Noa approached.

"You're doing well?" he questioned, taking a seat on the edge of her bed.

"I am. They've restored all my damaged bits that the nano messed up," she said wryly, fingering the blue-black lock of hair that had fallen once more into her face. "I hate to think I'm this vain, but I have to say, I really missed my hair."

He smiled at her. "I couldn't help but notice that someone else seems fond of it, as well."

His daughter, the Marine, actually blushed. "He does, doesn't he? Although, it's nice to know he seemed to like me even before."

Noa sat back, pleased at those words; then a frown crossed his face, and he leaned toward her again.

"But Khela, what's this I hear about him shooting the sister of one of his own officers?"

LISA RICHMAN & M. D. COOPER

AN UNEASY TRUCE
STELLAR DATE: 09.17.3246 (Adjusted Gregorian)
LOCATION: ESS *Avon Vale*
REGION: Galene, Tau Ceti

<She's asleep,> Kodi's voice quietly informed Terrance.

<I know. I just…want a moment with her, before we head down to meet with the FSTC and Galene's provisional government. Everything went well planetside? On the ring?>

<Yes,> Kodi assured him. <Tobias is still on the ring; he sent an update an hour ago. The colloidene rectification code has been successfully deployed in every major city. Ironically, Henrick's goons really **had** done a decent job of eradicating most nano, so cleanup's gone pretty smoothly overall. There are still pockets of corrupt nano here and there, but for the most part, it's been neutralized.>

<Something tells me the bigger problem on the ring is going to be building them back up to the level of tech they had before the phage.>

Kodi sent his agreement. <As for the planet…. Well. You know as well as I do what things are like down there.>

<Yes. I owe Calista one for stepping in and taking over for me down there so I could return to the Vale *for a bit*.> Terrance looked around at the medical bay and added, <We also owe Marta's medics for staying and helping Dominica set up centers where people can receive treatment to reverse the damage that the nano did to them.>

The soft, irregular click of claws striking the medbay deck drew his attention, and Terrance looked over to see the platinum-furred figure of a Proxima cat limping toward him.

<Beck,> he scolded, continuing to use the Link so as to not awaken Khela. <Didn't Marta say you shouldn't put any weight on that leg for another few days?>

He received the fleeting impression of an obstinate rebellion, but it was overlaid by a sense of curiosity and determination as the cat paused by his side.

<I sleep with your Person,> he announced, and gathered himself into a crouch.

Before Terrance could stop him, the big cat uncoiled, leaping up onto the bed where Khela lay. His landing was light and agile, despite the injury, and he settled next to her with a satisfied huff.

<Beck, she needs rest,> Terrance scolded.

He reached over to smooth Khela's hair back, his other hand still cupped around her cheek, where she'd turned her head into his palm.

The cat fixed him with baleful aqua eyes and announced, <We both rest.> Then he settled his chin on his forelegs as if that settled the matter.

<And she's not my person, Beck. She's a Marine who needed Marta's help to get better.>

<Smells like you.>

Terrance blew out a breath. <That doesn't make her mine, though.>

<You smell like her, too.>

Kodi's laugh sounded in Terrance's head. <I think you'd better quit while you're behind. Don't think you're going to win against a cat's logic. I'm sure Marta will relocate him if she feels he should be elsewhere. Speaking of relocating....>

The AI's voice warned him of Marta's approach even before Terrance heard the doctor's soft footfalls. He removed his hand from where it cupped Khela's head and felt his face heat a bit as he caught the doctor's knowing smile.

"I had the autodoc give her a sedative," Marta spoke softly. "She'll rest for a few hours and will feel much better when she wakes."

She made a shooing motion with her hands, and Terrance grinned and stepped away from the unit, moving outside the room. Marta followed.

As the door swished softly closed behind them, the doctor pointed to the exit. "Off with you. I know for a fact that I have a dozen patients or more landing soon, and I need all the space available to treat them. At least Beck's no longer taking up his own bed." She winked and then arched a brow at him when Terrance was slow to move.

<I think we've just been given our marching orders,> Kodi interjected, his tone droll.

"Don't tell me you two don't have anything better to do with your time, or I'll set you to work stripping bed linens and reloading injection ampoules."

Terrance raised his hands and backed out into the corridor. "Going! I have it on good authority that I make a terrible maid," he replied with a wink of his own. "I guess I'll just be on my way."

* * * * *

"C'mon, dude. Council's waiting—and I'm hungry." Jason grinned from his position inside the shuttle's hatch as Terrance broke into a slow jog across the *Vale*'s main cargo bay.

He nodded to the *Sable Wind*'s aft cargo compartment as he asked, "Is our freight loaded and ready, too?"

Jason nodded, and then ducked back inside to give Terrance room to enter.

The FSTC and Galene's acting president—a *legitimate* acting president—had requested a contingent of their 'Centauran guests' be present for this first official briefing. Terrance had asked Jason and Calista to join him, leaving Landon in charge of the *Vale*. In a surprising twist, the Galene contingent had also asked for Tobias by name. The Weapon Born had taken the elevator down from the ring earlier.

Terrance knew there was a story there, and he couldn't wait to hear it. In the meantime, he'd ordered a sampling of some of Enfield's most valuable trade items to be transported down with them. It was intended as a goodwill offering, in case any of the Galene officials took issue with the fact that Phantom Blade had exchanged weapons fire with GSC forces, however well-intentioned the actions had been.

As Terrance reached the shuttle's hatch, he felt the ramp beneath his feet vibrate from the humanoid frame that trailed behind him. He caught Jason's knowing smirk and released a long-suffering sigh as the XO turned to address the AI in Terrance's wake.

"I heard Landon assigned you to babysitting duty." Jason's voice held a trace of amusement, which Logan ignored as the profiler ducked his frame through the hatch and ordered the shuttle's ramp to retract.

<He was told—and I quote—'don't let those two get shot at again',> Kodi chimed in, as Terrance moved forward and began to strap into the copilot's seat.

Logan just grunted.

Jason shouted a laugh, slapped Logan's frame, and slid past him into the pilot's cradle. A moment later, the AI had settled into the point defense position just behind Jason, although Terrance knew the station would not be needed on this trip.

"You'd think we're all a bunch of incompetents, the way Landon's acting," Terrance grumbled, but he regretted his words the moment Logan stirred.

"I think he will always be overprotective," the profiler said, his tone pensive.

Jason shot Terrance a glance before saying in an affable voice, "Not a bad vice to have, I'd say."

Logan didn't respond, and the three lapsed into silence as Jason finished his preflight and Shannon released the bay doors. With a slight push, the rails upon which the shuttle was docked released the little ship, and they floated free of the *Vale*.

Jason expertly spun the craft and sent it on a gentle arcing curve toward the planet's surface and the city of Meshuggah, Galene's third largest, and the one least ravaged by both battle and phage. It was on the southernmost tip of the continent, beyond the elevator that had so recently seen combat.

And isn't that an appropriately-named place to hold a meeting about the recent state of events....

As they neared their destination, Terrance could see the *Avon Vale*'s captain standing on the roof of city hall, waiting for them at the edge of the landing pad with Tobi by her side. Calista's dark hair haloed around her, whipped by currents generated by the shuttle's thrusters, as Jason brought the *Sable Wind* to rest with a flourish.

As Terrance exited, he was amused to see the small group of admirers keeping Tobi company. Jason had told him that tales of Beck's heroics had spread throughout Galene, and a sighting of one of the cats usually drew a small crowd. Beck had made another trip down to the planet long enough to submit his testimony, but Marta had ordered the big cat back aboard the ship soon after.

Tobi had been happy to step in and accept accolades on his behalf, especially once she'd discovered the Galene equivalent of bonito flakes. The Proxima cat fairly preened with all the attention she was getting. She was sitting tall next to Calista, awaiting their arrival.

"How's Khela?" Calista asked as they disembarked.

She tucked an arm through his and pulled him off to one side for a moment, as Jason bent down to greet Tobi.

"Marta managed to remove most of Hana's fragments, and she's certain they'll no longer cause her any pain," Terrance told her as he watched the lean, muscular feline strop the pilot's legs once in greeting, then turn to glide gracefully toward him and Calista. "Although the doctor was less sure about whether she'd be able to pair with an AI ever again."

Calista smiled as the big cat butted Terrance's proffered hand with her head, and then reared back, wrinkling her nose.

<*You smell like the Brat,*> Tobi complained.

Kodi made a sound like he was clearing his throat.

<We, ah, left Khela in Beck's tender care.> The AI's voice was laced with a thread of humor, and Terrance heard Jason snicker at the mental image.

Tobi shot Terrance a baleful glare at the mention—and smell—of her nemesis.

<I *was* having a nice **day**.>

Calista covered a smile, and Jason hooted in laughter at the cat's words. Terrance heard Kodi apologize to Tobi as they headed toward the entrance of the government building.

* * * * *

Jason nodded amiably to Admiral Berrong as they entered the council chambers that the Meshuggah city governors had made available to them. The admiral smiled when she spied Tobi, and slipped her hand under the table. Jason hid a smirk as the big cat trotted forward, shamelessly taking advantage of yet another proffered treat.

Seated next to her was Senator Bryce Daniels, Galene's acting president. The man was pale, his arm encased in biofoam. Jason noticed Galene's surgeon general was seated next to him.

<He was one of the leaders in the Q-camps,> Calista explained privately. <Dominica operated on him when he was infected. Noa said she sewed him up in the middle of a strafing run by GSC fighters.>

Jason shot the woman an appreciative glance and returned his perusal to the others as they approached the table. Next to Dominica Gonsalves sat the man they'd come from Proxima to see: Noa Sakai.

Beside him were two frames; the AIs they had come to free. In an ironic twist of fate, it had been the AIs who had freed Galene. Bette had been the one to unlock the mystery of the phage, while Charley had been instrumental in the fight to secure Galene's main elevator.

Terrance told Jason how fiercely Charley had fought alongside them at the spaceport, coordinating with Landon on the *Avon Vale*. There was something about Charley, though. Something Jason's AI teammates hadn't told him. Something that elicited a sense of awe and respect every time they mentioned his name.

He made a mental note to ask Tobias about it later.

As though his thoughts had conjured him from the shadows, the Weapon Born materialized beside him, pulling out the chair to his left and seating himself.

"I see our Tobi-girl has herself a new conquest," Tobias said, his lilting brogue thick with amusement.

Berrong's eyes twinkled and her chin rose. "I recognize *that* voice," she greeted. "Hello, Tobias. You know they're calling you 'Henrick's Bane' up on the ring? I'm not sure what you did to that woman, but all we had to do to get her to spill her guts was threaten to send you in to question her."

Calista made a strangled sound as Jason fought—and lost—to keep the broad grin from spreading across his face. If it was possible for Tobias to look abashed, the Weapon Born did at that moment.

"Ah, it was nothing, lass. I may have lost my temper for a wee moment, is all."

The admiral tilted her head to one side. "It may have been a bit more than that, to hear her tell the story. Of course, you look a sight different, too, in your regular frame. I believe you were all kitted out in your battle rattle when she saw you last."

"Ahh...." Tobias began weakly, and Calista came to his rescue.

"I'm sure that has a lot to do with it, ma'am," she agreed, managing to maintain a straight face.

"Admiral," Terrance said from behind Tobias as he approached and seated himself, "I want to thank you for your timely intervention." He sounded every bit the corporate executive as his eyes traveled across Phantom Blade. "Without it, I'm sure we wouldn't be here today."

"And *we* wish to thank *you*, Mister Enfield." Bryce Daniels' voice was a bit reedy, but Jason could hear the statesmanlike qualities the man possessed. "Without the *Avon Vale*'s assistance, Galene's very future might still hang in the balance." His expression darkened, as he added, "And Henrick and deSangro would still be in power, instead of being held for crimes against humanity."

The man's eyes cleared and he smiled once more. "The phage may have bested us for a while, but Galene will bounce back. And in the process, we're proud to have made some new friends."

Jason saw Terrance's eyes glint with unexpected humor as the exec responded with a wink.

"Well now, I couldn't just allow a lucrative new market for Enfield Holdings to slip away. That wouldn't be very good business, now, would it?"

THE END

* * * * *

The crew of the *Avon Vale* has completed the mission they took on in Alpha Centauri by rescuing the last of the AIs the Norden Cartel kidnapped from the *New Saint Louis*.

Now a new goal lies before them. Build a network of trade and communication that does not center on Sol.

Their next stop? Epsilon Eridani

AFTERWORD

Working with Lisa on these books is, as ever, a true pleasure. She has a real passion for the characters, the story, and Aeon 14 itself. Working with her on the book is always a fun adventure for me, because though she and I plan out what will happen in the pages you've just read, her spin is always unique and interesting.

Which, in a nutshell, is why I love having other authors working in Aeon 14. They bring a perspective borne of unique experiences that I simply cannot have.

Sometimes I think I'm stretching their boundaries and they come back with a solution, or a means to achieve what we want that is really quite fascinating and well thought out. In this book it was the suspension of the nano in a colloid that really gave what we wanted to do with the nanophage legs, so to speak.

When Lisa proposed that solution, I knew we had a winner…and the folks in Tau Ceti were really going to be in for it.

Add to that the fact that sometimes people make mistakes that don't seem that bad—but later cause disasters—and things can go very, very wrong.

I hope you've enjoyed the journey thus far, and come along for the second leg, where the crew of the *Avon Vale* goes to Epsilon Eridani, followed by Sirius, and finally Sol.

Michael Cooper
November 2018, Danvers

THE BOOKS OF AEON 14

Keep up to date with what is releasing in Aeon 14 with the free Aeon 14 Reading Guide.

Origins of Destiny (The Age of Terra)
- Prequel: Storming the Norse Wind
- Book 1: Tanis Richards: Shore Leave
- Book 2: Tanis Richards: Masquerade
- Book 3: Tanis Richards: Blackest Night
- Book 4: Tanis Richards: Kill Shot (November 2018)

The Intrepid Saga (The Age of Terra)
- Book 1: Outsystem
- Book 2: A Path in the Darkness
- Book 3: Building Victoria

- The Intrepid Saga Omnibus – *Also contains Destiny Lost, book 1 of the Orion War series*

- Destiny Rising – *Special Author's Extended Edition comprised of both Outsystem and A Path in the Darkness with over 100 pages of new content.*

The Orion War
- Books 1-3 Omnibus (includes Ignite the Stars anthology)

- Book 1: Destiny Lost
- Book 2: New Canaan
- Book 3: Orion Rising
- Book 4: The Scipio Alliance
- Book 5: Attack on Thebes
- Book 6: War on a Thousand Fronts
- Book 7: Precipice of Darkness
- Book 8: Airtha Ascendancy (Nov 2018)
- Book 9: The Orion Front (2019)
- Book 10: Starfire (2019)

- Book 11: Race Across Spacetime (2019)
- Book 12: Return to Sol (2019)

Tales of the Orion War
- Book 1: Set the Galaxy on Fire
- Book 2: Ignite the Stars
- Book 3: Burn the Galaxy to Ash (2019)

Perilous Alliance (Age of the Orion War – w/Chris J. Pike)
- Book 1: Close Proximity
- Book 2: Strike Vector
- Book 3: Collision Course
- Book 4: Impact Imminent
- Book 5: Critical Inertia
- Book 6: Impulse Shock (Dec 2018)

Rika's Marauders (Age of the Orion War)
- Book 1-3 Omnibus: Rika Activated

- Prequel: Rika Mechanized
- Book 1: Rika Outcast
- Book 2: Rika Redeemed
- Book 3: Rika Triumphant
- Book 4: Rika Commander
- Book 5: Rika Infiltrator
- Book 6: Rika Unleashed
- Book 7: Rika Conqueror (Dec 2018)

Perseus Gate (Age of the Orion War)
Season 1: Orion Space
- Episode 1: The Gate at the Grey Wolf Star
- Episode 2: The World at the Edge of Space
- Episode 3: The Dance on the Moons of Serenity
- Episode 4: The Last Bastion of Star City
- Episode 5: The Toll Road Between the Stars
- Episode 6: The Final Stroll on Perseus's Arm
- Eps 1-3 Omnibus: The Trail Through the Stars
- Eps 4-6 Omnibus: The Path Amongst the Clouds

Season 2: Inner Stars
- Episode 1: A Meeting of Bodies and Minds
- Episode 2: A Deception and a Promise Kept
- Episode 3: A Surreptitious Rescue of Friends and Foes
- Episode 4: A Victory and a Crushing Defeat (2019)
- Episode 5: A Trial and the Tribulations (2019)
- Episode 6: A Deal and a True Story Told (2019)
- Episode 7: A New Empire and An Old Ally (2019)

Season 3: AI Empire
- Episode 1: Restitution and Recompense (2019)
- Five more episodes following...

The Warlord (Before the Age of the Orion War)
- Books 1-3 Omnibus: The Warlord of Midditerra

- Book 1: The Woman Without a World
- Book 2: The Woman Who Seized an Empire
- Book 3: The Woman Who Lost Everything

The Sentience Wars: Origins (Age of the Sentience Wars – w/James S. Aaron)
- Books 1-3 Omnibus: Lyssa's Rise

- Book 1: Lyssa's Dream
- Book 2: Lyssa's Run
- Book 3: Lyssa's Flight
- Book 4: Lyssa's Call
- Book 5: Lyssa's Flame

Legends of the Sentience Wars (Age of the Sentience Wars – w/James S. Aaron)
- Volume 1: The Proteus Bridge
- Volume 2: Vesta Burning (Fall 2018)

Enfield Genesis (Age of the Sentience Wars – w/Lisa Richman)
- Book 1: Alpha Centauri

- Book 2: Proxima Centauri
- Book 3: Tau Ceti
- Book 4: Epsilon Eridani (2019)

Hand's Assassin (Age of the Orion War – w/T.G. Ayer)
- Book 1: Death Dealer
- Book 2: Death Mark (2019)

Machete System Bounty Hunter (Age of the Orion War – w/Zen DiPietro)
- Book 1: Hired Gun
- Book 2: Gunning for Trouble
- Book 3: With Guns Blazing

Vexa Legacy (Age of the FTL Wars – w/Andrew Gates)
- Book 1: Seas of the Red Star

Building New Canaan (Age of the Orion War – w/J.J. Green)
- Book 1: Carthage
- Book 2: Tyre
- Book 3: Troy (2019)
- Book 4: Athens (2019)

Fennington Station Murder Mysteries (Age of the Orion War)
- Book 1: Whole Latte Death (w/Chris J. Pike)
- Book 2: Cocoa Crush (w/Chris J. Pike)

The Empire (Age of the Orion War)
- Book 1: The Empress and the Ambassador (2018)
- Book 2: Consort of the Scorpion Empress (2019)
- Book 3: By the Empress's Command (2019)

The Sol Dissolution (The Age of Terra)
- Book 1: Venusian Uprising (2018)
- Book 2: Scattered Disk (2018)
- Book 3: Jovian Offensive (2019)
- Book 4: Fall of Terra (2019)

ABOUT THE AUTHORS

Lisa Richman lives in the great Midwest, with three cats, a physicist, and a Piper Cherokee. She met the physicist when she went back to get her master's in physics (she ended up marrying the physicist instead).
When she's not writing, her day job takes her behind the camera as a director/producer.

If she's not at her keyboard or on set, she can be found cruising at altitude. Or helping out the physics guy with his linear accelerator. Or feeding the cats. Or devouring the next SF book she finds.

* * * * *

Michael Cooper likes to think of himself as a jack-of-all-trades (and hopes to become master of a few). When not writing, he can be found writing software, working in his shop at his latest carpentry project, or likely reading a book.

He shares his home with a precocious young girl, his wonderful wife (who also writes), two cats, a never-ending list of things he would like to build, and ideas...

Find out what's coming next at http://www.aeon14.com

Made in the USA
Coppell, TX
28 December 2019